WELL-TEMPERED CLAVICLE

Piers Anthony

Well-Tempered Clavicle

A Tom Doherty Associates Book

New York

This is a work of fiction. All of the characters, organizations, and events portrayed in this novel are either products of the author's imagination or are used fictitiously.

WELL-TEMPERED CLAVICLE

A Tor Book
Published by Tom Doherty Associates, LLC
175 Fifth Avenue
New York, NY 10010

www.tor-forge.com

Tor® is a registered trademark of Tom Doherty Associates, LLC.

Library of Congress Cataloging-in-Publication Data

Anthony, Piers.
    Well-tempered clavicle / Piers Anthony.—1st ed.
        p. cm.—(Xanth series)
    ISBN 978-0-7653-3134-2
    1. Xanth (Imaginary place)—Fiction.   I. Title.
PS3551.N73W44 2011
813'.54—dc22

                                        2011019919

First Edition: October 2011

Printed in the United States of America

0 9 8 7 6 5 4 3 2 1

In memory of our daughter

Penelope Carolyn Jacob

October 12, 1967–September 3, 2009

Contents

WELL-TEMPERED
CLAVICLE

1
IDEA

W hat's that?" Picka Bone asked, startled. His bone head was hollow, but this was normal for a walking skeleton, and he could see, hear, and think well enough. Magical creatures were not handicapped in the manner of mortal ones; they were not subject to the ills of flesh. As it happened, they were just completing their hourly tour of the cemetery they were patrolling.

"It's a living cat," his sister Joy'nt said. She was his age, twenty-four, with nice bones. "With a bird sitting on his head."

"That's what I thought it was. Don't live cats normally eat live birds?"

"Normally," Joy'nt agreed. "There may be an interesting story here."

"And we could use some interest in our dull routine." For that was a liability of their state: terminal dullness. Without the fear of pain or death, they seldom got exited. Intellectual interest was about all that sustained them, and they were not great intellects.

The cat was coming directly toward them. It was a nondescript male with blond fur, evidently mundane. The little bird was flapping its wings but not flying, as if trying to get their attention. It was a male parakeet with brownish feathers, another mundane creature. They halted right before the skeletons.

Joy'nt had a soft spot for animals, figuratively, as none of her was physically soft. She squatted and extended her bone hand to the cat to sniff. "What can we do for you, strange feline?" she inquired.

The cat scratched in the sand, smoothing it. Then he stroked a claw across it several times, forming some kind of pattern. In fact it was alphabetical letters.

"H-E-L-P," Picka read.

"Help?" Joy'nt asked. "How?"

The cat turned and went back the way he had come. The bird, still riding his head, cheeped and flipped one wing, as if encouraging them to follow.

"Got it," Picka said. "Show us where."

They walked through the graveyard, past the F and G gravestones that were shaped like the letters F and G to represent Effie and Gee, who had been hanged in effigy. Past the stone saying FOR PETE'S SAKE! in honor of a man who hadn't planned on dying. There were all manner of mildly amusing stones here. Picka and Joy'nt had wandered though the graveyard repeatedly, and each time discovered something they had missed before.

The cat and bird led them to a collapsed crypt they had not noticed; it was one of several rather old and worn structures scattered through the graveyard. This one had been open and empty, of no concern. The stone slab that formed the roof of the front portal had dropped down, sealing it off.

"In there?" Joy'nt asked.

The bird nodded. It was evident that these animals understood human speech, but could not speak it. Many animals were like that.

Now they heard a faint "Woof!" Something was in there!

Picka braced himself, got his bone fingers on the stone, and heaved it up and to the side. Walking skeletons had no muscles but were stronger than they looked, being magically animated. The portal was open.

A big dark mongrel mundane dog came out, tail wagging, glad to be freed. He joined the other two. The three were evidently friends, odd as such an association might be.

"You wanted to rescue a dog?" Picka asked the cat, surprised again.

"I think we deserve an explanation," Joy'nt said.

The three animals just looked at her. Maybe they were having trouble with the idea of an explanation, when they couldn't speak human.

"Let's trade," Picka said. "We'll tell you about us if you tell us about you."

The bird, cat, and dog exchanged glances. Then the bird nodded.

"First we need a better way to communicate," Joy'nt said. "I know just the thing." She fished in her hollow skull and brought out a roll of bone-colored paper. She spread this on the ground. "This is a magic marker made from dragon bone," she explained. "I got it from a man I met named Cody, who could decipher any code or language. It works only for living creatures, so I never had use for it before. Whoever wants to talk can put a hand, claw, or paw on it, focus, and it will print your thought. Try it."

The cat touched the paper with a paw. Words formed. I AM MID-RANGE CAT.

The dog tried it. I AM WOOFER DOG.

Finally the bird flew down and landed on it with both feet. II AAMM TTWWEEEETTEERR BBIIRRDD.

Midrange made a mewl of impatience. He touched the paper. JUST ONE FOOT, BIRDBRAIN!

Tweeter hauled up a foot. OOPS.

Woofer touched the marker. HA HA HA!

Joy'nt glanced at Picka. She had no eyes, of course, but her squared-off eyeholes could be expressive. "Now give our history, briefly."

"I am Picka Bone, son of Marrow Bones and Grace'l Ossein," Picka said. "This is my sister, Joy'nt. Our kind, the walking skeletons, originated in the dream realm of the gourd, but Esk Ogre found Marrow on the Lost Path and brought him out to Xanth proper. So Marrow and Grace'l are no longer scary dream figures, but regular Xanth denizens. Marrow once accompanied Prince Dolph on an adventure. That was when he met Electra, and later married her, and they got the twin sisters Sorceresses Dawn and Eve. Later Marrow got half a soul, which he shared, so we have eighth souls. So we feel obliged to do some good in Xanth. We have wandered all around, but living humans tend to avoid our company, so we have been unable to do them much good. We agreed to watch this graveyard for a month so the zombies could take a break. This is our last day; we don't know what we'll do tomorrow, but hope it isn't too boring. Our hollow heads get easily bored." He made a little screwing motion with a bone finger, as if boring into his skull.

Woofer looked blank. Midrange looked disgusted. Tweeter fell over with melodic laughter.

Picka had given them his personal history. Did they really understand any of it? Did they care? How would they respond?

The cat touched the marker. A column of print appeared. Digested, it was this:

"We are three pets brought from Mundania by the Baldwin family fifteen years ago. Our names are Woofer, Tweeter, and Midrange, as specified above. It seems the Baldwins liked music, so they named us after their speakers. We liked our family, but pets don't live forever in drear Mundania, so when we got old we migrated here, thanks to a dispensation from the Demon Xanth, for whom I once did a favor. Now we are back in our primes of life, but even a magic land can get dull, so we are looking for adventure. Woofer has a nose for that sort of thing, and he led us to this cemetery, and to this crypt. There is something interesting in there. But when Woofer went in, the stone fell down, trapping him. So we came to you to beg for help. You helped us, so we owe you a favor. What favor do you want, that we can do?"

Picka exchanged another eyeless glance with his sister. "We'd like to find something interesting to do tomorrow," she said.

"So would we," Midrange spelled out on the marker. "Maybe we all should share a great adventure."

"Agreed," Joy'nt said. "What adventure?"

"We hoped you would know," Midrange printed.

Picka tapped his skull with a knuckle. "Our empty heads are not great on ideas. In fact I'm not great on anything much. Joy'nt has the usual skeleton talent of disassembly and reformulation; she can form her bones into different configurations if she gets a good starting kick in the—" He caught his sister's warning glare. "Pelvis. But it doesn't work for me. I'm a defective skeleton. A complete nonentity, even among my own kind, which are not exactly live wires. So I'm not sure I'm even worthy of an adventure. But still I wish I could have one."

Tweeter flew across and landed on his shoulder bone. "Tweet!" he tweeted sympathetically.

"Thanks," Picka said. He was beginning to like the little bird.

Woofer woofed.

That reminded Picka. "What were you looking for in the crypt?"

Woofer wagged his tail and trotted back to the crypt. The others followed, Joy'nt lingering only long enough to recover her marker paper. The crypt was a large one, with room for them all. It had attracted the dog, who had the nose for adventure. There had to be something.

But Picka hung back. "We can't be sure what we'll find in there," he said. "Maybe the way that stone fell, sealing Woofer in, was a warning."

That made the others pause. "Yet it was open," Joy'nt said. "Whatever was inside could have escaped."

"Woof!"

"Woofer says no," Picka said. He was coming to understand these animals even without the marker paper.

"There should be a plaque on the entry stone," Joy'nt said. She looked around. "That must be it, fallen to the side. Maybe an ogre slapped at it in passing."

Picka went to look down at the flat stone. "Danger: Think Tank," he read.

"Think what?" Joy'nt asked.

"The stone is weathered," Picka said, "but that's what I read. Maybe it's an old storage tank."

"Then why bury it in a crypt in a graveyard?"

Picka shrugged with both his clavicles. "Maybe there's something dangerous in the tank, like a nest of nickelpedes."

Even the animals dismissed that. Picka's hollow head sometimes produced empty notions.

Woofer tired of the dialogue. He went into the crypt, sniffing for the tank. The others had no choice but to follow, after making sure nothing else could collapse to trap them inside.

There in the back was a large machine with caterpillar treads and a gun barrel. Picka recognized it from descriptions of bad machines in the dream realm.

"I thought those monsters were imaginary," Joy'nt murmured, awed. "No wonder they buried it."

"I understand such things actually exist in Mundania," Picka said. "Maybe this one escaped, got into Xanth, and someone put it away so it couldn't tear up our landscape."

"Well, now we know enough about it," Joy'nt said. "It is indeed dangerous. We'd better bury it again."

But Woofer was sniffing the tank. He found something on its back. It looked like an on-off switch.

"Don't touch that!" Picka cried, alarmed.

Too late. Woofer was already nosing the switch. It changed position with a brisk click.

The tank animated. A muted light came on somewhere inside. There was the sound of a motor running.

"I think we'd better get out of here," Joy'nt said, alarmed.

They scrambled out. The tank revved up its gears and followed.

"Maybe we should turn it off again," Picka said. "If we can."

"I'll do it," Joy'nt said. She ran toward the emerging tank.

Its turret turned. Its cannon oriented on her.

"Watch out!" Picka cried.

Joy'nt threw herself to the ground just as the cannon fired. An oddly shaped ball of light zapped toward her, touching the back of her skull as she dropped.

Tweeter flew toward the tank, going for the switch. The cannon oriented on him and fired again. The bulb-shaped ball caught the tip of a wing, and Tweeter spun out of control.

By the time they got reorganized, the tank was crashing out of the graveyard and into the surrounding forest. It was too late to stop it.

They compared notes. Neither Joy'nt nor Tweeter seemed to have been hurt, just disconcerted by the strikes. "Those light balls the tank fired," Picka said. "They looked like bulbs." Then he realized what it meant. "For ideas! It's a *think* tank. It makes people think of ideas."

This time Midrange and Woofer exchanged glances. Midrange went to Joy'nt. She brought out the marker and set it down for him.

He touched it with a paw. "What's your idea, Tweeter?"

Tweeter flew down and put one foot on it. "Picka Bone must have a talent."

Midrange touched it again. "And yours, Joy'nt?"

"That we should visit Princess Eve, who knows all about anything that isn't alive, to ask her what Picka's talent is."

"They are friends of ours," Picka agreed. "We knew them as children; they were three years younger than us. But two years ago Princess Eve married the Dwarf Demon Pluto, and became the Mistress of Hades. She may not be in Xanth now."

"But her twin sister, Dawn, would know," Joy'nt said. "We can go to Castle Roogna and ask her where Eve is now."

Picka was intrigued. "Let's do it. It may not be much of an adventure, but I'd really like to know about my talent, if I have one."

"We'll go too," Midrange printed.

"Of course," Joy'nt agreed. She was an agreeable person. So was Picka, actually; he was very even-tempered, and could get along with anyone who wasn't spooked by his appearance.

"Is there anything to eat? We're hungry."

"We skeletons don't need to eat; we're magical spooks," Picka said. "There's not much around the graveyard. Just a few palm trees holding coco-nuts containing hot nut-flavored cocoa, and some mints. Pepper, astonish, fig—"

"We'll forage for ourselves," Midrange printed.

Next morning when the zombies returned they set out as a party of five. Picka knew that all of them were glad to be doing something, even if it wasn't much. It gave them the illusion of purpose.

The graveyard was off the beaten path—in fact, there wasn't even an *un*beaten path. This did not bother the skeletons or animals, but they were wary, because there were many dangers in backwoods Xanth.

Not that the walking skeletons had much to fear. Dragons tended to leave them alone because they weren't very edible; even the marrow in their bones was dry and tasteless. Most living creatures spooked at the very sight of them.

The three living animals were protected by an amicability spell put on them by Nimby, the donkey-headed dragon form of the Demon Xanth, so that other creatures meant them no harm. They could still get in trouble on their own, as Woofer had, but that was his own fault.

Still, Xanth could come up with surprises, so they were careful. They made their way toward the nearest enchanted path, not hurrying, because hurrying could attract more attention than they cared for. This was a bit circuitous, because none of them knew exactly where the nearest enchanted path was.

Woofer, always sniffing things ahead, woofed. He was good at woofing. That meant he had found something halfway interesting. They went in that direction.

They came across a standing woman facing away from them. "Hello," Picka called. It was better that a stranger hear his voice first, so she wouldn't be as startled by his form.

The woman did not answer or move.

Joy'nt tried. "Hello. Can you tell us where the nearest enchanted path is?"

Still no answer. Then they caught up and saw the woman's front side. She was a metal statue!

"Woof," Woofer repeated in an I-told-you-so tone.

They inspected the statue at close range. It was solid iron, a marvelous image of a bare young human woman. Picka was not into bare human women, but did understand that this one was extremely well formed. He reached out to brush a fallen leaf from her conic left breast.

"Eeeee!" she squealed.

Picka fell back, startled. "You're alive?" he asked.

"I'm animated, like you," she said. "I'll thank you not to paw me."

"I can't paw you," he protested. "I have no paws."

She turned her head with a certain squeakiness. "You make no bones about it," she agreed.

"Who are you, and what are you doing here?" Joy'nt asked.

"I am the Iron Maiden, a statue animated by an ancient Magician King."

"He animated a statue?" Picka asked, amazed. "Why?"

"I never was quite clear on that. He simply said I was statuesque. But he was good to me; he had me sleep every night in his bed while he cuddled me. I told him the stork would never deliver to a statue, but he kept trying. I suppose he didn't want to be unkind to me, so he pretended it didn't matter. He was a very generous man."

It occurred to Picka that the old king might not actually have wanted the stork to pay attention, but he decided not to argue the case. "What happened then?"

"Finally he died, and his wife kicked me out and banished me from the castle. I don't know why she was so mean. I have been wandering in the wilderness ever since. It gets dull, so sometimes I pause and sleep."

"We wish you well," he said. "Do you know where the nearest enchanted path is?"

"What's an enchanted path?"

It occurred to Picka that the Iron Maiden was a bit out of touch, but again he decided to let it be. She might have napped for a long time; there was rust on her joints. "Never mind. Thank you for your time."

"You are welcome," she said. "If you happen to encounter any other man who would like someone to share his bed, I have experience."

"We'll do that," Joy'nt said briskly. For some reason she seemed impatient.

"Woof!"

"Woofer found a path!" Picka said.

They hurried to catch up to the dog. Sure enough, there was a crazy-looking path. It looped around trees, twisted across fallen logs, and seemed to be aimless. But it was a path, and surely went somewhere, so they decided to follow it.

Yet when Picka tried to put his foot on it, it writhed away from him. He tried again, and it retreated again. Joy'nt tried, and it avoided her also. This was a really odd path!

Then they saw a man walking along the path without difficulty. "How do you do that?" Picka called to him. "We can't touch the path."

The man looked at him. "I think I'm getting crazier by the minute," he remarked. "You look exactly like a walking skeleton."

"I *am* a walking skeleton."

"Now even my hallucinations are talking back. Well, I'll treat you just as if you are real. This is the Psycho Path. Only crazy folk can use it. You may not be real, but neither are you crazy, so you're out of luck."

Now it was making crazy sense. A crazy path for crazy people. No wonder they couldn't use it. "Thank you," Picka called as the man wandered away.

It was getting dark. "We'll never find our way in the night," Joy'nt complained. "We'd better make camp, and find something for our friends to eat."

That was right: the animals needed food and rest, even if skeletons didn't. They located a glade with a blanket tree, and fashioned several blankets into a warm nest. Then they scouted for a pie plant. But when they returned with slices of pizza and quiche, the blankets were gone. The animals hadn't done it; they were out scouting for water.

There were some drag marks indicating the direction the blankets had gone. Someone had taken them. They went in that direction, and soon discovered a man sleeping on the pile of blankets.

"You took our blankets!" Picka said indignantly.

The man opened an eye. "What?"

"Those are our blankets!"

"I don't know what you're talking about. I found these here."

"You dragged them here. See the drag marks?"

"Maybe someone dragged them here before I came. People are always accusing me of stealing. I don't know why."

Again, there was something odd. "Let's introduce ourselves. I am Picka Bone, and this is my sister Joy'nt."

"I am Rob."

Joy'nt angled her head in the way she had when she got an idea. "What is your magic talent, Rob?"

"I have no idea."

"Could it relate to your name? Rob?"

"I don't know what you're talking about," Rob repeated. "All I know is neither men nor women seem to like me much. I don't care about the men, but I'd really like to meet a friendly woman."

They let him be. Apparently Rob robbed people without knowing it.

Then Picka got an idea. "The Iron Maiden has nothing to lose," he murmured. "She's bare."

"And lonely," Joy'nt agreed. She faced Rob. "Follow that crazy path," she said. "I'm sure you can use it. It will lead you to a lovely maiden in need of company."

"That sounds great," Rob agreed. He got off the pile of blankets and went to the nearest twist of the path. He stepped on it. Sure enough, it worked for him. Soon he was walking purposefully toward the spot where they had left the Maiden.

"I think we just did a couple of lonely people a good deed," Picka said.

"And we got our blankets back," she agreed.

They hauled their blankets back to the original spot. Then Joy'nt dislocated her bones and formed them into a roughly block-shaped framework. Picka heaved the largest blanket over the top, forming a tent. Joy'nt caught hold of the edges with her fingers and pulled them taut. Picka folded the other blankets and placed them on the ground inside the tent. It was ready.

The three animals returned, their foraging finished. They paused at the sight of the tent.

"The tent is for you," Picka said. "So you can sleep comfortably for the night. Joy'nt made the framework and I put the blankets on. We thought you'd prefer a bit of shelter, after being out in the forest so long. It's safe; we skeletons don't sleep, so I'll be keeping watch for any mischief."

Surprised, the three checked it. Then Woofer and Midrange settled down beside each other on the blankets, and Tweeter perched comfortably on Joy'nt's skull. "Tweet!" he tweeted appreciatively.

Darkness closed in. Picka could see well enough without light, as most nightmare spooks could. He and his sister were not in the bad-dream business, despite their ancestry, but their nature remained.

In fact being a walking skeleton was a rather lonely business. There were no others of their kind in Xanth proper, as far as they knew, apart from their parents, which meant that he and Joy'nt were doomed to remain single and have no families. They hated that, but had no choice. They were technically monsters, not wanted around living folk. They made do, but at quiet times like this Picka had occasion to be bothered by it, and he knew Joy'nt felt much the same.

He heard a rumble. It was from the sky. He knew what that meant: Cumulo Fracto Nimbus, Xanth's meanest cloud, had somehow spied the tent and intended to ruin it with a good soaking.

Picka scrambled into motion. He had seen a tarpaulin tree near the blanket tree. He ran to it, harvested a waterproof tarp, and ran back to fling it over the tent. "Better get under cover," he warned Tweeter. The bird quickly fluttered down into the tent.

Fracto arrived and was furious at being balked. He loosed a drench-pour that instantly wet the tent and formed a puddle around it. Picka hastily fetched a stick and dug a trench around and away from the tent so that the water could not swamp it. They had pitched the tent on a small rise, so that helped. Fracto sent fierce gusts of wind, but Joy'nt kept firm hold on the edges of the tarp.

Fracto raged, but couldn't take out the tent. Finally he stormed off, defeated.

In the morning the three pets emerged, dry and rested. Picka pulled off tarp and blanket, and Joy'nt disjointed and reformed in her normal shape.

Tweeter flew to her shoulder and tweeted. She brought out the marker, and Tweeter touched it. "We are getting to like you."

"We like you too," she said.

They gave the animals time to forage and take care of whatever natural functions were necessary for living forms. Then they set off again. This time they came across an enchanted path. That made the rest of their journey easy.

They encountered a man walking the opposite way. He was juggling three balls of light. They paused to watch.

After a moment he noticed. The light balls vanished. "Are my eyes deceiving me, or are you walking skeletons?" he inquired. "We don't see many like you on the enchanted path, but I know you don't mean any harm."

"We are skeletons," Picka agreed. "I am Picka Bone, and this is my sister Joy'nt. Plus Woofer, Midrange, and Tweeter. We are going to Castle Roogna."

"It's not far," the man agreed. "I am Aaron. My talent is to make balls of light." He smiled. "They are easy to juggle, because they weigh very little."

"We noticed," Joy'nt said.

"Good luck in your visit," Aaron said. A light ball appeared in his hand. He tossed it up, and another appeared. He tossed that, and a third appeared. He resumed walking, juggling the three.

"Which is the thing about the enchanted paths," Joy'nt said. "No harmful creature can get on one, so travelers know they are safe, and don't freak out at the sight of us."

"That does make it easier," Picka agreed.

Soon they met another traveler. Like the other, he seemed slightly taken aback by their appearance, but not really concerned. "Hello. I am Champion. It is my talent to lend strength of body, substance, or character. But you folk don't look as if you need any of that."

"We don't," Picka agreed, and introduced the members of their party. "I hope I have a talent, and that I can find out what it is."

"I regret I can't help you there," Champion said.

"Do you know something?" Picka said as they moved on. "Normal human beings seem like nice folk."

"We just never got to know many," Joy'nt said. "They were too busy screaming."

"Even though we have left the bad-dream business behind," he agreed. "In fact we never indulged in it. I wish I could somehow have a normal relationship with regular people. But that seems unlikely."

"We are what we are," she agreed somewhat sadly.

When they approached Castle Roogna, three animals intercepted them: a dog, a bird, and a cat.

But Picka had seen such tricks before. "Hello, Princesses," he said. "We are looking for Princess Dawn."

The animals formed into three blossoming fifteen-year-old girls, almost identical triplets. They all wore little gold crowns. "We knew that," Melody said. She wore a green dress, and had greenish-blond hair and blue eyes.

"We told her you were coming," Harmony said. She had a brown dress, hair, and eyes.

"She's already packed and ready to travel," Rhythm concluded. She had a red dress, red hair, and green eyes.

"But all we wanted was to ask her where—"

Princess Dawn arrived. She was twenty and as lovely as sunrise. She hugged Joy'nt, then Picka, not at all put off by their form. They were, after all, friends from childhood. "It can't be told," she said. "My sister values her privacy. I'll show you the way." She glanced around, then dropped to her knees to pet Woofer, stroke Midrange, and lift a finger for Tweeter to perch on. They had evidently met before.

Then Dawn walked purposefully into the orchard. They followed. So simply, they were on their way again.

2
TALENT

We are private here," Dawn said, pausing in the center of the orchard. She took a deep breath, which was too bad, because it accented the unsightly mounds of flesh covering her surely sightly bones. "Now I need to explain some things before I take you to Hades."

"Hades!" Picka protested. "We need to see Princess Eve."

Dawn smiled. That, too, was unfortunate, because it distorted the skin around the front of her skull. But she couldn't help it; she was alive. At least it showed her nice teeth. "She's the Mistress of Hades, ever since she married Dwarf Demon Pluto. They have a castle in Xanth, but she spends a lot of time ministering to the lost souls of Hades. She won't be back in Xanth for several days. So we'll see her in Hades." She looked sharply at Picka. "Do you have a problem with that?"

"No. My eighth of a soul is not damned. But our living friends may."

Joy'nt held the marker, and Midrange touched it. "No. It's probably more interesting than Xanth." Actually, Picka knew, Dawn could have gleaned the cat's answer directly, because she knew everything about anything alive.

"It is indeed," Dawn agreed. "Fascinating to visit, but we wouldn't want to stay there. So pay attention to the ground rules. My pass will deliver us to the River Styx, where there will be a ferry. We will take the ferry, then follow the path to Eve's castle." She frowned. "Do not stray from that path. Anyone stepping off it will have literal hell to pay to get back on it. Once we reach the castle, it will be all right; Eve doesn't let any temptations in there."

The five of them nodded. They understood.

"Now gather together. We must all be touching when the pass is invoked, going in and coming out. I don't want to leave anyone behind."

They gathered together. Picka and Joy'nt held hand bones, while he put a hand on Woofer's back and she did the same for Midrange. Tweeter perched on Joy'nt's head.

Dawn brought out a square of colored paper and held it before her. She put her free hand on Picka's shoulder bone. "Pass, do your thing," she said. It seemed that no fancy archaic language was required to invoke it.

The scenery around them changed. The assorted fruit trees were gone. They were standing in a desolate dead forest beside a polluted river. Gray smog surrounded them.

There was a ramshackle boat moored at a rickety pier. A male figure sat in it. He looked at Dawn. "You again?" he asked in a tone of disgust.

"You know any other mortal princess with a pass?" Dawn responded archly. "Charon, ferry us across the river."

"Why?"

"Because I have a pass," she repeated. "We've been through this before."

"Your pass brings you here," Charon said. "It doesn't pay your ferry fee."

"*What* ferry fee?" she demanded.

"The one I'm invoking for mortal princesses, walking skeletons, and pet animals."

"Ridiculous! You have no authority."

Charon shrugged. "Then find a ferryman with authority."

Dawn's fleshly mouth thinned to an almost skeletal line. She was almost attractive that way. "Do you want me to tell my sister, who will tell Pluto, who will whip your arrogant ass?"

"My donkey is elsewhere," Charon responded, unperturbed, "and unafraid of the whip. This is Hades, remember. Meanwhile you can't tell your sister if you don't get to her."

Dawn considered. "What do you want?"

"Your hand in marriage."

The princess swelled as if about to burst, especially in the chest area, but managed to contain herself. "I'll give you half a smile."

"One good stork summoning."

"One kiss."

"And a feel."

Dawn turned about. "Gather together," she told the others. "We're returning to Xanth."

"Very well, one kiss," Charon agreed hastily.

"Done, you immortal lecher." She approached the boat. Charon stood. They embraced, he on the boat, she on the shore. He kissed her ardently.

"It's an act," Joy'nt said wisely. "They enjoy bargaining for smooches. Living folk are like that."

Picka rattled his bones in a shrug. He had never claimed to understand the ways of mortal folk.

Finally the two completed the kiss. Then Dawn turned to the others. "Get on the boat. We have been granted safe passage." She stepped on herself, as Charon made his way to the rear of the boat. He lifted one hand, and a long pole fell from the sky. It seemed to be clothed in thick flesh, oddly.

"If I may inquire," Picka said, "what kind of pole is that?"

"It's a meaty oar," Charon said. "Its muscle helps me propel the craft. The sky is full of them, if you know where to look."

"Abysmal pun on meteor," Dawn muttered. "Something should be done about the puns that infest every section of Xanth; they are now leaking into other realms."

"Something should," Charon agreed. "It's disgusting."

"That water," Picka said. "Doesn't it make you forget things?"

"That's the River Lethe," Charon said. "This is the River Styx."

"It is safe to touch this water," Dawn said, "but the River Lethe is an excellent example of why we must not stray."

Joy'nt got on the boat. Then Woofer scrambled aboard somewhat awkwardly. Midrange simply jumped, landing neatly in the center. Tweeter had the easiest time: he flew across to land on Joy'nt's shoulder bone. Finally Picka stepped on, and untied the mooring rope.

Charon pushed vigorously on his pole, assisted by its muscle, and the boat moved out across the dark water. The surface was quiet except for occasional ripples. Picka, curious, poked a finger into a ripple, and teeth snapped violently at it.

"Don't do that!" Dawn cautioned belatedly. "The monsters are there to prevent doomed souls from swimming back across and escaping."

"I have no fear of monsters," Picka reminded her, "being one myself. They can't hurt me."

"But you shouldn't tease them. They are just doing their job."

She had a point. He lifted his finger from the water, undamaged. "I apologize, monsters."

There was an irritated splash. The monsters were not mollified.

"Make yourself useful," Charon said gruffly. "Use the curse sieve."

"The cursive?" Picka asked, perplexed.

"The curse sieve," the ferryman repeated. "The River Styx has become polluted with expired curses, making the river monsters uncomfortable. We try to seine out a few each time we cross."

That made sense. Picka took the sieve and swept it through the water. It fetched in a mottled film of gunk. Picka dumped it in the cursor, which was a kind of sliding, blinking bucket in the boat. It grunted an expletive, but had no choice but to accept the foul stuff. There was an odor of musty rot. Some of the expended curses might have been puns, which would account for the stink. It was really too bad that folk did not take care to dispose of the curses properly, instead of befouling the environment.

Charon continued poling, sometimes rowing with the oar, and before long they came to the opposite shore. They disembarked in fair order.

"Remember," Dawn said. "Stay on the path."

Why was she making such a point of it? They had heard her the first time.

"I will see you on the return trip," Charon said.

"More's the pity," Dawn agreed.

He poled away, and they started down the path. Woofer led the way, eager to see and sniff new things. Midrange followed more sedately, and Tweeter was content to ride Joy'nt's shoulder bone. Dawn walked beside Joy'nt, and Picka was last. He looked at the motions of the two females ahead of him, which had similar sways. It was too bad that Dawn's pelvis was swaddled in flexing living flesh, instead of being more like Joy'nt's clean bones. She seemed oblivious to the way that spoiled her appearance.

"Isn't Charon a Demon?" Joy'nt asked Dawn.

"Yes, he is a Dwarf Demon, less powerful than a full Demon, but still infinitely beyond any person or creature of the mortal realm."

"He seems to like you."

"He does. Demons have a certain thing about mortal princesses."

"He even spoke of marrying you."

"His master Demon Pluto married my sister Eve. He'd like to marry me and gain equivalent standing, at least in that respect."

"But you don't want to marry him? I should think he'd be a catch worthy of a princess."

"Here is the thing," Dawn said seriously. "If I married Charon, I'd be associating with an inferior Demon, at least compared to Eve with Pluto. Eve and I have always been equal. Call it princessly foolishness, but I can't abide the thought of settling for less than she got."

"How could you match her?"

"Oh, a mortal prince would do, or some similarly spectacular man. If one exists."

"That's a problem," Joy'nt agreed. "I'd like to find a nice male skeleton, but I don't want to go live in the dream realm and become unreal."

Dawn nodded. "That's roughly parallel to my disinclination to enter the realm of Hades. It's too limiting." She sighed. "Sometimes I envy Jumper."

"Who?"

"Jumper Spider. He was swept into Xanth proper by a narrative hook, was put into manform, and wound up marrying the Demoness Eris, who is devoting herself to making him sublimely happy for the next few millennia. It's a complicated story. She's parallel to, and I think slightly ahead of Pluto, and not associated with Hades. If there were some other male Demon . . ." She shrugged. "Not much chance. They like mortal princesses, all right, but not on terms I'd settle for. So I'll have to look elsewhere."

It was a revelation to Picka that a princess and Sorceress could have the same sort of romantic problem as a walking skeleton: insufficient prospects. He had supposed that royal figures led charmed lives.

Meanwhile the path was winding through the desolate forest, skirting bleak rocks and ugly puddles. Picka could readily appreciate why Dawn would not want to live here. But that evoked the question: why did Princess Eve evidently like it? Or was she trapped here?

A figure appeared beside the path. It was a female skeleton! Picka was so surprised he stopped walking, staring at her lovely bones.

"Come to me, handsome male," the creature said. "I am Skimpy Skeleton. I'll bet you can really kick tail!"

This was a reference to the way walking skeletons reproduced: the male kicked the female in the posterior, who flew apart and her bones scattered across the near landscape. This was known as knocking her up. Then he selected a number of her smaller bones and fit them together into a baby skeleton. It was the way Marrow Bones and Grace'l had made him and Joy'nt. Such interaction was a truly exciting prospect.

"I am Picka Bone," he said, unable to think of anything else at the moment.

"Well, Picka, come kick me." Skimpy faced away and bent over, presenting her shapely pelvis.

He was sorely tempted, but cautious. "But we don't even know each other."

"We will in a moment," she said. "Come to me, lover."

Picka stepped forward, enthralled.

"No!" Dawn cried, tackling him. They fell together at the edge of the path in a tangle of bone and flesh.

"But—" he protested.

"She's not real," Dawn said. "She's just a figment crafted to tempt you off the path. Once you cross the line, she'll vanish and you'll be stuck in Hades."

"Oh, can it, you liar," Skimpy said. "Don't believe her, Picka. I will give you such a good time!"

Picka was still tempted, but knew that Dawn had no reason to deceive him. They had been friends for years. He untangled his limbs from hers and both of them stood on the path. "Forget it, spook," he said.

"Oh!" Skimpy exclaimed, furious. "I boned up on you for this? That really heats me." She burst into flame and vanished.

"Now I understand, I think," he said to Dawn. "You did warn us, but she was so . . . so . . . ."

"I know. You should see the handsome male princes who try to get me to cross the line."

"I know better now," Picka said. "Thank you for rescuing me."

"We're friends," she reminded him. "I mean to see you safely through. Besides, it's a nice pretext to visit my sister."

They went on, catching up to the others. There was already mischief. A male walking skeleton with powerful bones was tempting Joy'nt, making suggestive kicking motions. "Don't do it!" Picka called to her.

Joy'nt came out of her daze. "Oh, I knew better," she said. "I think."

"Well, I'll just go find a more amenable skeleton," the male said grumpily. He stalked off. And there was Skimpy beckoning him again, moving her pelvis suggestively. That made both Joy'nt and Picka wince, as it was supposed to.

Then came a female dog, woofing fetchingly at Woofer. "Get out of here, you bitch!" Joy'nt cried. That jolted Woofer out of his momentary trance.

A lovely furred female cat appeared, mewing enticingly at Midrange. But the others were on it, and shooed her away before she could do much damage.

Finally a brilliantly plumed bird addressed Tweeter, tweeting seductively at him. But he, having seen the temptations of the others, knew better, and ignored her.

The castle came into view. It was a forbidding edifice, massively squatting on a bleak mountain, overlooking a phenomenally ugly lake. Surly clouds roiled overhead, as if angry that the castle even existed. Picka could take or leave living scenery, but he was surprised that a human princess would choose to live in such a mean-spirited place.

Dawn made a quarter smile. "It's better inside," she said.

They approached the grim front gate. An armored guard glowered down at them. "Begone, intruders," he called. "This is forbidden; you don't have permission to access this castle."

Dawn brought out a small device. "My ocarina," she explained. "Eve and I have taken to music in the past two years. We each have our instrument. It's amazing what music can accomplish."

"What does music have to do with this awful place?" Joy'nt asked.

Dawn lifted the instrument to her mouth and blew into it as her fingers moved across a number of little holes in it. Sweet music emerged, a pleasant tune.

"Ooof!" the guard cried, covering his ears. "Stop it!"

Dawn paused, looking at him.

Defeated, he looked away. "Oh, go ahead and pass," he grumped.

"You're sweet," Dawn said. And to the others: "See? Music really does sooth the savage breast." She marched ahead, and the others followed. They had gained admission to the dread castle in a way Picka had not anticipated. But maybe it made sense that ugly spooks of Hades could not stand beauty.

Once they were inside, things changed. It took Picka a good moment and a half to realize what the change was: the environment had become nice. The grimness was completely gone. The hall was softly lighted with muted colors, and pleasant pictures of Xanthly scenes were hung on the walls. Notable among them were Castle Roogna, where Princess Eve had grown up, and the Good Magician's Castle.

"What a difference!" Joy'nt murmured.

"Eve isn't like the other denizens of Hades," Dawn said. "But it's not politic to advertise that."

They reached the main hall. There was music there, and dancing. In fact Princess Eve was conducting a dancing class, playing the music for it on an odd instrument.

"Panpipes," Dawn explained. "A series of pipes of different lengths, so they make different notes, bound together. The denizens of Hades like that music; it reminds them of satyrs, who are great players." She made a small frown/smile. "And not just with musical instruments."

They waited while the lesson proceeded. There were eight couples dancing in unison, stepping and turning in a set order. Picka was surprised by how handsome the men were, in living terms, and how lovely the women. They were garbed in suits and flaring dresses of pastel colors, each perfectly formed. They were smiling. That surprised him most.

"Hades is not a region of torment," Dawn said, again divining his thought. "It is more of a staging area for souls that have not yet decided where to go. Here they learn useful skills. My sister is helping with the song-and-dance aspect."

The dance ended. Only then did Eve turn to them, smiling. She hurried across to hug her sister. "So nice to see you again, Morning Sun!"

"Ditto, Evening Shade," Dawn agreed. "I'm here on business. Our friend Picka Bone needs to know his magic talent. I'm sure he has one. I can't help him, but you can."

Eve glanced at Picka. "Let's play for another dance. Two instruments are better than one."

Picka was perplexed. Why wasn't Eve answering?

Dawn brought out her ocarina. The two played a lively melody and the couples danced. It was very pretty, both music and dance. Picka almost wished he were alive, knowing that the way the women's skirts flared as they twirled, almost (but not quite) showing their panties would have thrilled him. But he wasn't, so they didn't. He was also impressed by how similar the two sisters were, other than one being bright and the other dark. They were of the same height and fleshly girth, with hair of similar length, and well-formed features. Stripped of the ponderous flesh, their bones would have been almost identical.

"She's right," Joy'nt murmured. "Two musicians do make for a better dance."

Even the three animals seemed impressed. They were all listening and watching.

The dance ended. Eve faced Picka. "Why don't you join us for the next one?" she asked.

Join them? "I'm not musical," he reminded her.

"That's what you think. Music is your talent."

He laughed, thinking she was making a funny. "What, clanking my bones?"

"Yes."

This was becoming less funny. "It's not nice to tease folk," he said.

Eve walked to him. "This way. First remove your shoulder bones."

"My clavicles? I need them to move my shoulders." He shrugged, demonstrating.

"No, you are special, Picka. You can spare those particular bones. Like this." She put her hand on his right shoulder, grasped his clavicle, and lifted it away from his body.

Picka was so surprised he just stood there. He had had no idea that the bone could come off.

"And then you use it to play a melody on your own ribs," she continued. "They are musical too." She demonstrated, tapping a rib with the bone. It made a fine clear note.

Again, he was too surprised to react.

"You have more than an octave," she continued, tapping all his ribs in turn to produce eight or nine different notes. "And the half tone on the other side. Your other clavicle has a different quality, and each end differs, so you can play different types of melodies. You can surely do overtones too. Try it." She handed him his clavicle.

Picka took it and tapped one of his ribs. It made a clear ringing sound. He was amazed anew.

"Try a melody," Eve said.

He tried to play a simple tune. Instead he got a series of wrong notes. Dawn put her hands over her ears.

"It may take a little practice," Eve said.

"A *lot* of practice," Joy'nt said, wincing.

"But we can get you started with something simple," Eve said. "Like maybe 'Chopsticks'." She lifted off his left clavicle and took back his right one. Then she used them together, striking two notes at a time in rapid order, repeatedly. From this series emerged a certain awkward melody. "Perfect that, then move on to more advanced pieces," she advised, handing him his clavicles. "You'll get there, in time."

"A long time," Joy'nt muttered.

Picka tried it. To his amazement he was able to duplicate the tune, and it sounded all right.

"See?" Eve said. "You catch on quickly. It's your talent. You can probably play any melody you hear. Try the one I just used for the dance."

Picka was dubious, but he tried. And the melody came out perfectly. The couples started dancing again.

In a moment Eve joined in with her panpipes. Then Dawn played her ocarina. Suddenly they had a three-instrument melody, and it was absolutely beautiful. The dancers danced brilliantly, with more verve than before. The twirls were more vigorous, and the skirts flared up so high that eight panties flashed in perfect unison. Picka was not a panty-gazing male, because panties only emphasized those lugubrious mounds of flesh, but the motions were such that the outlines of the underlying pelvis bones were clear, and that made him stare.

The melody came to an end, all three players synchronized. The dancers applauded. It had been a fine melody and a fine dance.

"And there you are," Eve said. "You have the potential to be a fine musician, Picka, rather than being a duffer like Dawn and me. Your magic not only enables you to play the notes, it enables you to memorize any tune you hear so you can play it yourself. You merely need to make an effort to hear a lot of music. I'm sure there will be other effects I haven't thought of that will make you better yet. You just need to apply yourself."

"I will!" he promised gladly.

"Now let me give you folk the tour of the castle. It was built to my specifications, but we receive few visitors from Xanth, for some reason." Eve made a cute moue. Then she glanced at the three pets. "We have an indoor garden with catnip, dog fennel, and bird branches. Right this way."

The three animals were immediately interested. They formed a cluster right behind Eve. Dawn, Joy'nt, and Picka followed.

It was a marvelous tour. The castle had everything, and there was no sign of the bleakness outside. Eve had made an enclave of pleasantness in an otherwise unpleasant region.

"And how is Pluto?" Dawn inquired as they walked.

"He's a great lover and a fair companion," Eve replied candidly. "He gives me anything I want, except maybe love. I'm not sure he's capable of that. But that's the nature of political marriages. They are for status and heirs and not much else."

"Heirs?"

"Oh, did I forget to mention that? I'll show you our one-year-old son Plato next."

She had forgotten to mention her baby son? Picka was not well-versed in living family relations, but that suggested that there was indeed a certain lack of something. They must have signaled the stork many, many times, because that was what living men and D/demon males liked to do when they got hold of lovely princesses, and the stork had responded. But ordinarily that would have been the very first thing a mother mentioned.

"Oh, Eve, I'm so jealous!" Dawn said.

"Well, you know what you can do about it, sister dear."

"Find a prince and let him signal the stork all he wants," Dawn agreed. "But is there a suitable prince?"

"One that matches a Dwarf Demon? I doubt it. But why don't you ask the Good Magician?"

"Maybe I should," Dawn agreed thoughtfully. "My nose is out of joint because you're suitably married while I'm a spinster."

A spinster at age almost-twenty-one? Picka trusted this was mortal humor.

"Isn't it awful," Eve said smugly. "We are victims of the Demon's spell."

"Demon's spell?" Joy'nt asked.

"When Great-grandpa Bink helped the Demon Xanth, way back when," Dawn said, "the Demon did Bink the favor of making all his descendants have Magician-caliber magic talents. But there seems to have been a glitch, because most of them are female. Apart from Grandpa

Dor and Father Dolph, they've all been girls, and it's getting worse. So we have the two of us, and then the three little princesses."

"And all those girls really have to scratch," Eve said. "Poor Dawn may be left out."

"That does it," Dawn snapped. "I'll do it, even if I do have to pay a year's service or do an equivalent mission."

"That's the girl. Now let's have that banquet my staff has prepared for you." Eve glanced at the pets. "All of you; you haven't eaten until you have feasted on what the chefs of Hades prepare."

That proved to be the case. It was a sumptuous meal for all except the two skeletons. However, they were used to that. Picka amused himself by lightly tapping his ribs with his clavicles, zeroing in on their nuances. Dawn had spoken truly: he had one and a half octaves, and the two ends of his two clavicles made different sounds as they struck the ribs: ringing, muted, firm, dull, so that he could achieve different effects with the same notes. It wasn't just his ribs; his thighs, shins, and knees had their own inflections, and his hollow skull made a drumlike sound.

"It really is a good talent," Joy'nt said approvingly. "I could never make music like that."

"I wonder." He tapped one of her ribs with a clavicle. It made a dull thud. So it was true: her bones were not musical.

The others returned from the banquet. Even the pets were impressed; it showed in their demeanors.

"I have decided," Princess Dawn said. "I am going from here to the Good Magician's Castle, to seek an Answer to the Question, Where is there a suitable Prince or equivalent for me? But first we'll get the rest of you back to Xanth so you won't be trapped here."

"Trapped?" Eve asked, frowning prettily.

"It's the abode of the dead!" Dawn said.

"True, but that's not their fault," Eve said. "There are some really nice souls here. You saw the dancers."

"Maybe when I'm dead I'll have a change of heart," Dawn said.

"And this castle is an enclave. Living folk can exist here." Eve glanced at the pets. "Which reminds me: we are short of nice living animals.

How would you three like to remain here, as my guests? My servants would love the privilege of catering to you endlessly."

The three animals exchanged about five glances, obviously tempted. But then they shook their heads. They preferred to return to Xanth.

"What about you skeletons?" Eve asked. "You remind me of my childhood, when we used to play together. Dawn and I would try to tempt Picka into human masculinity, without much success. Would you like to stay?"

Picka realized that despite the opulence, Eve was lonely. She had a castle in Xanth to which she could go at any time, yet she missed her friends. It seemed there was more to life than status.

Joy'nt answered for them. "We seek adventure to enhance our dull existences. Your castle is lovely, but there's no adventure in it. Xanth in contrast is full of challenging things. We are more likely to find adventure there."

"True," Eve agreed, dabbing at her face. Was there a tear there? But she didn't have any reason not to be happy, did she?

"I'll make sure all of you get safely back to Xanth," Dawn said. "Then I'll go on to see the Good Magician."

"I will go with you," Picka said. "Maybe I can help in some way."

"So will I," Joy'nt said. "There's bound to be adventure there."

"Woof!"

Dawn glanced at Woofer. "What, you too?" Then she nodded, because they were living creatures and she knew all about anything alive. "All three of you! That's wonderful."

"It's nice to have friends," Eve murmured, dabbing her face once more.

Picka saw it again. Princess Eve had everything, yet was sad because she lacked friends and adventure. She was a prisoner of her royal life. He never would have expected it.

"Well, the ferryman awaits," Dawn said. "This time I may have to give him a feel."

"Charon is making demands?" Eve asked sharply. "I'll speak to Pluto."

"Don't bother," Dawn said. "I can handle it."

"I'm sure you can," Eve agreed. Then the sisters hugged and separated, tearfully.

It was time to move on. Picka realized belatedly that they hadn't even seen Eve's son, Plato. They had all forgotten.

3
MISSION

The Good Magician's Castle was suitably impressive, with its moat, wall, turrets, and flags.

"It's never the same twice," Princess Dawn murmured. "Humfrey keeps magically renovating it. He always knows who is coming, and is prepared."

"But we decided to come here only yesterday," Joy'nt said. "How could he know in time to set things up?"

"He's the Magician of Information," Picka reminded her. "It's his business to know."

"Also, he sets up magical fields to nullify the talents of querents," Dawn said, "so they have to use their wits to get through. That means I won't be able to learn instantly about living things, and the two of you won't be able to reformulate your bones or play music."

"What about the pets?" Joy'nt asked.

Dawn glanced at the three animals. "They're really Mundanes, without magic, though they may develop talents some day. I don't think they'll be affected." She pondered half a moment. "Are you three sure you want to tackle this with us? Challenges can be frustrating and scary, and you really don't need to—"

"Woof!"

"Tweet!"

"Mew."

"Thanks, folks. I'm touched."

Picka realized that even though she was a princess and a Sorceress, not to mention being outstandingly beautiful for her species, Dawn was nervous about what she faced, and appreciated the moral support. It might come in the form of skeletons and animals, but they were friends, and that was what counted.

Dawn glanced at him. "I can't tell much about you, Picka, because you're not alive, but I have the feeling you understand more than you let on."

"I do get bone-headed ideas," he agreed.

"They are surely good ones." She kissed his skull. The effect was oddly pleasant, despite the meatiness of her lips. There was something *about* a beautiful young princess Sorceress. Maybe in time he would figure out what it was.

"Let's get on with it," Joy'nt said, a trifle tersely. It was almost as if something was bothering her.

"Indeed," Dawn agreed. She faced the castle, took a deep breath that momentarily accented the burdensome flesh on her chest, and marched toward the drawbridge.

The others followed. "Things should get interesting soon," Picka murmured to Joy'nt.

"Woof!" Woofer responded, wagging his tail.

There was a noisy babbling, as if a small crowd of human folk were walking and talking just ahead of them, but there were no people in sight.

Then Dawn halted. "There's a wall here," she said. "An invisible wall."

Picka stepped up beside her and extended a bone finger. It encountered some kind of panel. He tapped, and the babbling increased. "The wall is talking," he said, surprised.

"It is also blocking our way," Joy'nt said, feeling high and low. The three pets were also exploring the unseen surface: Woofer was sniffing the base, Tweeter was flying up to the top, and Midrange was clawing the surface. None of them seemed to be making much progress.

"If I were an ogre, I would simply crash through it," Dawn said. "But of course there would be a different Challenge for an ogre. There must be a less violent way past. We have but to find it."

"Walk around it," Joy'nt suggested.

"I doubt it's that simple, but let's see," Dawn said.

Dawn and Joy'nt walked to the left, while Picka and the three pets went right. The invisible wall continued, merrily babbling unintelligibly. They kept on, and it kept on.

Until they encountered another party. There were Dawn and Joy'nt, coming from the opposite direction. The wall had curved, closing a circle. There was no way around it.

"Or maybe not," Joy'nt said as they met.

"I wonder whether it's glass," Dawn said. "If so, we might be able to fracture it."

They checked around. There were bushes, trees, and rocks all around. Picka suspected that if rocks would crack it, there would have been no rocks here. But he picked up a stone, and bashed it against the wall.

The babble increased, sounding vaguely disapproving. But there was no crack. He struck it several more times, just to be sure, but it was impervious.

"So what's your idea, Picka?" Dawn asked. He had the impression she was suppressing exasperation.

He pondered, thoughts caroming across the interior hollow of his skull. Every idea seemed stupider than the prior one. In desperation he fixed on the stupidest of them all. "It's a sound barrier. A kind of invisible wall. Maybe there's a door through it."

They checked for a door. The invisible wall was smooth throughout—until Tweeter discovered a little hole, no bigger than a fingertip. "As doors go, that isn't much," Dawn remarked.

Then Joy'nt got a notion. "It's a keyhole!"

"A keyhole!" Dawn repeated. "Of course. Now all we need is the key."

And of course there was none.

Woofer went out amidst the trees, sniffing. He stopped by a small tree with greenish yellow fruit. "Woof!"

Dawn glanced across. "That's just a lime tree, Woofer. The fruit is bitter. You need sugar to make it into sweet pies, like—" She stopped, a bright bulb flashing over her head. "Keylime pie! There's the key! Woofer, you're a genius!"

Woofer wagged his tail.

They harvested a keylime fruit. Dawn brought it to the invisible keyhole. The wall's babbling increased, almost like a protest. It touched the indentation. There was a click. Then the invisible door swung open.

They piled through. They had navigated the first Challenge. It had been a joint effort, with Picka thinking of the door, Tweeter finding the hole, Joy'nt realizing it was a keyhole, Woofer finding the pun for the key, and Dawn putting it all into a notion. They had worked well together.

But there would be two more Challenges remaining. They might be more complicated.

The way to the drawbridge was now clear. They walked to it. Picka half expected it to lift clear of the moat before they got there, but it remained in place.

"I don't trust this," Dawn muttered. She set one foot on the nearest wood plank of the bridge.

"Boo!" a funny-faced man's head yelled, startling them all. It was a cartoon figure, all wires and hinges, with a head on a bouncy spring.

"Jack in the Box," Dawn said, disgusted. "Well, it's done; we'll go on."

But when she took another step, another head shot out of another box on the bridge. "Boo!"

"Oh, go away!" Dawn snapped, trying to brush by him.

But the figure flung his arms about her, trying to feel and kiss her. Doubly disgusted, Dawn lurched back, escaping him. "Bleep!" she muttered in a singularly unprincessly expletive that scorched the nearest planks.

"Let me try it," Joy'nt said. "There's nothing on me to kiss or feel." She stepped on the drawbridge.

Nothing happened.

Picka tried it, with no different result. It seemed it was Dawn alone who was barred. And of course she was the one who had to make it through.

So the second challenge was for Dawn to pass an obnoxious Jack in the Box. How was she to do it?

They considered. There had to be a way, because this was an arranged Challenge with an arranged solution. But what was that solution?

"There must be something nearby that will do it," Picka said, "just as the keylime tree was near the sound barrier. We just need to see it and understand it and use it."

They looked, but there was next to nothing in the immediate vicinity—only the planks of the drawbridge, nailed together, the heavy rope that hauled it up and let it down—the end of which was badly frayed beyond its terminal knot and would soon need replacement—and the assorted boxes, from any of which Jack could obnoxiously pop up.

Midrange sat beside the end of the rope, batting its loose fibers. Then he got an idea; they saw the bulb flash over his head. "Meow!" he said.

Dawn understood him. "The knot?" she asked. "That's the answer? I don't understand."

"Meow."

"Yes, the end is frayed. But how will that stop Jack?"

"Meow. Meow," Midrange said carefully.

"Frayed. Knot," Dawn repeated. "I still don't see—"

"Tweet!" Tweeter tweeted urgently.

"Put them together? Frayed Knot? I still don't see—"

"I'm afraid not!" Joy'nt exclaimed. "That's the phrase. Try it on Jack."

"Afraid not," Dawn repeated thoughtfully. "Could that actually be it? It's such an abysmal pun."

"Puns have power in Xanth," Picka reminded her.

"Well, let's see." Dawn put her foot on the plank. Jack popped out at her, leering. "I'm afraid not," she told him firmly.

Jack flung his ramshackle arms about her and drew her close for a smooch. She jerked back just in time to avoid it.

"Maybe it's not just the words," Joy'nt said. "Maybe you need the knot itself."

Dawn nodded. She reached for the knot and pulled on it. It came away in her hands, separating from the frayed rope.

She tried again. This time when Jack popped up, she thrust the frayed knot at him. "'Fraid not!" she said.

Jack recoiled. Some of his own wiring started fraying. The destruction was contagious!

"Well, now," Dawn said. She marched along the drawbridge, carrying the knot before her like a shield. The assorted Jacks shied away. They had found the solution to the second Challenge, thanks to Midrange and Tweeter.

The others followed her. The team had scored again.

Beyond the drawbridge stood an ugly tree. Its gnarly branches reached out like tentacles ready to grab a victim. It wasn't a tangle tree, however; the wood could not move.

"This is a bad idea," Dawn said abruptly. "We'd better go back."

What? The others stared at her.

"Let's go." Dawn started back across the drawbridge.

"Dawn!" Joy'nt protested. "We can't quit now!"

"What's the point?" Dawn asked. "There's probably no good prince for me anyway."

"But—" Then Joy'nt's attitude changed. "You're right. Why serve a whole year's Service for nothing?"

Dawn looked confused. "I didn't say that! I just—" Her features changed. "Yes, I did. I have better things to do with my life than waste it on drudgery for a year."

"This is ridiculous!" Picka protested. "How can either of you even think of quitting now?" But at that point he changed his mind. "Actually, it *is* a lot of trouble the Good Magician puts folk through, for obscure Answers. We shouldn't play his game."

"No!" Dawn and Joy'nt said almost together.

"That isn't—" Joy'nt continued.

"Yes, it is," Dawn said.

"This is crazy!" Picka said. "We're saying things we don't mean." But then he changed his mind. "Unless . . ."

"One at a time," Dawn said. "Bad thoughts are coming to us singly. Something is affecting our thoughts."

"What could that be?" Picka asked.

The three pets turned almost together to face the ugly tree.

"The Devil Tree! Why didn't I think of that?" Dawn asked. "I should have divined its nature immediately."

"Two reasons," Picka said. "First, your talent of knowing all about any living thing is nullified for these Challenges. Second, if you happened to think of it independently, the Tree would have changed your thought so you lost it."

"True deviltry," Joy'nt agreed.

Dawn focused on Picka. "Have I remarked that there seems to be more in your empty head than shows?"

"I believe you have," Picka said. "My skull is not clogged with meat, so my thoughts are free to rattle around freely."

"You're no meat head," she agreed.

"So why isn't the Tree changing both of your thoughts now?" Joy'nt asked.

"Because it's focusing at the moment on the pets," Picka said. "See, they are giving it a hard time."

Indeed, first one pet was turning away from the tree, then another, while the first one turned back toward it. The Tree was trying to turn all three away, but two were always focusing on it. The Tree's foliage was rustling with annoyance; it couldn't handle three simultaneously. That left Dawn and the skeletons to converse on their own.

"I am getting to appreciate that trio," Dawn said. "So now we know the Challenge: the Tree keeps changing our minds. How do we handle it?"

"Maybe if all six of us focus on passing it, it won't be able to balk us," Picka suggested.

"Let's try it," Dawn agreed.

They got together and concentrated on a single thought: PASS THE TREE. They started walking.

But Dawn broke ranks. "I can't do it!" she said, pained.

"Oh, fractures!" Joy'nt swore. "She's the one who has to do it; the rest of us are only Companions who don't matter."

"You matter," Dawn said. "But it is true that for this particular Challenge, I'm the one who has to pass."

"So we need another way," Picka said.

"There must be something to counter the Tree," Dawn said. "If we can fathom it, without the Tree diverting us."

"Maybe the pets can balk it again," Joy'nt said, "acting as a trio."

The pets got moving. They found a nook in the castle wall nearby, where there was a dining table and a place setting with plate, glass, silverware, and chopsticks. Evidently it was set up to accommodate any preference. Except for animals. Still, the three paused there expectantly.

"Chopsticks," Joy'nt said. "Maybe you can play a tune, Picka."

"No, my music talent is stifled here," Picka said.

"But you know, that could be a pun," Dawn said. Then she changed her mind. "No, of course not."

Picka exchanged a hollow eye-holed glance with Joy'nt. Dawn's mind had been messed with. That suggested that her original thought was apt, and the Tree did not want her to have it. What was there about the chopsticks?

Picka went to the nook and picked up the two little sticks. Immediately they jerked in his fingers, seeming to possess animation of their own. They rapped down on the table, chipping splinters from it.

"They like to chop!" Joy'nt said. "Well, maybe not."

So now Joy'nt's thought was being stifled. That confirmed it.

Picka took the chopsticks and carried them to the Devil Tree. He held them beside its trunk. They started chopping vigorously, chipping the bark.

GO AWAY! The thought was so strong that Picka stumbled backward. The Tree had evidently been so annoyed by the attack of the chop sticks that it forgot to make the thought seem like his own. But it did stop him from keeping the little sticks close.

"No problem!" Dawn called. "We're past it, thanks to your distraction."

Oh. Picka returned the sticks to the dining nook, then walked across to join the others. It seemed they had navigated the third Challenge.

A formerly hidden door in the castle wall opened. "Welcome, visitors!" a woman called. "Come on in."

"Hello, Wira," Dawn said. "It's so nice to see you again." The two women hugged. "And these are Picka and Joy'nt Bone, and the three former Baldwin Family pets, Woofer, Tweeter, and Midrange."

"Of course," Wira agreed. She petted Woofer, stroked Midrange, and proffered her shoulder as a perch for Tweeter. "Dara has treats for all of you."

"Dara?" Joy'nt asked.

"Magician Humfrey's Designated Wife of the Month," Wira explained. "She was his first, and doesn't mind returning one month in six, though she says that's about all she can take of him."

"A demoness?"

"He was young then," Wira confided. "She tempted him, but then became impatient, so he moved on to the Maiden Taiwan. It's a long story that we don't speak of much today."

"In Xanth a man is supposed to have only one wife at a time," Dawn said. "But in the course of a century or so Humfrey had five and a half different wives. So now they take turns. Ah, here we are."

They had arrived at the main reception hall. There was Dara, resplendent in a royal gown. But as they approached it shifted to an ordinary housedress, then to bra and panties, and on to a business suit.

"Oh, bleep!" Dara swore. "I forgot your friend is a skeleton. Illicit flashes won't freak him."

"True," Dawn agreed cheerfully. "He doesn't even like meaty panties."

Dara became a skeleton with glowing bones. That made Picka take note. He found himself leaning against a wall. Some time must have passed, because the three animals were finishing snacks that Picka had never seen served.

"Ha!" Dara said. "I did freak him out."

That made him wonder whether a demoness could be a good girl-friend for him. There were very few walking skeletons in Xanth proper, but many demonesses. Obviously they could be attractive when they tried. But then he realized that most Demonesses wouldn't have the patience to mess with a dull skeleton.

"So when may I see the Good Magician?" Dawn asked.

"Oh, you won't be seeing him this time," Dara said. "He's busy with something else. But I can brief you."

"Something else!" Dawn said, tiny sparks snapping from her eyes. "I went through this bleeping Challenges charade just to have him ignore me?"

"At ease, Princess," Dara said, not at all intimidated. "Humfrey asked me to explain your Service to you."

"When he hasn't even given me an Answer?"

"He says you'll find your ideal significant other by the time you complete the mission."

Dawn subsided. "He does arrange things that way, sometimes," she said. "So there is a suitable prince for me?"

"There is an ideal male for you," Dara said. "I'm not sure whether he's a prince, but Humfrey says he will be more than worthy of you, and you'll be well satisfied when the time comes. Now are you ready to learn about the mission?"

Dawn sighed. Her normally straight nose had become slightly crooked. It was evident she wasn't accustomed to being treated this way—no princess was—but of course the Good Magician was a rule unto himself. A whole complex of rules, as the matter of five and a half wives demonstrated. If she wanted her Answer, she would have to cooperate. "Yes," she said.

"Humfrey has learned, after a century or so, the whereabouts of Pundora's Box. He means to recover it."

"Pandora's Box?" Dawn asked. "Isn't that Mundane? It held all the blessings and curses, and when Pandora opened it they all escaped, which is why Mundania is such an awful place. What would the Good Magician want with it? It's empty, after all, except maybe for one blessing, Hope. We learned about it in Comparative Magic class." She yawned delicately, clearly not much interested.

"Pundora's Box," Dara repeated. "With a U. Pundora was the Xanth equivalent. When she opened the Box, all the confined puns escaped, and they have been infesting Xanth ever since. The only thing that will contain them for any length of time is the original box, securely closed.

But though it is possible to sweep up errant puns—if you have a strong stomach—that is pointless, because the Box has been lost. Until now."

Picka got interested. "So now those puns can be put back in the Box, and not soil Xanth anymore?"

"Exactly," Dara agreed. "It will finally be possible to clean up Xanth. 'Tis a consummation devoutly to be wished."

"But isn't Xanth mostly made of puns?" Joy'nt asked. "If all of them were taken out, there might not be much left."

"We'll be selective. Only the worst riffraff will be culled, at first. Then we'll see about what else is expendable."

"Once you recover the Box," Dawn said. "Where is it?"

"That is another story," Dara said. "Every time Humfrey got a fix on the Box, and sought to fetch it in, its location changed. It was almost as if the Box knew it was being tracked, and sought to escape. Which doesn't seem sensible. Why would the Box care? But though Humfrey knows just about everything about everything, somehow that knowledge escaped him. It was frustrating. It made him grumpy."

"For over a century?" Dawn asked. "That would explain a lot."

"It does," Dara agreed. "His grumpiness is legendary. All five and a half of us wives are highly aware of it. Now we know why. We must recover that Box, and not just because of the potential pun cleanup."

"Yes," Dawn agreed. "A way to reduce the Good Magician's grumpiness would be a significant service to Xanth. He might even start seeing querent princesses instead of snubbing them."

Dara smiled, evidently amused by Dawn's irony. "Even that, perhaps," she agreed. "I am glad you appreciate the importance."

"I do. So exactly where is the Box? I presume my mission will be to go fetch it."

"Not exactly. Pundora's Box is in Caprice Castle."

"What castle? I think I know all the castles of Xanth, but I never heard of that one."

"It's a feral castle, escaped from some long-forgotten Magician, never officially classified because it never remained in one place long enough to be identified. Legend has it that it seeks a worthy occupant, scaring off unworthy ones, so has a reputation for being haunted. But Humfrey says it was never haunted, just choosy. So it keeps traveling, looking, but is never satisfied. Maybe it likes being wild, and is only pretending to look for a suitable occupant."

Picka was interested again. "This castle—Caprice—is alive?"

"We don't think so, at least not exactly. It may be like you, Picka, animate without being alive. Possibly it derives from demon stock. It does seem to have a will of its own."

"And it travels," Joy'nt said. "How does it do that? Does it have legs?"

"No legs," Dara said, smiling again. "It merely fades out from one location and fades in at another. There's no implosion or explosion of displaced air. It's completely silent."

"Maybe it's illusion," Dawn said.

"No, it's quite solid."

"How do you know, if nobody can catch it?"

"Nobody catches it, but people have nighted in it on occasion. They report that it's an excellent host, with good food, soft beds, and all the other amenities. But when it goes, it goes, and they are left standing on empty ground." Dara paused thoughtfully. "They say that it seems to be studying them, in some manner. We suspect it is considering them for permanent occupation, but when they prove unworthy, it moves on. So it's still looking, as it has for centuries."

"You think I might be considered worthy?" Dawn asked. "That it might stay put for me?"

"We suspect that you might be half-worthy," Dara said. "The other half would be the Master, your husband. When you find him and marry him."

Dawn brightened. "You saw me coming! You're getting two birds with one arrow! I need a good man to catch that castle, and you're making me capture the castle in return for getting that man. What connivance!"

"Humfrey can be devious," Dara agreed. "Your mission will be to find and tame Caprice Castle. We suspect it will not be easy, even if it finds you worthy. This is a very choosy edifice."

"Let me see if I understand correctly," Dawn said seriously. "You can't tell me where this castle is, because it moves without a forwarding address. So I have to catch it on my own, persuade it to accept me, and nail it down so you can recover Pundora's Box."

"That is the essence," Dara agreed.

"How the bleep do you expect me to find it when it moves randomly?" Dawn demanded.

"Humfrey didn't tell me that."

"Which must be why he's not showing his gnomelike face." Dawn frowned, pondering. "Maybe I should decline to take this mission."

"But we really need to get that Box," Dara protested. "Xanth has survived so far, but it will be overwhelmed by idiotic puns if something isn't done soon."

Picka got an idea. "How does the Good Magician track the Box?"

"You are an empty-headed genius," Dawn said. She looked at Dara. "Well?"

Now Wira answered. She had been so quiet they had forgotten she was still there. "He doesn't track it constantly, just when he's in touch with someone who can track it. He gave me a small list of people." She produced the list.

"Let me see that," Dawn said, taking it. She looked at it. "Attila the Pun?"

"He hates puns, and destroys them relentlessly," Wira said. "Somehow he knows where they are. His subtitle is the Punisher."

"And where is Attila?"

"He moves about, seeking puns to destroy."

"So we have to track down Attila, so he can track down the Box," Dawn said. "And how to we do that?"

"He has a distinctive savage primitive odor. Woofer will be able to wind it from some distance, after Tweeter locates a region of freshly dead puns."

"So all the members of our party will contribute to the effort?"

"In time," Dara agreed.

"And is there anything else we should know before we start?"

"Yes," Wira said. "The Good Magician will see Picka and Joy'nt Bone now."

"He will see them but not me? Exactly whose Quest is this?" Dawn demanded. Now her nose was definitely out of joint.

"Yours. But the skeletons aren't normal people. They need some assistance."

"Still, if it's my Quest—"

"Some definitions," Dara said firmly. "You are the person with the Quest. But Picka is the protagonist."

"The what?"

"The viewpoint character. The one from whose perspective the Muse of History will relate the narrative. Protagonists warrant special attention, even if they are merely assisting the main enterprise."

"But I don't warrant that," Picka protested. "I'm just a no-account spook."

"For the moment, yes," Dara said. "But things may change."

Dawn's nose was bent so badly it was threatening to snap in half. "He's the main character of this narrative? How does he rate that?"

"Oh, it's a pretty standard convention. The protagonist needs to be an apt observer. Often a bystander can do that more effectively than the action figure."

"I am a bystander?" Picka asked. It was just as well he didn't have a nose, because it would have strained its joint.

"It is important to pick the correct bystander," Dara said patiently. "One who witnesses most of the most important activities. You happen to be that one."

"So he's along to notice what I'm doing?" Dawn asked, her nose relaxing somewhat.

"Yes, approximately. At least until he becomes an action figure himself."

Picka would have liked to learn more, but Wira was urging him and Joy'nt to follow her. So they left Dawn and the pets to question Dara, while the two of them followed Wira up the narrow winding stairway to the Good Magician's dingy office.

There he was, a small, wizened, and, yes, gnomelike man seated before a giant open tome, which he was perusing intently.

"Father Humfrey, here are Picka and Joy'nt Bone," Wira said, introducing them.

The Good Magician looked up. "Give them the spell," he said grumpily.

Wira delved into her pocket and produced two small spheres, which she handed to the two of them.

"What spell is this?" Joy'nt asked, looking at hers.

"Transformation," Humfrey answered. "When you invoke it, it will transform you to a living person, for one hour. Then you will revert to your natural state. You will not be able to invoke it again that day, so don't waste it."

"A living person?" Picka asked. "With meat on my bones?"

"Gobs," Humfrey agreed with the trace of a smile.

"Why would we ever want to do that?" Joy'nt asked, repelled.

"To conceal your identities, if the necessity arises." Humfrey frowned. His face was marvelously formulated for that. "Do not allow any other person to use that spell. It is for the two of you alone."

"We're not ashamed of our nature," Picka said. "We don't mind who knows we are walking skeletons."

But Humfrey had already returned his attention to his tome. He had tuned them out.

They put the spells into their skulls for safekeeping and returned to the downstairs room, bemused. Picka doubted they would ever use the spell. The very idea of living meat on his bones was sickening.

Dawn faced them as they returned. "I think we're done here," she said, evidently reconciled to her nonprotagonist status. "Let's go."

Picka was happy to agree. He was not entirely comfortable with the revelations they had received.

"There is a spell for Dawn too," Wira said, bringing out another small ball.

"What's this?" Down asked, hardly mollified.

"A transport spell. You can invoke it to transport yourself and anyone in physical contact with you instantly to any spot you choose. It is in a manner similar to your Hades pass. Do not invoke it unless it is quite necessary; it is not for casual use, but for emergencies."

"Only for emergencies," Dawn agreed, putting away the spell.

"You will want to stay the night," Dara said. "Fracto Cloud has located you and is waiting to drench you."

"Skeletons aren't afraid of water," Joy'nt said.

"But fleshly creatures don't always appreciate getting their clothing or fur or feathers soaked." Dara's expressive mouth twitched. "And we have tasty treats for each of you."

The interest of the pets intensified.

"Including some wonderful marble cake the Gorgon made by stoning a flour cake. It has a special edge."

Dawn threw up her hands in a mortal expression. She, being a princess, naturally loved special cake. "One night," she said gruffly.

4
TRAVEL

Princess Dawn was given a room of her own, while Joy'nt shared one with the three pets, who weren't easy being alone in a strange castle. That left Picka alone in his own room. He didn't need a room, as he didn't sleep, but he didn't want to be a bad guest, so he accepted it.

There was a knock on his door. He opened it, and there was Dawn in her nightie. "We need to talk," she said, brushing past him.

"If you wish," he said.

She sat on his unused bed, leaned against the wall, and lifted her knees. Her nightie reached only to her knees, so that her legs showed under it, and a section of her sunny panties. "Sit down," she said.

He fetched a chair and sat on it, facing her. What was on her mind? "Closer."

He hiked the chair closer.

She put her legs down and leaned forward so that her bright bra showed. She caught a chair leg, pulling it closer yet, so that he had to lift his weight to allow it to slide. Now his knees touched hers.

"You really don't notice, do you," she said.

"Notice what?"

"I just flashed you with my well-filled panties, and my well-filled bra. You never blinked."

"I can't blink. I have no eyelids."

"I think you know what I mean, Picka. Remember when we were children and we went skinny-dipping?"

"You and Eve floated on the water," he agreed. "Joy'nt and I sank." He still did not know what she had in mind.

"We splashed each other, and then you walked on the bottom and held me over your head so that it looked as if I was swimming without moving my arms or legs. Then I dived down and tried to tickle you, but your bare ribs weren't very ticklish. We wound up in a tangle of bones and limbs. I kissed your bare teeth. We had a ball."

"I don't remember the ball."

"Not a physical ball. I mean we had a lot of fun."

"Oh. Yes, we did."

"We were children—Eve and I were ten, you and Joy'nt fourteen. You were more responsible than we were, and made sure we did not get into water too deep."

"I remember. You wanted to swim too far out, and I had to fetch you back. You tried to make me lose my footing."

"I wrapped my legs about your skull," she agreed. "So that you couldn't see which way to go. It almost worked."

"Until you started laughing," he agreed. "Then I knew I was going wrong, and reversed direction and got you out."

"You were a spoilsport."

"I am sorry about that."

"I think I could do it better now," she said. "Because I wouldn't laugh."

"Perhaps."

"You doubt? I'll show you. Let me get my legs on your skull."

"But—"

She pulled him to her on the bed, then lifted her legs and locked them on his skull. His face was caught against the base of her belly. "Can you see anything?" she asked.

"No," he said into her bottom. "Your flesh is blocking off my eye sockets."

She relaxed. "So it really is true."

"Yes, you can hamper my vision."

She laughed. "That too."

She was leading up to something. "There is something else?"

"Picka, if I had done what I did with you just now with a living man, he would have freaked out so badly he wouldn't have recovered for a week! But you never even noticed."

"I don't understand. What didn't I notice?"

"My sister Eve, who is no better endowed than I am, showed the Dwarf Demon Pluto less than I just showed you, and he was so taken he married her. You saw my panties, into my bra, and I pressed my bottom against your face, and you suffered no male reaction at all."

He was perplexed. "Should I have?"

"When we swam, we were children, so you wouldn't have been turned on anyway. But now we're adults. And you still aren't turned on."

"I am sorry I disappointed you," he said contritely. "Maybe if I had known what you wanted, I would have done better. What did you want?"

"You didn't disappoint me, Picka. You proved that I can trust you."

"Of course you can trust me. We're friends."

"Yes, we are. That is extremely important to me."

"But why should my failure to appreciate your flesh matter? You know you are not my type. You said yourself, I don't like meaty panties. Was that intended to be humor?"

"Picka, I am a beautiful princess. When most men see me, they develop notions that make it difficult for us to relate as friends. So I have had very few friends in adult life, and those tended to be not exactly human, like Jumper the Spider. Even so, Eve managed to seduce him, and I could have too, if I had tried. But I couldn't seduce you."

"I'm sorry," he said contritely.

"Don't be! I need a male friend I can talk candidly with without having to worry that I'll turn him on and ruin it."

At last he caught on. "Living men want to summon the stork with you!"

"They do indeed. As you know, I can tell anything about anything alive. But when I'm with a man, and all he can think about is getting into my panties, I can't relax. His lustful thoughts override all else."

"You talent means you can't ignore his notions. I'm sorry I didn't realize. You do have a problem."

"But I don't have that problem with you. You don't care whether I'm clothed or naked, far or near. You just want to help me because you're my friend."

"Yes."

She kissed his skull. "I value that beyond words, Picka."

"You're welcome."

"Because we'll be going out into the wilderness, camping out, sharing dangers. You'll be seeing me clothed and bare, maybe carrying me soaking wet out of deep water. And I'll never have to worry about what you're thinking."

"Well, you can't tell what I'm thinking anyway, because I'm not alive."

"Which is why I needed to verify that you truly don't desire my flesh."

"I truly don't," he agreed. "But I do crave your friendship."

"And you have it."

"If that was what you wanted to talk about, now you can return to your room and get some sleep."

"Actually I had in mind to ask you what the Good Magician talked to you about. But then I realized that this was more important."

"He just gave us a spell to make us alive for an hour, in case we ever needed it."

"Why would you want to be alive?"

"To conceal our natures. I hope we never have to use those spells."

"I hope so too. If you became a live man, it would ruin our friendship."

Surprised, Picka worked it out. "Because then I might see you as an interesting woman."

"Not might; *would*. You would desire me."

"If you say so."

"Oh Picka, I hope you never have occasion to have your doubt destroyed."

"I hope so too." But he remained curious about one thing. "Surely you could get a palace guard, maybe a swordsman, or a swordswoman, to accompany you on your Quest. Why bother with walking skeletons or mundane pets?"

"I want friends, not guards. And if along the way I meet my ideal man, as the Good Magician indicates I will, I want to be with companions who understand and will not interfere."

"That makes sense."

"And I want to be with folk who understand me without condemning me."

"We don't condemn you! Why would you think that?"

"Because you know I'm jealous of my sister. She nailed her man, she married up, she has a son. I was left behind. We were always even. Now she's ahead. I hate that."

"But she does not seem happy."

"True. I think she misses our relatively carefree days of independence. I don't think I'd want her type of marriage. But still I'm jealous."

"But you were also jealous of the Good Magician seeing us instead of you. And of my being the protagonist."

"Outside I'm a princess. Inside I'm a female bleep. You do understand. Do you condemn me?"

"No, of course not. You're entitled to your living emotions."

"There you are. You are a very understanding, even-tempered person, Picka. You know me for a girl with private spites, yet you accept me anyway."

"Well, skeletons lack the passions of living folk. We don't have glands."

"Precisely."

"Do you still mind my being the protagonist?"

"Oh, it irks me. But if I can't be it, then I'm satisfied for you to be it, Picka. I'm sure you won't abuse your position."

"I hope I don't. I've never been a protagonist before. I'm afraid I might mess it up."

She laughed, relaxing. "I don't think it's possible to mess up something like that. You're just the observer. Just please don't leave me out of the story."

"I won't," he promised. "Now you really need to sleep, because tomorrow may be arduous."

"Yes." She got up and started toward the door. Then she changed her mind. "I'll sleep here."

"You are welcome. I don't need the bed."

"I know. I want more than your bed. Humor me."

"Skeletons don't have much humor either."

She lay down on the bed. "Lie down beside me. Put your arms about me. I will feel safe in your embrace."

She did not feel safe? Picka joined her on the bed and put his arms about her. She snuggled against his bones and went to sleep.

It was no burden to hold her, as skeletons did not tire. But he wondered. Why was she nervous about this Quest? Did she know something he and Joy'nt did not? Or was she simply dubious about trying to pin down a traveling castle? Regardless, he and Joy'nt would support her. After all, they were friends.

Picka's mind drifted. In his futile fancy he and Dawn were more than friends, and the holding was more than comfort. It was the beginning of romance.

He snapped out of it, knowing the notion was ridiculous. And saw a surprised day mare standing there. There was a girl on the mare's back. He could see them because he derived from their realm.

"What are you doing bringing a daydream to a skeleton?" Picka asked.

"Oh," the girl said. "My fault. I'm Debbie, and I got to ride a day mare for one day while she delivers daydreams. This one was supposed to go to a living couple. We must have gotten the address confused. I'm sorry."

"That's all right," Picka said, relieved. "It was a nice daydream, until I realized that it couldn't be for me."

"We'll get it right next time," Debbie said. "Bye."

"Bye," Picka said as mare and girl vanished.

Dawn stirred. "What was that?" she asked sleepily.

"Nothing," Picka said. That was true, but there was that in him that regretted it.

Belatedly he realized that the girl and mare had gotten more than the address confused. They had tried to deliver a daydream by night. That was a really curious mistake. True, he had been awake, because he never slept. But what could account for a foul-up like that?

In the morning Dawn woke, went to the pitcher on the table in the corner of the room, poured water into the basin there, stripped, fetched a washcloth, washed her copious flesh, found a towel and dried. Then she looked around. "I forgot my clothing!" she said. "Picka, would you fetch it for me? I don't dare go out and risk being seen bare."

"But I'm seeing you bare."

"You don't count, any more than my sister did when we were teens."

Picka suffered another realization: she missed the routine company of her sister. She didn't like being alone. She liked being with someone who understood her without desiring her body, just as she had told him. Somehow that was more meaningful when he confirmed it with his own understanding.

He went to her room for her clothing, glad to be of help. She had laid out underwear, heavy shirt, jacket, and trousers, evidently planning for travel rather than being princessly. That was probably just as well.

"I had the strangest dream last night," Dawn said when he returned. "It was that a night mare got lost and brought me a dream of romance that wasn't mine. Can you imagine that?"

"Maybe it was a premonition," Picka said. And wondered whether that could be true. Probably not.

"Yet it wasn't a black mare. More like a bright day mare." She shrugged, dismissing it. Picka didn't comment. She had been asleep, but had picked up part of the daydream. It was another indication that magic of any type could have devious aspects.

In due course their party set off in search of Attila the Pun. Woofer sniffed the air and oriented, his nose pointing north.

"North it is," Dawn said briskly. Picka noticed that she was no longer wearing her little crown, and her long fair hair was braided. She looked a lot like an ordinary lovely girl.

They followed the enchanted path north. Woofer moved in a dog trot, with Tweeter riding on his head. Midrange bounded along just behind. Then came Dawn and the two skeletons.

Soon they came to a rest stop where there were several odd wheeled machines. "Bicycles!" Dawn exclaimed.

"What are they?" Joy'nt asked. "Machine skeletons?"

"They are for riding on. They make travel much faster, as long as there's a navigable path. I'll show you."

Dawn fetched a bicycle, flung her leg over it, and pushed off. It moved, carrying her swiftly along.

The others just stared. They had never seen such a thing before.

"Try it, Picka!" Dawn called. "You can do it." She looped her machine around and returned to them, coasting to a neat stop.

Picka tried it, following Dawn's instructions. He put his pelvis bone on the seat, his hands on the handlebars, and pushed on a pedal with one foot.

It worked, to his surprise. The bicycle carried him smoothly forward. When it started to fall over, he turned the front wheel, and the bicycle stayed upright.

Joy'nt learned similarly. Before long the three of them were riding north, with Midrange riding in Joy'nt's basket and Tweeter perching on Picka's basket. Now their travel was much faster.

Still, it was a distance to wherever Attila was, and it became evident that they would not make it that day. Dawn and the pets needed to rest at night, so they pulled into a camping site and parked their bicycles. Seeing that, Woofer veered back to rejoin them.

"Midrange is nervous," Joy'nt said. "He doesn't want to camp here."

"Let me check with him," Dawn said, drawing her bicycle to a stop beside Joy'nt's. Picka joined them. "What's up, Middy?"

The cat meowed.

"Oh, my, you're right," Dawn said. "That could be dangerous."

"What is it?" Joy'nt asked.

"There's a massive, horrifying creature heading this way; she'll be here within the hour. We won't be comfortable sharing the camp with her."

"That's wrong," Picka said. "She won't hurt us."

"Maybe not bone folk," Dawn retorted. "But what about flesh folk like me and the pets?" She eyed him narrowly. "Besides, how do you know she's harmless?"

"Because she wouldn't be on the enchanted path otherwise."

Dawn stared at him with her flesh-filled eyes. "You're right! No hostile monster can use these paths. So we're all right, as long as we don't judge by appearances."

"How does Midrange know about the monster?" Joy'nt asked.

"It's his developing magic talent," Dawn said. "When Mundanes have been in Xanth a while, they start getting magic too. Middy's seems to be awareness of coming problems."

"That's interesting," Joy'nt said. "I wonder what Woofer's and Tweeter's talents will be?"

"We'll know in due course. But they can take many years to develop."

They resumed riding the short distance to the camp.

Three people were already by the shelter: two boys and a girl. "Do you want to share, Princess?" Joy'nt asked Dawn as they coasted in. "We can go on to another camp if we need to; it's not that late."

"This is fine," Dawn said. "But if you would, just call me Dawn, not Princess. I want to be one of the regular folk."

"*We* aren't regular folk," Picka reminded her.

"I will introduce you as harmless spooks."

"Accurate enough," he agreed amicably.

Dawn led the way. "Hello!" she called as she stopped and parked her bicycle. "I am Dawn. These are my friends Picka and Joy'nt. They are harmless spooks. Their family left the dream realm and no longer works in bad dreams."

"Oh," one of the boys said. "Okay. I'm Tom. These are Aliena and Aaron."

"You're not a boy," Dawn said shortly.

Aliena and Aaron looked surprised. They hadn't known.

Tom was surprised too, for a different reason. "How did you know?"

"It's my talent to know about things like that."

"You're right. I'm a girl. But I'm adventurous and very good at emulating a boy, and it spares me the looks of panty hunters. So I generally travel as a boy. I don't have two walking skeletons and a big dog to protect me."

"Oh, I forgot to introduce Woofer," Dawn said. "He's friendly. The bird is Tweeter, and the cat is Midrange."

"Oh, that's great!" Aliena said. "May I pet them?"

"Woofer yes," Dawn said. "Midrange maybe. Tweeter no."

Aliena immediately petted Woofer. "My talent is to change the color of trees," she confided. "See." She gestured to a small nearby tree, and it changed from green to blue.

"And mine is hot hands," Aaron said. "I can even start a fire with them, if I concentrate."

"You do look hot," Dawn agreed. But Picka could tell she was being cautious, because Aaron was looking at her with a bit more intensity than seemed proper. She was right: if it was a human male, it desired her.

"Why don't we take one side of the shelter, and you three take the other?" Joy'nt suggested.

The three looked into her hollow eye sockets, and hastily agreed. Spooks might be friendly, but they remained a bit scary to strangers.

They gathered pies from a nearby pie tree—pie trees were always to be found at enchanted camps—and Aaron used his hands to heat them until they were toasty. It was a nice meal.

Then Picka talked with Aaron while Dawn, Aliena, and Tom washed up on the clean pond. That way he was sure that Aaron did not peek at any panties or bare bodies. This was important for living folk.

After that, Aaron and Picka went to wash, though Picka didn't really need it, while Joy'nt made sure no girls peeked. It was all part of the social courtesy of such camps.

When they returned, Picka remembered something. "When does the monster arrive?" he asked Dawn.

"Oh, I forgot about that," Dawn said. "We should warn these three."

"Warn us about what?" Aliena asked.

"There's a horrendous monster coming. You may not want to stay here."

"Are you trying to get rid of us so you can have the shelter to yourselves?" Tom demanded.

"Not at all," Dawn said. "It's just that this creature may make you uncomfortable."

"A likely story. We'll stay."

"That's fine," Dawn said with a quarter smile.

"I don't know," Aliena said nervously. "If there's really a monster—"

"I'll burn it with my hot hands," Aaron said confidently.

Aliena laughed. "You do that."

Aaron glowered. "Just because I burned you a little, you don't have to be sarcastic."

"I apologize," Aliena said quickly.

"He tried to burn you?" Joy'nt asked.

"I didn't!" Aaron snapped. "It's just that when I get excited, my hands get hot. I can't help it."

"You got excited and burned her?"

"He didn't mean to," Aliena said.

"Exactly what happened?" Joy'nt asked.

"We were getting friendly," Aaron said. "But when she kissed me, my hands heated." He sighed. "That's happened before, with other girls. Each time I hope it will be different, but it never is. I can't have a girlfriend."

"So your talent is useful at times, but interferes with your social life," Joy'nt said.

"That's it exactly."

"Too bad you don't like skeleton girls."

"Oh? Are you interested?"

"I'd like a boyfriend. But you're not my type." That was, of course, the understatement of the day. It was almost impossible for any skeleton to have a meaningful romance with any living person, as Picka and Dawn had already determined.

Midrange mewed.

"Oh, she's coming," Dawn said. She picked up the cat and held him. "Now remember, this is an enchanted camp. Nobody hurts anybody here. So try to be polite."

They went out to meet the new arrival. It was just dusk.

Aliena screamed. Tom covered her mouth to prevent a similar reaction. Even Dawn seemed taken aback.

It was a truly horrendous creature. Her body was a ragged mass of fur, her head was a blank ball, but it was her arms that were truly repulsive. They were huge and multiply jointed, with spikes, and her hands were like metallic scoops.

"I'm SOGA, a refugee from the dream realm," she said. "May I share this lodging with you?"

"Hello, SOGA," Dawn said. To the others, she said, "SOGA stands for Sea of Gruesome Arms." Then to SOGA: "It's all right with the skeletons and me, but we don't know about the others."

"Skeletons!" SOGA exclaimed. "You're from the dream realm!"

"We derive from it," Picka agreed. "But we are longtime residents of Xanth proper."

"I don't want it near me!" Aliena said.

"But I mean you no harm," SOGA said. "I hate the way I look. All I want is to be loved. But who would ever love me?"

"Maybe we should give her a chance," Tom said.

"Thank you," SOGA said. She took a step forward.

"No!" Aliena screamed.

"Hold her," Dawn told Aaron.

Aaron stepped forward to intercept SOGA. "Don't try to come in. I'll stop you."

"But it's getting dark and I don't want to be alone at night," SOGA protested. She took another step.

Aaron grabbed her arms. "No."

"Please!" She struggled to get past him.

"Don't fight me," Aaron said. "My hands will get hot."

"I can't help it. I'm so lonely! And there are skeletons here. They'll understand."

"We do," Picka said. "But I think it has to be unanimous." Still, he wondered why Dawn had told Aaron to stop SOGA. His hands were likely to burn her.

"Please!" SOGA repeated, struggling again. Aaron resisted, and his hands heated. In fact, they became burning hot. They could see smoke rising from them.

Suddenly SOGA's fur caught fire. It puffed into a ball of flame and vanished in a noxious cloud. Worse, her head seemed to fall off.

"Oh, my clothing!" SOGA exclaimed. "I'm naked!"

Indeed she was. Her body, now revealed, was nymphlike, and her face under what was now revealed as a concealing helmet was elfin. She was an outstandingly pretty girl, except for her awful arms.

Aaron looked at her bareness, and freaked out. He froze in place. SOGA drew back, freeing herself. "I'm so embarrassed!" she said.

"I think we can handle this," Dawn said, setting down the cat. "Take my dress." She pulled it off and gave it to SOGA. The sight of her bra and panties didn't affect Aaron, because he was already freaked out.

"But why?" SOGA asked.

"Because you don't want to freak him out again," Dawn explained. "Put on the dress, snap your fingers, and kiss him. Meanwhile I'll go find another dress." She walked away.

Picka realized that Dawn was definitely up to something.

Evidently bemused, SOGA put on the dress, which fit her reasonably well because Dawn's figure was nymphlike. Then she snapped her fingers.

Aaron snapped out of his freak. "What happened?" he asked.

SOGA kissed him.

Little hearts flew out. In a moment Aaron drew back. "Let's find somewhere private."

"But my arms," she protested.

"You have arms?"

"Horrendous ones."

He yanked his eyes away from her face and clothed body. "Did I burn them?"

"No. They're too tough to burn. After all, they can tunnel through the ground. But they aren't pretty."

"You have other qualities."

"Use the shelter," Aliena said, evidently regretting her prior attitude. "We'll manage."

They went into the shelter.

"Who would have thought it," Tom said. "She does have scary arms, but the rest of her is something else."

"And it seems that all any man cares about is that something else," Aliena said wryly.

Dawn returned, wearing a newly harvested dress. "You knew that would happen!" Joy'nt said.

"Middy knew," Dawn said. "I merely followed his advice and let them discover each other. He simply needed to see more than her arms."

"He did," Aliena said. "I'm sorry I was so prejudiced. She seems like a nice girl."

"She is," Dawn agreed. "And right for Aaron, because his hot hands can't hurt her tough arms when he gets excited." She allowed half a smile to escape. "And he's very excited now."

After a brief but reasonable while, Aaron and SOGA emerged from the shelter. "We're in love," he said.

"Of course," Dawn agreed, as if that were only natural. Picka realized that the urgencies of living flesh were such that it might indeed be natural. The two knew almost nothing about each other except for the contact of their bodies, but it seemed that sufficed.

They took different sections of the shelter, with the new couple in one corner and the skeletons patrolling outside. The frequent sounds of kissing didn't seem to bother the three other females or the pets.

In the morning the people went their various ways. Picka, Joy'nt, and Dawn mounted their bicycles, following Woofer, and Tweeter and Midrange rode on or in baskets.

By noon they reached the great Gap Chasm. Picka and Joy'nt had seen it before, but it remained impressive. It was a huge crack in the ground, so deep that a few small clouds were floating in it below the normal ground level. Deep within it, they knew, ran the dreaded Gap Dragon, Stanley Steamer. Except that he wasn't dread to Dawn or the skeletons, who knew him from way back.

Woofer turned, heading east. There was no enchanted path there. They would have to tackle the rest of their trip by foot.

They put the bicycles by the edge of the chasm, for future use, and oriented on the unenchanted wilderness. The easy part of their travel was over.

Somewhere, not far away, was Attila the Pun.

5
ATTILA

They plowed into the wilderness south of the Gap Chasm, following Woofer, who was sniffing more avidly. That suggested that they were getting close.

Suddenly in the thicket they came to a sign: BEWARE THE BANKS. Woofer paused there, uncertain.

"What is it, Woofer?" Dawn asked, touching his back. Then she answered herself. "We are about to enter a region stiflingly thick with puns. They are so dense they are obscuring the smell of Attila. Woofer has lost the scent for the moment. We'll just have to forge through and hope he can pick up the scent on the other side."

They forged through. First they came to a bank of red sand that blocked their way. When Picka stepped in it, it stuck to his foot, making it icky red. He poked a bone finger into it and inspected it. "That's not sand," he said. "It's partly clotted blood!"

"Do you wish to make a deposit or a withdrawal?" the blood inquired.

"Neither," Picka said. "I have no blood, and want none."

"Then I have no interest for you."

"Don't you mean in me?" But the blood was silent.

"A blood bank," Dawn said. "It deals in blood. That's what the sign meant. We'll have to go around it."

They tried, but soon came to a mass of fog so thick they couldn't see through it at all. "A fog bank," Joy'nt said.

"We will pay the highest rate of interest," the fog said, blowing a waft of mist at them. "Store all your fog here."

They turned aside again, and came to a river. "Do you wish to deposit your water?" it asked.

"I think not," Dawn said, coloring slightly for some reason.

"A river bank," Picka said. "But why should we beware of this?" He dipped his bloodstained foot so he could wash it off.

A fish swam close. "Stop that!" it shouted in a very low voice. "You're polluting the water, and you aren't even a client!"

A talking fish? "Who or what are you?" Picka asked.

"I'm a bass, you numbskull. I have the very lowest voice of all fish, and those who eat me, cursed be their kind, develop similarly low voices. Now get your filthy foot out!" It lurched forward, snapping at a toe bone.

Picka couldn't pull his foot out fast enough, so he flung down his hand to push the deep-voiced fish away. His fingers struck two scales, and major and minor notes sounded.

"Musical scales," Dawn said, laughing as the bass swam indignantly away. "The sign was right: there are puns here."

"So it seems," Picka agreed. It also seemed he wasn't alone in having a musical body. He tried again to rinse his foot, but immediately two more fish attacked. One was long and fat, the other small and thin. Both made nasty bites that would have hurt, had his toes been flesh. "What are you?" he asked them warily.

"We are gar, bonebrain," the larger one said. "I am Ci-Gar, and this is my girlfriend Ci-Garette. We'll smoke you out." And smoke did seem to issue from them as they charged up for more nips.

Picka hastily pulled out his foot, which now had been washed clean. But when he put it down on the sand, it touched a rounded branch lying there. His thoughts started drifting, and he forgot what he was doing.

"Picka!" Dawn said, pulling on his arm. "Snap to!"

"What?"

"You touched a piece of drift wood, and your thoughts drifted."

"Oh." He moved away from the wood.

"Maybe we should take a break and reorganize," Joy'nt suggested. "So we don't blunder too much."

"Good idea," Dawn agreed. "Let's rest in that shed, and forage for lunch." She gestured to a shed they saw farther along on the river bank.

The pets were glad to agree. They went to the shed, which turned out to be filled with an odd collection of objects. There were fine coral combs, glossy mirrors, and an assortment of jewelry. "Who left these here?" Joy'nt asked, lifting a pretty earring.

"Stop molesting our things!" a voice called. There in the water was an angry mermaid.

Joy'nt dropped the earring. "I didn't realize these belonged to anyone."

"Well, they do," the mermaid said. "That's our water shed, where we store our things because it's hard to carry them with us. We don't have pockets."

"I'm sorry," Joy'nt said. "We skeletons don't have pockets either, and we don't use jewelry. I was just curious. Who are you?"

"I am Khari Saia," the mermaid said.

"I am Joy'nt Bone, and these are my brother Picka, and friend Dawn. Also three pets. We thought we'd pause here so the living folk could eat."

"That's all right, then," Khari said. They shook hands. "There are snacks a little further along the bank."

"Thank you. We'll go there."

The mermaid disappeared in the water, satisfied. They walked along the bank to the place she had indicated. It did look like a kind of picnic area.

Pea plants curled around a natural trellis, with many pods. Picka accidentally stepped on one. "Moo!" it protested, and squirted him on the skull.

"That's a cow pea," Dawn said. "Full of milk." She picked a pod and held it down for Midrange, who found it tasty.

Next to it was a rocky bar with assorted plants on it. "A salad bar," Dawn said. "But I think I'll pass it up."

"Why?" Joy'nt asked. "Isn't it edible?"

"In a manner. This is a bar where vegetables get drunk. I'm afraid it would do the same for me."

Near to it was a tea plant, with several little cups of tea. But Dawn passed this up too. "A person drinks this to deal with an infinite number of puns. But I don't want my pun sense dulled, because I'm pretty sure there are so many puns here because we're getting closer to Attila. He would naturally seek the thickest thicket of puns, so he could destroy them."

"That makes sense," Picka agreed. It did seem to be an unusually thick infestation.

"Here's a pie plant," Joy'nt said. "With several nice pies. That should feed you living folk."

"Maybe," Dawn said.

Woofer went up to snag a long-hanging pie in his mouth. But it avoided him, and his teeth snapped on nothing. He tried again, and missed again.

"That's what I thought," Dawn said. "This is an occu-pie. You can harvest it only if occupied with something else."

"Then how can you eat it?"

"I will focus on something else. Look, there's a set of crack-hers."

"Crackers?" Joy'nt asked.

"Crack-hers," Dawn said, picking up the metallic device. "You use it to crack open wall-nuts and similar." She applied the device to a nearby wall in the shape of a nut, and in half a moment had crunched off a section. There was a corrugated nut in it. "A man would have to use crack-his to manage it."

"Still more puns," Picka said.

"And here is our pie," Dawn said triumphantly. "I nabbed it while occupied with the wall. Have a good meal, pets. There's enough there for all three of you." She set it down on the ground.

The three pets eagerly dived in, sharing. Meanwhile Dawn harvested more wall sections, and then another pie. She also caught a bug that turned out to be a pop fly, made of soda. She had evidently had experience with this sort of thing before.

After eating, the living folk were ready to move on. Woofer still found the sniffing slow, because of the interference of the massed puns, but slowly advanced to the east. He stepped on some O-shaped mats. Immediately they broke into argumentative speech. "Our way is the only way to pursue peace!" one mat proclaimed.

"No, our way is the only way," another said.

"What are they?" Picka asked Dawn.

"I can't tell; they aren't alive."

Tweeter, flying overhead, tweeted. "You don't say!" Dawn said, laughing. "Those are diplo-mats? O-shaped mats that constantly argue their cases?"

It seemed that Tweeter had encountered such mats before.

They came to a small grove of palm trees. The palms had long fingers. In their midst was a handsome prince.

"Well, now," Dawn said, inhaling. Picka wasn't sure why she did that when she met a man, but it did seem to get his attention. "Hello, Prince."

"Hello, damsel," the prince responded.

"We are in search of a person somewhere in this vicinity," Dawn said. "Would you like to travel with us for a while?"

"I would," the prince said. "But I can't. I am the Finger Prince, governing this palm grove, and I may not depart it."

"Finger Prince?" Dawn asked. Then something overtook her, and she had to stifle a laugh. "Fingerprints!"

It was yet another pun. The prince had no reality apart from it.

"There is something amusing?" the prince inquired, frowning. Obviously he didn't get it.

"Not at all," Dawn said with a remarkably straight face. "But we must be moving on." Because though she was looking for a prince, this one was clearly not suitable.

They moved on. Picka hoped they would find Attila soon, because all these puns were becoming wearing.

Picka found a horn lying on the ground. At first he feared it was a stink horn, but its configuration was different. Was it meant to be blown?

He showed it to Dawn, who examined it carefully. "This is no longer alive," she said, "so I can't be sure. But I think it's a matter horn. You can blow it only for things that really matter. It must have come from the home of all such horns, Mound Matterhorn."

"Can you blow it?"

"I can try." Dawn put it to her lips and blew, but no sound came out. "It seems not. We're searching out puns, and they really don't matter." She set the horn down.

The thicket became thicker. Thickets liked to do that, always striving to become thickest. Small branches caught in Dawn's hair, yanking it into disarray. It was getting in her face, so she paused to put it straight. But somehow it just got messier. "I don't understand," Dawn fussed. "I never had such trouble with my hair before."

"Let me try," Joy'nt said.

"You know how to do hair?"

"I think so. Remember, I practiced on yours when we were children."

"That's right! I had forgotten. You had the touch. Do it now."

Joy'nt tried. But Dawn's sun-bright hair remained tangled.

Midrange meowed. "You saw this problem coming?" Dawn said. "But did you see how to fix it?"

Midrange walked a short distance to the side, and meowed again. "Work on it there instead of here?" Dawn asked. "How will that help?"

But they moved there, and Joy'nt tried again. This time she did the job perfectly, and Dawn's hair was neat again.

"Now this interests me," Dawn said. "Why did moving fix the problem?"

It took a while, but they unraveled the mystery. It seemed that they had been in a Hair-don't region. When they moved to a Hair-do region, then it worked. It was another pun.

Woofer woofed. "You found him!" Dawn exclaimed gladly.

So he had. There was a warrior man, clad in archaic garments, with a curved sword. Attila the Pun.

"He looks dangerous," Picka whispered.

"Not to me," Dawn said. She tightened her clothing and took a deep breath. She marched toward the man.

Attila said something unintelligible, lifted his sword, and charged.

"He's not friendly!" Dawn said, picking up on the obvious.

Picka jumped in front of her, grabbing for the sword. It would have cut flesh, but not his bone. It would have hacked him apart if it had struck with full force, but he had hold of it, and it was nullified.

"Death to all puns!" Attila cried, struggling to yank his sword free.

"I am not a pun," Picka said. "I am a walking skeleton. A night mare spook."

Attila paused. "So you are. What are you doing here?"

"We are here to recruit you to our cause," Picka said. "We need your help."

"I'm not interested. My mission is to destroy all puns, not to help with the causes of other people."

"We need to recover Pundora's Box," Dawn called.

Attila paused. "That relates," he agreed. "I have no love for that Box myself. I was once imprisoned in it."

"You were in it?" Dawn asked, surprised.

"It's a long story. Suffice to say that my girlfriend freed me. I love her, and hate that Box. But no one knows where it is."

"It is in Caprice Castle," Dawn said.

"I knew that. But that castle travels randomly."

"I am Princess Dawn. My mission is to capture and tame that castle, so we can recover the Box."

Attila considered. "No, I can't help you."

"But we need you to locate Pundora's Box," Dawn said, "so I can complete my mission."

"It's not her Box. Anyway, I can't take time off from *my* mission," Attila said. "This is the thickest thicket of puns in Xanth, and I must act swiftly to destroy them all." He advanced on a nearby pastree and viciously sliced it in half. Pastries flew out, dissolving into paste, which puffed into acrid smoke.

It seemed that his sword was what did it, magically nullifying any puns it cut.

Dawn, watching him, backed into a razor tree. Suddenly she was lifted up a good foot. It was a raise-her pun.

Attila whirled and slashed the tree, and the blades dissolved into vapor and dissipated.

"Oh!" Dawn said, stumbling into a windowpane. "Ouch!" Because it was actually a window pain.

Attila swung his sword, and the pain shattered into mist. Then he whirled and leaped, catching a pie that was floating overhead: pie in the sky. Then he stared ahead. "I see an enemy!" he cried, and charged at a spiny creature in nearby water: a sea anemone. Then he spied a legalistic document running along a branch with little feet, with the word DAVID on it. "I am the official aphid," it proclaimed. "I make things legal." Attila sliced it in half, and it dissipated. "An affidavit," he said, disgusted.

He was certainly efficient. But Picka knew these puns would keep, while Pundora's Box would be constantly on the move. They needed to get a fix on it. But how would they get Attila's attention, let alone his cooperation?

"There's another," Attila said, advancing on a jacket hanging from a branch.

"That's just a coat," Picka said. "Useful for a living person."

"The bleep it is! That's a turn coat. Wear it and you switch loyalties until you take it off." He slashed through it, and the coat dissolved into smoke. It had indeed been a pun.

"How may we persuade you to help us?" Dawn asked.

"I don't care about you," Attila said, hacking at a flight of stairs that were chained down to prevent them from flying away. In half a moment they did fly, in the form of fading smoke. "Just stay out of my way."

"Maybe he needs a woman," Joy'nt murmured. "Apart from his girlfriend."

"Oh, no!" Dawn muttered, appalled. "He *can't* be my perfect man!"

"I was thinking maybe me," Joy'nt said.

"But you're not his type."

"I have the transformation spell."

Dawn paused. "You would do this?"

"The spell lasts only an hour. I can stand it that long, I think."

Dawn nodded. "Give it a try, then."

Picka, Dawn, and the pets faded into a pun-expired section and left Joy'nt to make the effort. Joy'nt invoked her spell, and the transformation began. Flesh formed around her bones, thickening until it entirely

covered them, and thickening further. Finally there were no bones remaining in view.

Joy'nt was a fully fleshy bare woman. "She's lovely!" Dawn whispered.

It was just as well that she clarified that, because to Picka she was
hideous. Her nice white clean bones fouled by so much jiggling meat!
How could she stand it?

Meanwhile Attila was busy destroying puns. He was chasing down
a clucking sound, but every time he swept his sword through the spot it
seemed to come from, there was nothing, and the clucking came from a
bit beyond. He was getting frustrated. "Where are you?" he demanded.

"Cluck!"

He dived for the spot, but again there was nothing. He turned angrily to Dawn. "What's going on here?"

Midrange meowed. Dawn nodded, understanding. "It's a poultrygeist,
a noisy ghost chicken."

"That's the fowlest pun yet!" This time he not only swept his sword
through the spot, he charged on beyond, slicing back and forth. There
was a squawk and a puff of smoke. "Got you, you dumb cluck!" He had
caught up to the chicken's next roost, and taken her out.

"Attract his attention, Joy'nt," Dawn murmured.

"Ahem," the skeleton said.

Attila looked, expecting another pun. What he saw made him pause
appreciatively. "Hello, nymph. Are you looking for a faun?"

"I am no nymph," she replied. "I am Joy'nt, the walking skeleton."

"The bleep you are! I know a nymph when I see one. So get a run
on, because if I catch you I'll make exactly like a celebrating faun."

"Two things," she said firmly. Her firmness was emphasized by the
breath she took to speak. "I may look like a nymph, but I am not. I invoked a spell to put meat on my bare bones for one hour. So if you want
to do anything with me, you will have to do it within that time."

"No problem!" He advanced on her.

Meanwhile Picka noticed that Dawn was contorting herself under
her clothing. Did she have a bad fleshly itch?

"The second thing is that I won't do what you want unless you do what I want," Joy'nt said. "Which is to locate Caprice Castle. We can do that by zeroing in on Pundora's Box within it. Do we have a deal?"

Attila sheathed his sword and grabbed her by an arm. "Bleep no! Now I've got you and I will do what I bleeping well please with you."

"I doubt it."

He drew her in to him, trying to plant a bushy kiss on her face. She used her free arm to straight-arm that face. He tried to knock her arm away, but she was too strong for him. She did not depend on soft weak flesh to move her limbs; her bones were magically animated, and the flesh was mostly decorative.

"You're right," he agreed. "You're way too strong for a nymph. I can't use you."

"You can't use me unless I let you," Joy'nt said. "And I won't let you unless you lead me to Caprice Castle."

He let go of her arm and turned away. "I'll find a real nymph instead. Anyway my girlfriend will soon be returning."

"Joy'nt," Dawn called. "Put these on." She tossed her two items of clothing.

Joy'nt caught them and looked at them with perplexity. "What are they?"

"My bra and panties."

So that was what Dawn had been doing: removing her underwear without taking off her outer clothing. But what was the point?

Joy'nt considered for a good three-quarters of a moment. Then she smiled. She quickly stepped into the panties, then snapped the bra around her chest. "Attila!" she called.

The man turned. "What? Are you ready to do it my way?"

Joy'nt also turned, showing the backside of her panties. They were meatily full, and so was the bra. Picka was disgusted.

Attila said nothing more. In fact he wasn't moving. What had happened to him?

"He has freaked out," Dawn murmured.

Oh. He was a living man. That meant that undergarments made him freak. Joy'nt had used the oldest weapon in the book to subdue him. But what else could she make of it? A freaked-out man couldn't help them any more than a defiant one.

"Now face him and snap your fingers," Dawn called.

Joy'nt did so. Suddenly the man snapped out of it. "What happened?" he asked dazedly.

"I made you freak," Joy'nt said. "And I'll do it again if you don't cooperate." She seemed to be enjoying this exchange despite the clumsy overload of flesh.

"You're bluffing. All I have to do is shut my eyes." He demonstrated by closing them tightly.

Joy'nt approached him. "And I will open them," she said. She put her fleshy hand to his face and brushed upward on his eyelids.

He stared at her bra. "I'm not freaking out!" he exclaimed. "You can't affect me partway. That means I have control." He grabbed her arm again.

"Inhale," Dawn said.

Joy'nt inhaled. Attila's eyes started to crystallize. "Okay, okay! You've got power! What do you want?"

"I want your cooperation," Joy'nt repeated patiently. "You must come with us, orienting on the Box and Caprice Castle, and I will make it worth your while."

"But there are gazillions of puns remaining to be destroyed here."

"They will keep. Once we recover the Box we won't need you anymore. Then you can return here and abolish them all."

Attila considered. "Okay. Let me at you."

"Nuh-uh," Dawn said. "Her favors will be parceled out in limited manner, so that you can't take them all and then renege on the deal."

"Bleep!" he swore. Dawn had, of course, fathomed his intention and acted to prevent it. "How much for a kiss?"

"Just your agreement to locate the castle," Dawn said.

"Okay! I agree."

"Uh, I don't know how to do a fleshly kiss," Joy'nt said to Dawn.

"Just stand here and hold your lips firm," Dawn said. "He'll do the rest."

"I sure will!" Attila grabbed her and jammed his face against hers.

Joy'nt seemed uncertain, but gradually she gained confidence and kissed him back. Picka could tell by the attitude of her body. It was almost as if she liked it. That was of course unimaginable. She had to be acting the repulsive part, for the good of the mission.

At last it broke. Joy'nt smiled, a facial maneuver she was getting better at. "You see? You can't take it by force, but you can have it if you play by the rules."

He nodded eagerly. "How much for a feel?"

Joy'nt looked at Dawn. "Get a good bearing on Caprice Castle."

Attila turned Joy'nt loose and turned around, concentrating. "I usually focus on close puns. That Box is far away. Lots of other puns between me and it, running interference. I don't know if I can."

Joy'nt took his hand. She shaped it so that only his forefinger projected. She touched that to her bra.

Attila stiffened. "But I'll sure as bleep try!"

"I'm sure you will," Dawn agreed. Picka realized that Joy'nt was an expert at managing men. It wasn't just that she was beautiful; it was the way she rationed out her favors for maximum effect. Her technique was marvelous.

Attila focused, and slowly oriented northward. "It's that way."

"True," Dawn agreed. Picka knew that it was not that she knew the castle's location, but that she could tell that the man was being honest. Her talent was truly Sorceress level in its power and nuances. "One hand, outside," she said to Joy'nt.

Joy'nt moved his hand and held it so that it lay flat against the outside of her bra-ed breast. A wisp of steam rose from the contact; it was clearly potent. Attila froze in place, on the very verge of freaking out. He was plainly in a subdivision of male heaven.

"That's enough," Dawn said after an indecent interval. "Now we shall start traveling toward the castle. There will be further limited feels along the way."

Joy'nt removed the hand. There was a faint imprint on the bra where the heat had seared it. Obviously it had not been painful to either party, however.

Attila offered no further objection. But Joy'nt did. "I think about half my time has been used, maybe more. The spell expires after an hour. Then I won't be able to do it. But the journey will take maybe several days."

"That's right," Dawn said. "Bleep. We'll have to make sure he understands." She turned to Attila, who was coming out of his fond daze. "Joy'nt can be like this for only an hour at a time. Then she will revert to her natural skeletal form. Tomorrow she can flesh out for another hour. Can you accept that?"

"One hour a day, and all I get is feels? Let me have the whole thing."

"No. The moment you get the whole thing, you'll buzz off in search of a nymph. You don't get it until we're standing inside Caprice Castle."

"That's not good enough. I demand satisfaction within the hour. Bare bones are no use to me."

Dawn considered. "Feels vary in strength. A panty feel can leave you floating for several hours."

"And then I'm back with a skeleton," he retorted. "It might be worth it if she were a real nymph, or a woman who could commit. Like my difficult girlfriend. But a skeleton? I don't think so."

Evidently he did not take his girlfriend too seriously, as Joy'nt had surmised. He wanted all he could get. Picka understood that some living men were like that.

"It's all we have to offer," Dawn said.

He gazed at her cannily. "Not necessarily. *You're* not a skeleton."

"No way!" Dawn snapped. "I wouldn't settle for a—" She broke off.

"For a what?" Attila demanded.

"Never mind. I suppose I could let you look at me without touching, during Joy'nt's off-hours."

"Just peeks? It's not worth it. Considering that it's only one pun to be destroyed."

"No. You can't destroy Pundora's Box. We need it."

"It's a pun," he repeated. "I exist to destroy puns, especially that one. You want me to settle for one hour a day, and then not get to destroy one of Xanth's biggest puns? You're crazy."

"You're mighty choosy, considering."

"There you go again. Considering what?"

Dawn was clearly nettled. She said something she shouldn't. "Considering that you're a pun yourself. Attila the Pun."

Attila paused, working it out. "Somehow I never thought of it that way. I *am* a pun. Therefore I must be destroyed." He drew his sword.

"No!" Joy'nt cried.

But Attila lifted his sword, then stabbed it through his own body. Immediately that body went up in smoke. The smoke floated away, dissolving. Even the sword puffed into vapor.

True to his nature, Attila had destroyed the Pun.

Picka, Dawn, and Joy'nt shared a glance of pure chagrin, with maybe a small admixture of guilt. They had ruined their chance to pursue their mission.

"I think I could have liked him, for an hour a day," Joy'nt said. "He was so appreciative." Then her flesh puffed away, leaving her skeleton. The bra and panties, suddenly without fleshly support, dropped to the ground.

That seemed appropriate. Their mission had abruptly become a mere skeleton of itself.

6
GRANOLA

The three human-style folk sank into a mottled purple funk, which was one of the worst types. They might have remained in it indefinitely, but the pets lost patience and took action.

Tweeter sat on Picka's skull and tweeted mercilessly. He would not shut up. Midrange went to Joy'nt and prowled all over her bones. Woofer went to Dawn, nosing her butt. "Woof!" he said imperatively.

"Can't you see we're in a funk?" Dawn demanded. "Go sniff out some food or something, and leave us alone."

"Woof!" he repeated insistently.

"What is bothering you?" she asked, annoyed.

"Woof!"

"Oh, you have something to tell me? What is it?"

"Woof!"

Her eyes widened. "You think you are developing a magic talent? Let me check." She touched his back. "You're right. You can sniff out any living thing, or will be able to when your talent matures. We thought it was Attila's acrid smell you tracked, but it was the beginning of your talent." She shook her head. "Too bad we can't just have you sniff out Pundora's Box."

"Woof!"

"But maybe you can sniff out the one who will find it for us? If only we knew who that is."

"Woof." He nosed her pocket.

"But there's nothing in there except—" She broke off, a dim bulb flashing. "The list of names! I had quite forgotten."

"The names!" Picka said.

Dawn pulled out the paper. "The second name is Granola." She looked up. "But isn't that a breakfast food?"

"Woof."

"But also a name," Dawn agreed. "And you can sniff that person out?"

"Woof!"

She leaned forward and hugged him. "We're back in business, Woofer, thanks to you."

"Which way is this Granola?" Picka asked.

Woofer sniffed the air, then pointed his nose north.

"But that's where the Gap Chasm is."

"Woof."

She nodded. "The Gap Chasm it is. We'll go back to where the enchanted path crosses it, because that's where I know a way down into it. I'll have to clear it with Stanley Steamer, the Gap Dragon, so he doesn't steam any of us."

Picka knew that was a good precaution, because though fire dragons were impressive, Stanley's steam could quickly cook a living person.

They organized, then headed northwest toward the crossing. Soon they encountered a small furry creature heaving rocks around. It ignored them, and didn't seem to be dangerous. "What is it?" Joy'nt asked.

"I can't tell," Dawn said. "It's not alive. But it's acting like a wood-chuck."

"Don't woodchucks chuck wood?"

"Yes. So this must be a rockchuck."

The creature glanced at her and nodded. Then it returned to chucking rocks.

"How much rock could a rockchuck chuck, if a rockchuck could chuck stone?" The voice came from one of the chucked rocks.

"Could chuck what?" Dawn asked.

"Boulder, pebble, gravel, sand—"

"Rock?"

"Whatever," the rock agreed irritably.

"So nice to meet you again, Metria," Dawn said with feigned niceness.

The rock expanded into a cloud of swirling smoke, which in turn formed into a sultry, shapely female demon form. "How did you know it was me?"

"It was a lucky guess."

Metria frowned. "People get suspiciously lucky around me." She glanced around. "Who are your friends, and what are you up to?"

"These are Picka and Joy'nt Bone, and the erstwhile Baldwin Family pets Woofer, Tweeter, and Midrange. We're on a quest for Pundora's Box."

"Oh, the Good Magician stuck you with that chore? Lotsa luck, Princess."

"We may need it," Dawn agreed. "I don't suppose you would like to help?"

"Me? I'm almost never helpful. It's against my principles."

"You won't make an exception? We're having a real problem."

"No exception." Metria puffed into bad-smelling smoke and dissipated like a used pun.

"I have heard of Metria," Picka said. "She's always mischief. Why were you so polite to her?"

"Because she prefers to do the opposite of what you want. It's called reverse psychology."

"So you really wanted her to go away?"

"I did. We're going to have enough trouble locating and recruiting Granola, without Metria putting in her three cents."

"How many cents?" he asked.

"Four, five, six, seven, eight—"

"Two?" Joy'nt asked.

"Whatever," Dawn said crossly. Then they all laughed.

"I heard that," Metria said, reappearing. "You are up to something interesting, after all."

"Oh, bleep!" Dawn swore. "I forget that you can never be sure a demoness is really gone. My worse."

"Your what?" Metria asked.

"Worst, awful, mistake, error, miscue—"

"Bad?"

"Whatever!"

Even the demoness had to laugh this time.

"So I suppose now we are stuck with you," Dawn said.

"I'm not sure," Metria said thoughtfully. "I can't tell whether you are pretending to be mad to be sure I'll stay, or whether you really want me to go, as you said before. You might have known I was still listening."

"True," Dawn agreed.

Metria eyed her. "You are being most annoying."

"It must be awful to have someone else emulate your specialty."

The demoness puffed into momentary flame. "That does it. I'll stay until I'm sure I'm wanted. *Then* I'll go."

"You will have a long stay, then," Dawn said.

"Bleep you! You're as bad as your sister."

"I am not!" Dawn retorted. "I'm worse than my sister."

Picka had no idea how much of this was serious. Dawn was no slouch with intellectual fencing. "Why don't we just ignore her?" he suggested.

"Ignore me?" Metria demanded. "You can't ignore me!"

Picka ignored her.

She puffed into smoke, then reformed as a skeleton with marvelously nice bones. "Ignore this!" she said, presenting her shapely pelvis for a kick.

Picka tried, but couldn't keep his eye sockets off that evocative tailbone. She did know how to tempt a skeleton.

"What would you do if he kicked your donkey?" Joy'nt asked. "Fly apart and let him make a baby skeleton out of your smaller bones? Or simply dissolve into smoke like the annoyance you are?"

"I'm not sure. Let's try it and see."

Picka gave in to temptation. He kicked her tailbone so hard that she exploded into a blizzard of bones. Then they dissolved into smoke, which coalesced into the fleshly Metria form. "The latter," she concluded.

But she had given him a wicked thrill in the process. He knew that demonesses liked to tempt mortal men into summoning the stork with them. Now he knew that demonesses could tempt skeletons too.

"You're pitiful," Joy'nt said.

Metria glared. "How so?"

"You're married to a mortal. You have a half-mortal son. But you're still out tempting other males instead of being a decent wife and mother. How can anyone respect you?"

"Oh, bleep!" Metria said, and faded out.

Dawn shook her head. "And I thought a demoness couldn't be shamed."

"I was just mad because she has what we all want, a decent family, yet she treats it like dirt. She deserves to be shamed."

"I heard that," Metria's voice repeated from supposedly empty space. But it did not sound triumphant. The demoness knew she *had* been shamed. There was no more from her.

"Where were we?" Picka asked. "We had something in mind before she distracted us."

"We were heading north toward the Gap Chasm," Dawn said. "Following Woofer, who is sniffing out Granola. Whoever she is, whatever her talent is."

"So we were," he agreed, remembering. The demoness's temptation had jogged that information loose from his skull.

They marched on northward. Joy'nt walked beside Picka. "I can't blame you," she said. "Temptation is hard to ignore."

"You suffered it too?"

"Yes. When I had flesh, and Attila looked at me, and put his hand on my borrowed bra, I really wanted to do more with him, even though

I didn't much respect him as a person. That flesh—there was just something about it."

"You looked horrendous," Picka said. "Covered in all that bulging meat."

"I know. I was disgusted—but also intrigued. Attila was so *eager*. He was really turned on. That gave me power over him, but also made me want to . . . to take it to the next level."

"The next level?"

"To summon the stork with him."

"But you're a skeleton! Skeletons don't summon storks."

"True. But in that moment I wanted to, and I think I could have. Using that flesh. Maybe the storks would have ignored it, but I still wanted to make the signal. Just as you wanted to kick Metria's tail despite knowing she wasn't your kind."

It was an apt point. "Our forms of the moment, and the forms of those we interact with, do have impact," he agreed. "That is surely a useful lesson."

"Yes."

"I hope you find a nice male skeleton," he said. "And that I find a female skeleton who is as nice as you, only who isn't you."

"I understand completely. But on this mission, we're helping Dawn find Pundora's Box, and maybe her ideal prince."

"Yes. We're her friends, and we will help her."

"Tweet."

They had forgotten Tweeter, who was now riding on Picka's shoulder. "And a nice lady bird for you," Picka added.

"Tweet," Tweeter agreed.

They made it back to the stop where they had parked the bicycles. "Too bad we can't use these again," Joy'nt said.

"Unless Granola is actually north of the Gap Chasm," Picka said. "Then we can ride them across the invisible bridge and on."

"No such luck. See where Woofer is pointing?"

The dog was standing at the brink of the gulf, looking down. That meant that Granola was inside the chasm.

"We can use the cycles," Dawn said. "I happen to know a secret about the Gap. Watch, then follow." She fetched her bicycle, mounted it, and rode it to the brink of the chasm.

Then she went off the edge.

Picka and Joy'nt both leaped to stop her, but were too late. They peered down into the void.

And there was Dawn, riding down the sheer side of the chasm. It was as if she were cycling on level ground, but she was going down.

Now Picka remembered. "Some folk know routes where gravity changes. Naturally Dawn knows."

"A fall won't hurt us the way it would her," Joy'nt said. "Still, we could break some bones. Let's try it cautiously."

They tried it carefully, wheeling their bicycles over the brink by hand. They made the turn and stood facing down, not falling. "It's working," Picka called to the pets. "Come join us."

Tweeter, flying in the chasm, came to a landing on the wall, and did not fall. He tweeted reassuringly. Then Woofer and Midrange tried it. It worked for all of them.

Picka and Joy'nt mounted their bicycles and rode down, while Woofer and Midrange bounded along after them. It was fun, once they were sure of it.

Dawn was waiting for them at the bottom. "Now you know," she said. "Don't tell; the Gap Chasm would lose much of its effect if every-one knew about this."

They agreed not to tell. Then they started cycling across the base of the chasm. Picka expected to see the dread six-legged Gap Dragon steam-ing toward them, but he must have been patrolling some other section.

The base of the Chap Chasm was actually nice scenery, with as-sorted bushes and trees growing. Pleasant paths wound through it, and they cycled along these. Woofer led the way, his nose in the air rather than to the ground, oddly.

Dawn slowed and stopped. The others stepped with her. "Is there a problem?" Joy'nt asked.

"Just something odd," Dawn said. "I have been here a number of times before, and have a fair idea of the layout. We just passed something I don't recognize. I want to check, just in case it's important."

She walked to the nearest bush and touched it. "Oh, all right," she said, smiling.

"What did the bush tell you?" Picka asked.

"A car pet passed by here. See, there are the marks of its tread." She indicated a kind of aisle pressed into the ground, leaving it even. "It rolls along, winding up and unwinding as it goes. When it rolls up tight, it looks like a Mundane vehicle. It seems it had a run-in with Stanley Steamer, the Gap Dragon. Stanley tried to steam it, but car pets like steaming; it helps clean them. It rolled right into Stanley, upsetting him. Stanly tried to bite it, but its fabric was impervious. But then it ran into a bog and lost traction. Stanley pulled it out. After that they got along all right. Now it's Stanley's pet, and stretches out and turns red when the dragon returns from a hunt."

"A red car pet," Skully said.

"So it seems," Dawn agreed with two-fifths of a smile. "We don't need to be concerned. Sorry for the interruption, Woofer."

"Woof!" The dog resumed his dog trot.

He led them to the opposite wall, then along it. They came to a section where there was a large natural ledge, about twenty feet up, beyond which the cliff rose again. "This section isn't navigable," Dawn said. "We'll have to go further along to reach the vertical trail out."

"After we find Granola," Picka said.

"Of course. It's curious that she should choose to live down here. She must have made a deal with Stanley Steamer, because nobody intrudes here without authority."

"Where *is* the Gap Dragon?" Joy'nt asked.

"I'm not sure. I can whistle for him if you'd like to meet him."

"Not necessary," Picka said quickly. The skeletons had little to fear from steam, but the pets could be in trouble.

Woofer paused beside the ledge. He glanced up, but there was nothing to see. The ledge was empty.

"Does Granola live here?" Dawn asked the dog.

Woofer shrugged uncertainly.

"She's here sometimes, but is away at the moment?"

"Woof."

"She's here now?"

"Woof."

"But we don't see her," Dawn said, frustrated.

To that Woofer had no answer.

"Maybe there's a cave," Joy'nt said.

"Where?" Picka asked. "The cliff is blank."

"It might have its entrance covered by illusion," Dawn said. "But in that case, Woofer could lead us to it."

Woofer remained where he was, looking up and sniffing. It was odd.

Tweeter had been hovering overhead. Suddenly he tweeted and fell some distance before righting himself. "Tweet!"

"You banged into something," Dawn said. "Something invisible?"

Tweeter flew back, carefully, then came to a landing and perched on something. Ten feet high. Invisible.

"An invisible perch?" Dawn asked, perplexed. "That's new."

"Is it relevant?" Picka asked. "We're looking for a person, not an invisible perch."

"Tweet!"

Dawn was taken aback. "What?"

"Tweet!" the bird repeated emphatically.

"Well, I'll be tweeted," Dawn said amazed. "Who would have thought it?"

"Thought what?" Picka asked, frustrated.

"That Tweeter is perching on an invisible foot."

"An invisible foot! But it's ten feet high!"

"And there's nothing on the ground," Joy'nt said.

Dawn nodded. "I believe it must be the foot of an invisible giant. Maybe a sleeping one. Maybe with one leg dangling off the edge of that ledge."

"An invisible giant," Picka said, amazed. "No wonder Woofer couldn't reach it; he couldn't fly."

"Woof," Woofer agreed, evidently glad to be vindicated.

"But is that giant Granola?" Joy'nt asked. "There's no bad smell. Well, there must be some odor, because Woofer found him, but no stench."

"True," Dawn agreed. "An invisible giant is reputed to smell like a hundred fat men sweating in unison."

A bulb shaped like a glowing little skull flashed over Picka's head. "For a male giant, yes. But what about a female giant?"

"As far as we know, nobody's ever encountered a female invisible giant," Dawn said. "But I suppose they must exist, to propagate the species. The storks prefer to deliver to couples."

"What kind of stork could deliver a giant?" Joy'nt asked.

"A giant stork," Picka answered, regretting that he could not smile. He could grin with his bare teeth, but that wasn't the same.

"Is it really Granola, or is she a captive of the giant?" Joy'nt asked.

"If I could reach that foot, I could find out," Dawn said.

"There may be a simpler way," Picka said. "Just make a clamor and wake the giant."

"And get stepped on?" Joy'nt asked. "That would be awkward for us, and worse for Dawn and the pets."

"We can stand up against the cliff," Dawn said. "Where a foot is unlikely to land."

That seemed to make sense. They lined up against the base of the cliff. Then they set up a clamor, with Dawn, Picka, and Joy'nt yelling, Woofer woofing, Midrange yowling, and Tweeter tweeting.

There was an answering sound, as of some huge stirring. "HUGH?"

"It's us, down here," Dawn called. "A party of six assorted creatures. Are you Granola?"

There was more stirring, then a thunk that shook the cliff as a monstrous foot banged into it. "I am Granny Ola, Granola for short. Who are you?"

"I am Princess Dawn," Dawn called. "I am on a Quest for the Good Magician. My friends the walking skeletons and animal pets are helping. I may need your help too."

"Now that's interesting," Granola said. "Let's talk. I will lie down so as to be on your level."

"Thank you!" Dawn called back.

There was a rumbling and shaking of the ground as the giantess got down off the ledge, then dropped to the ground beside them. They saw small plants and foliage flattening as her body pressed down on them. Then her voice came from about head height, because her head was on the ground. "I have lived a long, dull life," Granola said. "I always longed for adventure, but opportunities for female invisible giants are few. How do you think I might help you, Princess?"

Dawn explained about the Quest, and the name on the list. "So if you have any way to locate Caprice Castle, we need you," she concluded.

"I confess to being intrigued," Granola said. "I am not familiar with this Caprice Castle, probably because it has no fixed location. Locating it should be a diverting challenge. But I am not at all sure I can help you with that."

"The Good Magician evidently believes you can help," Dawn said. "He may be old, obscure, and grumpy, but he is never wrong. There must be a way."

"I have heard of him," Granola agreed.

"Do you have a magic talent?" Picka asked.

"I do, but that's a story in itself, because we giants all have the same magic of invisibility. That prevents us from alarming too many mini-sized folk. So my talent was inflicted on me. I doubt it would be useful in this context."

"Maybe our challenge is to figure out how it can help," Joy'nt said.

"What is it?" Picka asked.

"It is to find whatever I seek in the next to last place I look for it."

There was a silence of at least a moment and a half as they digested this. "I don't think I understand," Joy'nt said. "I thought anything looked for was always in the last place looked, because then you stop looking."

"Normally it is," Granola agreed. "That's why this is a curse. It is frustrating as anything. It is my *pun*ishment." There was a special emphasis on the first syllable.

"Is that really a pun?" Dawn asked. "It seems more like a paradox. Something impossible."

"Maybe Litho didn't properly understand the definition of a pun."

"Litho?" Dawn asked. "As in the Demon Litho, associated with rock?"

"That one," Granola agreed grimly.

"I think we had better hear your whole story," Dawn said. "Even the peripheral involvement of a Demon is mischievous news."

Picka knew she was serious. Her sister had married a Dwarf Demon, and possibly not entirely happily.

"It's not much of a story," Granola said. "You might be bored."

"We have patience," Picka said.

"It was this way. Several centuries ago, when I was young and lithe, said by some to be the prettiest teen invisible giantess of the region, I lived only for excitement and adventure. I discovered that I could turn male giants' heads merely by the way I walked." She paused half a moment. "I should clarify that we giants can see each other, and when we are young we don't wear much if any clothing. There's really no need, since others can't see us anyway. We're related to the transparents, except that we aren't ghostlike and of course we are larger. So things show, for those who can see us, like giants and demons."

"We understand," Dawn said.

"There was some kind of a party going on, so I went to look. In those days I liked to spy on human affairs. It's amazing what an invisible person can see if she gets close enough and keeps quiet enough and doesn't smell. I knew all about summoning the stork, just from watching folk at the fringes of parties. I had never done it, but I knew about it.

"Then just as this one was getting interesting, I felt a hand on my shoulder. I jumped, because I hadn't known any other giant was there. And it turned out to be the Demon Litho, who had been watching me while I watched the small folk. Demons of any kind can change their size, of course."

"Of course," Dawn agreed.

"Litho had rock under Xanth. But he also had a small separate planet. He offered to take me there for a visit. But I was wary, not certain exactly what he might want of me in return. Males of any type tend to have limited perspectives on the uses of females. So I told him no."

"Good for you," Dawn murmured.

"That was when I learned that Demons don't like to take no for an answer. He was so angry that his planet exploded into a million fragments. Now there's no planet there, just the asteroid belt. Naturally I fled.

But just before he exploded he cursed me to have to spend the rest of my life with a nasty pun or equivalent, like a paradox. That's how I came to have my talent. It drives me to distraction when I think about it, so I try not to. I think if I had known what a frustration it would be, I might have visited his planet. After all, he was reasonably handsome."

"It may not be such a bad curse," Dawn said. "I think you were right not to get involved with him. He might have trapped you on that planet and made you do nothing but signal the stork twelve times a day."

"It would not be a curse at all, if I could only use it," Granola said. "But I never find anything I look for, because it's always in the place I looked at just before I stop looking."

"Can't you go back to the prior place?" Joy'nt asked.

"No, because then that becomes the last place I look at, and it's no longer there. I know I'm close, but I can never actually find it."

"That's why Litho did it," Joy'nt said. "He got very close to you, and wanted you, but he couldn't quite get you. So he cursed you similarly."

"I suppose so," Granola agreed. "But why don't you think it so bad?"

"Because I think we can get around it and make it useful. You were trying to use it alone, but if you had company, you might be able to locate things."

"I don't understand."

"Maybe we can demonstrate. Picka, why don't you hide something somewhere around here? Joy'nt, you can help Granola look for it."

"I will hide this blue pebble I just found," Picka said, picking it up.

"Don't look," Dawn told Granola. "Nobody look."

Picka walked in a general circle beyond the cliff, passing behind several trees. He tucked the pebble into a knothole in a branch on a snowshoe tree. The snowshoes were melting before they matured, in this warm weather. He walked on, completing his circle, then rejoined the others. "I have hidden it."

"Now look for it," Dawn told Granola.

The giantess got up carefully, but the ground still shuddered with her movements. "I will carry this branch, so you know where I am going," she said. A branch rose from the ground and hovered.

First she looked along the cliff. "Not here," she said.

"I will mark this spot," Dawn said. "First place looked."

Then Granola walked around a tree. "Not here."

"I will mark the spot," Dawn repeated, going there. "Second place looked."

Granola tapped the ledge she had been sleeping on. "Not here. I give up; I can't find it." She got back down on the ground, rejoining their level.

"Then this is the next-to-last spot you looked," Dawn said, going to the snowshoe tree. "And now I see it! In a knothole in a branch. I can't think why I didn't see it before."

"Because if you could see it," Picka said, "you would have found it before she looked in the next place. The curse prevented you, even if it was in plain sight, which it was."

"Which it was," Dawn agreed. "But once she gave up looking, and I remained here, I could see it. Because while the curse may prevent Granola from seeing it, it lacks staying power with me. It got spread too thin and lost focus."

"Amazing," Granola said. "You are the first person to have been able to make use of my talent."

"So you *can* help us," Dawn said. "Will you?"

"Yes!" They were almost blown over with the force of her exhalation.

"What would you like in return for your help?"

"Just participating is more than enough. I'm an old giantess who has lived her life and don't have many material needs. All I ever lacked was a mission and excitement. You have shown me how to finally use my talent! That's a greater reward than I ever anticipated. So please, don't change your mind. Let's just get on with the search."

Dawn glanced at the others, including the pets. "Is this okay with the rest of you?"

All of them nodded agreement.

"Then I think we have a deal," Dawn said, satisfied.

7
MUSIC

T ell me what you are looking for," Granola said.

"Pundora's Box," Dawn reminded her.

"Oh, yes, of course. That's in our recent fables." There was a pause. "I don't know where it is, but I have an idea where to look. But it's not close to here."

"So we'll travel there." Now Dawn paused. "But we won't be able to keep up with you even if you take very small steps. Would you be willing to carry us?"

"Certainly. I'll put you in my handbag."

"All right. Where is it?"

"Right here." There was a thunk on the ground before them.

"It's invisible too!" Joy'nt exclaimed. "Of course."

"I made it from my own hair. Our skin, nails, and hair are all invisible. When we eat, the food is visible until it enters our bodies; then our skin hides it. So we don't waste our hair, so we can carry things without being seen by visible folk."

"That makes sense," Dan agreed. "But how do we find it?"

"Woof!"

They laughed. Of course Woofer could sniff it out.

Picka went to it first. He discovered a massive bag taller than he was. It did seem to be made of hanks of hair. He felt the side, which was loosely braided. He caught hold with his finger bones and toe bones and climbed up. Soon he was able to peer into it from the edge.

There was an assortment of visible things inside. Fruit, giant hair-pins, a huge hankie, a similarly enormous comb, a bottle of perfume, a monstrous pair of sandals, gloves. Even a tremendous bra and panty. She was a woman, all right. There was only one thing he couldn't identify: a sort of hexagonal bellows with handles on the ends.

Picka climbed over the top and dropped inside.

"Hey!" Joy'nt exclaimed. "He vanished!"

"He is in the bag," Granola explained reassuringly. "It conceals whatever is inside."

But Picka could see them clearly. "I'm inside," he agreed loudly, "but I can see you, Joy'nt."

Soon Joy'nt and Dawn joined him. "Your underwear is not invisible," Dawn called up to the giantess.

"That's my original underclothing," Granola said. "Later I wove replacements out of my hair, and those are invisible. But I didn't throw away the old ones, in case I should ever need them again."

"That does make sense," Dawn agreed.

"My early, visible clothing I got from a helpful wear-wolf," Granola continued. "She was a bitch who could conjure clothing."

"She was a what?" Joy'nt asked, startled.

"A female wolf is a bitch," Dawn explained. "She would be affronted if you called her a girl."

"She would indeed," Granola agreed. "Her brother was a where wolf; he could tell where anyone was at the moment. I envied him, because my own talent is so clumsy in comparison."

"What is the bellows?" Picka asked.

"That's my concertina. I like music in my private time. I won't play it if it bothers you."

"Not at all," Picka said, gratified. "We like music too. Dawn has an ocarina, and I . . . well, I have my bones."

"Bones?"

"I discovered recently that I can play notes on my ribs," Picka explained, hoping she wouldn't laugh. "Any tune I hear, I can play. I haven't done it much."

"But do you like music?" Granola asked.

"Actually, I find I do," Picka said, embarrassed. "Now that I have discovered I can play a tune."

"And you, Princess?"

"I love it," Dawn said. "I'm not great at it, but my sister and I really enjoyed our sessions together."

"And you, Joy'nt?"

"I know nothing about music, alas," Joy'nt said.

"Long ago I found a pair of maracas. They are way too small for me to use, but I didn't want to waste them, so I saved them. Would you like to have them?"

"I don't know," Joy'nt said, taken aback. "What are they?"

"Small gourd-shaped rattles on sticks. You shake them, and they make a sound. They can keep a beat. That can enhance the music made by other instruments. They are in my handbag somewhere, if you delve for them."

Joy'nt delved, and in no more than a moment and a quarter found them. She shook them experimentally. They made a pleasant dry-seed sound. "I like it," she said.

"Then let's make music," Granola said, pleased.

Picka saw Dawn consider. He knew she wanted to get on with the mission. But it was getting late in the day, and they still hardly knew the giantess. This could be a way. "Yes, let's," she agreed, bringing out her ocarina.

They climbed out of the handbag, and Granola reached in to bring out her concertina. She was invisible, but it was visible, so it seemed to be floating in midair and playing itself. Picka realized that this could be a reason she didn't play it often, or at least not by daylight. They settled in a half circle before the invisible giant and readied their instruments.

They heard a stirring as Granola sat up so she could play her concertina, and the instrument rose up higher. At least it gave them a better notion exactly where she was. "What song?" she asked.

"What do we all know?" Dawn asked in return.

They considered, and found that they did not have any songs in common. What were they to do?

"What about 'Ghost of Tom'?" Joy'nt asked. "That's pretty simple. Picka and I know it, and we could teach it to you. It's a Mundane song that got picked up by the night mares because it's useful for bad dreams, but it's really rather pretty."

"How does it go?" Granola asked.

Picka removed his clavicles and bonged them on his ribs. He knew the tune, so played it perfectly the first time. Joy'nt sang it with him. They weren't great vocalists, but they were able to do it with the help of his perfect notes.

Have you seen the ghost of Tom?
Round white bones with the flesh all gone.
Oo-oo-oo-oo-oo-oo-oo-oo!
Wouldn't it be chilly with no skin on!

"I like it!" Granola said. Then she played it on her concertina, perfectly. The concertina fairly danced as it expanded and contracted; she was getting into the feel of the melody.

"It's really a round," Joy'nt said. "One person sings the first line, then the second does the first while the first goes on to the second, and so on. It's fun."

"I'll start," Granola said, and played it.

Dawn started playing her ocarina as Granola moved to the second line. Then Picka started. Finally Joy'nt started, singing it as she shook her maracas. It got confused in the center, with all four parts going, but then it cleared as they finished one after the other. The main sound was the oo-oo, which was the highest part.

Then Woofer augmented it with his own howling. Oo-oo-oo! Midrange joined in with his own yowl. Tweeter retouched it with tweets.

They concluded in order, with Granola finishing, then Dawn, then Picka, then Joy'nt, solo at the end, singing and shaking her maracas.

They paused, mutually impressed. Then Granola spoke, as the concertina settled to the ground. "That was wonderful! You are all musicians!"

"No, I'm just a dabbler in this respect," Dawn protested. "It's an easy tune."

"I always liked it," Picka said. "So it's easy for me too. You really know how to play that concertina, Granola."

"Well, I have had a century or so to practice. But I never played with anyone else before, and am amazed how compatibly it worked."

"I'm not a singer," Joy'nt said. "But all I had to do was keep time with the rattles, and the song is familiar, and the rest of you were so good that it was easy for me to keep the melody."

"Well, I'm really not an expert either," Granola said, "but I know competence when I hear it, and the three of you did very well. You too, pets. That helped me. I think we make a nice foursome. Or sevensome, with the pets. Who would have expected it?"

"A princess, two walking skeletons, and an invisible giantess," Picka said. "Plus three expressive animals. That does seem hard to believe."

"Let's try another," Granola said. "We might even be able to get into parts."

They consulted again, and managed to come up with melodies all of them could play. Picka really enjoyed it, because he knew each new tune forever the moment he heard it. He had half feared that others would laugh at the way he bonged on his own ribs, but Granola was all admiration. It did seem that music was their common ground with the giantess. It no longer seemed odd to be with her.

They played together, developing a four- or five-part harmony of sorts. Joy'nt sang soprano with increasing confidence, also shaking the maracas. Dawn played alto on her ocarina, reveling in the music. Granola played tenor on her concertina with verve. Picka bonged on his ribs, feeling more at home with this mode; they did have nice ringing tones that filled out the bass range. And the three pets added their harmony, fleshing out the whole.

As they played, they became louder, singing, blowing, and striking their notes more proficiently. It was such delight! Picka had never before realized how transporting music could be, especially when he was making it himself. It seemed to make him become more than he had been before, a creature of artistry.

They completed another piece, finishing together with a flourish. Then Dawn saw something. "Well, now," she murmured.

The others looked. There was the dread Gap Dragon, green, six legged, breathing wisps of steam. He had been listening to the music.

"I think it is time for introductions," Dawn said. "Folks, this is Stanley Steamer, the terror of the Gap Chasm. Stanley, these are Picka and Joy'nt Bone, and the invisible giant Granola."

"We know each other, of course," Granola said. "He gave me the ledge to sleep on in peace."

"And we know *of* him," Picka said.

"And the three Baldin Family pets, Woofer, Tweeter, and Midrange," Dawn concluded, "who are helping me on my mission for the Good Magician."

Stanley blew out a nonthreatening waft of steam, acknowledging.

"What brings you here, Stanley?" Dawn asked. "Were we making too much noise?"

The dragon blew out a steam ring.

"Oh, you like the music!"

He liked the music.

"So you don't mind if we camp here tonight?"

He didn't mind. That was just as well, because darkness was closing in.

The pets foraged for food, not threatened by the dragon. So did Dawn, harvesting a pie from a pie plant. So did Granola, harvesting another pie. It was interesting to see it disappear into the air where her mouth was, becoming invisible.

"Don't you need more than that?" Joy'nt asked. "You're so big."

"I hardly eat more than a normal person does," Granola explained. "I think most of the food energy goes into making ordinary folk visible. I don't need that, so eat less, proportionately."

"I suppose that's no more unusual than the way we skeletons don't have to eat at all," Joy'nt said.

"Anything is possible, with magic," Dawn reminded them.

Except, Picka thought, for a skeleton to make it with a fleshly woman, as Dawn had ascertained with him. Why did that bother him?

Then they settled down for the night. Dawn and the three pets chose Granola's handbag, because it was protected and comfortable. Picka and Joy'nt had no need of safety or comfort, so simply collapsed at the base of the cliff.

"Picka," Joy'nt murmured.

"That's me," he agreed.

"Stanley's still here."

Picka peered into the darkness and discovered it was true. He hadn't thought to look before; he has simply assumed that the dragon had departed when the music finished. "Why?"

"I don't know. He can't be hungry for our dry bones."

"Maybe we can ask him," he suggested.

"I'll try." She faced the dragon. "Stanley, why are you still here?"

The dragon looked at her, then puffed a jet of steam that curled into a question mark. He was unable to speak Human, and without Dawn to translate, they could not understand him.

"Bring out your magic marker," Picka suggested.

Joy'nt brought it out. She got up and approached the dragon. "If you put a foot on this paper, it will print your thought," she said.

Stanley put a front foot on the panel. MUSIC.

"You liked our music," Picka said. "We picked up on that. It seems that music soothes the savage beast as well as the savage breast. But we're not playing music now."

Stanley touched the panel again. WANT A SONG.

"We can surely play it, if we know it," Picka said. "When the others get up in the morning. What song?"

POOF THE MAGIC DRAGON.

"Oh, one about a dragon! Of course. But Joy'nt and I don't know it. We know one about spooks and skeletons."

Stanley looked disappointed.

"Can you tell us how it goes?" Joy'nt asked.

Stanley touched the panel again. This time a series of notes and words appeared.

"I can read the words," Joy'nt said. " 'Poof the Magic Dragon lived by the ocean.' But not the notes."

"I can read them," Picka said, surprised.

"I didn't know you could read music."

"I didn't know either," he said, excited, "but I discover I can. I can play this melody." He took off his clavicles and played on his ribs.

Stanley perked up, wafting steam. That was the melody.

"You can pick up the tune from my playing," Picka told Joy'nt. "Then you can sing it for him."

She did, and soon they played and sang the whole song for the dragon. Stanley was so contented he almost floated on a bed of soft steam.

Dawn poked her head over the end of the invisible handbag. "You're playing without us?"

"We didn't want to disturb you," Picka said, embarrassed.

"As if music could do that," Granola said.

"So let's do this right," Dawn said as they joined the dragon and skeletons. It was dark, but that hardly mattered; they could sing, play, and howl without light.

They got the words and tune, then did it in style. Again the dragon almost floated. It was a nice song.

"That was fun," Dawn said when the finished. "We have another song in our repertoire." She glanced mischievously at the dragon. "Which of us was best, Stanley?"

The dragon turned his head and wafted out a waft of steam. It found Picka, bathing him in temporary warmth.

"That was supposed to be rhetorical, steam snoot," Dawn said with mock severity. "Everybody contributes to the joint effort, so no one is best or worst."

Stanly wafted her with steam, just hot enough to make her step back as it illuminated her. "You are arguing with me, steam-for-brains?" Dawn demanded. "I'll have you know I'm a princess."

"But he's right," Granola said. "Picka is the best. Without his perfect notes and cadence, the rest of us would be sloppy. He makes all the rest of us better."

"I wouldn't say that," Picka protested.

"You don't need to," Granola said. "You are the heart of this ensemble."

"But I hardly know music! I merely repeat what I hear or read. I've only been at it a few days."

"The more credit to you. You will surely be a very fine musician when you achieve your full potential."

"That's right," Dawn said thoughtfully. "We should help you get there, Picka. I am a Sorceress, and it took me time to develop my full powers, and I may not have done so yet. It may be similar with you and music. We owe it to you to help you get there."

Picka shrugged. "There's really no need. I just want to help you find Pundora's Box."

"You are modest and well-tempered," she said, "and very musical. So while you're helping me find the Box, I'll try to help you find your full talent. We all will."

Picka shrugged. "Thank you. I do like music, though I never knew how I liked it before Eve identified my talent."

Dawn found him in the dark and kissed his skull. He wished she wouldn't do that. He didn't like direct contact with meat, yet did like her touch, so it mixed up his emotions.

Now Stanley Steamer departed, satisfied. Dawn and the pets returned to the handbag. That left Picka alone with Joy'nt again.

"Am I really good with music?" he asked her, uncertain.

"Yes. When you play, I can sing and shake the maracas better, because you are perfect in key and timing and I can follow that. It's the same for the others. I don't know how good you can be, but you are very good now."

"Thank you," he repeated, hoping she was correct.

In the morning the living folk aroused and did their ablutions. Then Picka and Joy'nt joined the others in the handbag, and Granola got to her feet and began her search.

Picka and the others peered through the invisible fabric of the handbag as it swayed grandly more than twenty feet above the ground.

Picka knew that some invisible giants were so big that their feet flattened whole trees, but Granola was only the height of a typical tree and did not do any such damage. She walked between and around trees, and her tread was light so as not to thud. Thuds would call attention to her, and none of them wanted that.

Granola found a slope she knew and ascended rapidly out of the chasm, passing several clouds on the way. Picka realized that clouds were lazy; some of them floated below normal ground level when they could get away with it.

They sailed up out of the gulf and over normal land, finding a trail and following it north. The giantess had a good stride and made excellent progress on the level.

"Where is she going?" Joy'nt asked.

"Somewhere in the Region of Fire," Dawn said, fathoming that from her proximity to Granola. "But of course the castle won't be there."

"Then why go there?"

"Because she has to look in more than one place in order to have a next-to-last place."

"Couldn't she simply look in a likely place, then look at another about ten feet away?"

"That's tempting," Dawn said, "but she has tried. The curse can't be so simply cheated. Every place she looks has to be a likely one. She thinks the castle could hide in the Fire Region before moving on. It might not be there now, but might have been there in the past."

Joy'nt nodded. That just might make sense.

In due course they saw the firewall delineating the boundary of the Region of Fire.

Granola halted. "I don't think we can safely pass through that," she said.

"We skeletons might," Picka said.

"I'm not sure," Dawn said. "What heat does it take to cremate bones?"

Picka climbed out of the bag and approached the firewall. He poked a finger at it. The tip of his finger began to char. "That heat," he said, retreating.

"Yet I understand there are living natives of the Fire Region," Granola said. "How do they manage?"

"They must be acclimatized," Joy'nt said.

"And they would be on the other side of the firewall anyway," Dawn said.

"Woof!"

"Oh, you can find a fire resident on this side!" Dawn exclaimed, pleased, patting his shoulder. "Maybe that will help."

Woofer set off, sniffing the hot air, and they followed. The dog led them away from the firewall and into more normal terrain, with hooded witch grass, hungry tangle trees, wise sage plants, fresh egg plants, and other routine vegetation.

They came to a house keeper, keeping three young men and two women. They were having a party. The others held back while Dawn went ahead with the dog.

Woofer went up to the woman, who had red hair and looked hot. "Why, here's a dog!" she exclaimed, wisps of smoke on her breath. "What are you up to?"

Dawn joined them. "This is Woofer, who can sniff out living folk. We are looking for someone who can cross the firewall."

"That's me," the woman agreed. "I am Furn. I can walk on fire. I live in the Region of Fire. I just happen to be out here in the cold visiting my four siblings." She nodded toward the others.

"I am Dawn," Dawn said. "I need to check something on the other side of the firewall, but I can't cross it without getting burned. If you could cross it and check for me, I'd be grateful."

"I can do that tomorrow when I go home," Furn said. "Today I am visiting." She gestured to the four.

This time the others introduced themselves. "I am Airic," the other woman said. "I can walk on air."

"I am Peat," a man said. "I can walk in earth."

"I am Wyck. I can absorb any liquid, becoming its color."

"I am Quantum. I can be in two or more places at the same time."

"Well, now," Dawn said, "most or all of you could get past the firewall, I think. By walking on the fire, or high over it, or through the earth beneath it, or maybe by absorbing so much liquid that it would quench the fire that tried to burn you. Or simply by being on each side of the firewall without crossing it."

"Of course," Airic said. "That's how we visit our sister. What's your point?"

"I would really like to check a certain spot inside the Region of Fire, to see if anything is there."

The five siblings exchanged about four and a half glances. "We can check it tomorrow when we see Furn home."

"I would really prefer to do it today."

"Then you will have to make it worth our while," Peat said.

"Maybe I can trade you something for it."

"We really don't need anything," Wyck said. "We are already doing what we like, which is visiting with our siblings."

A bulb flashed over Dawn's head. "What about entertainment?"

"What kind of entertainment?" Quantum inquired, eyeing her in what Picka suspected was a disturbing interest.

"A song."

They all laughed. "What would we want with a song?" Furn asked.

"This is a special one, done by a remarkable ensemble." Dawn paused, then made her offer: "Suppose we do the song for you, and if you find it worthwhile, then you'll check that site beyond the firewall for us."

"And if we don't like the song?" Airic asked.

"Then we wait until tomorrow."

"That seems fair," Pete said.

Dawn signaled the others. They moved up to join her.

In three to five moments she had introduced them. The siblings seemed amused to see the skeletons and animals, but where quite impressed with what they did not see: the giantess. But there was no doubt of Granola's presence, because she made her footfalls heavier, shaking the ground.

"Let's do 'Ghost of Tom,' in the four parts," she suggested.

They set up and started in, doing it as the round it was. The three pets contributed their howls and tweets. First Granola's concertina, up over their heads. Then Dawn's ocarina joining in. Then Picka's clavicles on his ribs. That made the siblings take notice. Finally Joy'nt with the maracas, also singing.

Picka could see the siblings reacting as the piece proceeded. It was weird and beautiful, because of the extreme diversity of the players and the surprising competence of their music. Music had real power, he realized, not merely over a creature like the Gap Dragon, but over regular people too. The siblings were profoundly moved.

Joy'nt completed her part, and the round ended. There was half a moment of silence.

"You win," Wyck said. "We'll check your site now."

They set out for the firewall. Airic walked high in the air, chatting with Granola, whom she had come to respect. Pete waded knee-deep through the earth. The others were satisfied to walk on the ground with Dawn and the skeletons.

"Exactly what are we looking for?" Quantum asked Dawn.

"A traveling castle. We don't actually expect it to be there, but we have to look."

"As you say," he agreed dubiously.

They came to the firewall. Furn walked right through it, stepping on flames. Airic walked so high she could cross above it. Pete walked down into the earth and disappeared, passing below it. Wyck drank a huge amount of water, turning translucent, then marched through with a fierce sizzling and burst of steam. And Quantum simply stood in place, quivering. But now he looked less dense. He had fissioned, and his other self was on the far side of the firewall.

Soon they returned. "No castle there," Furn reported, and the others agreed. "Just a flat field of fire."

"However," Airic added, "there is a kind of broad pattern vaguely resembling the foundation of a castle. So it might have been there, once, eons ago."

"Thank you," Dawn agreed, unsurprised. "Now we'll look in the next place."

"Before you depart," Peat said, "could you do another song for us? You really are a fine ensemble."

"Gladly," Dawn said. "What song would you like?"

" 'Flaming Passion,' " Furn said quickly.

Picka consulted with her, getting the melody. Then he played it for the others. Then the group of them did it in improvised four-part harmony. They were good, and getting better; even the flames of the firewall danced in time with the music.

This time the siblings applauded. "We don't understand your mission," Quantum said, "but we do thrill to your music. Thank you."

"Welcome," Dawn said. Then she and the others piled into Granola's handbag and disappeared from the view of the siblings. The giantess walked away, leaving the siblings amazed. Music had won the day, even if they hadn't found the castle.

"We have checked the first site, as well as we could," Picka said. "We knew it wouldn't be there, because it won't be at the first site. But how many sites should we check?"

"This does get a bit devious," Dawn said. "Could we check the next site, then quit, and return to find it in the Region of Fire? I have a problem with that, and not just because we can't get to that site ourselves."

"Maybe we should check as many sites as we conveniently can, today, then stop," Joy'nt suggested. "Then go back. I have a feeling it won't work if we try to arrange it too obviously."

Dawn nodded. "You are surely correct. Let's take a nap while we travel, those of us who can do so."

The three pets agreed. Dawn and the pets settled down to sleep, while Picka and Joy'nt watched the passing scenery outside the handbag.

It had been an interesting, if inconclusive start. However, the discovery of their common appreciation of music made the past night and day seem worthwhile.

8
KNUCKLEHEAD

G ranola slowed. Picka could see why: they were now sloshing through the Region of Water.

The giantess lowered the handbag so that it floated on the water. "I think this is the place," she said, "but it gets too deep for me ahead." Indeed, she was already standing waist deep, by the feel of it.

"How do you know where to look?" Picka asked.

"It's just a feeling. Mostly it's wrong, of course, but it's all I have to go on. I have to trust that I will pass by the castle at some point, even if I don't know it at the time."

That did seem to make sense. The castle could not be at the next-to-last place she looked—unless she passed it on the way to the last place—so her feeling had to be accurate to that degree.

"I don't see anything but water," Joy'nt said.

"Neither do I," Granola agreed, "but this is where my feeling leads me."

"Tweet."

"Well, you can check, Tweeter," Joy'nt said, not needing a translation. "I agree that the local birds should be familiar with this area. Maybe they will have useful information. See what you can learn."

Tweeter flew up, and soon disappeared into the sky.

"Maybe it's below," Picka said. "I could go down to look."

"You'd get lost," Joy'nt told him. "And if you plunged to the bottom of the lake, how would you ever return to the handbag? You wouldn't even be able to see it."

"I have some thread," Granola said. "It would seem more like a cable to you. You could lower yourself on that, and follow it back when you're done looking."

Dawn woke. "Are we there?" she asked. "Why didn't you wake me?"

"You looked too comfortable sleeping," Picka said. "You and the pets. Except for Tweeter."

"Well, we don't want to sleep through the key sites. It's my mission, after all."

Joy'nt found the thread. The giantess was right: it was more like a cable. They tied it to the concertina so it couldn't pull free, and Picka tied the other end around his backbone. He was ready to explore the depths.

Tweeter returned. "Tweet!"

Dawn pursed her lips. "That is serious news," she agreed. "You say the local birds report that there's a haunted shipwreck below this spot, so no fishermen come here for fear of it."

Evidently a lot could be conveyed in a single tweet.

"What have we to fear of haunts?" Joy'nt asked. "What can they be—the ghosts of drowned sailors? They're more likely to be spooked by us than we by them."

"I agree," Picka said. "I'm going down."

"The wreck is at the base of the slope that starts beyond Granola's feet," Dawn said. "Too deep for her, but there's plenty of cord."

"Got it," Picka said. He was slightly nervous, but he refused to let the others know it.

"Be careful," Joy'nt murmured. She knew it, because she was his sister and knew him well.

He climbed over the edge of the floating handbag and dropped into the water. His bones were solid, with few air spaces, so he plunged straight down, the cable stretching out above. The upper reaches of the water were light, but the lower reaches were increasingly dark. Fortunately he could see well enough in darkness, as his vision was magical rather than physical.

Meanwhile his hollow head was pondering. A haunted wreck? Could that actually be Caprice Castle? That didn't seem likely, but why else would the giantess be drawn here? If she stopped looking after the next site, this would have to be the place. So he intended to inspect the wreck very carefully.

Something glowed nearby. He peered at it. It was an illuminated blob of translucent flesh, smelling faintly of gasoline. A petroleum jellyfish. A bit farther down was a large blob in the shape of a bean: a jellyfish bean. Interesting; he had wondered where such creatures came from.

Farther down, there were no more fish. Picka made a lipless smile. Even the fish were wary of the wreck!

Then his foot bones touched something. Was it the wreck? No, it was merely sloping seafloor. He walked down it, knowing he needed to get to the bottom. His sight was adjusting, and he could see the dim landscape.

And there ahead was the looming shape of a ship. It looked as if it had settled on the seafloor to rest for a while, before resuming its journey. Its prow still angled boldly forward, and its deck was canted at a stylish angle. Nothing fearsome there.

Then he saw the figure pacing the deck. Round white bones with the flesh all gone. A walking skeleton. So that was the spook!

"Ahoy!" Picka called. He knew the sound carried well through the water.

The figure paused, then turned. "Hoy!" he replied.

Picka came to the ship and scrambled up onto the deck. "I am Picka Bone."

"I am Skully Knucklehead."

They shook bone hands. "I am looking for Caprice Castle."

"Never heard of it. This is Shadow Shipwreck."

"What are you doing here?"

"That's a long story."

"Tell me anyway, and I'll tell you mine."

"I was working the night shift of the coast of Xanth, acting in bad dreams for errant sailors. They spend a lot of time sailing and the night mares can have trouble catching them for their dreams, so I had to be handy in case a dream needed shoring up. I've been to all the ports: C for bringing in fish and marine life; D where ships can only leave; M where things get shipped in; X where they are shipped out; Car, where vehicles are stored; Pass, where workers pass the time of day; Purr for cats; Trans for shipping fat; and so on. One ship was caught in a storm, and the mare lost her footing and lost part of a dream, so I had to get out there on an emergency basis and remake it on-site, as it were. But then the ship sank, and I was caught in it and ripped right out of the gourd realm. The sailors died, of course. The mare escaped, but I was stuck here. I couldn't swim to the surface, and the lake bed seems endless. So rather than get lost worse, I waited here, figuring they would miss me and come for me, and take me back to the gourd realm. You must be my rescuer."

"No, I'm not," Picka said. "I am on a mission with Princess Dawn, seeking Caprice Castle and Pundora's Box. We had information that it might be here, or perhaps was here recently, or maybe will be here in the future."

"It hasn't been here since this ship went down," Skully assured him. "I would have noticed."

"Then I had better return and report."

"You're really not from the gourd?"

"No. My father was, but I have always resided in Xanth proper."

"You can still be my rescuer. Take me back with you, and in due course I'll find a gourd and reenter the realm."

"I can do that," Picka agreed. "I just have to follow my rope back."

They set off, following the rope. Soon the wreck was behind and they were at the slope. It was too steep to walk up conveniently, so they grasped the cord and hauled themselves along. When the remaining distance was straight up, they climbed hand over hand until they reached the lighted shallow section.

"Some legs," Skully remarked.

Picka looked. Granola's two legs were invisible in air, but translucent in water, so they showed. "That's Granola, the female giant who is part of our company."

"A princess and a giantess," Skully said. "You have an interesting taste in company."

"Plus a Mundane dog, cat, and bird. And my sister, Joy'nt Bone."

"Remarkable!"

"We just happened to get together. We all do our parts. We haven't made much progress so far, but we'll keep trying."

They reached the surface, and took turns clambering into the floating handbag. "Caprice Castle is not down there," Picka reported. "But I found the haunt: Skully Knucklehead."

"Hello," Skully said.

"This is Princess Dawn," Picka said, beginning the introductions. "A Sorceress."

"Another walking skeleton!" Dawn said, surprised.

"And my sister Joy'nt."

Skully and Joy'nt exchanged eyeless glances. A bone in the rough shape of a heart floated up. They were impressed by each other.

"Oh, my," Joy'nt murmured.

"Woofer, Tweeter, and Midrange."

The pets presented themselves.

"And Granola Giantess, whose handbag we are in."

"I want to join your company," Skully said immediately. "I'll help any way I can."

"Why, because you saw Joy'nt?" Picka asked sharply.

"Yes."

Picka turned to his sister. "What do you think of this?"

"Let him join," she said eagerly.

They considered. "Do you have any useful abilities?" Dawn asked.

"Maybe. I'm not a normal skeleton. I can't reconnect my bones. That's why I worked on special projects; my own kind didn't want to associate with me. But I do have a magic talent instead."

"You do!" Picka said, interested. "So do I. We're both outcasts."

"Mine is that I can form my bones into different things, like armor or weapons. What's yours?"

"Music. I can play notes on my ribs."

"What use is that?"

Picka was taken aback, as he hadn't thought of it that way. "It helps makes friends. What use is yours?"

"I can form bone weapons to protect other folk. All I need is for someone to tell me what's needed."

"You can't see for yourself?"

"Not always. I'm rather boneheaded."

"That makes sense," Dawn said, laughing. She glanced up. "What do you think, Granola?"

"Sometimes animals smell me and attack my ankles," Granola said. "I don't like that."

"I'll protect your ankles," Skully said.

Dawn glanced at the pets. "How do you three feel?"

"Woof."

"Tweet."

"Purrr."

It seemed they were amenable.

Thus it was decided: Skully could join them.

"So Caprice Castle is not here," Dawn concluded. "Let's try the next site."

Granola heaved up the handbag and waded back the way she had come.

"This is something," Skully said, peering out through the fabric of the bag. "I never traveled this way before."

"How have you traveled?" Joy'nt asked.

"Mostly I rode night mares, so they could take me to the dream sites where I was needed. They can pass through trees and run across water, you know; they're very swift."

"So you're directly from the gourd!" she exclaimed, thrilled.

"Yes. Until that accident with the sinking ship."

"How did you get solid?"

Skully paused. "I am solid now, aren't I! I never thought of that. How did your family get solid?"

"Somehow it happened when our parents left the gourd. We think it occurred naturally when they spent too much time in Xanth proper. Solidity just came to them."

"Well, I was caught on the ship, beneath the sea, for several years. So I had time to absorb matter, I suppose. I didn't realize it was happening."

"Can you go back to the gourd now?"

"I don't know. I thought I could, if a night mare returned to the wreck to fetch me. Now I'm not sure. I may have been spoiled for that. That's unfortunate."

"Maybe it happened at the outset," Dawn suggested. "Because if you had been a figment, like a night mare, you should have stayed at the surface of the lake, instead of being drawn down in the ship. You would have passed right through the timbers."

"I would have," Skully agreed, surprised. "I didn't know."

"Maybe that's why the night mares didn't come for you," Picka said. "They knew you'd been polluted with matter, so they would no longer be able to carry you."

"That makes me feel better about them," Skully said. "I thought they had deserted me without reason. So I guess I'm stuck here permanently."

"Do you really mind?" Joy'nt asked coyly.

He looked at her. "Not anymore."

Joy'nt actually blushed. It wasn't supposed to be possible for flesh-less skeletons, but her bones turned faintly pink. She was definitely in-terested.

Now they were moving over land as the giantess forged south. They came to the Gap Chasm. She walked down a path she knew, across the base, and up the other side. Then she continued through the jungle. It was evidently a long trip.

"We might as well nap again," Dawn said to the pets. They were glad to agree. The four of them settled down for a snooze.

That left the three skeletons to get to know each other better. Picka demonstrated his music by playing on his ribs. Skully showed him he could grow his arm bones big and wide, like clubs. Joy'nt was impressed, making a little show of it. Picka was privately amused, and a bit jeal-ous. She had found a prospective companion. When would he find one, if ever?

The giantess slowed. They were on an almost featureless plain. There was only a single ragged outcropping of rock.

She stopped beside the outcrop. "This is it," she announced, setting down the handbag.

The others piled out and looked around. There was nothing. Woofer sniffed something interesting, perhaps a scent trail, but it led to the foot of the outcrop and stopped. "Woof," he remarked, disappointed.

"So maybe the castle was here once," Dawn said. "Or will be here in the future. But not now."

That seemed to be it.

Midrange yowled. "Danger?" Dawn asked. "What kind?"

The cat was unable to say. It was simply urgent that they get away from here quickly.

"But we haven't finished looking for the Box," Joy'nt protested.

Then they heard something. It sounded like a troop of men marching. "Hup two three four! Hup two three four!"

As they watched, the troop marched around the outcrop. It was a formation of round red cherries with little feet, led by a pineapple who called the cadence.

"Company halt!" They stopped before Dawn's party, apparently coincidentally.

That made Picka nervous. He was dubious about coincidences.

"Today's drill will be on detonations," the pineapple said. "When you get hurled into an enemy camp, what do you do, Bomb One?"

"Explode?" the first cherry answered hesitantly.

"Well, sure, fruitbrain! But is that all?"

"All?"

"Lesson number one: there's a stupid way to do it and a smart way. I'm here to teach you to be smart. If you detonate on contact you may take out one aggressor enemy personnel, or none. Your effort will be largely wasted. That's the stupid way. Instead you should hold off a while, survey the situation. Move a few yards over and you may be able to take out three or four. A lot more bang for your buck. That's the smart way."

The assembled cherry bombs bobbed, getting it. Picka remained nervous, not trusting this. But what could he or the others do, except keep quiet?

"Any questions?"

"Some of us have short fuses," Cherry Bomb Number Two said. "We *have* to detonate on contact. That's the way we're made. So how can we pick our targets?"

"Short fuse, my fruity fundament!" the pineapple exclaimed impatiently. "Stifle it, red neck. You can hold off until you hit the right target."

The cherry bombs were silent. They had been given the word.

"Now for a practice run," the pineapple said briskly. "All we need is an enemy troop." It looked around, spying Dawn's group, as if coincidentally. Of course the thing had seen them all along. "And I believe we have one. Company, attack!"

The cherry bombs started marching forward.

"Get out of here!" Dawn cried.

They scrambled for the invisible handbag, but several cherries were crowding between them and the bag. One touched Joy'nt's moving foot. It exploded into a ball of fire and roiling smoke, just missing her. It had been a stupid bomb.

"Not that way!" the pineapple bawled. "Get smart, you dumbbells!"

The others were determined to be smarter bombs. They surrounded Joy'nt, closing in.

Skully charged in to join her, his arm bones expanding into clubs. He swung at a cherry, knocking it into the air. It exploded, harmlessly. He swung at another, knocking it into the main formation. It detonated, setting off the others, and there was a fusillade of explosions and a surging cloud of smoke.

Meanwhile Dawn and the pets made it to the handbag, and Joy'nt was approaching it.

"No, no!" the pineapple shouted, running to intercept her. "Get organized!"

Skully leaped to reach the pineapple first, swinging his club. He caught the pineapple on the crown.

There was a horrendous explosion. The pineapple and Skully flew into pieces.

Picka watched, appalled. Skully had saved Joy'nt at the cost of his own existence. The smart-bomb menace was gone, but at what price?

"No!" Joy'nt cried. She ran to fetch a stray bone as it landed some distance away. She picked it up and went after another.

Of course! Picka started fetching scattered bones himself. Dawn and the pets caught on, and joined the effort. The bones were smoking hot, some charred, but they were all in the area. They just had to find and collect them.

Soon they had a pile of battered bones. Then they started fitting them together, toe bone to foot bone, foot bone to ankle bone, leg bone to knee bone, thigh bone to hip bone and so on up. All that was missing was one finger bone they were unable to find. When they put the skull bone on the neck bone, Skully animated. "What a headache!" he exclaimed.

"You're back!" Joy'nt said, hugging him.

"Well, you know a walking skeleton can't be destroyed by dismemberment," Skully said. "Not if he has friends."

That about covered it. Skully had proved himself in more than one sense. He was burnt and battered, but before long his bones would heal.

They piled back into the handbag and Granola started walking again.

"Picka and Joy'nt have partial souls," Dawn said, "so they do decent things. But you, Skully are directly from the gourd. What motivated you to sacrifice yourself like that?"

"Actually I have some soul," Skully said. "We all do. It's desiccated and so thin that it's hardly noticeable, but it's there in the marrow. We are, after all, derivatives of living human lineage, way back in our past."

"So you are," she agreed, surprised. "I never thought of that. All human-related creatures have souls, including crossbreeds and derivatives. I suppose I assumed that skeletons are dead, so their original souls departed."

"Most of our souls do go," Skully agreed, "but a little fraction remains." He shrugged. "I never had much use for it. But then Joy'nt was in danger . . ." He made a gesture of helplessness.

Picka had been a bit jealous of Skully's interest in Joy'nt, but the incident of the smart bombs had defused it. Skully was worthy. Now if Picka could just find a similarly worthy female walking skeleton . . .

"Are you at all musical?" Joy'nt asked Skully.

"Not a musical bone in my body."

Picka realized what she had in mind. "Music is what you make of it. Anyone can be musical in his fashion. Just form an arm into a hammer and bonk your skull, keeping the cadence."

"I guess I could do that," Skully said. "But why?"

Dawn smiled. "We are a musical group. It's not just Picka. We'll show you." She looked up. "Granola, can you play while you walk?"

"Yes, if it doesn't freak out the local wildlife," the giantess responded.

"The wildlife might appreciate a good freaking," Skully remarked.

"Then let's do it," Dawn said. "You might as well know the company you are keeping."

They did "Ghost of Tom" again, sure that Skully would like it. He did; by the time the last refrain finished, he was happily bonking his skull in time.

"I like it," Skully said. "Including the animals. It is a rendition like none other. I'm just a hollow head, but the rest of you are good at it."

"It came upon us more or less coincidentally," Dawn said. "I liked to play tunes with my sister, and when we discovered Picka's talent we just got into it."

"I'm not a reliable judge," Skully said, "but you seem like the finest musician I've heard, Picka."

"I just repeat songs I've heard." But Picka was coming to like Skully better.

They played other songs, enjoying the harmonies. "You know, what we need is a book of songs," Joy'nt said. "Then we could really improve."

"After we find Pundora's Box, we can look for a good music book," Dawn said.

Granola slowed. They were approaching the next site.

This turned out to be by the bank of a river. A young woman stood there. She looked frustrated.

Granola stopped some distance away, amidst a grove of trees. She set the handbag down gently.

"Maybe I had better go first," Dawn said. "Our full company might startle her."

"Three walking skeletons and an invisible giant?" Picka asked. "Whatever makes you think that?"

"Woof!"

"You're right, Woofer," Dawn agreed. "A woman with a friendly dog should not spook anyone."

Dawn and Woofer got out and walked toward the river. The others remained hidden, listening.

"Hello," Dawn called. "Where are we?"

"Woof," Woofer added.

The girl turned. "Crymea River."

"I never heard of that river."

"No, *I'm* Crymea River. My talent is to build a bridge and get over it. But there's nothing on the other side that I want, so I'm left with nothing to do."

"Oh," Dawn said, disconcerted. Evidently the girl had misheard her query. "I'm Dawn. This is Woofer. He's a dog."

"I noticed."

"My talent is to know about living things. We are looking for a . . . a castle. Have you seen it?"

Crymea laughed. "Not here! I'm sure I would have noticed. Are you sure you don't need to cross the river?"

"Not unless the castle is there."

They both gazed across the river. No castle was visible. "Why do you think a castle should be here?" Crymea asked.

"It's a complicated story. The essence is that the castle seems to travel, so it's hard to locate. But we're trying."

Crymea smiled, not taking her seriously. "Good luck."

Dawn turned and returned to the grove. "I think we had better give up the search for today," she said. "It is getting late."

Midrange stirred. "Meow."

"We should cross her bridge?" Dawn asked. "But the castle is not across the river; we looked."

"Mew."

Dawn shrugged, not completely pleased. "If you say so. That means I'll have to introduce the group."

"Mew."

"Come on, folk," Dawn said. "Midrange says we need to do it."

They climbed out of the handbag. Dawn went ahead to warn Crymea, then signaled the others to advance, including the giantess.

The girl was plainly amazed to see them, and more than a trifle nervous. "Woofer Dog you've met," Dawn said briskly. "This is Midrange Cat, and Tweeter Bird. Picka Bone. Joy'nt Bone. Skully Knucklehead. And Granola Giantess. She's invisible."

"Then how—?"

"Hello, Crymea," Granola said from above.

"Uh, hello, Granola," Crymea said faintly.

"We have decided we need to check the other side of the river after all," Dawn said.

"You want my bridge!" Crymea said, abruptly overjoyed.

"Yes. Granola won't be able to use it, but the rest of us can."

Crymea turned to face the river. She spread her arms wide. From her fingers issued streams of vapor that arched across the river and touched the far bank. The arches thickened and sent tendrils to interconnect. Soon a ghostly bridge formed.

The image shimmered and intensified. There it was: a lovely arch spanning the river.

"But it's illusion," Dawn said.

"Not to me," Crymea said. She stepped on the bridge, and it supported her weight.

"I wonder," Joy'nt said. She put a foot on the span—and it sank through it to the ground below. It was indeed illusion.

"Meowrer," Midrange said.

"Midrange would like to cross with you," Dawn told Crymea.

"That's fine," the girl said, pleased. She bent to pick up the cat, then walked on across the span. Midrange seemed quite interested in it.

"We'd better see what they're up to," Dawn said.

They piled into the handbag, and Granola carried them across the river, keeping up with the girl and cat.

"Meow!" Midrange said urgently.

Crymea stopped. "But we're not all the way across yet," she said.

"There must be something," Dawn called from the bag. "Midrange can tell when something important is about to happen."

"I hope it's not getting dunked in the river," Joy'nt murmured. "If Crymea lets go of him, he'll fall right through the bridge."

"Woof!"

They looked at the dog. Woofer was sniffing avidly, his nose pointing to the water. "What is it?" Picka asked.

"He doesn't know," Dawn said. "Just that it's something we ought to know about."

They all peered down into the river. It wasn't deep here, and they could see the bottom. It was irregular, except for a series of flat sections, as if some very large creature had waded through it.

"Giant steps," Granola said. She knew about such things, of course.

"What do we care about some other giant?" Picka asked.

A skull-shaped bulb flashed over Skully's noggin. "Not a giant," he said. "A castle!"

"Castles don't walk," Joy'nt reminded him.

"But they do settle. At least Caprice Castle does. It must have been here not long ago, and those are the marks of its foundations where they flattened the river bottom."

The others stared at him. "I believe he's got it," Dawn said. "That's why Midrange knows, and what Woofer smells. The taint of the departed castle."

"So now we know we're getting close," Picka said. "This may be its last site. We just need to move on to its present site."

"But where would that be?" Joy'nt asked.

"The rocky outcropping," Skully said. "Woofer was sniffing there."

"But that would be the site before this one."

"No," Skully said firmly. "That's the site *after* this one, for the traveling castle. It has a different schedule. Our next-to-last stop."

"But it can't be traveling backwards in time," Picka protested.

"Not backwards. We're just following its trail back."

A glance of wild surmise circled the group. "That just might be," Dawn said.

It seemed that Skully had come through again.

"Are you satisfied?" Crymea asked.

"Yes, I think we are," Dawn said. "Thank you for your help. Your bridge enabled us to see our first direct evidence of the castle we seek."

"That's good," Crymea said, pleased again. She held Midrange up as the bag swung close, and he scrambled in.

Then they were on their way back to the next-to-last site, thanks to Crymea, Midrange, Woofer, and Skully.

9
CRUSH

Granola hurried, and they made it back to the outcropping before nightfall. And paused, amazed.

The massive rock formation was gone. It was simply a level plain.

"Are we sure this is the right place?" Joy'nt asked.

"Yes," Skully said. "Here are the pineapple fragments." He picked up a small metallic scale. "And here's my missing finger bone." He picked it up. It had evidently gotten wedged under a stray stone and been hidden before.

"So what happened to the outcrop?" Joy'nt asked.

"And where is the castle?" Dawn asked.

Then a mutual glance almost crashed in the center of their circle. "The two were the same," Picka said, putting it together. "The castle was masked as the outcrop. That's why Woofer sniffed to the edge."

"But why didn't Midrange react?" Joy'nt asked.

"Meow."

"There wasn't anything to react to," Dawn translated. "He anticipates significant events, but we weren't destined to find the castle at that time."

Now Midrange became agitated. "Meow!" he said imperatively.

"Oh, my," Dawn said. "Now something is about to happen here. He doesn't know exactly what, except that it may be life-changing." She paused. "And the only folk here with lives are you three pets, and me."

"And me," Granola said from above.

"And you, of course," Dawn agreed. "One or more of us will be significantly affected."

"And not any skeletons?" Picka asked. "But we're working together. What affects one affects the others."

"Mew."

"Some more than others," Dawn translated. "There's a threshold."

"Let's hope it's good," Joy'nt said. "Meanwhile, night is looming and you living folk will want to eat and rest. So you can be prepared for that happening."

Dawn looked around. "You're right. Unfortunately there's nothing much here to eat, and no shelter. We may have to go to another area where we can forage."

"But the happening might happen while you're away," Skully pointed out. "You living folk need to stay here so you won't miss it."

"Good point," Dawn agreed. "We must remain for it, all of us, whatever it is. We don't know which living creature will be affected."

"We three skeletons can forage," Picka said. "We know what food is, even if we don't need it ourselves. We'll find something and bring it back."

"That is kind of you."

The skeletons set out, walking in a widening spiral, searching for anything edible. It was increasingly dark, but that did not bother them. The plain had been warm, almost hot by day; now it was cooling and stray breezes were stirring as if just waking up. It might get cold; the smaller living folk would need some sort of shelter.

"Joy'nt," Skully murmured.

"Yes?"

"May I . . . hold your hand?"

Picka stayed out of it. Hand holding was one of the customs skeletons shared with living human folk. It was a strong signal of mutual interest.

"Yes," she replied faintly. She was surely blushing again; that remained a good trick for a skeleton, and signaled burgeoning emotion.

So they walked connected, their finger bones intertwined. Picka's feelings were strongly mixed. He was glad for his sister; she had found a worthy male skeleton. But he was also jealous again. Why couldn't he encounter a nice female skeleton? He knew his chances were diminished, because he could not reconfigure his bones the way normal skeletons could. Female skeletons would consider him to be handicapped. Yes, he could play music on his ribs, but that seemed likely to make him a laughingstock among his own kind, rather than a prospective partner. So even if there were other skeletons out in Xanth proper, he would still have a problem.

"There's a garden ahead," Joy'nt said. She was good at picking up on such things, even when distracted by interdigitation: the twining of finger bones.

"Just what we need," Picka said. "But if it is tended by a human, we should be cautious about approaching."

"It's dark," Joy'nt said. "I can call out, and maybe they won't realize my nature until I have had a chance to reassure them. Then we can make a deal for some fruits, vegetables, or pies."

"Seems apt," Picka agreed.

There was a trim little fence around the garden, which appeared to be irrigated. The odors of growing vegetables and fruits and pie plants wafted out on a passing breeze. Inside the enclosure was a neat little cottage shaded by decorative trees. The property was like a verdant island in the barren plain. Someone had gone to some trouble to establish it.

Picka and Skully lay down outside the fence, while Joy'nt walked around to the gate. "Hello!" she called.

"Who is there?" a living woman's voice answered from the house.

"I am Joy'nt Bone. I would like to talk with you about getting some things to eat."

The cottage door opened and a figure emerged, silhouetted by the spilling light from the interior. Female, slender, garbed in homegrown blouse and skirt. "I am Doris. You may not want to associate with me."

Picka exchanged an eyeless glance with Skully. She thought *they* would be wary of *her*?

"I am not concerned," Joy'nt said. "I am a walking skeleton. I am friendly, but you may be alarmed by my appearance."

"Come on in," Doris called. "I know you are telling the truth."

Joy'nt opened the gate and entered the yard. "How can you be sure of that?" she asked.

"It's my talent. No one can lie to me; I always know the truth when a statement is made. There are folk who are uncomfortable with that."

"Why should they be uncomfortable?"

"Social conventions. Most folk don't want the truth. They prefer to be falsely flattered. I can't do that; I have to stay with reality. They regard that as unkind candor. So its easier to live apart."

"That's too bad."

"No, that's good. It relieves stress. I can be my own person without stressing others or myself. Now, why do you need anything to eat? Skeletons don't eat, do they?"

"We are part of a party on a special mission," Joy'nt said. "Five members are living, three nonliving. We make music together. The living ones need food and rest."

"True. Who are they?"

"Granola, Dawn, Woofer, Midrange, and Tweeter."

"A giant, a princess, and three pet animals! That's a remarkable party!"

"How did—"

"My talent, remember? You answered with a partial truth, but I knew the real case. Why didn't the living folk come here themselves?"

"Something is going to happen that will be life-changing. So they have to remain there for it."

"I would like to meet them," Doris said. "I don't get to socialize much, and they sound interesting."

"I don't know . . ."

"I will bring a basketful of good food."

"Done," Joy'nt agreed. "My companions are outside the fence. They are skeletons too."

"Are they friendly?"

"Yes, if you are."

"True. Bring them in while I gather food."

Picka and Skully entered the enclosure and introduced themselves to Doris. "We like your garden," Picka said. "We can't eat anything in it, but it's a pleasant place."

"Thank you. I wish one or both of you were alive."

"I have a spell to make me fleshly for one hour," Picka said, "but that would be futile. You are not my type."

She laughed. "Indeed I am not! But if you should encounter a suitable fleshly man who is in need of a woman who will always know the truth about him, please do send him my way. I'd love to have company—and perhaps romance."

"We will do that," Picka promised.

In due course the four of them were walking back toward the camp of the living, with a big basket of food. Joy'nt filled Doris in on things, as she fathomed them anyway.

Soon they heard music. Granola and Dawn were playing their instruments, and the pets were joining in.

"And you three are musical too?" Doris asked.

"Picka is," Joy'nt said. "I just shake the maracas, and Skully bonks his hollow head, keeping the beat."

"Let me hear."

Picka unlimbered his clavicles and played on his ribs as they walked. Joy'nt and Skully joined in in their fashions.

"You *are* good," Doris said appreciatively. "Especially you, Picka. But I suppose if you turned fleshly, you wouldn't be able to play your ribs."

"True," Picka agreed. It was another reason not to invoke the conversion spell.

They rejoined the others. Joy'nt introduced Doris to Dawn and the pets.

"What is that scent?" Dawn asked, sniffing. "Is there a horse nearby?"

"Just perfume I distill from garden herbs," Doris replied. "Mainly horseradish. I like horses."

"Oh. Of course." Picka realized that Dawn was embarrassed about suggesting that Doris smelled like a horse. She did, but it seemed that as perfume it was all right.

Doris opened the basket she had packed. There were pies, sandwiches, milk pods, tsoda water and boot rear for the people, and dog biscuits, catnip, and birdseed. A wonderful repast. "There's even some genuine moon cheese," Doris said proudly. "I have a friend whose talent is to summon cheese from the moon." It was obviously genuine, because it had a green cheesy smell and looked like a full moon: a bare human bottom.

"That needs to be spanked," Joy'nt muttered.

"Oh, thank you!" Dawn exclaimed. "How may we repay you?"

"Just play some beautiful music. I seldom get to hear it."

"We can do that," Dawn agreed. "It's not relevant to our mission, but it's fun."

"That's not true," Doris said. "It is essential to your mission. In fact it will help you tonight."

"You can know the truth even when we don't know it?" Dawn asked guardedly. Picka could tell she was miffed by the girl's presumption.

"At least I know an untruth when I hear it," Doris said. "You said music was not relevant to your mission, but it is. I knew it the moment you spoke of it."

"How will it help us tonight?"

Doris paused, focusing. "I'm not good at fathoming things directly, only at knowing the truth of anything spoken. You are looking for something. Music will summon it. That exhausts my insight."

"It is nevertheless some insight," Dawn said.

They took out their instruments and played several sprightly melodies. Doris was evidently enchanted.

"But it's hard to see how this relates to our mission," Dawn said.

Doris shrugged. She must have learned not to argue about truth. "Now I must go home, before the chill of night sets in. Thank you for the music." She turned about and departed with her empty basket. The odor of horses lingered briefly.

"The chill of night," Dawn murmured with an anticipatory shiver.

"We're not equipped, and there are no blanket bushes in the neighborhood."

"We could search for some," Picka said.

"Did you see any before?"

"No."

"I have a small blanket in my handbag," Granola said.

They checked. What was small for the giantess was huge for regular-sized folk. They took it out, and Dawn and the pets wrapped themselves in its folds.

There was a distant roll of thunder.

"Oh, no!" Dawn breathed.

"If rain comes, I can turn over my handbag to serve as a shelter," Granola said.

"But what about you?" Picka asked. "Won't you get wet?"

"I'm used to it. I go largely naked, and have considerable body mass; water just runs off me without chilling me unduly."

Reassured, they settled down. "That was an interesting statement Doris made," Skully said. "About music bringing the castle."

"Music will summon Caprice Castle?" Joy'nt asked, amazed. "I had missed the significance."

"That could be life-changing," Dawn agreed. Any annoyance about Doris had dissipated. Had she really provided them with the answer to their search? "So let's make music!"

They went through their limited repertoire as the night progressed, ignoring the cooling and the gusting winds. The scents of day were being replaced by those of night. But too soon they ran out of the ones they had rehearsed, and no castle had appeared. "Will it accept re-used songs?" Dawn asked.

"We are talking about it as if it is a conscious entity," Skully said. "Does that make sense?"

"If it masked itself as a rocky outcrop to conceal itself from us, then it must be conscious," Dawn said. "It must have motivation of its own. It may be that we'll never find it unless it chooses to be found."

"And music might make it choose," Joy'nt said. "So music *is* relevant."

"If we just have good enough offerings," Picka said.

There was another roll of thunder, closer, and a gust of wind that was verging on cold. Rain seemed increasingly likely.

Dawn focused on him. "Can you improvise?"

He was taken aback. "I don't know. I have just been playing what I have heard. I don't think I'm creative."

"Try it."

He shrugged, which was tricky without his clavicles on, and tried.

The music flowed. Melodies came to his fingers and resonated from his ribs. He was lost in the marvel of it, transported by the wonder of his own expression.

The others simply sat in a circle around him and listened. They seemed to be entranced. The breaths of Dawn and the pets were fogging, but they did not seem to notice.

The first drops of rain spattered on the ground around them. The living folk would have to take shelter, now. But Picka, caught up in the mood of the music, played on.

Then something happened. Misty walls appeared before Picka's gaze, like the ethereal strands of Crymea's bridge. They thickened, becoming opaque.

He kept playing, fearing that if he stopped, so would the manifestation. The walls continued to solidify.

When Picka saw drops of rain splashing against those walls, he knew they had solidified. "It's here," he said, pausing his music.

The others looked around. "Oh!" Dawn said, surprised.

The castle was definitely there. It ascended into the darkness, the glass of its windows glinting in the lightning flashes. The storm was inhaling, about to blast them with full force.

Then interior lights came on, illuminating the complete castle. It was magnificent.

"We had better go in, if it lets us," Dawn said.

"It that wise?" Joy'nt asked. "To let the storm drive us in before we know anything about this castle?"

Dawn paused. "Excellent point."

There was a horrendous crack of thunder.

"But I'm willing to gamble on its goodwill," Dawn said.

"But what of Granola?" Skully asked.

"There's a large sheltered courtyard I can use," the giantess said.

They hurried to the front gate, which was open. In between one and two moments they were under cover, as the rain sluiced down outside. It was a suspiciously close call.

It occurred to Picka that life-changing could be a euphemism for life-ending, but it did not seem expedient to mention that at the moment.

They were in a high-vaulted passage. Alcoves lined it, containing paintings and statuary. The paintings were of Xanthly scenes: beaches, forest, fields, and some of the Gap Chasm. The sculptures were of ordinary Xanth creatures: dragons, griffins, fauns, nymphs, nickelpedes.

"This castle travels," Joy'nt said, "and collects pictures of what it sees."

"As castles go, it's a competent one," Dawn agreed.

There were doors along the way but they were closed and locked, so they continued down the hall. It led to a curling stairway, which took them to a similar hall a flight up. There they found three doors open, providing access to bedrooms. All the other doors on this floor were closed.

"Bedrooms?" Dawn asked. "We're looking for Pundora's Box."

"We are evidently guests," Picka said. "Tonight it wants us to sleep."

Dawn explored the first bedroom. There was a king-size bed, properly made with the sheets turned down invitingly. There was an attached bathroom, with a tub full of soapy water. "Oh, that is tempting!" Dawn breathed.

They checked the second bedroom. Its bed was without sheets or blankets; it was just a big square pad. There was no bathroom. "Good for two skeletons," Skully remarked.

"Yes," Joy'nt agreed, her bones turning pink again.

"Take it," Dawn said. "I'll take the bath."

"I'll explore elsewhere," Picka said.

"The bleep you will," Dawn said. "You're with me."

"I am?"

"We'll talk while I have my bath."

"Oh."

The third bedroom was for the pets, complete with old blankets, sandboxes, water, and a perch.

Joy'nt and Skully took the pad. The pets were happy with their room. Dawn led Picka into the other bedroom, closing the door behind them, then into the bathroom. She stepped out of her clothing, dumped it into the available laundry chute, and got into the bath. "Just right," she said, sinking luxuriously into the water. "Caprice Castle knows how to entertain royalty."

"Are you sure we can trust it?"

"I can't be quite sure, because it's not a living thing. But if it wanted to trap us or hurt us, why would it hide from us, then come to us when you played such excellent music? It has to have some other agenda."

"What would that agenda be?"

"My guess is that it wants a suitable occupant, like a king or queen. Or someone with an outstanding talent, like you. When we showed it that we had something it might want, it came to us. Now it's looking us over."

"What if it doesn't like us?"

"Then it will depart, leaving us behind. So we had better complete our mission, finding Pundora's Box, before the castle decides we're not good enough for it."

"But you did not let me search at this time."

"The castle does not want us to search right now. That's why its doors are closed—except the ones for sleeping. Tomorrow it will surely give us better access. I'm glad to have the chance to clean up, rest, and sleep."

"But I have no need of these things."

"You will, Picka, when you invoke your flesh spell."

"I'm not going to do that!"

She reached out of the tub and caught his wrist bone. "Oh, yes you are! Do it now."

"But—"

"Must I humiliate myself? Then here it is: I have a sudden crush on you, Picka. It happened when I listened to you improvise. Your music was just so beautiful, so perfect, it captured my heart. So at this moment I like you—in fact, I love you, and I mean to have you."

"This is nonsensical!" he protested. "I'm not your type. That's why you associate freely with me."

"That's changed. Now I want you, Picka, at least for one hour. Invoke the spell, or I'll haul you into the tub and soak your bones."

"But if I invoke it, I'll see you in a different way."

"A male way," she agreed. "That's the idea."

"What idea?"

"I want you to become capable of feeling what I feel. So you will understand."

"I don't think this is something I want to understand."

"We princesses are an imperious lot. When Princess Rhythm got a crush on Cyrus Cyborg, he did not take her seriously, because she was only twelve years old. So she invoked a spell that aged her a decade and hauled him into a love spring. *Then* he understood."

"It's not a matter of age. You are almost twenty-one. It's that I'm a walking skeleton."

"Which is why it is time to invoke the transformation spell," she said patiently. "Do it."

She would not yield. He brought the spell out of his cranium and invoked it, fearing he would regret it.

Suddenly he was clothed in living flesh. It spread across all his bones, covering his limbs, ribs, skull, and everything. His skull filled with substance, and so did his pelvis. He had meat in places that hadn't existed before. It threw him off balance, so that only her grasp on him kept him upright.

"Very good," she said approvingly. "Now get into the tub with me."

"But—"

She hauled on his wrist, and he tumbled forward, splashing into the water. She caught his stray limbs and got his clumsy body arranged. He struggled to get out, but she held him and kissed him on his now-meaty mouth.

It was like getting clubbed on the skull. His head seemed to explode into rapture. Nothing existed except that ardent contact of his lips and hers.

After an eternity-long moment she drew back. "Now behave, or I'll kiss you again."

"But—"

She kissed him again. This time not only did the new flesh of his head seem to swell, a new organ inside his rib cage started thumping vigorously. What was going on?

She drew back again. "Now will you stay in place?"

"But—"

She caught his now-meaty hand again and put it against her fleshy chest. His new heart muscle beat violently again, seeming to swell in his chest. So did some of the flesh farther down.

"Had enough?" she asked.

"No, I—"

"Then I will give you more." She wriggled forward, bringing her wet skin up against his. She wrapped her arms around him and held him close, so that her sculptured chest pressed tightly against his while her midsection squeezed his most swollen flesh. She wriggled and did something, relieving the lower pressure, though there was no room there. It was almost as though she had taken his flesh into hers. An impossibility, of course, because her flesh was solid throughout, not spaced between bones the way his body normally was. "Now?"

"I don't—"

"You never learn." She kissed him on the face, and squeezed him below, rhythmically.

His entire being erupted into incredible rapture. He found himself kissing her while something else gloriously surged into her. It continued for several eternal moments, then subsided blissfully.

"What happened?" he gasped.

She laughed. "Let's finish our bath, and I will take you through it again, in slow motion."

The bath turned out to be halfway pleasant, as she washed him and rinsed him. He was beginning to get used to being buried in meat.

Then they got out and dried off, using the big towels the castle provided. There was new clothing laid out, but she demurred. "We have less than an hour, now. We'll stay bare."

She took him to the bed, and they lay on top of it. "I know skeletons do it differently," she said, "but for the moment you are in my realm. Living folk like to make love."

"I don't understand."

"Like this." She rolled over and came up against him. She was marvelously soft. She kissed him, and it transported him again. Then, step by step, she took him through the process of making love, explaining it along the way.

By the time they completed it a second time, he understood the burgeoning emotion he felt. "I love you!"

"Yes, for now."

Then the hour expired, and he reverted to his natural state. "Oh, my," he said, appalled. How could he have done such fleshy stuff?

"But for that time, you did understand what I meant when I said I loved you," she said. "Because you felt it too. Now you are back to normal, and the living feeling is gone. But I remain as I am, and my feeling has not faded. I just wanted you to understand, even if you don't feel it yourself at the moment."

"I understand," he agreed, fazed. "I think."

"So now we can talk sensibly, and decide our future."

"Our future!"

She caught his hand again, making him lie beside her on the bed. "Picka, that can be anything. We may complete my mission and part ways forever, or we may continue our association and possibly even marry."

"Marry!"

She squeezed his finger bones. "Let me make something clear to you, Picka. I am a princess and a Sorceress and a lovely female living human creature in my own right. I am not accustomed to hearing the word 'no' from any man. I will marry whom I choose. We need to determine whether I will choose you."

"But you're not my type! You have all that, that—"

"All that disgusting flesh on my bones," she agreed. "You are perhaps the only kind of humanoid male who would see it that way. I was not romantically interested in you before we discovered your music. In fact, I wanted to be sure that you did not see me as a desirable creature."

"I remember," he said. "You climbed all over me."

"How would you have reacted if I had done that when you had flesh on?"

He visualized the way she had flashed him with her bra and panties, then wrapped her legs about his head so that his face had been blinded by her lower belly. He had not understood how arousing that would have been for a fleshly man; now he did. "I would have wanted to summon the stork with you."

"Yes. And when you had flesh on, you did do that, though I took a potion that prevented the signal from going out. And there's the irony."

"Irony?"

"I wanted to be sure you had no romantic or sexual interest in me, so that I could trust you not to get all eagerly male. Now I want exactly such interest, and you can't give it. I never thought of myself as foolish, but I have put myself into a truly foolish situation."

"I'm sorry."

"I brought it on myself. Now we have to figure out what to do about it."

"I'll be your friend until you find a handsome living human prince. Then you can forget me."

She shook her head. "Unlikely, and not just because there don't seem to be any suitable princes available at the moment. Picka, I fell for you because of the absolute beauty of your music. You will only get better, musically, and my love will intensify accordingly. I know you for a thoroughly worthy male, surely better than any prince I might encounter. I don't *want* to forget you."

"But—"

"But it's impossible. I know. Unless you should be willing to convert permanently to a fleshly man."

"Then I could not play my ribs. I would lose my music."

She sighed. "True. But I'm not sure I want to convert to a skeleton, if that were even possible. So we have a problem."

Picka pondered. "Dawn, we are friends, and I do like you, and after that hour I do understand your feeling. If you wish to marry me, I will do it. I could invoke the spell once a day."

"I don't want you to marry me out of friendship, Picka. I want you to fall madly in love with me. Your prospects for finding a suitable female skeleton are about as dim as mine for a prince. We might make a couple of convenience. An odd couple, but a couple. Can you consider that?"

"Yes. But I can't promise love."

"I am going to court you, Picka. If I can make you love me, in your natural state, then we'll reconsider marriage. Is that fair?"

"Yes."

"Then lie here beside me as I sleep. Be tolerant when I wake and kiss you. If it is possible to arouse love in a skeleton, I mean to do it. Just give me a fair chance."

"Of course." He believed in fair chances, even when the odds were impossible.

She lay back and closed her eyes, but continued holding his hand possessively. Soon she was breathing evenly in sleep.

She was a beautiful creature of her kind. She was, as she said, a princess and a Sorceress. She had a crush on him. She intended to win his love along with his passion. But was it possible for him ever to love her back while in his natural form?

He didn't know.

10
CAPRICE

In the morning Dawn woke and kissed Picka on the skull. He had not slept, of course, but he had spent the time pondering, wishing he could be what she wanted him to be. She was a good person, a worthy partner. But she was *alive*.

"And you are not," she said, divining his thought though she could not fathom things about the un-alive. "It is a challenge."

"I will give you some privacy to get dressed," he said, remembering that she had preferred it in the past.

"Nu-uh. You'll watch everything. Maybe it will impress you."

He did not argue, not wanting to make her feel bad about her chances of impressing him in that manner.

She got up, washed, and dressed, all in his sight. He recognized that she was an extremely sightly creature, one of the prettiest in Xanth. But there was no obscuring the fact that she was simply not his type. All that meat on her bones! Only if he invoked the transformation spell would she impress him, and then only for an hour. It wasn't worth it.

"I had hoped there would be more of a lingering effect," she said.

"I remember how impressed I was when I had flesh," he said. "But now that I am myself, I know better."

"Let's go out and see whether this hospitable castle serves breakfast."

It did. Dawn and the pets had a nice breakfast, and food was sent out for Granola in the courtyard.

When they were finished, they blinked, and the dirty dishes and crumbs were gone. It seemed that all chores were magically accomplished.

"Now it is time for our mission," Dawn said. "Somewhere in this castle is Pundora's Box. I thought it would be easy to find, once we got in the castle, but now that I see the size of the premises I'm not so sure."

"We can split up and search many areas at once," Picka suggested.

"No. We must not forget that we are in a castle whose nature and loyalties we do not properly understand. We should search in pairs, and the pairs should be in constant touch with the others."

"This is sensible," Skully agreed. "Joy'nt and I will pair."

"And Picka and me," Dawn said. "And the three pets. That leaves Granola to search outside, just in case."

They went to work. Now all doors were open. Picka and Dawn searched the higher turrets first, looking in closets, under beds, even behind hanging tapestries. The castle was well-appointed throughout, but there were no boxes.

"This is such a nice castle," Dawn murmured. "I wouldn't mind living here."

"It does seem suitable for a princess," Picka agreed.

"Yes. But a princess does not rate her own castle until she marries; it's an unwritten rule." She glanced sidelong at him. "So all I need to do is tame this castle, find Pundora's Box, and marry you."

"Maybe we'll find that Box." Picka was being careful, trying not to annoy her.

She laughed, with a trace of bitterness. "We'll start with that, anyway."

By noon they had gone over all the upper sections, admiring the well-kept chambers, but finding no Box.

"I just realized," Picka said. "There are no puns in this castle."

"They probably stay well away, lest they get caught and boxed."

"Do puns make decisions?"

"Some do. Remember Attila the Pun? But more likely they have simply been swept out. Caprice Castle may not like puns. It would hardly be alone in that."

They returned to the ground floor.

"Woof!"

"Woofer!" Dawn said gladly. "What have you found?"

"Woof."

"A book? We'd better check."

They followed the dog to a small chamber where Tweeter and Midrange waited. There on an ornate pedestal was a single book. Dawn picked it up, glancing at the cover. *"History of Caprice Castle,"* she read. She looked up. "I think this is something we all need to share."

They located Skully and Joy'nt, who had been searching the basement levels with no success. Then they went out to the courtyard, where Granola also had not found anything. Picka, Joy'nt, and Skully dropped their bones on the ground, and the three pets lay down beside them, ready to listen.

Dawn settled on the rim surrounding the fountain and opened the book. She began reading aloud. Her words sailed out across the fountain, and the water there formed into a picture. The group of them watched, amazed.

"You have lost the wager, Pundit," the dramatic voice of a Demon said.

Pundit bowed his head, acknowledging. Demons lived for status, and that was won and lost solely by Demon wagers. The bets could be on anything, often foolish chance—like whether a human child might sneeze before evening, or the course of a scouting ant. Demons generally did not interfere; they merely watched with demonic patience, for an instant or a millennium. Whatever it took.

"Your status is already beneath notice," the voice continued. "Therefore we impose an alternate penalty. You are the Demon of Puns, as lowly a venue as can be imagined. You are barely a Mini-Demon, minuscule to us though still more powerful than any mortal creature or low-caste demon. You will gather and confine every pun in the universe. Only when the universe is without free-ranging puns, apart from yourself, will your penalty be expiated."

Pundit nodded.

"This must be accomplished without fanfare or public notice, because puns are notorious for detesting restrictions. If they catch on that they are being hunted, it will be impossible to catch them all. That is all."

Pundit nodded again, and vanished. The scene faded.

Dawn looked up from the page. "I didn't know there was a Demon of Puns."

"It does explain a lot," Granola said. "No wonder they are so tenacious."

"But how does this relate to Caprice Castle?" Joy'nt asked.

"Pundora's Box is here," Skully reminded her.

"Oh. Yes. I forgot."

Dawn resumed reading, and again her words touched the fountain and became a scene. This time it showed Demon Pundit flying between planets, looking for something. "First I need a suitable site for a toxic waste dump," he said. "Where can that be?"

He peered down. "There," he decided, and descended toward a world the shape of a peninsula. "No one will ever think to search for a pun here in the Demon Xanth's domain."

Dawn paused, and the picture froze motionless. "Is this making sense? Xanth is overrun by puns!"

"The History may explain," Picka said.

"I hope so." She resumed reading, and the picture resumed animation.

Demon Pundit landed on a barren plain. He struck the ground with one finger and it cracked open, forming several large fissures. Indeed, even the least important Demon had gross power. He tapped it again, and a pit formed, so deep that the bottom was not visible. "Here is my toxic waste site," he said, satisfied. He snapped his fingers, and the hole filled in, leaving only a manhole cover.

He looked around. "Now I need a mechanism to transport the captive puns here. One that that does not arouse suspicion. So I will make it blend in with its surroundings, and enable it to travel silently."

He concentrated, and Caprice Castle formed, perched directly over the deep dump. Picka realized that this was the origin of the magic castle: it had not been built, but magically crafted by the will of the Demon. That explained a lot already.

"And I need an occupant to work my will while I am occupied elsewhere," Pundit said, "so I won't have to tend to the tedious business of actually collecting egregious puns. Five minutes of that would turn my stomach, but the job will require years of it, because puns have infested every unsupervised corner of the universe. Now how can I best set this up, so that others won't notice what is being done?"

He pondered, and the intensity of his thoughts caused steam to rise from his head. The steam interacted with the cooler air above, and formed a dense cloud. Demons seldom had to think, and it was obviously an effort. The cloud roiled and darkened, and lightning jagged from one side to the other. Then the entire cloud went up in a nova flash: the Idea.

"Music," he said. "I will fathom the music that relates to the pundamental nature of all puns, irresistibly summoning, weakening, and pacifying them so that they can be confined. Only puns will relate to that special aspect; others will hear it as merely melody, and won't realize what else it is accomplishing. It will siphon out the puns without anyone realizing."

But there was an aspect missing. "I will need a suitable musician," he concluded. "Someone apt enough to be able to master this special aspect, which will not readily be invoked. Someone who won't advertise his ability, or abuse it. Where can I find such a person?"

Pundit cast his awareness out in a widening circle, exploring the primitive life of this backward world. He found a musician, a highly talented piper, but ugly in feature, so that others did not want to associate with him. That seemed ideal.

Pundit summoned the musician by conjuring him abruptly to the new castle. "Here is the deal," he said, speaking from seemingly empty air because he did not care to reveal himself to this inconsequential mortal. "You will play your pipes to summon puns, which you will confine so that they will no longer bother regular folk. You will proceed from place to place, conveniently transported by the castle, cleaning out all puns, leaving the region clear of them. In return you will be allowed to reside in this nice building, all your needs provided, and you will be rendered handsome so as to impress any maidens who see you. You will not age while you occupy the castle. Once you have completed the chore, confining all puns, you will become immortal and permanently handsome. Just see that those captive puns are never released. Do you agree?"

"Sure," the homely man said without hesitation.

For the following century or so Piper did his job, traveling around the universe collecting puns. He piped them into a bag, and when the bag was full he dumped them into a nondescript box in the castle basement. He was always careful to seal the basement vault during his absences, in case the pun box should leak. It would be a shame to have any hard-won puns escape. When he had enough, he would dump them in the toxic waste site.

Along the way he encountered assorted maidens who were charmed by his music and his looks. In fact, he discovered that the same music that pacified puns also pacified maidens. He brought them to private spots for romantic nights. But he could not bring them into the castle itself; only he and the puns could enter. That was frustrating, but he could handle it. The mass of puns in the basement box swelled.

Then he captured a very special pun. Her name was Pundora, and she was more beautiful than any natural girl could ever be. Just the sight of her made him tremble with desire. He wanted to embrace her and spend romantic nights with her. He knew he shouldn't, because she was a pun, but he couldn't help himself. He let her out of the bag and took her to the main bedroom, where they had a phenomenal night.

But he had not entirely lost his wits. In the morning he played his pipes, rendering her eerily passive, and put her in the box with the other puns. Then he went out to collect more puns.

So it continued, with Pundora confined by day, and released by night to share his bed. It seemed ideal to him.

But not, for some reason, to her. "You think I'm good only for one thing!" she complained.

"And very good at that," he agreed.

"Well, I don't like being constantly used and boxed. I want to have more of a semblance of a life, as I had before you captured me. Let me go."

"I can't do that," he said reasonably. "You are a pun, and I am obliged never to release a pun."

"At least let me stay in the castle while you go out collecting," she wheedled.

"No. It's against the rule."

She sat on his lap. "Pretty please?"

"No." But he was weakening.

She opened her blouse, showing her overflowing bra under his nose. "With honey on it?"

"No." But it was getting hard for him to breathe.

She pulled her skirt out so that now her full panties sat on him, heating his flesh. "With kisses and squeezes on it?" She flexed her bottom.

His will broke. "Very well. But stay out of mischief while I'm out."

"Oh, thank you!" she exclaimed, kissing him ardently. She was extremely pleased, and excellent at showing it.

After that session she had to change her blouse, skirt, bra, panties, and socks, which had become hopelessly compromised. Piper hardly noticed. He felt as if he were in danger of floating away.

So that day he left her free in the castle while he went out collecting.

When she was alone, Pundora went straight to the basement. She opened the vault, and then the box. She untied the straps that bound it closed, unlocked the lock, and pried up the lid.

The compressed puns burst out explosively. They whirled around the chamber and siphoned out of the basement. They poured out the castle windows. In no more than half an instant all of them were gone.

Except one. "Pundora!" he exclaimed. "You did it!"

"Attila the Pun!" she replied. "I had to rescue you! You are my one and only love."

They embraced and kissed. They made love. Then they too fled the castle.

When Piper returned with a new bag of puns, he discovered the disaster. All the puns of a century's labors had been lost. But that was not the worst of it. Demon Pundit learned of the loss.

"You have failed!" he intoned from the air. "You are banished from these premises."

Piper fell down in supplication. "Please! I was deceived. It won't happen again. Give me another chance."

Pundit relented half a notch. "Here is your chance: You will be banished until you succeed in marrying a beautiful mortal princess who will come to the castle and manage it in your absence, so that never again will it be untended."

"Thank you!"

"I'm not finished. You deserve some token punishment, so that you properly appreciate the value of what you sacrificed. Until that time, you will be a monster."

"But then how will I ever win a lovely princess?"

"Consider it a challenge." Then magic power flashed, and Piper became a monster. In fact, he had been changed into something vaguely resembling his instrument: musical pipes.

Castle Caprice faded, leaving Piper alone on the ground, an awful blob of foul-smelling, musical goo.

Dawn paused in her reading, and the picture froze again. "Challenge? What lovely princess would ever let such a monster touch her?"

"There must be some theoretical way," Picka said. "Demons always make sure their wagers can be won, even if the chance is so unlikely as to seem worthless."

"True," Dawn agreed.

"Pundora's boyfriend," Skully said. "Did you catch that? Attila the Pun!"

"He did refer to a girlfriend," Joy'nt agreed. "Could that still have been Pundora?"

"We know what happened to Attila," Picka said. "I wonder whether we can track Pundora? She is certainly relevant to this History."

"Let's find out," Dawn said. She returned to her reading.

The scene shifted to Attila and Pundora. He was shaken by his recent captivity, and not pleased by the manner she had rescued him. "You nighted with Piper? Then I'll night with other girls, as I choose."

"I did it to rescue you," she pointed out.

"You should have found some other way."

She was plainly not pleased, but she dropped the issue. "What do you plan to do now?"

"I hated being jammed in with all those abysmal puns. I'd like to be rid of all puns!"

"But you and I are—" She broke off, reconsidering. "Dating," she concluded.

"In an open relationship."

Again, she stifled her objection. "So let's go somewhere far, far away and be happy."

But his thought had not finished. "In fact, I think I'll make it my life mission to destroy puns. That way I'll never be jammed in with those wretched things again." Now he paused. "But it occurs to me that you and I are—"

Pundora grabbed him and kissed him. "In love!" she repeated. She proceeded to distract him most effectively, so that his thought never achieved its likely conclusion.

That was the way it was thereafter. Whenever Attila was in danger of realizing that he himself was a pun to be destroyed, or that she was, she distracted him out of it. This had the incidental advantage of keeping him too busy to pursue other girls, so he was true to her despite his shallow male nature. Thus they had an enduring relationship.

Dawn paused again in the reading. "Uh-oh," she said.

"We caught up to Attila while Pundora was away," Joy'nt said.

"And acquainted him with the paradox of his nature," Picka said.

"And inadvertently abolished him," Dawn concluded.

"I wasn't there for that scene," Skully said, "but it is my guess that Pundora will not be pleased."

"With reason," Dawn agreed heavily. "But what can she do?"

"She's not exactly a woman scorned," Joy'nt said. "But she may be equivalently dangerous."

"True," Dawn agreed again. "I wish I had held my tongue."

"At least there's a bright side," Picka said. "It set us up to find Granola, who is really better for our mission than Attila would have been, and nicer too."

"Thank you," the giantess said appreciatively.

Dawn resumed reading. This time the narrative followed Piper, the banished monster. He looked like a giant mass of bubbling goo, which was not surprising because that was what he was. He traveled by blowing jets of gas out of his underside, and honked by blowing gas out of his topside. He ate by settling on anything organic, dissolving it with digestive acids, and taking it in. This process evidently generated the gas he used, and the way ordinary creatures avoided him suggested that it was a smelly process. In fact, there was a whiff of stink horn in the air as they watched the scene. He was a monster in every sense.

But he could still play music. His multiple gas vents were organ pipes, and as time passed he became increasingly proficient in blowing them. They heard the music as he practiced, and it was powerful, covering a vast range of notes. He could make phenomenal harmonies.

"Piper must be the best musician in Xanth," Dawn murmured, impressed.

Picka could only agree. He could hardly aspire to music like that.

"More than that," Skully said. "With that ugliness and stink, you'd think he couldn't get close to anyone or anything. But look how he forages."

They saw. Piper could run down plants without difficulty, but animals were trickier. Yet he developed a way. He retained his ability to musically summon, weaken, and pacify puns, only now he used it on animals. So when he was hungry, which was often, he played his irresistible music and lured them in to be consumed. It was ugly but effective.

He could impress regular people too. Sometimes he would pause at a village, and summon the villagers for a musical recital. They came and sat and listened, pacified but appreciative. It was certainly better than having him raid the village, as it was not feasible to oppose him. His music made them unable to resist. Sometimes he lured in maidens, and they half-willingly submitted to his sticky touches because of the magnetism of his music. His form was no longer human but his taste in maidens was unchanged. They were disgusted afterward as they washed and scrubbed to get the goo and stink off, but that was when the compelling music no longer sounded. Again, it was better than having him raid, and perhaps consume them. No villagers spoke of it afterward, partly from fear, partly from shame.

Princesses, however, forewarned, remained well clear. They did not want to get goo-ed, no matter how lovely and evocative the music. Only ugly princesses, trolls, ogres, or disfigured humans allowed themselves to be reluctantly courted, and they did not qualify to abate his curse. So Piper's quest for a suitable princess was balked.

Dawn paused again, and the picture faded. "I'm not sure this actually helps us tame the castle," she said.

"There must be more about the castle," Granola said.

Dawn resumed reading. This time the text was about Caprice Castle. It had lost its occupant, and Demon Pundit seemed to be occupied for the moment elsewhere, so it was without direction. However, it was resourceful and set about improving its lot, as it were. What it wanted was a worthy occupant, preferably a prince or king, and a suitable plot of ground to occupy. It had never had its own ground, which was one reason it was compelled to constantly travel. So it traveled, searching somewhat randomly for these things. When it saw a nice piece of land it considered the location, but on closer inspection there was always something wrong with it. When it encountered a prospective occupant, it might allow that person to enter and spend a night, while Caprice studied that person carefully. If the person proved to be unsuitable, Caprice simply moved on, leaving him behind. There were scenes of frustrated one-night occupants standing on the ground where the castle had been. So far, no prospect had proved to be sufficiently worthy. But there was always hope.

"We're prospects!" Dawn exclaimed, interrupting her reading. "It's watching us!"

"Well, you *are* a pretty princess," Joy'nt said. "You should qualify."

"It wants a couple," she said. "I will have to marry Picka first."

Picka had given up trying to dissuade her. He shrugged.

"It doesn't want just *any* couple," Granola reminded them. "Does it consider Picka worthy?"

"How can we know?" Dawn asked.

"Maybe there's more in the History," Joy'nt suggested.

Dawn resumed reading. This time there was a surprise: the scene seemed to be contemporary. It was of Pundora, returning to discover Attila gone.

"What happened here?" she demanded. "Did some hussy steal him away from me?"

There was an answer from a potato lying on the ground. "You might say that," it said.

She glared at it. "You're a common tater, aren't you?"

"Commentator," it agreed. "My eyes see everything."

"So what happened here?"

"Princess Dawn saved me from getting baked."

"I mean, what happened to Attila?"

"I am getting to that," the potato said. "Attila was destroying puns at a great rate, and was about to do the same to me. But Princess Dawn distracted him just in time, as she tried to recruit him to join her Quest. She certainly saved my peel. I'd have been chips for sure."

Pundora inflated dangerously. "Was she pretty?"

"Luscious," the potato said with a certain relish.

"So did she take him away?"

"Not exactly."

"Stop teasing me, or I'll mash you!"

Cowed, the potato let her have it: "She told him he was a pun, and he destroyed himself."

"The female dog! After all my work to distract him from that realization. The nerve!"

"Too bad for you," the potato said with scant sympathy.

"So Princess Dawn cost me my man," Pundora raged. "I'm going to make her pay!"

Dawn paused. "So it seems I have made an enemy."

"You had better stay away from her," Joy'nt said.

"We had better find out what she plans to do," Skully said.

Dawn resumed reading in the remarkable tome. The picture reanimated.

Pundora pondered a good three moments, then hit upon a nasty plan. They could tell it was nasty, because a mean little cloud formed over her head and rumbled menacingly.

She went to Piper. "A word, monster."

He was surprised. He honked, then played a series of notes.

"Wait a moment," she said. "I have a spell here somewhere that can enable me to understand monster talk, at least for a little while." She found it and invoked it. There was a small flash. "Now try it again."

He played the same notes over, but this time she heard them as words. "You're Pundora! I haven't seen you since you betrayed me and cost me everything. You were foolish to come within range of my music." He played a deadly chord, stunning her where she stood.

"Wait!" she squeaked. "Don't wipe me out! I came to help you!"

"You can never make up for what you cost me, you treacherous traitor! I'm going to goozle out your gizzard." He slid toward her on a carpet of goo.

"Yes, I can!" she cried desperately. "I can help you capture a beautiful princess!"

Piper paused, interested despite his ire. "How so?"

"Princess Dawn," she said. "I've been spying on her. She's trying to capture Caprice Castle. She might marry a walking skeleton and do it."

The monster was taken aback, as were those watching the image. "Why should a walking skeleton be considered worthy to occupy that supremely choosy castle?"

"Because he's musical! He's really good. And the castle seeks a musical master, so it can resume its original job. He might qualify."

Piper considered. "Good enough to master the key melodies?"

"I don't know. But it's possible, isn't it? Do you want to gamble that he isn't?"

Piper came to his decision. "I will destroy him and marry her. Then the castle will be mine, and I'll be handsome again, and have a princess to play with endlessly."

"And it will be even better for you than before," Pundora agreed. "See, I am helping you."

"Why?" he demanded. "You're a shallow, selfish creature, seductive but untrustworthy. Why should I trust you now, when you betrayed me before? Why do you come to me with this news? What's your angle?"

"Dawn destroyed Attila the Pun," she said simply.

"Ah. Now I get it. You are a vengeful female, using me to get back at the one you hate. You figure that my desire to recover my appearance and status will override my anger at you."

"Exactly," Pundora agreed. "You never loved me, you just used me, so your anger with me lacks staying power. Your desire to become hand-some and successful is far more enduring, and you are not entirely stupid, so you will do what it makes sense for you to do."

She had a point. "Very well. Tell me where this princess is."

"I can lead you to her. But she's a moving target, chasing after Ca-price. It may be a long chase."

"You mean I have to keep company with you for a prolonged period? Without smooching you or eating you?"

"You may smooch me," Pundora said, coming close, "but not eat me, because you need me to lead you to her. I didn't really mind your touches before; I merely loved Attila better. Do we have a deal?"

"I am no longer handsome as I was before."

"But I remember how you were, and my rage is great. Try me with-out your compelling music."

He extended a pseudopod and touched her provocative chest. She didn't flinch. He wrapped another pseudopod around her bouncy bottom. She accepted it. He heaved up a section and smeared goo on her face. She kissed him, showing no aversion. She was serious. She figured she would be safe from him as long as she gave him whatever he wanted. And that he wanted her luscious body, for the interim.

Pundora was cynical, but no dummy, and she had nerve. As she said, her rage was great. Perhaps as great as his own rage. She understood him.

"Deal," he agreed. Just in time, because the understanding spell was fading out. His music became merely music again.

However, Pundora had made the deal she wanted. She would have her revenge, with the help of the monster.

The narrative paused. Dawn looked pale. "I don't like this," she said.

The others nodded soberly. It was not a nice situation.

11
NICE BONES

I t is ugly," Picka agreed. "You have a bad enemy." Woofer growled in agreement, Midrange showed his claws momentarily, and Tweeter fluffed his wings. None of them liked it.

"If I had known, I never would have told Attila he was a pun," Dawn said glumly. "But though I know anything about anything living, my talent has limits. I can't use it on you walking skeletons, because you're not alive. And I can't use it on someone who isn't in my immediate sight. So I didn't know about Pundora. I understand why she hates me; I destroyed her lover. Now I fear there will be no way to deal with her, because I can't bring back Attila."

"You will have to deal with Pundora," Skully said, "because otherwise she will lead Piper to you, and that will be serious mischief."

"How does Pundora know where Dawn is?" Joy'nt asked.

There was a surprised silence of a generous two moments. Finally Dawn interrupted it before it could try for a third moment. "I never thought of that! Maybe she's bluffing."

"I doubt it," Skully said. "She knows Piper will eat her if she deceives him again."

"Maybe it's in the History," Granola suggested.

Dawn focused on the book again. The picture formed, showing Pundora in the period soon after she had fled Caprice Castle with Attila. She was having a dialogue with another woman.

"This is my territory," Pundora said. "I have been foraging here for years. It's where I found my man."

The other woman was tall, lean, and grim. "Xanth has no territories that can be enforced, and men are not properties. My name is Steel, and I will forage here if I choose."

"Well, my name is Pundora, and I don't like being balked. Suppose I call my man and have him roust you out?"

"He would have a problem," Steel said sharply. "My talent is to become any magic weapon I choose."

"Oh? What weapon can match this, when dealing with a man?" Pundora asked, opening her blouse and inhaling.

"This," Steel said cuttingly, becoming a long razor-edged sword. It flashed for a moment, then reverted to the woman.

Pundora reassessed the situation. "Did you say your weapon-forms are magic?"

"Yes. For example, a sword might cut through metal, or glow bright enough to illuminate dangerous darkness."

"But if you become the sword, who wields it?"

"Anyone I choose to allow. That's what makes me attractive to men: I can give them what they most truly desire: effective violence."

"Attractive in other ways than romantic," Pundora said musingly.

"Why would I want anything romantic? I prefer violence. The problem is finding men who are properly committed to it, instead of merely indulging occasionally."

"My man is committed to destroying puns—all except me. Can you become a pun-destroying sword?"

"Readily."

"Then let's make a deal. Let me give you, in the form of the sword, to him to use against puns. You will enable his unceasing violence, for he is a violent man. I will enable his romance when he's not violenting."

"That seems good to me. I like to be in the center of action."

Then Steel became a magic sword, and Pundora took it and presented it to Attila. He tried it, and loved it; he no longer had to stomp on puns, getting stinky pun squish on his boots. Now he could simply touch them with the blade, and they puffed into smoke and dissipated. It was a long and mutually beneficial association.

Right up until the time Dawn approached him for her mission, lost her temper, and spoke the words she regretted.

Then Attila self-destructed, leaving the sword unwielded. Steel was desolate, for she had never been handled with such consistent violence before.

Until Pundora made her another deal. "I need to track the lady dog princess who did this, so I can wreak cruel vengeance on her," Pundora said. "Can you become a weapon that will enable me to find her?"

"How about a magic mirror oriented on her," Steel suggested, interested. "I never thought of a mirror as a weapon, but really it is, for this purpose. Of course you would have to bring me to her, to zero in."

"But that's the problem. I can't bring you to her if I can't find her. Using the mirror to identify her is fine, but that won't bring me to her. I will need an indication of direction."

Steel pondered. "Maybe there's another way: a mirror oriented on beauty."

"How will that help? I have beauty of my own."

"But maybe not the beauty of a princess."

"Maybe not," Pundora conceded grudgingly.

"Try this: hold the mirror up and say 'Mirror, mirror, in my hand, who is the fairest in the land?'" She became the mirror.

Somewhat dubiously, Pundora held her up. "Mirror, mirror, in my hand, who is the fairest in the land?"

The mirror went blank for an instant, then formed the picture of Princess Dawn. It was working!

"But this merely identifies her," Pundora said, "as before. I still need to locate her."

Steel reappeared, with Pundora's hand still on her leg. "Turn the mirror so that the image is clearest. That will be the direction of the subject." She returned to mirror form.

Pundora rotated the mirror, and soon found the clearest image. "Good enough!" she said. She had the wit not to say that this technique should have worked as readily when the mirror oriented specifically on Dawn. Steel was stronger on talent than on common sense. "Now to put the rest of my evil plan into place. This will require a strong stomach, but I believe I can manage it, for the sake of vengeance." And she went for her dialogue with the monster.

Dawn stopped reading. "That certainly clarifies things," she said. "Now what do we do about it?"

"We are in Caprice Castle," Joy'nt reminded them. "We need to complete our mission by finding Pundora's Box and taking it to the Good Magician. Then you can return to Castle Roogna, Dawn, where you will surely be safe from angry puns and lecherous blobs."

"Good thinking," Dawn agreed. "Picka and I did not find the Box in the upper reaches. The pets did not find it on the ground floor, and I gather Skully and Joy'nt did not find it in the cellar." Dawn glanced at the last two, her mouth quirking. "You *were* searching?"

"Yes," Joy'nt answered, though the slightly pink cast to her bones suggested that that was not all of what they had been doing. "There's no Box there."

"Something must have happened to it after the puns escaped," Picka said. "We know Pundora and Attila did not take it."

"The castle has been traveling around Xanth for an indefinite time," Skully said, "occasionally entertaining visitors. Anyone could have taken it."

"I don't think so," Dawn said. "The Good Magician said it was in Caprice Castle, and he would not be wrong about a detail like that. So it must be here, somewhere."

"We'll just have to search harder," Picka said. "Our mission is not complete until we find the box."

Dawn sighed. "It's a nuisance. Let's relax with a song, then resume the search. There may be closets or dungeons we haven't explored."

The others were glad to agree. They selected a song and played it with a certain tired enthusiasm. Then they had Picka improvise again.

He did so, really getting into it, enjoying it as his melodies filled the courtyard and made the fountain quiver.

And Caprice Castle faded, leaving them sitting on the barren plain.

They stared at each other, appalled. "It dumped us!" Dawn exclaimed indignantly.

"In the middle of our music," Granola said.

"Not necessarily," Skully said. "It may be that it can't remain in any one location for long, so it was time to move on."

"I don't buy that," Joy'nt said. "That is, it may be limited, but it has the option of taking occupants along with it, doesn't it? It could have taken us, but chose not to. So it rejected us."

"Maybe," Skully agreed. "But we don't really understand its motives. Maybe it was afraid that this time we would find Pundora's Box, and it didn't want that."

"Why wouldn't it?" Dawn asked.

"If we found it, we would have taken it away. That might leave the castle with no hope of reestablishing its original mission of storing puns."

"It wanted us to become regular occupants!" Dawn said. "To stay here, instead of leaving."

"Then why dump us?" Joy'nt asked. "That's no way to encourage us to stay."

"I have another reason," Picka said. "One I don't like."

"Out with it, bone head," Dawn said fondly.

"The one who occupies the castle must collect and store puns. Music is used to fetch them and pacify them. But it has to be superior music, if I understand the History correctly. Piper could do it, but maybe we could not."

"But you are becoming a fine musician," Granola said.

"Not fine enough, it seems. My music brought the castle, but when Caprice had another chance to listen and assess its quality, it concluded that it wasn't enough. So it departed."

The others looked at him. "Bleep," Dawn muttered. "I have a horrible feeling you're right. We were judged and found wanting. So now it's looking for other prospects."

"Bleep," Granola echoed. That surprised Picka; he had never before heard the giantess swear.

"And meanwhile Piper the Music Monster is looking for Dawn so he can marry her and recover the castle," Skully said. "So we had better not stay in one place too long, until we develop a new plan of action."

"We should be able to stop him," Picka said. "He may be able to stun and pacify living folk, but we're not alive. He may not have counted on that."

"Still, its best to avoid trouble if we can," Joy'nt said. "Where can we go next, if only to a nice safe place so we can think about things?"

"I don't know, but I can look," Granola said.

They piled into the handbag, and she heaved them up and started walking. It was a gray day, matching their mood. To have come so close, then lose it!

After a time, Granola spoke. "Things are dreary all over, except for one little spot where the sun is shining. Shall I go there?"

"Why not?" Dawn asked. "It won't last, but we can delude ourselves with foolish hope for a little while." She was evidently feeling pretty negative.

They gazed ahead to see the spot. It was a hill with a copse of trees, and a house on top. A beam of sunlight speared down to brighten it, and only it. Picka distrusted this, but decided not to comment.

Granola came to the hill, which was big enough to hold her, and set down the handbag. They climbed out.

The door to the house opened and a young man emerged. He saw them and paused. "Oh, no! I knew death would come for me some day, but three deaths and a maiden? Whatever could I have done?"

"Not death," Dawn called. "These are walking skeletons, my harmless friends, and three animal friends. I am Dawn." She did not mention Granola; that might have been complicated.

"Oh. I am Skyler. I have heard of walking skeletons, but didn't know they existed outside of bad dreams."

"We saw your sunny hill, and thought it would be a nice place to rest. We'll move on if you prefer."

"No, that's all right. My talent is to turn gray days into sunshiny ones, or at least the section around me. Or to imbue sad folk with sunny feeling."

"I could use that," Dawn said. "My talent is to know things about people, and I can tell you're nice. But I feel someone else here."

"That's my sister Shy Violet. She blends into the scenery at will, when there's a violet near. So I make sure to keep violets growing here."

A girl appeared. She had been standing by the house, blending perfectly into it. "Hello," she said shyly. "You're very pretty."

"Thank you," Dawn said. Her beauty had been confirmed by the manner Pundora was orienting on her: fairest in the land. Probably her twin sister Eve, similarly lovely, was not in Xanth at this time. Or maybe it was that Eve's beauty was dark rather than fair.

Once the brother and sister got to know the skeletons somewhat, they relaxed. Then Dawn introduced Granola. That was another shock for them, but they handled it.

They wound up in the house, except for the giantess, telling a limited version of their adventure. "So we just wanted a safe haven to relax for a few hours," Dawn concluded. "We will have to depart before the monster catches up. He doesn't seem to travel swiftly, so we think we have at least a day. Once we go, he will change direction to orient on our new location, so you won't see him."

"That seems just as well," Shy Violet said, shuddering.

Dawn and the pets joined them for supper, with a pie passed outside to Granola, while the skeletons helped out by splitting some wood for their stove. It seemed it got cold when Skyler wasn't making the sun shine; maybe that was to make up for the warmth. Magic often did have side effects.

As dusk loomed, the sunlight finally faded, as the two environments did not get along well together. Picka, Dawn, and Midrange took a walk around the hill, admiring the shifting view. Midrange led the way; there was something significant in the offing.

They passed a large tree, and almost collided with a young woman in a strange outfit. "Oh!" she said. "I was expecting someone else."

"Other than a woman, a skeleton, and a cat?" Dawn asked.

"Only a cat." She looked at Midrange. "But I don't think you are she."

"Midrange is a tomcat," Dawn said.

"Yes. I am Clair Voyant. My talent is to know things. I heard that there is a cat with the same name and a similar talent, so I came here to meet her."

"Midrange knows things," Dawn said. "Maybe your talent oriented on him."

"Maybe. I'm sorry I bothered you."

"Meow."

"Midrange says this is the place," Dawn translated.

A second cat appeared, a female. "Mew," she said.

"And there's Claire," Dawn said. "Sammy Cat's girlfriend."

"Too bad, Midrange," Picka murmured. "She would have been perfect for you."

Midrange shrugged as if it didn't matter. Cats were good at that.

Claire Cat and Claire Girl met and chatted, in their fashions, oblivious to the others. Picka, Dawn, and Midrange moved on, letting them be.

There was a spare bedroom in the house, and the siblings insisted that Dawn and Picka take it. "Thank you," Dawn said before Picka could demur. Skully, Joy'nt, and the pets went outside to join Granola.

"We should not have imposed," Picka reproved Dawn when they were alone. "We don't need this bedroom."

"We are not imposing," she said. "There was something they did not tell us but I picked up, because of my talent. This room is haunted, at least with respect to Shy Violet. A male spook is pursuing her. She's seriously frightened."

"Ah. I will speak to him."

"Do that. He doesn't come until she gets in bed in this room. She has to flee to join her brother. She hates that."

"We will be ready." Picka stepped into a closet and stood still.

Dawn stripped to her underwear, then to bare flesh, donned one of

Violet's nighties, and lay on the bed. In the darkness it wasn't clear who she was.

The spook came. He was a gaunt ghost with large hands. "Noow yooo aare miiine!" he whispered sibilantly, putting those hands on Dawn.

Picka stepped out from the closet. "One moment," he said, tapping the ghost on the shoulder. He could do that, because he was a spook himself.

The ghost jumped, astonished. "Whoo are yooo?"

"I am a friend of Shy Violet," Picka said. "I hate it when she gets haunted by some other spook. Do you know what I do to spooks who bother her?"

The ghost was daunted. "I didn't know she had a—a friend."

"Now you do know," Picka said. "I am going to tie you up in such a knot you will never get loose." He started twisting the ghost's substance like a sheet. He could do this because he had more substance than the ghost and was much stronger.

"No, no, I'll go!" the spook cried. "I thought she was . . . was available."

"Not to the likes of you." Picka twisted further.

"Please! I'll go away and never return!"

"No problem. You will never return anyway, once I finish with you." He twisted some more.

The ghost wrenched desperately away. In a quarter of a moment he was gone, and unlikely to return. Ghosts did not much like getting twisted; it ruined their lines.

Dawn sat up and applauded. "Very good, Picka! I think you scared him off permanently."

"That was the idea."

"Now invoke your spell."

"Dawn, I don't think—"

"Bring it out," she said, throwing off the nightie.

He did, but still tried to protest before invoking it. "It makes me want you for an hour, but there's no future in it. When I revert, I know you for what you are: a fleshly creature."

"Not your type," she agreed. "Well, if you don't want me, let's see what that spell will do to me." She snatched it from his hand and pressed it against her body.

"No!" Picka cried, too late. He had no idea what such a spell would do to a living person. It could be lethal.

Dawn's living flesh melted away. Suddenly there was nothing left of her but bones.

Beautiful bones.

Picka had never realized exactly how lovely her bones were, because of their unsightly contamination with flesh. Now he saw her in all her bare-bones glory. He was instantly smitten.

"Oh!" she said, liplessly. "I'm naked!"

"You're beautiful," he reassured her. "You have become a walking skeleton."

Her marvelous square eye holes gazed at him. "The spell—it had the opposite effect on me. It transformed me into your kind!"

"For an hour," he agreed, trusting that was true. He knew she would not want to be a permanent skeleton. Mortal maidens liked to be thin, but not that thin. Generally.

"Then let's make the most of it." She came close and tapped her skull lightly against his, in the skeletal version of a kiss.

He was profoundly affected. "Dawn, did it affect your feeling for me?"

"No. I still want to marry you." She eyelessly eyed him again. "So, how do you like me now?"

"You have the nicest bones I have seen. I am utterly smitten."

"Well, that's progress. Now will you marry me?"

"No."

"No? I am not accustomed to that word. I'm a princess."

"That's it. You are a living human princess. I'm a nonentitious skeleton. We have only our friendship in common."

"But you do love me now?"

He sighed. "I think I have always loved you, Dawn, in my fashion. Maybe that's why a day mare once brought me a daydream of romancing you. But I am nothing but a skeleton, not even a royal one. I always knew there could be nothing between us except friendship. Now I have seen your lovely bones, and I wish there could be more. But there can't be."

"I disagree. This transformation spell can give us similar-form interaction, an hour at a time, in your form or mine. There are other spells, like accommodation, that can enable similar interactions."

"For limited times."

"Picka, we can associate as ourselves most of the time. We don't have to be making constant love. I love and respect you as what you are, a walking skeleton with an even temper and a wonderful musical talent. Isn't that enough?"

"It's not enough. I am not worthy of you. Even if we were of similar kind, I would not warrant your romantic attention."

"Oh, for bleep's sake! What *would* make you think you were worthy?"

Picka considered. "I suppose if I were a prince or equivalent."

"Princes are overrated. Sometimes they are required, yes; when Jumper Spider became a prince it made him eligible to marry the Demoness Eris and rescue her from confinement. But I don't have to marry a prince."

"You don't?"

"A man of equivalent status would do."

"Like what?"

"Like being the finest musician in Xanth."

Picka laughed. "I am not that. Caprice Castle found me wanting."

"Not yet," she said earnestly. "But you can improve. I'll help you."

"But we're still not each other's types!"

"First things first. Let's make you worthy, in your own estimation. Then we can worry about types."

"This is ridiculous."

She tapped her skull against his again, and little hearts radiated out from the contact. "How's that again?"

"Ridic—"

She rattled her arm bones against his, sending a vibration through his whole body, distracting him with romantic passion. "I don't think I heard you, Picka."

"Ri—"

She intertwined her finger bones with his and squeezed. All powers of resistance left him. "What?"

He surrendered. "I love you!"

"That's what I thought you said," she said, satisfied. She tapped her skull against his again, and this time he tapped back, avidly. It was impossible to resist her, at least in this form.

After that it was sheer bliss—until a seeming instant later, when she reverted to fleshly form. Suddenly a naked living woman was in his embrace.

And it made hardly any difference. Once his love had broken through and been expressed, it remained, regardless of her form. Her flesh was no longer objectionable.

"Does this disgust you?" she asked, kissing his skull with her fleshy lips.

"No," he confessed. Not anymore.

"Or this?" She stretched out against him, full length, her fleshy pelvis against his bone pelvis.

"No." In fact, now he discovered he liked the contact.

"I think I am becoming accustomed to that word 'no.'"

"Oh, Dawn! You made me love you. What am I to do?"

"Just keep loving me, Picka. The next challenge is to make you worthy in your own eye sockets. It's time to practice your music."

"But—"

She fetched her ocarina and played a melody. He was obliged to unlimber his clavicles and play the same melody. It was evident to him that he was better at it than she was; he was a better musician than she. Not that he would say it to her.

"You're better than I am," she said, "but I think not as good as you can be. We need to get you good enough so that Caprice Castle accepts you. Then we can summon it again and complete the mission."

"This is all for the mission!" he exclaimed, not entirely pleased.

"That too," she agreed. And somehow that made it all right.

Then he improvised, and she put away her instrument and slept. She smiled in her sleep, and that made him feel good. She was indeed beautiful, whatever her form. He still felt unworthy of her love, but he was satisfied to do what she asked, and to labor to be the best musician he could be. To maybe become worthy of her. Then they could perhaps tackle the problem of their differing types. After all, as she had said, a spider had married a Demoness. Anything was possible, with enough magic.

He played a love song, and Dawn smiled again. It was wonderful being in love. He had never experienced it before, partly because he had known no female skeletons. He had never anticipated love with a living woman, but it had happened, and it colored his whole existence.

After a while he leaned down and touched her fleshly head with his skull, lightly, in a skeleton kiss. She turned her face and kissed him in fleshy style, then pulled him down with her. He could no longer play music, but it didn't matter. Nothing mattered except being close to her.

In the morning they reported to Skyler and Shy Violet that the amorous ghost was gone. "Picka warned him away," Dawn said.

"But ghosts don't accept warnings," Violet said doubtfully. "I escaped him before only by merging into the scenery."

"They do when a skeleton friend of yours twists their sheets into knots," Dawn said. "You should have no further problem."

"Thank you!" Violet said gratefully.

"We heard music," Skyler said. "It was beautiful."

"Picka and I like each other," Dawn said. "We are of different types, as you may have noticed, so we play music together."

"That's so romantic," Violet said.

"Thank you for your hospitality," Dawn said. "Now we must be on our way, before the Music Monster tracks us down here."

"It is too bad you can't twist the monster up like a sheet," Violet said.

"Too bad," Picka agreed.

They stepped out into the sunlight, which always shone on the hill.

They got into the handbag with the others, and Granola heaved them up high. They waved farewell to Skyler and Violet.

"Where to?" Skully asked. His skull and bones looked as though someone had been tapping and rattling them all night.

"I think I know," Granola said. "I suffered a revelation during the night."

"So that was the flash we saw," Joy'nt said. Picka realized that he and Dawn, inside and distracted, had not seen the flash she spoke of.

"Revelation?" Dawn asked.

"Pundora's Box. I believe I know why we couldn't find it. It was in the next-to-last place we looked, which I believe would have been a look by one of your interior parties."

"Yes," Dawn agreed. "We checked the turrets, the cellar, and the ground floor, while you checked outside. Where do you think it was?"

"We were looking for the wooden box we saw in the History," Granola said, "but that was only a convenience. It couldn't possibly hold every pun that exists. The real container is the castle itself, especially its cellar, which can be sealed off."

"Caprice!" Dawn exclaimed, amazed.

"Caprice," Picka agreed, seeing it. "We searched it, then went outside, where Granola was still searching. So her search was the last, and ours was next to last."

"And we didn't see any puns because all of them had escaped," Joy'nt said.

"And that little wooden box doesn't matter," Skully said. "Someone may have used it for firewood. Pundora may have opened it, but first she opened the sealed cellar, the real storage place."

"And that is why the Good Magician wants me to tame the castle," Dawn concluded. "Because it is the Box."

"Now we know," Granola agreed. "So I think we had better search for the castle again, hoping we can find it by strategically backtracking as we did before."

"But finding it isn't enough," Picka said. "We have to convince it we are worthy to occupy it. And we're not."

"Not yet," Dawn said. "So it's time to practice our music—you especially, Picka. So that when we do catch up to it, we are good enough to hold it."

That seemed to make sense. But Picka feared it would be no easy accomplishment, if even possible.

Nevertheless, he agreed to practice. So they moved along, playing their music. If the folk they passed wondered, well, let them wonder. The mission was important.

12
CHAMELEON

Granola forged southward, pursuing her notion of a likely place, though they all knew it couldn't be the first site she checked. But there wouldn't be a next-to-last site until there was a first one.

The others tired of singing or playing music, but Dawn insisted that Picka keep practicing regardless. She was happy to explain to the others. "I love Picka, and he loves me." She made a three-quarter smile. "It took some work in bed to convince him, and some magic, yet I finally persuaded him. But he needs to be worthy. So if he becomes the best musician in Xanth, he'll be worthy, won't he?"

The others, seeing the way of her thinking, agreed. So Picka continued to improvise, and had to admit to himself that he was improving. He could feel it. But would he ever be good enough? How could he or anyone else tell?

Granola came to a mountain. She found a route to climb it, carrying them upward. When they reached the top she set down the handbag so they could get out.

They were on a high level plain, a mesa, that dropped off sharply on the sides. "This is Mount Rushmost!" Dawn exclaimed. "The dragons' retreat."

"I just came where my muse led me," Granola said.

"Caprice could have stopped here," Picka pointed out.

"Woof!" Woofer was smelling something.

They looked in the direction his nose was pointing. There was a tent pitched near the brink. Someone else was here.

"Maybe we had better check this out," Dawn said.

"Suppose they're unfriendly?" Joy'nt asked.

"Picka will protect me," Dawn said confidently, and started walking.

Picka hurried to catch up. "You have a lot of confidence in me."

"You can wring the sheet of a ghost. You can surely handle ordinary folk."

"You're imperious!"

She glanced sidelong at him? "You just now realized that? What did you expect when you set out to love a princess?"

"I didn't set out to—"

She kissed him on the noggin. "I'm teasing, Picka."

There was an appreciative murmur behind them, including a woof and tweet. The others were following, of course. They could see that Dawn had already taken over Picka's attention and existence, and was managing him in the standard manner.

A figure emerged from the tent, coming to intercept them. It looked like a girl with wings.

"Hello!" Dawn called.

"Hello," the girl replied. "You don't belong here. None of you do."

Dawn paused, assessing her. "Who are you to say?"

"I am Mim Barbarian, a winged monster. This is Mount Rushmost, the sanctuary of winged monsters. No nonwinged monsters are allowed here without special dispensation. Please go away before I summon a guardian dragon."

"We can't do that yet," Dawn said. "I am on a mission for the Good Magician, and it brings us here at the moment."

"You don't seem to understand. I see that three of you are monsters, but without wings; one has wings but is not a monster. You can't be here."

"*You* don't understand," Dawn said unevenly. "We have passing business here."

"No, you don't. Go, before I kick you off the mountain."

Picka could see that Dawn was not taking this well. It was that princessly aversion she had to being balked. He tried to intercede. "We are looking for a castle. We'll be leaving soon."

"There are no castles here. Never have been. Probably never will be. Dragons don't live in castles. Go."

Dawn started to swell. Picka was afraid she would burst. "Maybe we can qualify as winged monsters," he said quickly.

"I doubt it," Mim said. "This is your last warning. I can change my wings into anything, including weapons. I don't want to have to use them." She spread her wings, and they became shining swords.

Dawn opened her mouth as if about to identify herself. That would ruin the anonymity of their group.

"Think of us as having invisible wings," Picka said desperately. "You can't see them, but we can fly."

"I doubt it," Mim repeated.

"All I need is to say the magic words to invoke them," Picka said. "Which are, 'Granola, be my wings. Make me fly.'"

"Ludicrous," Mim said. She did not know that there was an invisible giantess with them. She thought granola was cereal.

Picka spread his arm bones and flapped them in the manner of a bird. Granola, standing behind him, reached down and put her fingers around his waist. She lifted, gently, and he rose into the air.

Mim stared. "It's true!"

"It's magic," Picka said. "The rest of us can do it too." He lowered his arms, and the giantess obligingly set him back on the ground. That freed her to lift someone else.

"It's a stupid demonstration," Dawn said. "But if it will cut short this bureaucratic hassle . . ." She spread her arms and sailed upward.

After that the rest of them demonstrated their ability to fly, one by one. Even Woofer and Midrange. The dog evidently enjoyed it, the cat less so.

"So you can fly," Mim said with resignation. "But what about the bird? He can fly, but he's no monster, as I said before."

Now Dawn helped. She knew all about Tweeter, because of her talent. "Tweeter, I know you don't like to show your power, but this time you'll have to. Remember when you stomped the ground and made it shake? Monster feet? Do that now, in the name of our Granola magic."

Picka did not know about this stomping, but evidently Dawn did, and so did Tweeter. But did Granola?

"Make the ground shake," Dawn said encouragingly.

Tweeter stood up straight, lifted one tiny leg, and brought it down hard on the ground.

The ground shook. Granola had caught on, and stomped in time with the bird.

"Harder, Tweeter," Dawn said.

Tweeter stomped again. This time the ground shuddered so hard it was like an earthquake. The rest of them had trouble keeping their feet.

Dawn opened her mouth to order worse.

"Okay, okay, he qualifies!" Mim said hastily.

Dawn smiled, and the sunlight seemed to brighten. "That is so nice of you, Mim." She turned to the bird. "Try to dampen your tread now, Tweeter. We don't want the mountain to collapse."

Tweeter nodded amenably. They had made their point.

"Get your business done and go," Mim said shortly. She surely suspected she had been fooled, but at this point she just wanted them gone. She went back into her tent, in effect dismissing them.

"We shall," Dawn agreed. She glanced around. "I don't see any castle, so I suppose we can go, now that we've made our point."

They could have gone at any time, but Picka knew that Dawn had been unable to back off from a challenge to her authority, even though she was anonymous. It was a character flaw, but it came with the territory of being royal.

"Woof."

"You smell something?" Dawn asked him.

Midrange spoke. "Meow."

"Something significant?"

Tweeter flew up high, looking around. "Tweet!"

"Well, then, let's go see," Dawn agreed.

They headed on across the mesa. Soon another tent appeared, concealed before because it was the same color as the ground.

"Hello!" Dawn called.

A man emerged. "Dawn!" he exclaimed, surprised.

"Great Grandpa!" she exclaimed, running to hug him.

Great Grandpa? The man was not nearly old enough.

Then Dawn introduced him. "This is Great-grandfather Bink. He was youthened a while back. He's actually ninety-four. He's Grandpa Dor's father, who was Dolph's father, who is my father. It's all legitimate."

So it seemed.

Bink looked at the others. "I see you are keeping unusual company, Dawn."

"Yes," she said proudly. "This is Picka Bone, my fiancé."

Bink was evidently a man of the world, but even he was surprised. "I suspect there's an interesting story there."

"There is," Dawn agreed. Then she introduced the others, including Granola.

"Remarkable," Bink agreed. He did not seem as surprised as others had been; he had evidently been around.

"But why are you here alone?" Dawn asked. "And how did you get the winged monster girl to let you stay?"

"I am not alone," Bink said. "And I had your father Dolph introduce me."

"He assumed dragon form!"

"Exactly. They concluded that the grandfather of a dragon qualified as a de facto dragon, at least for the time being."

Dawn smiled, appreciating the device. Picka knew about Dolph's shape-changing ability, because Dolph had once traveled with his own father, Marrow Bones. "So whom are you traveling with now?"

"My wife, of course." Bink faced the tent. "Girls, come meet our great-granddaughter's friends."

Two women emerged. One was almost as lovely as Dawn herself. The other was breathtakingly ugly. Dawn's pretty jaw dropped. "Great-grandma Fanchon," she said. "Great-grandma Wynne. How is this possible?"

"Let me explain for your friends," Bink said. "My wife Chameleon is a changeable woman. She normally has three forms: Fanchon, who is extremely smart but not pretty; Wynne, who is lovely but not smart; and Chameleon, who is a compromise, being ordinary in both respects. She cycles among forms in the course of a month. I long ago learned to live with it." He took a breath. "But recently Chameleon had the misfortune to walk through a Double You, and got split into her two most extreme forms. We find this problematical, so are on a Quest to get her recombined. We were told that this could happen here on Mount Rushmost. We hope that is true. We are not enjoying the split."

Picka could see why not. Two wives, one with all the brains, the other with all the looks?

"But isn't it twice the fun to have two wives?" Dawn asked.

"For whom?" Fanchon asked, frowning. She frowned well. "This ignorant ignoramus has no romantic interest in me. All he can look at is Window-head here."

"Thank you," Wynne said. It seemed she was not smart enough to realize that the pun on her name was insulting rather than flattering. "I like his interest." She hugged Bink, and kissed him.

Bink did seem to like her attention. Wynne was very shapely in the fleshly manner. His hands stroked her body in the human male fashion.

"I think I'm going to vomit," Fanchon muttered. "It's the triumph of matter over mind."

"I am beginning to see the problem," Dawn said. "Men can be frustrating to deal with, because all they are interested in is one thing."

"And that thing is not intelligence," Fanchon said.

"Actually, my favorite is the compromise," Bink said. "The midpoint, Chameleon, who is neither too smart nor too pretty, but a perfect meld. She does not repulse me with her attitude or her body. And there's only one of her, so her components can't quarrel."

"Your two halves quarrel?" Dawn asked the two, surprised.

"She's such an idiot," Fanchon said.

"She's so ugly," Wynne said.

"But you're both parts of one woman," Dawn protested, "who changes with the tides of the moon. This way, you can offer your husband beauty *and* brains."

"We'd rather merge and be the way we were," Fanchon said. "Then we won't have to talk to each other."

"Or see each other," Wynne agreed.

Picka was beginning to see why Bink wanted them reunited.

"If you don't mind my asking," Joy'nt said, "how did you get here? This is a pretty remote and dangerous spot for a regular man and two women. It's not on an enchanted path, and there are monsters."

"Oh, we're safe enough," Wynne said. "Thanks to Bink's magic."

"Nuh-uh, dummy," Fanchon warned, too late.

"He has magic?" Joy'nt asked.

Dawn exchanged a glance with her great-grandfather. "Can I tell them? They're good friends."

Bink shrugged. "Try it and see."

"I'm not sure about this," Fanchon said. "Bad policy."

"If it's harmful, she won't be able to do it," Bink reminded her.

There was something odd about this. What was there to tell? Picka had always understood that Bink had strong magic, but no one knew what it was.

Dawn faced the others. "Bink cannot be harmed by magic." She paused, as if almost startled, then continued. "Part of it is that if anyone else knowing that would harm him, they won't be allowed to know. So few people know. I know, because of my talent. But I would not be able to tell, if it was not all right. So it seems it is all right."

"Or perhaps such knowledge by this group will help him," Fanchon said. "This is interesting indeed."

"So if there's bad magic, Bink blocks it off," Wynne said. "And we're safe."

"I don't understand," Joy'nt said.

"Say there's a hostile dragon charging one of us," Fanchon said. "A dragon is a magic creature, so can't hurt Bink. So Bink steps in between, and deflects the dragon, and we're safe."

"But suppose something nonmagical threatens?" Joy'nt asked. "Like a swordsman?"

"That's why his talent normally needs to be concealed," Fanchon said, "so that enemies won't focus on nonmagical means. If there is magic in the revelation, that magic is blocked. So normally enemies don't know, and his talent is effective."

"We're not enemies," Picka said. "We won't tell."

"But your actions might give it away," Dawn said.

"It remains curious why Dawn was allowed to tell *you*," Fanchon said. "I have never seen this before."

"Why are you here?" Wynne asked.

"That's a complicated story," Dawn said, "but we'll tell you a simplified form. I am on a mission for the Good Magician to tame Caprice Castle, which is also Pundora's Box, which can hold all the abysmal puns so they won't infest Xanth anymore. But to do that I need to marry Picka, and he needs to become Xanth's finest musician. So we're working on that while chasing the castle. But meanwhile the castle's former occupant, Piper, was changed into a monster, and he can only be redeemed if he marries me. So he's chasing us, with the help of his mistress, Pundora."

"But why here?" Fanchon asked alertly.

"Granola's talent is to find things in the next-to-last place she looks," Dawn said. "This is one place. We can't have a next to last before we have a last, so we have to search in more than one place. It gets tricky."

"I can imagine," Fanchon said. "What made her select this place?"

"I just have a feeling," Granola said.

"Because this is the place we came to solve our problem," Fanchon said. "I doubt that it is coincidence that you came here too, at the same time, so that we could meet. Your feeling must relate somewhat in the manner Bink's talent does."

"I wouldn't know," Granola said.

"Otherwise it would be an astonishing coincidence. I am not a believer in such coincidence, where magic is involved. Our destinies are somehow linked."

Picka saw that the women's intelligence was functioning. She was right: there had to be magical guidance. This should have been a routine stop, and it seemed it wasn't.

"Maybe we should explore this further," Dawn said. "To search for some hint why we met here."

"We were told to come here," Bink said, "but we were delayed a day by a misadventure."

"We would not have made it here yesterday," Dawn said, "so that delay must have been for a reason."

"Indeed," Fanchon said.

"Tell us about it," Dawn said.

"Wynne suffered a revelation," Fanchon said, her mouth twitching eloquently. Obviously she had not valued it. "Bink decided to follow up on it. So we borrowed a large flying carpet from the Castle Roogna closet and set off for Mount Rushmost."

Picka pictured the scene as she spoke, having become accustomed to that from the Caprice Castle History book.

The three of them were sitting on the carpet, Wynne in the lead, then Fanchon, and Bink third. They sailed up, circled Castle Roogna, and headed south. All went well for a while.

But soon a floating menace spied them: Cumulo Fracto Nimbus, the worst of clouds, who liked to rain on parades. This was not exactly a parade, but with a pretty girl leading it, it was equivalent in a minor way. Fracto was not the only entity who liked to see a pretty girl get soaked. Bink could not be harmed by magic, but his talent did not regard wetness as harm, so he could get rained on.

They veered to the side, trying to avoid the storm, but Fracto chased them. So they glided down to a rest stop on an enchanted path. They got under cover just before the storm struck. They rolled up the carpet and parked it beside the door.

There was a girl there, another refugee from the storm. She was compact and cute, with naturally curly hair. "Hello," Bink said, his attention caught in the male fashion. "I am Bink, and these are my, um, friends Fanchon and Wynne. We are traveling south, hoping to solve a problem."

"I am Eunice. My talent is toe change words by adding a silent E. For example, if there were a cub here, I could change it to a cube. But the effect lasts only while I am touching it."

"That is interesting," Fanchon said. She was interested in everything. "You could make a tub into a tube, or a can into a cane."

"Yes. Or a dam into a dame, and a gam into a game." She touched her leg, which abruptly became far more interesting.

"I do that," Wynne said. "Men notice."

"I cane imagine," Eunice agreed wryly. Fortunately her spoken "can" did not become a literal "cane."

"What we'd like to do is change this storm into a sunny day," Bink said. "So we can resume our flight."

"I cane try," Eunice said. "Could we think of the water coming down as being like an open faucet? I might convert that long enough fore you toe get safely away."

"I am not following this," Fanchon said, irritated about encountering anything she couldn't follow.

"I can't say the exact word until I'm ready toe change it," Eunice said, "because it happens automatically. But let me try it."

Perplexed, they followed her to the door. She stepped out into the pouring rain, getting instantly soaked. "Tap!" she said loudly.

The water sluicing down on her changed into colored streamers. They piled up around her.

"Tap became tape," Fanchon said. "But only the water that actually touches you. The rest of the storm remains."

"I was afraid of that," Eunice said, coming back inside. She was dripping wet. "Oh! I'm shivering!"

Bink grabbed a towel from the rack. "Take off your clothes. I'll dry you."

"*We* will dry her," Fanchon said, taking the towel from him. "You go face away."

"The only bare girls you can see are us," Wynne said. She was not bright, but she did have a grasp of the fundamentals, and did not want him ogling Eunice's fundament.

Bink knew better than to argue. When it came to him and any other woman, Fanchon and Wynne were of a single mind: No Way. He took another towel, lay on his back, and laid the towel over his face. As it turned out, the towel was slightly porous, and he was able to see vaguely through it.

The two stripped Eunice and rubbed her dry. Bink saw her bare body, but the filter of the towel blurred the details enough so that he didn't freak out. He was partly sorry; he had noticed young women ever since his rejuvenation. He loved Chameleon, but still liked looking. Ah, well.

They garbed Eunice in bra, panties, and a dress available in the closet. The panties made his eyeballs heat, but not a lot. "Now you can look," Fanchon said.

He lifted the towel off. "I'm sorry I couldn't help," he said.

Fanchon took the towel. "This is porous!"

"Is it?" he asked innocently.

"And his eyeballs are warm," Wynne said.

"That's too bad," Eunice said. But she did not seem annoyed, for some reason. She sat delicately on the bed he vacated.

"Well, we're stuck with her till the storm abates," Fanchon said.

"'Til it goes," Eunice agreed. "Oops."

For when she said "'til" it converted to "tile"—or more correctly, it converted the material of the bed she was sitting on. Since it was a textual word, the bedspread become a big tile covered with text: textile. A messed-up conversion.

The three of them gathered around the text tile, intrigued, trying to read the tight print. It was microscopically small, line after line, as if a larger text had been condensed to a small one. They lifted up the edges, peering close.

"I'm so sorry," Eunice said, rising. "I messed up the material. Let me get away from it and it will revert."

"No, this is interesting," Fanchon demurred.

But Eunice was already stepping away. The text abruptly drew to-gether, as though passing through a funnel, returning wherever it had come from.

They, holding onto it, were drawn along. They found themselves in limbo, the world swirling around them, with only the text tile remain-ing stable. It was carrying them along, wherever it was going.

"It can't be harmful," Bink said, "because—"

"We know," Fanchon said. "You can't be harmed by magic. But what about us?"

"Stay close," he said.

The tile landed on ground covered in text. In fact, it settled into a square depression, completing an interrupted pattern.

"It must have been ripped out of the ground here," Fanchon said, "when the spell went wrong."

They looked around. Not only was the land seemingly made of text, so were the trees, from trunks to leaves. Everything seemed to have been shaped from Mundane newspapers, with the text remaining prom-inent.

A man approached, walking along a text path. He too seemed to be formed of wadded text. He wore a wide-brimmed hat folded from news-paper, and had a big star-shaped belt buckle. "You ask him," Fanchon murmured to Wynne. Bink knew why: no man ever ignored Wynne.

"Excuse me, sir," Wynne called. "Can you tell us where we are, please?"

He glanced at her, and paused, exactly as any man would. "This is Text Us, of course."

"What is Text Us?" she asked stupidly.

But the man was not annoyed by her dullness. No man ever was. "This is the world of written text hidden behind written words, of course. Every word ever written exists here."

"Oh, that's so impressive," Wynne said fawningly. "What do you do here?"

"We all have related talents," the man said proudly. It was easy to be proud when Wynne was admiring a person. "Correcting, erasing, locating, altering words. There is constant work for we Textans to do, and we do it very well."

"That's wonderful!" Wynne enthused, breathing deeply. She might not be head-smart, but she was body-smart.

"Ask him how we can get out of Text Us," Fanchon whispered.

"How—"

"Who would ever want to leave Text Us?" the man demanded. "It's the greatest state in the universe!"

"Oh, I'm sure it is," Wynne agreed, swinging her long hair enticingly. "You are so smart!"

Bink almost smiled, seeing the Textan's eyes following that hair, and his ears soaking up her admiration. It was of course an act, but Bink himself always fell for it. Wynne's nymphly qualities were compelling.

"Of course it is," he agreed gruffly. "I'm just an ordinary Textan; we're all smarter than average."

"Thank you," Fanchon said crisply, stepping in front of Wynne. The man immediately lost interest in the dialogue, and departed. It was a system the two had worked out, and it worked well enough.

"There must be a way out of here," Bink said, "but it seems the natives don't see the need. We'll just have to find it ourselves."

They explored the great state of Text Us. Everything was made of compacted text, as they had seen. The natives were busily working on text rocks, using sharp text tools to inscribe obscure changes. They were remodeling text houses, correcting errors in the walls and windows. Obviously there was a lot of work involved in maintaining the text archives.

"But this is not doing us any good," Fanchon fussed. "There has to be an exit."

"We got here via a 'til becoming a tile, touching textile," Bink said. "Is there a tile becoming a 'til to reverse the process?"

"Backwards," Wynne said. "Text Us backwards is Sutxet."

"That's ridiculous," Fanchon snorted.

But suddenly they were swirling amidst textual fragments that swept them up into chaos. They grabbed on to one another to stay together as the realm sundered around them.

And they were abruptly back in the cabin they had left, landing in a tangle on the bed.

"It worked!" Wynne squealed.

"So it did," Fanchon muttered. "Out of the mouths of babes and idiots . . ."

"Well, it did!"

"Don't start," Bink said quickly. "Let's just bid farewell to Eunice and be on our way."

"Where is Eunice?" Fanchon asked, looking around.

"And where is the carpet?" Wynne asked.

There, where the rolled carpet had been, was a note. Bink fetched it and read it.

I HAV GON FOR HELP, LEAVING THIS NOT OF EXPLANATION. EUNIC.

"Her written words delete the silent E," Fanchon said.

"So we'll just have to wait until she returns," Bink said. "Bringing back our carpet."

"But we are supposed to be on Mount Rushmost today," Fanchon protested. "We can't wait."

"It's awful wet out there," Wynne said, peering out. Then: "What's this?"

Bink looked. There was a line of streamers where Eunice had flown away on the carpet, getting rained on. "Tap equals tape," he said.

"But the tape should have reverted to water after she stopped touching it," Fanchon said.

They considered that. "It got waterlogged," Wynne said.

"That is so stupid!" Fanchon said. "Yet apparently also true. They were too wet to change. They'll revert to water when they dry, ironically."

"We'll have to walk," Bink said.

"And how will we climb the sheer cliff to the mesa?" Fanchon demanded. "That is the winged monster retreat for a reason: only winged creatures can reach it."

They mulled it over, and decided they would just have to wait for

Eunice's return, hoping they could then make it to Mount Rushmost in time.

"If she returns," Fanchon said.

"But she left a note," Wynne said.

Fanchon considered, and decided not to make a logical issue that could only aggravate things. "So we'll wait."

They waited, but Eunice didn't return. Disconsolate, they slept in the shelter, as the rain continued. Bink would have liked to embrace Wynne, but Fanchon's presence nixed that. It wasn't that Fanchon wouldn't understand; it was that she *would.*

In the morning the storm had finally given up. And Eunice returned, with another passenger.

"Sorry I'm late," she said. "The rain made me lose my way. But I brought help. Note that you seem toe need it any more. You made it back one your own." She was still adding E's to words that could take them.

"But not in time," Fanchon said sharply. "We have missed our rendezvous."

Eunice nodded. "Maybe my friend cane help with that."

They looked at the other person. He was a grossly corpulent man. "Hello, folks," he wheezed. "I'm fat."

"We can see that," Fanchon said sharply. "Who are you?"

He smiled. "I get that a lot. That is my name as well as my condition. But Eunice rescued me from a fate worse than fat, as it were."

All three of them were perplexed. "You still look fat," Wynne said indelicately.

"Like this," Eunice said. She opened her shirt to reveal her nice bosom. The other women, caught by surprise, did not have time to prevent it, so Bink got an eyeful that came delightfully close to freaking him out. "I tempted Fate." She stepped into Fat.

And Fat became Fate, a gaunt hooded man who was plainly much taken with her. He kissed her ear.

"Wait tile we're alone," she murmured.

"As Fate, I can guarantee that your delay will not interfere with your mission," Fate told them. "You may proceed on it now."

"Ludicrous," Fanchon muttered. Then she reconsidered. "Still, crazy as it may seem . . ."

They took the carpet and soon were in flight, leaving the lovers in the shelter. It seemed their tryst was fated.

"But we didn't complete our mission," Bink concluded. "We arrived a day late, and there was nothing."

"We fear the text misadventure has cost us our answer," Fanchon said. "Unless you folk have it."

Dawn looked blankly at the others. No one had an answer.

Picka made an effort. "If repeating the word backwards got you out of Text Us, could reversing the Double You put you back together?"

"The letter W backwards is the same letter," Fanchon snapped.

"I was thinking of the opposite meaning," Picka said. "A singlet."

A look of wild surmise ricocheted around the group. "Do we have a singlet?" Bink asked.

"Sure," Wynne said. "It's just a loose-fitting jersey for when I exercise." She delved into her purse and hauled out the garment.

"This is just crazy enough to make sense," Fanchon said.

The two women stood together, Fanchon behind Wynne, and Bink pulled the stretchable garment over their heads and shoulders. As he did, something strange happened: their heads merged, then their necks and shoulders. As he drew the singlet down, their bodies continued to come together. They became single above, double below: the head and arms of an ordinary woman, with four legs. It was working.

Bink continued pulling the singlet down, stretching it to cover their legs. When he got it to the ground, only one woman remained. "Chameleon!" he exclaimed, hugging her.

"It's so good to be back!" she said, kissing him.

"And it was your boneheaded idea," Dawn murmured, kissing Picka's skull.

"Thank you."

Bink and Chameleon disengaged. "So our advice was correct," he said. "Our solution was here."

"It was just a guess," Picka said.

"We are duly appreciative anyway," Bink said. "What can we do for you in return?"

"There's really no need," Picka said.

"Let's celebrate with a concert," Dawn said. "Then we'll go our separate ways."

That seemed good. They brought out their instruments and played a round of "Ghost of Tom." Chameleon clapped her hands, somewhat in the manner of Wynne, and even her Fanchon aspect seemed impressed.

Then they paused. Something ugly was poking its snout over the brink of the cliff.

13
MONSTER

H e climbed the cliff," Dawn said, aghast. "Using his goo."

Mim flew across to intercept the Music Monster. "You can't come here," she protested. "You have no wings."

Piper ignored her. He continued to slide up and over the edge, making a right-angle turn without difficulty. He was huge and black and gelatinous, and he smelled like a putrid stink horn.

"Get off this mountain," Mim said imperiously, hovering right above him.

The monster shot out a black pseudopod that circled her waist and drew her down toward him.

Mim's wings became swords that lashed down. One cut off the pseudopod; the other hacked a slice off the top of the monster. Freed, she landed neatly on her feet beside Piper. "Now will you get out?" she demanded.

The two sections of monster slid along the ground and rejoined the main mass. More pseudopods shot out at her, catching her legs. She wind-milled, losing her balance.

Skully ran forward, his arms becoming massive swords. He hacked off the new pseudopods, freeing Mim. "Better get back," he advised. "This thing can't hurt me, but might hurt you."

"Thank you," she said somewhat faintly. It was obvious that she did not like accepting help, but realized that she did need it.

The three pets moved toward the monster, but Dawn waved them back. "That thing is dangerous," she said. "Stay out of harm's way, so we don't have to be distracted by concern for you."

That made sense to them, and they retreated.

"This is what wants to marry you?" Bink asked Dawn.

"Yes." She looked ill.

"That stinks," Chameleon said.

"That too," Dawn agreed with a third of a smile. "Literally."

"Then we had better dissuade him," Bink said. "In this manner we can repay the favor you have done us."

"I'm not sure he can be dissuaded. Look at what he was doing to Mim."

The monster completed his turn, and was wholly on the mesa. Now another figure came into view, riding his rear portion. A lovely young woman.

"Pundora!" Joy'nt cried. Picka realized that of course she would be with the monster; she was guiding him, using her friend Steel in the form of a magic mirror.

"And who are you?" Pundora asked, stepping onto the mesa.

Dawn nerved herself and stepped forward. "I am Princess Dawn, and these are my friends. We have no use for you."

"I wasn't asking *you*," Pundora said arrogantly. "I know who you are, you murderess; I've been tracking you. You destroyed my boy-friend. For that you must pay." She turned to face the skeletons. "But I don't know about you freaks."

"We are walking skeletons," Picka said. "We are helping Dawn with her mission."

"Well, forget it," Pundora snapped. "She will soon marry Piper and be miserable ever after. That's my revenge."

Bink stepped forward. "And I am Bink. I owe my great-granddaughter a favor, so I will stop the monster from coming after her. I suggest you go back the way you came, and never bother her again, and save us all trouble."

"Great-granddaughter!" Pundora said derisively. "You're barely old enough to be her father!"

Bink didn't debate the point. He simply went and picked her up and carried her back toward Piper. "Go. We are asking you nicely."

Pundora made a screech of impure outrage that sounded like a cross between an injured hoot-owl and a deflated frog. The mirror appeared in her hand. It converted to a sword. She struck at Bink.

The sword somehow went askew, missing him, and Pundora almost lost her grip on it. She tried again, and again it missed. "What?" she demanded. She tried a third time, determinedly, but somehow to no better effect.

The sword became the woman Steel. "It's no use," she said as she dropped to the ground. "Some kind of ambiguous magic protects him."

"The nerve!" Pundora snapped, outraged. Then she thought of another tack. She ripped open her blouse. "Look at this!" But the view did not freak him out; in fact, it seemed to have no effect. Pundora was amazed. So was Chameleon.

Bink carried Pundora to the monster and dumped her down on his back. "Go," he repeated.

Now the monster reacted. He had evidently been as surprised as Pundora by Bink's action and immunity. He lashed out with a pseudopod. And missed.

"It's that bleeping magic," Pundora said, disgusted.

Picka was standing beside Dawn. "Why didn't her bosom freak him out?" he asked.

"He can't be harmed by magic. Pundora is magical. If he had freaked out, he might have been vulnerable. So his talent did not let it happen."

"Still, he might freak out if there was no threat of harm?"

"Yes. Wynne could do it."

Or might have, if she had continued to exist separately. Still, it was an interesting distinction, confirming what Dawn had told them about her great-grandfather's magic.

"Get off the mesa," Bink said. He stooped, put his hands under Piper's front section, and heaved up. But his hands slid sloppily through the jellylike flesh. He couldn't get a grip on the monster. It was an impasse.

"Maybe if we three skeletons act together," Skully said.

They tried it. Picka, Joy'nt, and Skully lined up before Piper and hunched down together. They braced against the ground and pushed at the gelatinous substance.

And found themselves walking into it. The substance gave way before them, and closed in around them. They were mired in it up to their neck bones.

"Uh-oh," Skully said. "There's acid."

Picka felt it too. The juice was gradually eating into his bones and joints. Soon it would dissolve the joints, leaving the bones disconnected, and then it would slowly digest the bones.

"We had better get out of this," Joy'nt said urgently.

They waded out. The flesh couldn't hold them any more than they could hold it. It was another impasse.

"I can do it," Granola said.

"No," Picka said. "That acid would hurt your living flesh, unless you have protective gloves or a solid tool to push with."

"I will find one," the giantess said. They heard the sound of her footfalls as she hurried away.

"What is that sound?" Mim asked.

"That's just the invisible giant," Chameleon answered brightly.

"A giant?"

"Part of their party."

Mim turned to Dawn. "There's an invisible giant in your party?"

Picka realized that they were in trouble. "Well—"

"Who can pick up a person and make him seem to fly?"

"Uh—"

"So you're not really winged monsters."

"We confess it," Dawn said. "We had to do our business here. We did do it. We would have been gone by now, if the monster hadn't come."

"I will summon the dragons," Mim said grimly. "They will roast it and vaporize it. Then we can settle this issue of misrepresentation." She brought out a summoning horn.

"Stun them!" Pundora cried.

Suddenly the monster was making sound. Air blew from myriad vents in his substance, and each vent was a pipe that played a single note. The notes merged in chords, and the chords formed a melody.

Mim stood still, stunned, unable to blow her horn. So did Chameleon. So did Dawn. So did the three pets. Only Bink was immune.

"It's the stun music," Picka said. "Affecting living folk. Except Bink."

"And reel her in," Pundora said. She seemed unaffected, either because she was a pun rather than an ordinary living creature, or because the monster was able to exclude her from the effect. Neither reason was encouraging for the others.

Then the music changed. Dawn looked horrified, but took a step toward Piper. She was being compelled.

"No!" Bink cried. He strode to Dawn, picked her up, and carried her away from the monster.

"Do the others," Pundora said.

The music shifted again. Mim, Chameleon, and the three pets started walking toward the monster. Bink couldn't rescue them all.

"Picka!" Dawn cried. "Stop the music! You can do it!"

Picka unlimbered his clavicles and started playing his ribs. He played the same dire melody he had just heard. It was totally new music to him, with amazing implications, but it *was* music, and he could play it. It seemed that only a superlative musician could play the magic music, but he had evidently passed that threshold.

The living folk paused, torn between the two sources of summoning music. It was working!

Piper increased the volume. The people and pets resumed motion toward him.

Picka played harder, opposing volume with volume. People and pets paused again.

"Take them!" Pundora said.

The monster slid forward, the music unceasing. The people and pets, anchored where they stood, could not retreat. Picka knew that if the acid had slow effect on skeletal bones, it would have rapid effect on living flesh. The targets would be painfully dead in minutes or even seconds.

He had to do more. But what?

"Can you stun *it*?" Bink asked, setting Dawn down.

Picka tried. He copied the music Piper had used to freeze the living folk before, and directed it at the monster. Could he do this also? It was so new and different!

Piper's music paused. Again, it was working!

The people and pets came to life, fleeing the monster. But now Piper oriented on Picka. He played loud stun music.

Picka was unaffected. "You can't stun me," he said. "I'm not alive."

"Change your tune," Pundora told Piper. "He has some soul. Focus on that."

The music changed again. Suddenly it *was* affecting Picka. He could feel his bones being stilled. It became difficult to play his ribs, because his arms were slowing. Without that motion, he could not play his own music.

"Try harder!" Dawn cried.

For her, he could try harder. He concentrated all his will. Slowly his arms revived, and his playing regained strength. The process fed on itself, his increasing power of music providing better control of his bones.

Piper played harder, but now Picka was braced, and played harder too. It wasn't loudness so much as the magic element; the music summoned surrounding magic and directed it like a weapon. Piper was attacking, Picka was shielding, preventing the deadly theme from touching his bones. But he was also learning the nuances of the attack music, and playing it back at the monster. It was still another impasse as the two of them strained against each other, unmoving.

"Ho!"

Picka turned his head to look, without abating his magical effort. Bink, watching the struggle, had stepped back to the mesa drop-off and lost his balance. He was windmilling his arms, trying to recover, but not succeeding. Picka could not help him; it was all he could do to fend off the monster's attack.

But Joy'nt and Skully were free. Skully picked her up and hurled her toward Bink. She dissembled in midair and formed her bones into a chain. She reached out with one arm and caught hold of Bink's extended leg as he toppled off the edge. Then Bink dropped down out of sight, trailing Joy'nt's linked bones.

Skully had hold of one of Joy'nt's feet. As Bink's weight dropped, the bone chain went taut, and Skully was jerked forward. "Some help here!" he called.

Chameleon and Dawn leaped to catch his feet as he slid past them. Woofer caught Dawn's skirt in his teeth and set his four feet to braking. Midrange did the same with Chameleon's singlet. Tweeter flew over the brink, peered down, and tweeted.

"Oh, all right," Mim said, understanding him. She caught hold of one of Chameleon's feet and braked also, her own feet digging two little trenches in the soil. Her wings became stout poles with splayed ends that dug into the ground, generating a lot of drag.

The motion slowed, and halted. They had stopped Bink's fall.

Bink helped himself. He climbed up along Joy'nt's chain of bones and scrambled over the brink. Then he pulled her dangling portion up to join him. "Thanks!" he gasped. "I'm not proof against a physical fall."

The others relaxed. Woofer and Midrange let go of the skirts, which had come half off, baring portions of their panties and bottoms. Dawn and Chameleon quickly pulled their skirts back up as if ashamed, though in truth their bottoms were freakingly beautiful.

The monster's attack intensified, and Picka had to struggle again to fend it off. He realized that it had eased during the distraction of Bink's fall.

"You let those panties freak you!" Pundora told Piper, disgusted. "Instead of finishing him while he was distracted, you idiot."

Picka realized that it was so. Piper remained a human being despite his monster form; the sight of lovely human women's panties had indeed distracted him. That had given Picka invaluable resting time.

But now the battle was on again. Piper's music was pressing him hard, and he was slowly losing purchase. The monster had had plenty of time to perfect his ability, while it was new to Picka. Learning to play the kill-music was one thing; playing it well was another. He was in trouble.

A fallen tree trunk forged through the air toward them. "What's that?" Chameleon asked.

"Granola," Dawn said. "She found a tool."

The trunk came down to push against the monster. Piper started sliding toward the brink.

"An invisible giantess!" Pundora said. "I smell her perfume. Stun her! Stun her hard!"

The monster reoriented his music. The tree trunk stopped moving. Then there was a loud crash, as Granola fell backward to the ground.

"Bleep," Dawn said, wincing.

There was a loud honk. Mim had finally blown her horn. The distraction of stunning the giantess had meant the monster had momentarily released the others.

"Oh, bleep!" Pundora complained. "She's calling the dragons!"

Picka was relieved. The dragons could come and toast the monster, winning the battle.

"Finish him off before the dragons come," Pundora said. "You have to get rid of him before you can concentrate on the others and capture the princess."

Piper redoubled his effort. His vents blew out a phenomenal medley of notes. The music surrounded Picka, battering him, driving his control back. His arms slowed again, and his notes became faint.

"She's guiding him," Dawn said. "We have to silence her."

"I don't like attacking a woman," Skully said.

"You don't have to." Dawn abruptly charged Pundora.

"But she's not exactly alive," Joy'nt called, following her. "You won't know everything about her. You're not a fighter."

"Thats what you think," Dawn called back.

Pundora saw her coming. She drew out her mirror, which became the sword. But Dawn was upon her before she could swing the sword. Dawn grabbed the hilt, wrenching it away, and it fell to the ground.

Then it was a human-style catfight, with clawing, scratching, and hair pulling. The two fell to the ground, rolling over, trying to gain advantage.

"Meow!" Midrange called.

Dawn heard and heeded. She let go of a hank of hair and caught at the skirt. She yanked it down, exposing Pundora's panties. "Look at this, monster!" she cried.

Piper did. His music diminished. He had surely seen those panties many times before, and handled them, but this was a forbidden public view, far more enticing.

"Oh, yeah?" Pundora screeched. "Take that!" And she yanked down Dawn's skirt.

But that, as it turned out, was a tactical mistake. If Piper was half-way freaked by Pundora's panties, he was wholly freaked by Dawn's panties. She was, after all, the beautiful princess he wanted to capture, tame, and marry. His music died away.

"Oh, for bleep's sake!" Pundora exclaimed. She yanked Dawn's skirt back up, then her own. Then she wrenched herself away from Dawn's grip and retreated. "Take out the skeleton!" she called. "Now!"

The monster's music resumed and intensified. Picka had to struggle again to fend it off. He was dismayed by the increasing force of Piper's attack against him; the monster was getting his number, as it were, and might indeed finish him off.

Midrange meowed with further advice.

"Right," Dawn agreed. She pounced on the fallen sword.

But it changed into the woman Steel. "I'm not serving you," she said. "You're destined for a soft regal life. Not much excitement there." She followed Pundora.

So much for that ploy. It had seemed like a good idea, because the loss of the aid of the sword/mirror would have stripped away Pundora's ability to track Dawn.

Dawn had to retreat. Her clothing was torn in strategic places, her fair skin was scratched, and her hair was an utter mess.

But the reprieve she had won for Picka was vital, because now the first dragon was arriving. It was huge, with fire jetting from its snoot. It glided to a landing before the group of people.

"Toast it!" Mim cried, gesturing to Piper. "It's an intruder, and dangerous."

The dragon nodded and oriented on the monster. It inhaled.

"Pacify it!" Pundora cried. Her clothing, skin, and hair were in similarly bad shape. It had been an even fight.

The music shifted, and the pressure was off Picka. That was an enormous relief, because he had been near complete wipeout. The attack had not been physically debilitating, so much as magically. All he could do for the moment was rest and recuperate. And watch the face-off between dragon and monster.

The dragon paused in mid-inhalation. Piper's magic was freezing it in place, so it could not blast out its fire. The versatility and power of the monster was frightening.

But all Piper had done was stop the dragon, not defeat it. That obviously wasn't enough. It was simply another stalemate.

"Now slide forward and goozle out its gizzard," Pundora said.

The monster slid forward, literally, like a giant snail, his music not pausing. The dragon was in trouble.

Picka had to rejoin the fray. He was tired and weak, magically, but he couldn't just watch the dragon, who had come to help them, get goozled.

He resumed playing his music, directing the killing theme at Piper.

"Bleep!" Pundora swore. She lifted her recovered sword and charged Picka.

Skully intercepted her, his arms formed into swords. She had to turn to fend him off. In half a moment they were embraced, neither sword effective. But it took up Pundora's attention, which meant she couldn't attack Picka or direct Piper.

Picka intensified his music to the extent he could. It was a relatively feeble effort, but it had to be parried or it would be effective. The monster shifted his music to fend off Picka's attack. Picka felt the terrible power battering his bones. He could survive this for only seconds.

The dragon, freed, exhaled. A blast of fire shot out. It missed the monster, because the dragon had not yet had time to reorient, but the next one wouldn't miss. Not even the monster could handle a torching like that; he would be roasted in place.

The music shifted again. The dragon froze. Picka renewed his attack.

"Bleepity bleep!" Pundora swore villainously, causing the nearby grass to smolder. "We can't handle both together. We have to get out of here."

Piper seemed glad to agree. He slid away from the dragon and Picka. Both advanced at the same rate, alternating their attacks.

Pundora got on the monster's back. His rear portion went over the brink and folded down to contact the cliff, sticking to it. He continued around that turn, still fending off Picka and the dragon with sharp alternate musical thrusts.

"This isn't over!" Pundora screamed as she slowly disappeared over the brink. "We'll be back when you're not ready, meatless head!"

Picka and the dragon moved to the brink and looked down. The monster was sliding slowly down the wall, getting out of range of Picka's music. The dragon was unable to bend his snout down far enough to catch them. They had escaped.

"We won!" Chameleon said, thrilled. No one contradicted her; it wasn't worth it. But they all knew that it had been a lucky and mixed victory at best. The monster could have defeated them all, without the dragon, or defeated the dragon without Picka's countering music.

"I was not eager to have you folk here," Mim said, "but I must say you fought well to preserve the sanctity of the mesa."

Picka opened his jaw to protest that it was their own hides and bones they had been preserving, but caught Dawn's warning look, and was silent. For one thing, the monster would not have come here if Dawn and Picka had not been present.

"We will be moving on as soon as we recover from our effort," Bink said smoothly. "Thank you for your timely assistance, Mim. You may have saved my life."

"That's all right," Mim said. "I couldn't let you just drop. Your grandson would never have forgiven me."

His grandson Dolph, who could assume the form of a winged monster, Picka remembered.

"Thank you, Stover," Mim said to the dragon. "You did good work, stopping that stinky thing." He nodded and spread his wings. He launched himself off the cliff, and in two-thirds of a moment was gone.

"Now about that giant . . ."

"Granola!" Dawn cried. "She may be hurt! She took a bad fall." She ran to where she judged the giant lay.

"We apologize for deceiving you," Picka said. "We should not have done that."

"You should not have," Mim agreed. "But now that I have seen what you are up against, I am inclined to let it be. You were desperate."

"Well—"

"She's all right," Dawn called. "Shaken up, but not badly hurt. A day's rest should help."

"Take that day," Mim said gruffly. Then she walked back to her station, leaving the rest of them alone.

"Now I know why my talent allowed itself to be revealed," Bink said. "It was my own folly; I was so busy watching the action that I backed off the cliff. That's a nonmagical danger. I would have fallen and died, had Joy'nt and the rest of you not acted."

"But you wouldn't have been distracted, had the monster not come after us," Joy'nt said.

"Me," Dawn said, returning to the group. "It came after me. It was my fault."

"And I would not have been comfortable having you abducted by the monster," Bink said. "So I'm glad I was here. Quite apart from the fact that Picka solved Chameleon's problem."

"I never thanked you for that!" Chameleon said. She came and hugged Picka. "We're so grateful!"

"You're welcome," Picka said, embarrassed.

"But before we separate," Bink said, "I want to know what Pundora meant when she said they would be back. Surely not back here, where Dawn won't be, but the dragons will."

"Remember," Dawn said. "Piper wants to marry me. So he'll chase me until I find a better way to discourage him. He just won't stalk me when there's a big dragon near."

"Ah, yes," Bink agreed. "And I think that now he will be stalking Picka Bone as well, because—" He paused. "Is it Bone or Bones? Your father Marrow is Bones."

"We are Bones too," Joy'nt said. "Either one of us is Bone; the two of us are Bones."

"The plural," Bink agreed, nodding. "At any rate, now the monster knows that Picka can stop him musically, and wants to marry Dawn, so he is a rival to be eliminated."

"I really didn't stop him," Picka said. "He was overwhelming me. Only the savage presence of the dragon prevented Piper from wiping me out."

"Ah, but your effort was enough to divert him from the dragon," Bink said. "And it was, I believe, your first effort of magical music. He knows you will improve. So you are definitely a threat."

"Not much of one, I fear."

"We'll train you," Dawn said confidently, "so you can get good enough to take him on alone."

"I appreciate your confidence in my potential strength," Picka said weakly.

"And I still owe you a favor," Bink concluded.

"Consider it done," Picka said. "You tackled Pundora so she couldn't heckle me."

"But I did not get rid of her." Bink paused thoughtfully. "Though she was a pretty interesting armful."

"Bink!" Chameleon protested.

"Not as interesting as you," he said quickly. "And of course she's magical, so she was unable to freak me out and make me vulnerable. Anyway, my effort was wasted, so the debt is unpaid."

"There's no need—" Picka began.

"Maybe there will be another opportunity in the future," Bink said. "I will keep it in mind."

"Your approval of our union will do, Great-grandpa," Dawn said.

Bink frowned. "Now be reasonable, Great-granddaughter! I'm willing to slay a monster, but this is beyond the pale." But he was unable to keep his face straight, and they all dissolved in laughter.

They went to Granola, who was sitting up. "You tried," Dawn told her. "You helped. We really appreciate that."

"I was stunned before I accomplished anything," Granola said.

"We all were," Dawn said. "All living creatures, including the dragon. And the skeletons had problems too. You couldn't help it. That's one formidable monster."

"He is indeed," Granola agreed. "We shall have to consider carefully before we engage him again."

"And we will have to meet him again," Joy'nt said, "because he is after Dawn."

"Meanwhile, you need to rest, Granola," Dawn said. "We'll leave tomorrow."

"We don't know where we're going next anyway," Picka said.

"That favor," Bink said suddenly. "I just thought of it. Picka will need to practice his music. I know a fine musician in Rap Port who may be able to help you. His name is GoDemon, and he can make music from anything. If he can't help you, maybe he will know who else can. I will write you an introduction."

"Thank you," Picka said. "Maybe he will know how I can improve enough."

Bink wrote out the note and gave it to him. Picka stored it in his head. He wasn't at all sure that anything could help him enough, but he had to try.

After that Dawn remade her hair so as to look presentable and kissed Bink and Chameleon farewell, and the pair got on their flying carpet and departed.

"Mim accepted our apology and gave Granola a day here to recover," Picka said.

"That's a relief."

They set about foraging for a meal for those who needed to eat, then had another musical practice session. It was a nice conclusion to a highly mixed day. They had learned how deadly serious their mission had become.

Picka hoped he would be able to measure up.

14
RAP

In the morning, reasonably rested, they piled into Granola's handbag and lifted off the mesa. The giantess returned to the steep path she had found, unnavigable by any ordinary-sized creature, and brought them down to normal ground level.

Then she strode rapidly to the north and west, heading for Rap Port. She could move at ten times the speed of ordinary folk, but it was a fair distance, including navigating the Gap Chasm, and they would have to camp for the night before getting there.

"Oh, bleep!" Dawn swore. Picka had not realized how much she swore, before getting to know her better.

"What's the matter?" Joy'nt asked.

"I've got a Worry Wart," Dawn said, showing her left hand. Sure enough, there was a freshly grown wart on her little finger. "No wonder I've been edgy about things."

A Worry Wart. Picka knew of them. They infected living creatures, and made them worry unnecessarily, or exaggerated legitimate worries. Sometimes they formed because of worry. "You must be nervous about having to marry the monster," Picka said. "That gave you the wart."

Dawn nodded. "Could be. But now I'm worrying worse. Besides, it looks awful. I need to be rid of it."

"Touch it," Joy'nt suggested. "Fathom its nature, including what will abolish it."

"Good idea!" Dawn put her right forefinger on the wart. "It can be abolished by pressing something loathsome against it. Like rotten bean curd or a puke snail. Too bad we don't have any."

"Like the flesh of the monster?" Skully asked.

"Yes, actually. But I don't dare get near the monster."

"So we'll keep alert for something else loathsome," Picka said.

They found a nice section of beach near the Gulf that marked the southern edge of Xanth in this region. Xanth was a peninsula, and indeed there was a coastal town they passed called Peninsula, but this was actually a projection to the west that once connected deviously to Mundania.

"There should be something interesting here," Granola said as she set them down. "I'm not sure what. I don't think it's the castle."

"We don't need to look for the castle again until we know we can win it," Dawn said.

"But if you marry Picka—"

"I'm not a good enough musician," Picka said. "The monster is plainly better, apart from his kill-music. So the castle wouldn't choose me."

"Would it choose Piper, if he married Dawn?"

"I detest saying it," Dawn said, "but I think it would. I am determined to see that doesn't happen, but if the monster should catch me unprotected, I'd be lost. When he played that summoning music, I was unable to resist. I felt awful, but I was powerless. Picka has to protect me from that fate."

"And I'm not strong enough," Picka said disconsolately. "The monster can be stopped only by music, by a better player than he is, and I'm not."

"Yet," Dawn said.

Picka did not want to say that he doubted he would ever be good enough. "I'll try to improve."

"But enough of this pointless worrying," Dawn said, glaring at her little finger. "We have to forage for this and that."

Dawn and the pets explored the beach, looking for pie plants and puke snails. Picka, Joy'nt, and Skully followed an enchanted path inland, looking for materials to make a shelter for the smaller living folk. Granola sat by herself, resting, for she had walked a long way that day.

The skeletons rounded a turn and almost collided with a human woman. "Eeeeeeek!" she screeched, putting more E's into it than seemed humanly possible.

A young man in diving gear came charging in from the ocean surf. "What is it?" he called. Then he saw the skeletons. "Uh-oh."

"We're not enemies!" Joy'nt said hastily. "We're just passing through, on our own business."

"It talks!" the woman said, her amazement stifling her screams for the moment.

"Of course we talk," Picka said. "We're citizens of Xanth."

"Of what?" the man asked.

Dawn arrived. "A human being!" the woman said, visibly relieved.

Dawn knew the situation the moment she got in range. "You're new to Xanth," she said. "Both of you."

"I was diving," the man said. "Then there was an accident. I'm not sure what happened after that. I heard the scream, and came to help if I could. Then I saw these . . . these . . ."

"Introductions are in order," Dawn said. "I am Dawn." She gestured to the woman. "This is Tracy Berry McLian, age forty-five, from Mundania."

"You didn't have to mention my age," the woman murmured.

Dawn turned to the man. "This is Anthony Liaw, age twenty-eight, also known as Pirate. He's not really a pirate, it's a nickname. He loves the water."

"Oh, yes!" Pirate agreed fervently. "I'm a marine biologist."

"The two of you do not know each other, but you have this in common: you have come rather suddenly to Xanth, a land that is literally magical. You will both have considerable adapting to do. I suggest that you get to know each other, because you both remember Mundania, a land that is considered a fable here in Xanth. In time you will get comfortable here, and be able to make your own lives."

Dawn indicated the three skeletons. "These are my friends Picka Bone, his sister Joy'nt Bone, and Skully Knucklehead. We are traveling to Rap Port to study music." Dawn took a breath, and Picka noticed that Pirate noticed. Dawn had that effect on living men. "You may have noticed that my friends are walking skeletons. Xanth is a magic land, and such things exist, though they are less common in Mundania. You will encounter other strange things."

"Please," Tracy said somewhat plaintively. "I would prefer simply to go home now."

Dawn shook her head. "I am sorry to tell you that you can't go home. I must also tell you that you should not wander alone in the wilderness here; while the skeletons won't hurt you, there are other creatures who will. Stay on the enchanted paths, like this one; you are safe on them, and there are rest stops with facilities and food. The people you encounter on them will be friendly."

"Why can't we go home?" Pirate asked.

Dawn's mouth was grim. "Because in Mundania you are dead."

"Oh!" Tracy exclaimed.

"That accident," Pirate said. "It was worse than I thought?"

"Worse," Dawn agreed.

He sighed. "Well, at least there's a fine sea here. I did think some of the fish were odd."

"Quite odd," Dawn agreed.

"Actually, I know of Xanth. I just didn't expect to find myself in it."

Tracy also sighed. "The same here. I just wasn't assimilating it before." She looked intently at Dawn. "I believe I recognize you now. You are Princess Dawn."

"I am," Dawn agreed guardedly.

"How is your sister Eve?"

"She's married."

Tracy looked at Pirate. "I suppose if that's the way it is, we had better make the best of it."

"I agree," he said. He looked around. "I had better find some better clothing. There should be some growing on bushes somewhere."

"Yes," Tracy agreed. "I think I could become accustomed to this land. May I travel with you, Pirate, at least for a while, until we acclimatize?"

"By all means. At least the two of us will know we're not crazy, regardless what the natives may think."

"Regardless," Tracy agreed. They walked back along the path together.

"We must be on our way," Dawn said. "We don't want to spook anyone else."

"Thank you for unspooking the new residents," Joy'nt said. "They may have read about Xanth, but I suppose it's different actually being here."

But hardly had they started back toward the beach when there was another scream. "Oh, bleep!" Dawn swore. "More mischief. We'd better check."

They ran along the path. The two Mundanes had stopped. Pirate was absolutely still, while Tracy was just concluding her scream.

Then they saw why. "Metria!" Dawn exclaimed. "As if we didn't have trouble enough already."

The Demoness was standing in the path, blocking the way, in all her lushly flesh. She wore only the scantiest of skimpy bras, and burstingly tight translucent panties. Pirate had freaked out, and Tracy had screamed because that was what women did when they encountered blatant sexuality.

"What are you doing here?" Metria demanded, twitching her torso in a manner that made even Picka and Skully stare.

"We're camping," Dawn said. "And these are two Mundanes trying to proceed safely to a shelter. Why are you harassing them?"

"I'm not harassing them. I just wanted to make a card with them."

"A what?" Tracy asked.

"Deck, play, sell, trade, share, transact—"

"Deal?"

"Whatever," Metria agreed irritably.

"Well, you won't make progress as long as you're freaking them both out," Dawn said just as irritably. "Put something on."

"Spoilsport," Metria muttered. Clothing formed around her, almost covering her assets.

Dawn snapped her fingers, and Pirate came out of his freak. Tracy came out of her different freak.

"What deal?" Dawn asked suspiciously.

"Well, I found this man who copies talents, only they aren't as strong as the originals, and he can only get rid of one by giving it to someone else. I like him, but I can't get close to him with that talent."

Picka knew that when the demoness liked a man, she could be extremely naughty.

"What talent?" Dawn asked.

"Summoning stink horns."

Dawn and the skeletons had to laugh, partly with relief. "Why did he absorb that talent?" Picka asked.

"He was just experimenting, teasing me. But now he can't get rid of it, because no one else wants to take it. So I'm trying to find someone to take it."

Pirate, no longer freaked, was interested. "I don't have a magic talent. I'd like to have one. Even that. I presume a person doesn't *have* to bring a stink horn when he doesn't want it."

"But it can be hard to get rid of a stink horn," Dawn said. "And it can detonate at any time."

Pirate shrugged. "Still, it's magic. I think it could be great to discourage an attack by a dragon or savage person."

"You want that talent?" Metria asked.

"Sure."

The demoness lifted one hand and snapped her fingers. Sparks flew out, making a burning sound. One spark set fire to what turned out to be an invisible curtain. It flared up and dissipated in smoke. Behind it was a man, looking a bit surprised to find himself here.

"Dan, I found a taker," Metria said. "For the endowment."

"For the what?"

"Ability, strength, aptitude, capacity, power, gift—"

"Talent?"

"Whatever, you idiot! This man will take the stink horn summons."

"Oh." Dan smiled. "Welcome to it. Come here."

Pirate stepped up. Dan took his hand and shook it. "Now it's yours."

"Let's get out of here before he changes his mind," Metria said. She opened her arms, embraced Dan, and puffed into smoke, which slowly floated away. Both of them were gone. Picka suspected that the Demoness would not let go of the man until she had seriously smooched him.

"Were they fooling me?" Pirate asked.

"Don't invoke it!" Dawn warned.

But as usual in such cases, she was too late. A small hornlike object appeared in his hand.

"A stink horn!" Picka exclaimed. "Touch it to your wart!"

"That is loathsome enough," Dawn agreed, surprised. "May I have the horn, please?"

"Sure." He handed it to her.

"Thank you." Dawn carefully pressed the horn to the wart. The wart sizzled with indignation, then puffed into foul-smelling mist. It was gone. "It worked!"

But the pressure on the horn had ruptured it. Now the stink spread out in a stomach-churning cloud, enfolding Dawn.

"Get away from here, before you get stunk too!" she cried.

Pirate and Tracy hastily retreated and were soon gone. But the skeletons were too close, and all three got stunk.

"We'll have to wash off," Joy'nt said distastefully.

The hurried to the beach. There were the three pets. Woofer took one sniff and backed away howling. Midrange climbed a tree. Tweeter flew high into the sky. There was an audible sniff from the invisible giantess as she too retreated. None of them could stand the stench.

They dived into the water and busily scrubbed one another off. Dawn had to remove and throw away all her clothing. The skeletons scooped up handfuls of sand to scour their bones. There had been small fish in the water; they fled so rapidly they left wakes. The water itself took on a dirty brown hue, and reeked. It looked disgusted.

"That talent will certainly be effective as a defense against predators," Skully remarked.

"Indubitably," Dawn agreed, striding naked from the water in search of new clothing.

"I wonder whether it would be possible to make stink horn pie?" Joy'nt mused. Now that the odor had mostly faded, they were able to joke about it, though even the humor seemed dirty.

In time they were able to settle down on a new, unsullied section of the beach, having found food, poles, and blankets for shelter. It had been more than enough of an incidental adventure.

"But at least I'm no longer worrying," Dawn said, unworried. She eyed Picka in that disconcertingly direct way that living eyeballs had. "Time for your music practice."

They had their session, with Dawn paying special attention to Picka's contribution. "Get it sharp," she said. "Loud. Fast. Coordinated. And practice on those summoning and pacifying themes. You really need those."

"But I would have to use them on you," Picka protested.

"Do it. The monster will."

So after the others were done, Dawn took her stance some distance down the beach, and he played the summons. She resisted. He adjusted in that way he became aware of, and she started walking toward him. He intensified it, and she ran toward him.

"You've got it!" she said breathlessly. "But now try to pacify me."

Picka played the pacification theme. Again Dawn resisted. Again he adapted, and she wilted. In fact she fainted. Oops.

There was a huge thud. It was the giantess. She too had fallen on the beach.

"Next time see if you can focus on one person at a time," Joy'nt suggested as they did their best to revive Dawn and Granola.

"And step up the power in easy stages," Skully said.

"Why didn't Granola come toward me, if she was being affected too?" Picka asked.

"Maybe she was," Joy'nt said. "But she was sitting, so all she did was lean forward."

Before long the two revived, no harm done, because the sand was soft. But it had been a useful object lesson. In future he would practice the magic music with caution.

The next morning they washed again, to scrub off any remaining stink, and resumed their trek to Rap Port. "I hope Tracy and Pirate acclimatize well," Joy'nt said.

"And that he doesn't have to defend them with a stink horn," Skully said. They all laughed, but with wrinkled noses.

They knew when they were approaching Rap Port. Not only was it a port town, with boats sailing close, it had the fast musical beat of its nature. All the inhabitants seemed to be playing musical instruments, or rapping on objects, or talking in fast rhyming patters. It sounded something like, "This is the town that can't be beat; we are playing on our feet."

Fortunately the patter faded as they progressed beyond the town limit. The folk there seemed much like others, going about their business. Granola stepped carefully, trying to minimize the sound of her footfalls so that no one was alarmed.

"Now we need to locate GoDemon," Dawn said. "Woofer?"

"Woof!" The dog poked his head over the edge of the handbag and sniffed enthusiastically. Granola wasn't good for this, because of the nature of her talent; they didn't want to have to double back to check the next-to-last place. The natives would surely become aware of something going on as the giantess treaded back and forth.

"Woof!" Woofer had located the scent.

They went in that direction. It led to an extended campus whose entry sign was R U M.

"Rum?" Skully asked.

"More likely initials," Picka said.

"Are You Mad?" Joy'nt asked with the thought of a smile.

"Meow."

"Midrange says it stands for Rap University of Music," Dawn said. Indeed, there was the fast beat of music permeating the region.

They followed Woofer's nose until they came to a residence at the far edge of the campus. There was a house shaped like a big drum. That was the place.

Dawn got out and went to the door. She knocked. Soon a large gruff human man with some evident demon ancestry answered. "Do you mind?" he demanded. "I'm setting up to teach my next class."

Dawn smiled and inhaled.

"But perhaps I can spare a moment," GoDemon said. "Do I know you? You seem somehow familiar."

"My name is Dawn. I don't believe we have met before."

"There is a princess named—"

"I have a friend who needs some musical advice," Dawn said, continuing her breathing.

"Let him sign up for a class."

"This is a bit more complicated than that. He may not have much time."

Go opened his mouth to protest, but she took a deeper breath, fastening him in place. She beckoned Picka forward.

Go saw him. "What mischief is this?" he demanded. "I'm a musician, not an exorcist."

"Play a tune," Dawn murmured.

Picka quickly unlimbered his clavicles and played "Ghost of Tom."

Go's jaw dropped slightly. "Now, that's new! His own ribs!"

"He can do it well," Dawn said.

"I doubt he knows the first thing about real music, let alone the second thing."

"Play the summoning music," Dawn said.

Picka played it.

Go nodded. "That's well beyond the first thing," he admitted. "Where did he learn that?"

"From Piper the Music Monster," Dawn said.

"Oh, bleep! We don't want that creature here."

"Precisely," Dawn said. "The monster wants to catch, tame, and marry me. I need you to train Picka Bone here so that he can fend off that attack. Can you do that?"

"Only the finest musician in Xanth could do that. The Music Monster is a legend. An ill one."

"Then make Picka the best," Dawn said.

"You have no idea what you're asking! It would take years, if the skeleton even had the potential."

"Days," Dawn said. "We need it in days."

"Impossible! The very notion—" He paused, because Dawn had taken a really deep breath. "I'll do what I can."

Dawn was a Sorceress, but Picka realized that she had drawn on a different type of magic to persuade the musician. She was mistress of the art of being female.

And so, in due course, the four of them were in Go's house demonstrating their music, while he considered options. He grudgingly acknowledged that Picka had potential, after Picka accurately played all tunes Go tried. Go's way of making music was interesting: he could evoke it from anything, literally. He could tap the floor, and it resonated musically. He could tap his fingers against the wall, and music emanated. He could tap his own teeth, and they played notes, much in the matter of Picka's ribs. He could even wave his hands through the air, and sustained notes sounded. He was good at it, very good. He was, in fact, a master musician. But Picka matched anything he produced, after hearing it once.

"I am impressed. But whether it is enough, I doubt," Go said. "Your opponent is the most formidable creature I know of; he's had many years to achieve his potential."

Picka privately agreed with him, but Dawn didn't. "Why not?" she asked. "Picka learns rapidly."

"Because I can take him only up to my level, if he is capable of reaching it," Go said seriously. "But the monster is beyond that level. The monster is Xanth's finest musician. Neither I nor anyone else here can match him. So the task may be hopeless."

"It can't be hopeless," Dawn said, "because otherwise I will have to marry the monster."

"Your reasoning is understandable," Go said, "but not logical."

Picka agreed with him again. The man was sensible as well as being an excellent musician. Their case was hopeless.

"Teach him what you can," Dawn said firmly.

"But there is not time to do more than barely acquaint him with the techniques, let alone enable him to practice enough to become proficient with them."

She leaned forward persuasively. Her blouse was coincidentally loose at the top. "Please."

"I will do what I can," Go repeated, his eyeballs sweating.

Picka saw that Dawn knew everything about GoDemon, so understood exactly how to manage him. She was managing Picka similarly, despite not being able to use her knowing magic on him.

That evening, after Go's class was through, he worked with Picka. The other members of the group were out setting up a suitable place to camp inconspicuously. "You do have significant potential," he said quietly, "but I would not be doing this if it were not for your friend's persuasion."

"I know," Picka agreed. "It is hard to say no to a princess."

"So she *is* the princess. I wondered. She certainly has a touch managing people."

"She does," Picka agreed.

"First, you need to know chords—that's several notes played together. You have been playing a single note at a time, and while that is perfectly adequate for most musical purposes, it will not suffice against the Music Monster's massive chords. He can play any number of notes together."

"He can," Picka agreed. "But I have just my two clavicles."

"However, each clavicle has two ends. You can strike with both ends simultaneously to make chords. Try it."

Picka tried it. He lost his grip and a clavicle dropped to the floor.

"Like this." Go took a stick of similar size, held it in the middle, and struck two books simultaneously. They rang with two different notes.

Picka tried again. This time he managed to strike two ribs together without dropping the stick. He could do it, but knew that it would indeed take time to do it well.

"I regret that we have not the time to rehearse you in this aspect,"

Go said. "But you can do that on your own. The next thing to practice is parts."

"Parts?"

"A piece of music normally has four parts, or voices: soprano, alto, tenor, and bass. Your group has done some of that, with a different person taking each part."

"Oh, yes. It's a nice effect."

"You must learn to do the four parts yourself."

Picka stared at him, knowing that if he had had eyes, they would have been wide. "I don't think I—"

"Like this." Go took his two sticks and stood before a row of books. He used the two ends of the two sticks, striking four notes at a time. The sticks almost seemed to whirl in his hands as he played four-part melodies simultaneously. It was beautiful.

Picka was amazed. "And you are *not* Xanth's finest musician?"

"Not," Go agreed. "That honor belongs to the Music Monster, as I said before. Now you have demonstrated the ability to play anything after hearing it once. Play this."

Picka tried. Had he been fleshly he would have been sweating, because this was the most difficult musical challenge he had faced. But to his faint surprise, he managed it. Not nearly as well as Go's version, but adequate.

Go nodded. "Only my top students can do that, and none of them succeeded on the first attempt. You are remarkable."

"I wasn't sure I could," Picka admitted. "And I didn't do it well."

"The fact that you did it at all bodes well for your future as a musician. Again, you must practice on your own time. Learn the individual parts of each song, play them separately, then play them together. Only when you can do any four-part harmony well will you be able to even think of rivaling the monster." He paused, considering. "But you just might."

"I will practice," Picka promised.

"Now the kill-music, as we call it. This is dangerous to others, so you must use it with extreme caution."

"I know. I practiced it yesterday, and a member of our party fell down."

"Precisely. The monster doesn't care whom he harms, but you must care. The best you can do is learn to match the monster's skill in this respect. That will block his ability but not defeat him. You can defeat him only by becoming a superior musician."

"I have encountered him. I don't think I'll ever be that good."

"You love the princess?"

"I do," Picka confessed. "Though she is not my type, nor I hers."

"Then you will do what is necessary to accomplish your purpose. If it is possible."

"Yes."

"She will see that you do."

"Yes."

Go drilled him on summoning, pacifying, stunning, and repelling music. Picka had not encountered the last before, but appreciated its advantage. It meant that if any living creature menaced their party, he would be able to drive it away musically. That could be as useful a defense as a stink horn, and less smelly.

"There is also the opposite of negative music," GoDemon said. "That is healing music. That can be very good, when the need arises." He taught Picka the healing theme. Picka practiced it, appreciating its value, though at the moment he had no need of it.

"One more thing," Go said. "There is an aspect that perhaps only I know about, and I do not use it, because it is dangerous. But I suspect you will need it."

"I need anything I can get," Picka said.

"Most varieties of kill-music are emotional in nature, generating attraction, fear, avoidance, and so on. They work only on living, feeling creatures, and have no effect on inanimate things. But one type does. This one can weaken the bonds of matter itself, causing collapse. Practice it only well away from ordinary things, and use it only when the need is dire."

"Why would I want to make anything collapse?"

"I hope you will never want to. But I will teach you the theme. What you do with it will be your own responsibility."

Go took him out back, into a separate enclosed garden area. He set up a block of stone on a wood table. Then he stroked the wood to evoke an eerie music.

The stone cracked, fractured, and dissolved into sand. The wooden table was unaffected, being organic.

Picka tried it on another stone, copying the theme. It cracked, but did not disintegrate. "I don't seem to have it, quite," he said, disappointed.

"You have it, Picka. You simply need practice to build up your proficiency with it. Remember: far from anything you value. This theme is dangerous, because it can bring down a stone house, or theoretically a mountain."

"I will." Picka could see that this was a singularly potent type of music. "Thank you."

"Now I have informed you what you need to accomplish," Go said. "You will practice on your own, and with luck and application succeed in becoming the best that you can be. You no longer need my advice."

"But I do!" Picka protested. "You have shown me techniques that I never imagined before."

"Yes. But you can do it by yourself, in time. And you must do it far from here. I cannot afford to help you further."

"Why?"

"Because the Princess Dawn is staying close to you, and the monster is stalking her. If your party remains here any length of time, the monster will come. We do not want that. It would be great mischief."

Ah. "Yes, Piper will come. He travels slower than we do, but he is determined."

"So you understand why we must be promptly rid of you."

"I understand," Picka agreed.

$$\overline{15}$$
BATTLE

S o that is why we must depart first thing in the morning," Picka told the others.

"I will persuade GoDemon to relent," Dawn said.

"No, he is correct. Piper will come, and it could be great harm for the town. We must not inflict this on it. Go has taught me what I need to know; I can practice it anywhere. We must leave."

Dawn sighed. "Morning," she agreed reluctantly.

They were camped in a town park, in a section not normally visited because stench puffers, related to stink horns, grew there. It didn't smell too bad as long as no one stepped on a puffer. They were careful not to.

They did not practice their music that night, because they were in the invisible handbag and the natives would wonder if music seemed to come from nowhere. Instead Dawn, Granola, and the pets ate their meals, and did their attendant natural functions in another section of the park. The business of constantly eating and eliminating seemed botheringly inconvenient to the skeletons, but that was one of the penalties of life.

As they returned, a man did pass their way. "May I help you?" he inquired. "I am Mike. My talent is to make any rolling thing come up the way you want it. Such as dice."

"Can you make a gooey sliding thing go away?" Picka asked.

"Sorry, no."

"We are sorry, then; you can't help us."

Mike walked on, disappointed. "Too bad the monster doesn't roll," Dawn said. "We could make him come up upside down, and jam his pipes in the dirt."

Then they settled down in the handbag. Skully and Joy'nt interlocked bones, the pets curled up or perched, and Dawn had Picka form a close circle with his arms so that she could rest her head on it. Granola slept sitting, as was her custom.

Woofer woke in the night. "Woof," he woofed quietly.

"You smell something?" Picka asked, not disturbing Dawn from her slumber.

"Meow," Midrange said.

"I don't like the sound of this," Joy'nt said. "We can't translate as well as Dawn can, but something's up."

"Can you fly up and check it, Tweeter?" Picka asked.

"Tweet," the bird agreed, and flew up into the moonlit night.

"Maybe it's just a stray Rapper passing by," Joy'nt said.

"Woof," Woofer said negatively.

Tweeter returned. "Tweet!!"

Dawn woke. "The monster!" she exclaimed. "Tweeter, wake Granola. We have to get out of here."

Tweeter started to fly up again, but then fell back into the handbag, stunned. He landed beside Woofer, whose head had dropped to his paws. Midrange was also still.

"Bleep," Dawn whispered. "I am almost paralyzed."

Now they heard the distant music. Piper was coming here, and using his stun music to prevent their escape. Tweeter couldn't fly, Woofer and Midrange couldn't run, and Granola would be unable to stand.

"It is up to us to stop him," Picka said. "We skeletons are the only ones who can move."

"We'll go out and take him on," Skully agreed.

"Be careful," Dawn whispered. Picka realized that it wasn't because she was trying to be quiet, but because it was all the strength she could summon.

"We will," he assured her. Then the three of them climbed out of the handbag and went to face the music.

Now they heard music from GoDemon's house. The musician was using his ability to nullify the monster's sound.

They hurried to the house just as Go emerged. "He's coming," Picka said. "Dawn can't move."

"Can you carry her?" Go asked.

Picka hadn't thought of that. "I could. We skeletons are magically strong. But the monster's already here, and would follow us through the town. I think we simply have to fight him."

"Easier said than done," Go said grimly. "You try to fend him off. I'll alert the townsmen." He hurried away, rapping on his own clothing to make defensive music.

By this time it was clear where Piper was: sliding in from the east. He wasn't trying to conceal himself; he was simply advancing, using his music to stun the natives so they couldn't resist. Maybe he expected to nab Dawn before anyone realized, and carry her away before effective resistance materialized.

But the pets had sensed him coming, giving a little bit of warning. Not much, but maybe enough.

Picka, Joy'nt and Skully advanced three abreast to tackle the monster. Piper would have to pass them to reach Dawn, and they would not allow that.

"Bet we need more than just our bones," Skully said. "We know we can't stop him physically."

"I hope to stop him musically," Picka said. "The best I can hope for is to slow him. If you see he is going to get by, run to carry Dawn away from here. She's what he's after."

The monster hove into sight. It was dark, but the skeletons could see well enough. Maybe Piper had not thought of that aspect.

"Turn slightly left. We're getting close."

The dark form veered slightly left, orienting more accurately on Dawn.

"Pundora!" Joy'nt said. "Bleep."

Picka got an idea that flashed momentarily over his skull. "If we can get her away from him, he'll be much less effective."

"We'll do it," Skully said. "Cover us."

Picka played stun music directed at the monster. That got Piper's attention. His antenna aimed at Picka. Picka's ability might not match that of the monster, but it could not be ignored.

Skully and Joy'nt ran to either side, avoiding detection. Then they made a coordinated charge in from those sides. "Haaa!" Joy'nt shrieked, charging from her side, coming right up to the monster's fringe, waving her arm bones.

"Bleep!" Pundora said. "It's those other bones. Ignore them."

Picka continued playing his stun music, covering the action with the firepower of his mean theme. Piper shook it off, but it was an obvious distraction. Maybe like that of a hornet buzzing a man whose hands were occupied.

Skully leaped in from the other side. He stepped into the monster's jellylike flesh, reached out, and grabbed Pundora, who had been watching Joy'nt. "Eeeek!" she screamed, in a perfect emulation of a distressed maiden.

Skully lifted her high and slogged on through the monster's substance. In two and a half moments he came out the other side, beside Joy'nt. He ran on, carrying the struggling woman.

"Bleep!" Pundora cried, more outraged than frightened. "Unhand me, you ridiculous spook!"

"Give me a kiss, you luscious nymph," Skully replied, putting his skull toward her face.

"You pervert!" she screamed. "You're a bleeping skeleton!"

"And you're a lovely female pun. Come on, you know I'm more your type than the monster is."

Pundora puffed up like a balloon, but was so annoyed that she couldn't think of anything to say.

Joy'nt ran alongside them, not trying to conceal her amusement. She knew Skully had no interest in Pundora, and was just trying to make her so mad that she could not decide on any effective counter. He seemed to be succeeding.

Meanwhile Piper was indeed disoriented. He paused in place, barely fending off Picka's music. He could think for himself, and had done so for a long time, but had evidently become accustomed to Pundora's initiative. Should he follow her, or continue with his original objective?

"Follow Pundora, you idiot," Picka called helpfully.

In the confusion of the action, with the distraction of Picka's stun music, that evidently made sense to Piper. He swerved to follow his accomplice.

"Oh, for pity's sake!" Pundora said. "Don't bother with me! I'll handle this bucket of bones myself." She twisted about and managed to drop to the ground.

But Skully was not so readily evaded. He grabbed her again, this time by the hair, and dragged her on down the street. She was unable to escape without sacrificing a copious hank. She jerked, but could not free herself. "No fair!" she complained.

"Ah, but all's fair in love and war," Skully replied. "Are you sure you won't kiss me?"

"I wouldn't kiss you if you were the last skeleton in Xanth!"

But then the road terminated in a dead end walled in by houses. All doors were closed, of course. There was nowhere to go.

"Let her go," Joy'nt said. "We'll help Picka."

Skully let go of Pundora's hair and ran back, dodging around the surprised monster. He and Joy'nt ran back along the alley while Piper recovered Pundora.

Picka met them. "Maybe we can block them in," he said. He played destruction music really loud. The walls on either side wavered. Then blocks started falling out.

It was working! He had already improved significantly from his first effort.

Meanwhile Piper, having picked up Pundora, was turning and starting back out of the alley.

Picka played more destruction music, perfecting the theme. More stones crumbled and fell. Then the walls on either side collapsed, filling the alley with rubble.

"Wow!" Skully said. "You trapped him!"

"I hope so," Picka agreed. "We'll still need to figure out how to destroy him."

Then Piper came sliding over the top of the rubble wall.

Picka clapped a bone hand to his skull bone. "I forgot he can climb! My effort was wasted."

"You can still oppose him with the regular kill-music," Joy'nt said.

"I will have to, if I can."

He tried, but the monster simply blocked it with his own, stronger music and continued advancing. Picka and the others had to retreat. They knew that neither Piper nor Pundora would allow another attack on Pundora; such a surprise worked only once.

Steadily Piper advanced, and as steadily they retreated. The monster was simply stronger, physically and musically, than Picka.

"Go carry Dawn to safety," Picka told Skully grimly. "She will not be able to flee on her own, and I can't hold him back."

Skully started moving, then paused. "Too late."

"What?" Picka asked, still focusing on the repulsion music he was using to slow Piper's advance.

"She's been summoned."

And there was Dawn, passing them as she walked toward the monster. She did not look happy, but she did not pause.

"Grab her!" Picka said. "I can't do it; I have to focus on the music."

Skully tried, but Piper blasted out extra music, and Dawn leaped forward, avoiding the skeleton. In a moment and a half she reached the monster. Pundora reached down to haul her up on the creature's back with her. It was indeed too late.

Now other townsmen appeared. They were carrying flaming torches, illuminating the night.

"Give me those," Picka said. He reshouldered his clavicles and ran to snatch two from startled townsmen. Then he turned and charged the monster, swinging the torches. He jammed them into the creature's jelly-like flesh. There was a loud hissing as the fire burned it.

Piper shrank back, his music ending in a dreadfully sour note. That stopped his magic. He had been caught totally by surprise, and had been hurt.

Picka scrambled up to grab the woman on the monster's back. He wrapped his arms about her and heaved her up. He ran to the side, carrying her clear.

Once he got her far enough away, he set her down. "Are you all right?" he asked.

"Why Picka, I didn't know you cared."

It was Pundora! He could see in the dark, but not as well as in daylight. He had gotten the wrong woman. Pundora, of course, realizing his intent, had neither resisted nor protested. She was giving Piper time to carry Dawn away.

His first thought was to run back after the monster. But his second thought suggested that he might be able to make something of his mishap. Without Pundora, Piper would have trouble managing. He had trouble focusing on his deadly music and on physical strategy simultaneously. Picka knew how that was. Keep Pundora away from the monster, and the creature was unlikely to go far. Especially not when surrounded by angry torch-bearing townsmen.

"On second thought, you may be as good as she is," Picka said. "You have similar flesh."

"Ha. Ha. Ha," she said. "You're as funny as your form. You must be made of funny bones."

"Piper can't have you. I will take you away forever."

"The bleep you will, you emaciated freak!" She backed away from him.

Picka dived to catch her again. He heaved her up and flung her over his shoulder. He started walking away from the action.

"Put me down, you bleeping bleep!" she cried, pummeling his tailbone with her fists.

"I'm sure in time you will come to appreciate me," he said. "After all, what use will Piper have for you, now that he has Dawn?"

"Yes, that's my revenge on Dawn. She has to marry the slime monster. It serves her right."

She had to be bluffing. "So you might as well come with me. You'll never see Piper again."

She wriggled and heaved and managed to topple to the ground.

She fled instantly. So he had been right: she was not finished with the monster.

But she wasn't finished with this town, either. Two approaching townsmen intercepted her. They grabbed her by both arms. They knew her for an enemy, but she was also a beautiful woman.

"Unhand me, oafs!" she cried.

"Don't be like that," a townsman said, hauling her in for a kiss.

"Wretch!" she screamed. "Don't you dare kiss me."

"I won't," the other townsman said. He put his hand on her bottom for a good feel.

"Lout!" she yelled, swinging her fist at him.

This had gone far enough. Picka did not like to see a woman being mistreated, even a nasty one like Pundora. "Don't molest her," Picka called. "She's a prisoner of war. Take her to a safe place."

"Aww," a townsman said, but he obeyed.

They held Pundora firmly by the arms and started marching her away. She struggled to get free, but couldn't.

"Then again . . ." she said flirtatiously. She was obviously scheming to get free of them, using seductive wiles. Picka hoped the townsmen would be too smart for that, but he doubted it. They were, after all, living men, whose savvy stopped where female beauty began. She would soon enough get free of them.

Picka ran himself, but not after Pundora. He could see better in darkness than she could, and soon he was well away from the others. But before he reached the monster, Skully was before him. "I got her!" Skully said. He had Dawn in his arms.

"Thanks!" Picka said. He took Dawn, who was barely conscious. The monster had truly stunned her.

He had to get her farther away from Piper. But the monster was in the town, doing who knew what damage, and only Picka's music would balk it for long. What was he to do?

"Take her far away from here, so Piper can't get her," Skully said.

"Joy'nt!" Picka called.

His sister heard him and came to him. "You got her!"

"Yes. Skully rescued her. She can't fight Piper herself. I need to go and help the townsmen drive him away."

"Got it," Joy'nt agreed. She took Dawn by the hand and led her away. The stun seemed to be wearing off, but slowly.

Picka ran back to brace the monster. He found him where he had left him, on the street surrounded by townsmen. But the townsmen were not attacking. They were simply standing in place under their flickering torches. They had all been pacified.

It was an impasse. Pundora had not yet rejoined Piper, and Piper was using his music to hold the townsmen at bay. Neither could make progress at the moment. But the arrival of Pundora would change that, as she provided the direction the monster was missing.

Picka unlimbered his clavicles and began to play. He played nullification music, countering the pacification music. The townsmen began to stir. One of them threw his torch at the monster.

Then something odd happened. Just before it reached the monster's flesh, there was a short bleat of dissonance and it snuffed out.

A second townsman hurled his torch. This too winked out.

Piper was musically dousing the torches! Picka had not known he could do that, and probably GoDemon had not known either.

Skully joined him. "Can you do that?" he asked.

"I think I can, now that I've heard the music for it. But I don't want to put out any torches."

"If the monster can put a fire out, can he start one?"

Picka was surprised by the thought, and his music hesitated. That allowed the monster's music to gain advantage. "Maybe he can. That would be another inanimate effect."

"You had better learn how, then, so you can give him a better hotfoot."

"I can't invent such music. I have to hear it first."

"Then get him to play it."

"How?"

Skully considered. "Maybe you can trick him. Set him up to set you back by blasting you with fire."

"But he knows that skeletons aren't much subject to fire. It would have to be a very hot, enduring blast, like that of a large fire dragon. He won't waste his effort."

"He might, if he thought you were foolish. Without Pundora to advise him, he might be fooled."

It made sense. "She'll be back any moment now. I need to act fast."

"A mattress!" Skully said. "I'll fetch a mattress you can use to shield yourself, maybe muffling his music."

"But a mattress wouldn't be much protection. It would readily burn!" Skully nodded.

Then Picka caught on. "Fetch it!"

Skully ran off, while Picka continued to advance slowly against the monster, interfering with his pacification music so that every so often a townsman was able to throw another torch. Because there were many brave townsmen, Piper had to focus intently, and that enabled Picka to match his music. If it had been just the two of them, the monster would have driven Picka steadily back.

Skully reappeared, carrying a mattress. "I explained to a townsman," he said. "He gave me this old one."

But there was a problem. "I can't hold up the mattress and play my ribs at the same time."

"That's right! My oversight. Okay, I'll hold it, shielding you."

They advanced, Skully holding the mattress between them and the monster. "Say, this really helps!" Picka said loudly. "He can't see me to focus on me, as long as the mattress shields me from his view."

"When we get close enough, I'll start chopping off his legs," Skully said. He did not clarify how he would do that while using both arms to hold up the big mattress. With luck, he would not need to.

There was a strange new musical theme. Could that be it?

Suddenly a fireball formed right over the mattress. It was so hot it made the straw and fabric burst into flame.

"Oh, our plot is ruined!" Skully cried loudly. "I'll beat it out!" He threw down the mattress and flailed at it with his widened arm bones.

The music repeated. Another fireball burst, igniting more of the mattress. "Oh, horror!" Skully cried. "The monster is outsmarting us!"

Picka, though, now had the tune and could duplicate it. But he didn't, because he didn't want the monster to realize his mistake.

Pundora reappeared and ran to join Piper. Her hair was wild; she evidently had countered the foolishly amorous townsmen and had to fight her way free. They must have been tenacious. Probably the darkness had prevented them from seeing her bra or panties, so she had been unable to freak them out by mere sight. That would account for the delay.

That made him wonder about her. With her body she could have fascinated almost any mortal man. Why did she bother with the monster? Could her need for vengeance be that great? Well, how would Picka himself feel if someone killed Dawn? He would probably be dedicated to destroying that person to the exclusion of all else. Pundora must really have loved Attila. So her attitude was understandable.

The woman leaped onto the monster's back. She whipped out her mirror. "Princess Dawn is that way," she said, accurately pointing. Piper immediately turned that way.

This was mischief. Dawn would never be safe as long as Pundora could track her. Why hadn't he thought to take away that infernal mirror while he had Pandora? He knew why: because it wasn't just a mirror, but a collaborating woman who could not be dissuaded.

But that was a long-term threat. Right now he simply had to stop Piper from following Dawn. At least he had a new weapon to do it.

He played fireball music. His first effort was wild; the fire formed high in the sky and flared out in half a moment. His second was better, closer to the monster and lasting longer. His third was right on target, right over Piper's head-part.

The monster extinguished it immediately, of course. But that effort caused him to forget the townsmen. They tossed in several more torches.

"Stun them!" Pundora cried. "Stun them all, hard enough to last!"

The townsmen fell to the ground and lay still. They were out of it.

"Now take out Picka!" Pundora said. "You can't win the princess until you get rid of him, because she loves him. Run him over, dismember him, dissolve his bones! Then you'll be able to go after Dawn."

Unfortunately, she was exactly right. She was again providing the strategy the monster needed to win. Picka should never have let her re-join the fray.

The monster, freed of distractions, oriented on Picka. Another fire-ball flared. Picka put it out, but it was a struggle because he was not proficient in this new music. He backed away.

Piper advanced, hurling more fire. Picka felt the searing heat; any living man would be severely burned, or already dead. Picka himself would soon enough be singed; the blasts were too close, too fierce. He retreated farther.

"We need help," Skully said, and ran away. That was his idea of helping?

"See, his false friend's deserting him," Pundora cried gleefully. "Fin-ish him off!"

Picka got marginally smarter and sent a fireball not at the monster, but directly at Pundora. It burst right over her head and singed her hair before Piper put it out. But then she hunkered down, becoming much less of a target, and the monster was on guard, so that ploy was no good anymore.

The monster continued to advance, and Picka continued to retreat. His music was protecting him, and he was getting better at it with this necessary practice, but he was still far from good enough. He was in deep doubt he would ever be good enough. Piper was simply the better musician, and that included the kill-music, fireballs and all.

He was, ultimately, doomed. Even if he survived this encounter, he would be at a similar disadvantage in the next—and there would be a next, because the monster would never quit until Picka was destroyed and Dawn was possessed.

Then Skully returned. There was someone with him. "See? I told you," he said. "Fireballs!"

"So I see," the other replied. "I had not known of this particular as-pect. The monster has grown more formidable than I realized."

It was GoDemon, who had gone to organize the townsmen. "I need help!" Picka said. "He is too strong for me."

"And for me," Go agreed. "But let's see what we can do together."

He was holding a torch to light his way. Now he fingered it, and music surged forth.

The monster halted. Because Go's music was countering the stunning the townsmen had received, and they were clambering back to their feet. They picked up their fallen torches and resumed stalking Piper.

Picka played his music with new vigor. Fireballs flew at the monster, one after the other, barely getting extinguished before singeing Piper's tender flesh.

The monster had no choice. He had to retreat.

"Bleep!" Pundora cried villainously. "Bleepity bleepity bleep!"

"That girl's got a foul mouth," Go remarked as they slowly walked forward, playing their music.

"We tried to separate her from the monster," Picka said, "because she enables him to attack us effectively. But we failed."

"Why does she support him?"

"Dawn inadvertently destroyed her boyfriend, Attila the Pun. She's furious."

"Battila?"

"No, Attila."

"I encountered a Battila once, a caped warrior. Maybe they were brothers."

They were coming to the edge of town. There was a brushy area beyond it. "Set fire to the brush!" Pundora told the monster. "That'll distract them."

Piper directed his magic to the brush. One bush after another burst into flame. In no more than two and a half moments there was a raging brushfire. There was a nasty wind blowing it toward the town.

"Oh, bleep!" Go swore. "We have to stop that fire."

Picka tried, but he could douse only one spot at a time, while this was a savage line. The best he could do was make temporary holes in the firewall.

The townsmen got to work, fetching buckets of water from the harbor. Each bucketful was small, but there were many of them, and soon they got the fire under control.

But while they were doing that, Pundora and the monster made their escape. It would be useless to try to go after them in the night.

"At least we beat them back," Skully said.

GoDemon, worn and weary from the effort, looked at Picka. "I think you will understand why you will not be welcome here, hereafter. We can't afford to suffer more attacks like this."

"We understand," Picka said.

"Go somewhere else, practice your music, handle the monster," Go said. "You know enough to do it, Picka. All you need is to practice and get as good as you can be."

"I fear the monster is better than I will ever be," Picka said morosely.

"I am not sure of that. You have remarkable aptitude. At any rate, you have to try."

Picka had to agree.

They went to find Joy'nt and Dawn. They had rejoined Granola and were hidden high in the air. Picka bid farewell to GoDemon, thanked him for the instruction, and he and Skully climbed into the invisible handbag and disappeared. The townsmen were amazed.

Inside the handbag Dawn, fully recovered, flung her arms around Picka and kissed his skull. "You saved me!" she exclaimed.

Technically, Skully had saved her from the monster, but Picka elected not to argue the case. It was enough for now that he had learned powerful new music magic, and that they had managed to fight off the monster.

It had been a close call, though, featuring the massed power of two music magicians and many townsmen. Just as it had been when they had had the participation of the big fire dragon. Picka remained deeply uncertain that he would be able to do the same alone.

And he knew the monster would be coming after them again.

16
ADORA

G ranola set them down near the north coast of Xanth. "I have a place to go, but I'm tired," she said apologetically. "I need to rest. I did not participate in the action at Rap Port, but I was unable to relax while the rest of you were in danger."

"Understandable," Dawn said. "It was tense for all of us. But where is it you have in mind to go, since we have not decided on another thing to search for?"

"It is in the northeast corner of Xanth, a kind of community, I think. I have no idea why we might be interested, and of course unless it's the next-to-last place we look, we won't find anything there. But at the moment anywhere that's well away from the monster appeals to me."

"We understand," Picka said. Then he got an idea. "I think I know what to look for next. Maybe it's crazy, but GoDemon mentioned a person." He shook his head. "No, it's ridiculous."

"Now you have me interested," Dawn said. "What person?"

"Battila. I thought he meant Attila, but he didn't. Someone he met once. It must be a coincidence of names." The idea was flitting around, but not settling anywhere.

"I wonder," Dawn said. "I am dubious about coincidences. It sounds too much like Attila."

"I wonder whether Battila is anything like Attila," Joy'nt said. "Whether—" She broke off.

"Whether he might resemble Attila enough to interest Pundora," Skully said.

That was the idea. "If she got interested in someone else, she might desert Piper," Picka said. "Again. I think she really loved Attila, so isn't interested in anything but vengeance. But if she found someone else who was a lot like him, maybe then she would have another thought."

"Let's face it," Dawn said. "Attila the Pun destroying himself was crazy, but logical on his own terms, and it happened. This Battila might be similarly crazy yet logical. I think we should check him."

"I think I am already headed there," Granola said. "Of course I won't find it immediately."

"Now that too is interesting," Dawn said. "Picka had an idea he didn't know about, and you responded to it before he figured it out. We seem to be interacting more meaningfully than we realize."

"We're a team," Joy'nt said. "I think I'll almost be sorry when this mission ends and we go our separate ways."

"I'll go with you," Skully said immediately.

She laughed. "Of course. But what about Granola?"

"We'll make beautiful music together," Picka said. "Dawn, Granola, and I. Maybe we could travel around and give concerts."

"I'd like that," Granola said.

"Speaking of which," Dawn said, "we need to practice." She eyed Picka in that living eyeball way she had. "By that I mean *you*. You have to get as good as you possibly can be, or better."

"Yes, dear," he said meekly.

They all laughed. But there was a current of nervousness in it because they all knew that the challenge might be more than they could handle. Piper was a monster, but he was also Xanth's finest musician. How could anyone defeat him musically?

"Let's forage for something to eat," Dawn said. "Then we'll practice."

They piled out of the handbag and the pets quickly explored the area, searching for food. The skeletons looked too, caring about the welfare of their friends.

Midrange returned to Dawn. "Meow!"

"A significant encounter? Where?"

Midrange led them to a path through the forest. "Mew."

"In five minutes? We'll be ready." They settled down to wait.

A young woman with a flowery basket came down the path. She wore a hood that shaded her face, full clothing, and shiny boots. The skeletons quickly faded into the background, knowing that they were too likely to spook an innocent living person, while Dawn and the pets held their ground. "Hello."

The woman saw her. "Oh, hello. I'm Adora. Are you looking for food for you and your animal friends?"

"Yes, as it happens," Dawn agreed, quickly introducing herself as Dawn and the pets. "How did you know?"

"No one comes here without an appetite, because this is where the best reci peas grow."

"Recipes? We were hoping for pie plants."

"Oh, those are farther down the path," Adora said. "But they lack the variety of the reci peas. With reci peas you can make anything."

"Thank you. Right now we'll settle for the pies instead of the peas." Then Dawn did a double take. "Oh, my!"

"Oh, you saw my face!" Adora said, chagrined, pulling her hood tight.

"Its more than that," Dawn said. "My talent is to know things about people. But you have me confused. Are you male or female?"

"Female, of course. But my head isn't." Adora threw back her hood to reveal her head.

Picka and the skeletons were taken aback. The girl had the face of a bull. She was otherwise finely formed; in fact, her body was quite cute by living standards. But the head was quite another matter.

"You resemble the Minotaur," Dawn said.

"I am a female Minotaur," Adora said. "Adora Bull." She drew up her skirt to show that her boots were actually formidable hoofs.

"But how can you be a female bull? You should be a cow."

"Nobody cows the Minotaur," Adora said. "Anyway, I'm his daughter, so I carry his surname: Bull."

"Ah, now I understand."

"Now if only I could find a male of my species who is not my father or a sibling—"

"Sibling?"

Adora grimaced, which was impressive with the bovine face. "It seems my father liked the ladies, and they were impressed by his, um, masculinity. I have numerous half brothers and sisters with similar heads—Terri, Horri, Capa, Flexi, Practica, Lova, Misera, and maybe others I don't know about. Also those with human heads and bull bodies: Tough Bull-ies, rich Bull-ion, speeding Bull-et, stalwart Bull-wark, newsy Bull-etin, river-browsing Bull-rush, and so on. None of them are prospects for romance, of course."

"I see the problem," Dawn agreed. "But you know, different species can make it together, if they like each other and have accommodation spells."

"Really? I've never seen it. No boy will kiss me."

"I think it is time for you to meet my friends," Dawn said. She turned. "Picka?"

Picka stepped forward.

"This is Picka Bone, my fiancé," Dawn said.

"But he—you're—" Adora ran out of dashes and had to start over. "He's a walking skeleton!"

"So he is," Dawn agreed with half a smile. "Maybe I hadn't noticed. I like his musical talent."

"Musical talent?"

Picka unlimbered his clavicles and played a brief merry tune.

"I-I-I have a talent too," Adora said, evidently nonplussed, if not completely minussed. "I can open Doors. The problem is, I can't control where they lead." She gestured, and a Door appeared in a nearby tree trunk. She opened it. Beyond it was a rocky beach beside a tempestuous sea. "I have no idea where that is. If I went there, I would not be able to return here. The next Door would go somewhere quite different. So I don't use my talent much; it's not safe." She closed the Door, and it vanished. The tree seemed unaffected.

"Random travel," Dawn said thoughtfully. "We might have use for that."

"Oh? You like to travel?"

"Not exactly. Anyway, Adora, as you see, you don't have to find a perfect species match. A cowboy would probably do."

"A cow boy for a bull girl," Adora agreed. "That does seem to make sense. Thank you."

Dawn glanced at Picka. "Do you think we should invite her to travel with us for a while? It might enable us to change locations rapidly if we needed to."

Such as when the monster caught them by surprise, as had already happened twice. "Yes. But what could we offer her in return?"

"A search for a cowboy. Woofer might be able to sniff him, if he was anywhere in the area."

"It seems worth a try," Picka agreed.

"Then let's forage for pies, and explain our situation to Adora. I'll do the pies; you explain."

So Dawn and the pets moved on, while Picka explained to Adora in a carefully edited version. "It's complicated, but we are a kind of musical group with a challenge: to defeat the Music Monster and win Caprice Castle," he concluded. "Your talent could help us escape. Our talents could help you find your man. Does this seem fair?"

"Yes. I'd feel safer stepping through Doors if I had competent company."

"But it may be dangerous," he warned. "The Music Monster is vicious."

"It's not danger I fear, but getting lost alone."

"Then it is time for you to meet our other companions. Joy'nt, Skully?"

The two stepped out.

"More skeletons!" Adora said.

"My sister, and her friend. There's one more: Granola. She's an invisible giantess."

"Amazing," Adora said appreciatively.

Dawn returned, carrying several pies. The moment she got close to Adora, she knew the situation. "You'll like Granola," she said.

"I must go explain to my landlord," Adora said. "He'll be relieved to see me go."

"I'll go with you." Dawn said. "I can explain as much as is needed." She glanced at Picka. "You come too, but stay out of sight." She handed the pies to Joy'nt. "Save one for me."

Joy'nt and Skully went to rejoin Granola, while Dawn went up the path with Adora. Picka followed, but stayed well off the path, out of sight. He knew that it wasn't that Dawn was ashamed of him, but that she didn't want to freak out the landlord.

"Where is this?" Dawn inquired as they walked.

"South of Jacks on Ville," Adora said. "That's another reason I don't fit: I have the wrong name."

"It's a nice name."

"But here every man is named Jack, and every woman Jackie. Their children live in boxes and jump out when called: Jack in the Boxes. They play nothing but jacks. They wear jackboots, ride jackasses, and keep jackals and jackrabbits for pets. They use jack-o'-lanterns for light, carve with jackknives, and cook jackfruit in jackpots. They don't like foreigners."

"I can imagine," Dawn agreed. "We would not fit in well either."

They came to the landlord's house, and Dawn went to the door with Adora and explained that she would be going away with Dawn's group. Picka saw that the man wore a solid jacket and didn't give jack for their opinion on anything. So Adora was soon departing, carrying a bag with her meager belongings.

Midrange had been right: it was a significant meeting. Adora and Dawn's group could do each other some good.

Dawn introduced Adora to Granola and explained her talent. "I thought it could be useful, if we were caught again by surprise."

"Could I fit through one of those Doors?" Granola asked. "We wouldn't want to get separated and not be able to find each other again."

"Oops. I never thought of that."

"I could make a big door," Adora said. "Big enough."

"That should do," Granola agreed.

They showed Adora how the handbag made its occupants invisible. They had a supper of pies and milkpods, then had a music practice session that thrilled Adora, and settled down for the night. Picka and the skeletons kept watch, as usual.

In fact, Picka walked out some distance from the handbag so he wouldn't disturb the others, and practiced alone. First he played a predator-repulsive theme so that nothing nasty would come. Then he made fires and extinguished them, sharpening that aspect of kill-music. He cracked stones into piles of sand. He summoned bunnies and squirrels, pacified them, then repelled them. But mainly he tried to get better as a straight musician, because that was the only way he could ultimately compete with the monster. He was improving; he could feel it. He still doubted that he ever would be able to match that level, but he had to try. For Dawn's sake.

"It's utterly beautiful," Adora said.

Picka was startled. He had not seen her approach in the darkness, though he could have had he been more alert. "I was trying not to disturb you living folk."

The bull head smiled. "I felt this weird compulsion, and had to yield to it. Then I discovered it was you."

"I was practicing on animals, not people."

"I am part animal. That must be why I felt it and Dawn didn't. It also happens I can see better in darkness than regular people can, so I wasn't concerned."

Oh. "I apologize."

"Don't. I was restless anyway, because of the magnitude of the change in my life. Suddenly I am consorting with skeletons and an invisible giant. That takes time to get used to."

"I could play pacification music to make you relax and sleep."

"Please don't. I felt it before, but was able to resist it, maybe because I am only part animal. I will return now, and probably sleep."

"I'll return too," Picka said. "I have practiced enough tonight."

"This monster you speak of," Adora said as they walked back. "He must be some musician, if he is better than you."

"He is," Picka agreed morosely. "But if you should encounter him, as you may while you are with us, stay as far away as you possibly can. Piper—that's his name—is as dangerous as he is ugly. I seem to be the only one who can fight him, with my music, and the best I can do is thwart him when he's focusing on some other challenge. Alone, I can't match him, let alone defeat him."

"I will remember. But if he does come after you, I will try to remain close enough to open a door for you and the others, so you can get away from him. That is the only way I can repay your kindness to me."

"That will do," Picka agreed. He liked Adora, but of course that was her nature: to be adorable.

"If you don't mind my asking, why do you have to fight the monster? I mean, I know he's chasing you, but why?"

"He wants to marry the princess, so he needs to eliminate me and overpower her. A woman, Pundora, has her own grudge, so is helping him. He won't stop until he wins—or we do."

"Oh! that's awful!"

Picka shrugged. "It's just the way it is. That's why I warned you about him. He's not after you, so will probably ignore you unless you get in his way. Just be careful. Very careful. He can enchant you with his music so you can't resist."

"Now I understand," she said. "Thank you."

They reached the handbag, and Picka helped her scramble up to its rim and over. In the course of that he got an excellent look up under her skirt. He winced; she was such a nice person, and couldn't help that there was so much flesh on her bones. He had developed a tolerance for Dawn's flesh because he loved her, but other flesh still turned him off.

They settled down, and this time Adora slept soundly. Picka was relieved.

"She followed you out?" Joy'nt inquired.

"I played animal-summoning music, and she responded, being part animal. I didn't realize."

"You are still learning the potentials of that music."

"Joy'nt, give me your honest opinion. Can I ever get good enough to defeat the monster alone?"

"Oh, Picka, I hate to say it, but I doubt it. That thing simply has so many pipes and so much power! But don't give up; there's always a chance."

"Thank you." She had echoed his own assessment.

In the morning the living folk finished off the pies, pods, and snacks, did their attendant ablutions, and were ready to travel. The group of them rode in the handbag, and enjoyed seeing Adora's awe as it sailed up and across the landscape. "We're really invisible from outside?" she asked.

"Granola, could you take a couple of us in your other hand for a moment?" Dawn called.

"Readily, if you will trust me." The giantess reached down with her free hand.

They located it by touch, then Dawn and Adora climbed onto it and were lifted away as if flying. "Oh!" Adora exclaimed. By the time the two returned to the handbag, Adora was convinced.

"You know, this is the weirdest adventure, and you are the weirdest collection of folk I never imagined being part of. But I'm thrilled to be here, and though I hardly know any of you, I think I like you as well as any others I have met. Maybe it's because none of you see me as unusual, with my bull head. I mean, a Mundane bird, cat, dog, three walking skeletons, a lady invisible giant, and a princess—you are all as different in your ways as I am in mine. So you accept me. I really like that, and will be sorry to leave you."

"Princess?" Dawn inquired guardedly.

"Oh, bleep! Did I just put my hoof in my mouth? I'm so sorry!"

"I identified myself only as Dawn. Did you recognize me?"

"No, I—I don't know what to say."

"My fault," Picka said. "I forgot we hadn't told her that detail, and referred to you as the princess."

"Why didn't you say that?" Dawn asked Adora.

"I—didn't want to—I'm sorry."

"She didn't want to put Picka on the spot," Joy'nt said.

"You *are* a nice girl," Dawn said, and kissed her on her furry ear. "It's all right. But please don't refer to me that way to others. It would be hard for me to relate on a personal basis if they knew, and could interfere with our mission."

"I understand. I will. I mean, I won't." Adora was still flustered.

Granola slowed, then stopped. "I believe we're here." She set the handbag down, carefully so as not to make a noise.

They peered out through the bag. They saw a glade filled with enormous mushrooms. A man with a sword was hacking them apart. Pieces were flying up and out. One landed in the bag.

Skully caught it. "It's a slice of bread!" he said, amazed.

"Let me see," Adora said. She took it and bit into it. "Yes, it is. A big edible piece. Mind if I finish it?"

"Welcome," Dawn said. "There's evidently plenty more where that came from. But why would a man want to hack apart growing loaves of bread?"

"A crazy man," Adora said. "Maybe his mother was scared by a giant loaf, so he hates all loaves."

"Or his father was a loafer," Joy'nt suggested.

"Stranger things happen in Xanth," Dawn agreed. "Let's move on."

"I apologize for the miscue," Granola murmured, lifting the handbag. She carried it a few of her steps, which would have been ten times as many of their steps. "But I'm sure that what we want is somewhere around here. Maybe Woofer will be able to sniff it out."

"We can try that," Dawn agreed.

Granola set the bag down again. They looked out again.

There was a cheerful-looking man sitting at a table loaded with pies, milk pods, boot rear, and piles of cookies. It was perhaps not surprising that he was obese.

"I'll start," Dawn said. "Maybe with Woofer."

No one argued. She was the normal one, who wouldn't spook a stranger. Woofer would be there to guard her if she needed it.

They helped Dawn and Woofer make themselves presentable and scramble out, quietly, behind a beerbarrel tree. They walked around it and approached the table, reacting as if surprised to discover it there.

"Hello," Dawn said. "Are we intruding?"

"A pretty girl and handsome dog like you two can never intrude," the man said genially. "I'm Fattila the Fun. Are you hungry? Have some pie, and I may have a dog biscuit here somewhere."

They joined him at the table. "Thank you. I'm Dawn Human, and this is Woofer Dog. We were looking for someone named Battila. Are you related?"

"Pretty much," Fattila agreed. "We're a wide family." He patted his belly. "Though I'm the widest. I gathered breakfast for the others, who should be along soon. I'm sure they'll be glad to meet both of you. Try not to be nervous if some stare; we don't get to see many young women or Mundane dogs as pretty as you."

Sure enough, a group of others approached the table. They paused when they saw the two visitors, but Fattila waved them in. "We have guests this morning. Dawn and Woofer. I'm sure they have an interesting story to tell. Introduce yourselves."

The others came on in and settled around the table, taking food. The men did look mostly at Dawn, while the women looked at Woofer. "I'm Gattila the Gun," one said, showing his formidable weapon. "Don't worry; I use it only for target practice."

"I'm Rattila the Run," the next said. "I'll be happy to race you anywhere."

"Don't do it," the next said. "It's a rat race. I'm Nattila the Nun. I'm sure you'd like it in our nunnery."

"And don't do that," the next said. "Once you go there, you'll never get out of the habit. I'm Sattila the Sun. I can really brighten your day."

"He means *his* day," the next said. "Forget about habits; he'll get you out of your clothing so he can tan your bare flesh. I'm Hattila the Hun. If you need a fancy hat, I have it." Indeed she wore a very fancy hat.

"And I'm Pattila the Un," the last one said. "It used to be Pun, but Attila stole my name, leaving me with his vowel. If I ever catch him, I'll take it back."

"You can take it back now," Dawn said. "Attila is no more."

They all looked at her. "What happened?" Pattila asked.

"He was smiting puns. When he realized he was a pun himself, he smote himself and puffed into nothingness."

Fattila shook his head. "I always knew he would come to no good end. He was always too serious."

"We were actually looking for Battila," Dawn said.

"Battila the Bun," Gattila said. "He slices bread. He must have found another loaf and been too busy to come here this morning."

In the handbag, Picka turned to Joy'nt. "Battila the Bun! He's the one we saw before."

"The next-to-last place Granola looked," she agreed.

Dawn stood. "Thank you, all of you. This has been enlightening."

"We'd be happy to entertain you here," Rattila said, eyeing her torso.

"No, I think he is the one we want." Dawn and Woofer returned to the hidden handbag.

"How does Battila deserve such luck?" Sattila asked as they departed.

The others were ready. The moment Dawn and Woofer rejoined them, Granola lifted the bag and headed back the way she had come.

They were in luck. Battila was still finishing off the buns. Now Picka realized that he looked a lot like Attila. Maybe it was the attitude.

"I believe this could work, if we can talk him into it," Dawn said.

"That means he'll have to meet the rest of us," Picka said.

"Yes. let's give it a try."

Dawn glanced at Adora. "This could be awkward, possibly even dangerous, and you are not familiar with our maneuvers. You had better remain in the handbag, and Granola can lift you out of the way if there's an immediate threat."

"As you wish," Adora said. "But if I see the need for a Door, I'll make it."

"That will be fine," Down agreed. Picka knew she simply did not want Adora in the way if things got complicated.

They piled out and approached the man as he chopped up the last bun. "Battila?" Dawn called. "I have a proposition for you."

"Well, now," he said, gazing at her. "I'm interested."

"Not me," Dawn said hastily. "There's another girl you might like."

"Ah, but will she like me?" Battila asked. "Girls can be notoriously choosy."

"They can be," Dawn agreed with the hint of a quarter smile. "Maybe we can arrange for the two of you to meet."

"Any time."

There was a crashing in the brush. "She's this way," Pundora's voice called. "But he'll be with her. Remember, you have to eliminate him first, or she won't accept you."

"They've found us already!" Picka said, amazed.

"That magic mirror must have known where we would be before we got here," Joy'nt said. "So they could travel through the night and intercept us."

The monster burst into view. "There they are!" Pundora cried from his back. "Get him now! Wipe him out!"

Piper cruised directly toward Picka, making surprising speed, his music revving up. His flesh was almost liquid, flowing across the terrain, the pipes emitting massed musical notes. It was impressive and frightening.

Battila was caught in the middle. He drew his sword and faced the monster. "Get away from here," he called to Dawn. "I'll cover your rear, so to speak."

"No, don't try to fight the monster!" Dawn cried as she and Picka ran to get there.

But Battila was already striding toward Piper. "Time to face the music, doughboy!" he said. He was clearly no coward.

"No!" Picka and Dawn cried almost together, coming up behind Battila. But it was too late; they could not avoid the monster regardless.

Then Adora appeared right between them as she scrambled out of the handbag. "Here's your Door!" she cried, gesturing.

A huge Door appeared in the ground before her. It opened downward, and they jumped in.

But Battila avoided it. He ran around the edge toward Adora. "I'll save you, maiden!" he called. He sheathed his sword, swept her up in his arms and jumped into the pit.

Then Granola jumped too, following them, and the door closed above them just as the monster arrived.

The group of them landed on a flowery hillside, scattered in assorted awkward positions, but unhurt. The giantess had managed not to land on anyone.

Battila was still holding Adora. "That was the bravest thing I ever saw!" she exclaimed. "You swept me up without even knowing me."

"Well, we were about to be introduced," Battila said. "I couldn't let that gooey monster get you before we had a chance to get to know each other."

Picka exchanged an eyeless glance with Joy'nt. Battila thought Adora was the girl he was supposed to meet!

"Oh, that's not—" Adora started to protest.

Battila, ever a man of action, stifled her protest by kissing her on the mouth. A little heart flew up.

"Oops," Joy'nt murmured.

"She was right," Battila said. "You are another girl I could like. But how do you feel about me?"

"Haven't you noticed?" Adora said. "I'm a bull head."

He looked again. "Why so you are. Hoofs, too, and with the cutest body I ever saw. And I guess it was your magic that made the Door that saved us all. What's your point?"

She looked halfway flustered, but not cowed. She kissed him. This time two little hearts flew up.

Dawn, witnessing this, made a minor gesture of throwing up her hands. "I'm sure you'll be very happy together," she said.

Their plan had messed up, but it wasn't a complete loss. They had found Adora a romance.

17
DIVERSION

Battila and Adora were happy to remain on the sloping field, where there was plenty of grazing and some buns growing. They were hardly aware of the others. So soon enough Granola was carrying the group back toward the brothers. Because they needed to fetch another one for Pundora.

"Meanwhile, as we travel, practice your music," Dawn told Picka. "You didn't have a chance to unlimber your clavicles that last time, but it was close; next time you'll have to fight the monster off."

"I know it," Picka agreed. "But I'm still not at all sure I'll ever be good enough to—"

She grabbed his clavicle and bonged him over the head with it. It made a surprisingly mellow note. "I won't listen to that. You are bleeping well going to get good enough."

"Yes, dear," Joy'nt said for him, and they all laughed. But it was serious business.

"Work on the chords," Dawn directed. "That's one area Piper has you beat."

Hardly the only area. Picka played chords by using both ends of his clavicles simultaneously. He could play up to four notes that way, rapidly improving.

"We have done some four-part harmonies," Granola said from above. "Can you do more than one part yourself?"

Picka tried it, and succeeded. It was like playing special chords. "That's beautiful," Dawn said appreciatively.

"What about the parts of a round?" Skully asked.

Picka tried to play two voices of "Ghost of Tom," but got so fouled up that a clavicle flew out of his hand when he started the overlapping second voice. "It seems not," he said regretfully.

"But suppose the monster can do it?" Dawn asked. "You can't afford to be inferior in any respect."

Picka tried again, and again. Chords were one thing, parts another, but this was a single melody done in four overlapping stages. It required a different type of musical coordination. He failed repeatedly, which was not a thing he liked.

"You can do it," Dawn said.

"But it—"

She kissed him on the skull. "Don't make me get mushy."

He tried again. This time he succeeded, at least in part. He managed to overlap the first and second voice for a few beats before losing it. Nevertheless, the others applauded. It was, after all, progress.

After a while they paused for what Dawn called a rest stop. It seemed she was not about to perform certain natural functions while they bounced along in the handbag. Granola set them down, and Dawn climbed out. "You too, Picka," she said.

He had learned not to try to argue with her. "I need a place that is safely private for five minutes," she said.

He looked around. This particular section was hilly and sandy without any private spots.

Then a woman walked by. "Hello," she said. "I am A Sist. Is there anything I can do for you?"

"I can't tell her nature," Dawn murmured.

Picka did not quite trust this. "I don't think anyone else can do what she needs at the moment. Why do you want to help?"

"I am a minor demoness," she replied. I used to be D Sist, interfering with people. Then I interfered with a donkey-headed dragon, and suddenly I was reversed, and now I must help anyone once before moving on."

"Ah," Dawn said. "In that case, where is there a private spot for a natural function or two?"

"Over there," A Sist said, pointing.

Picka looked. There was a ring of bushes that he hadn't noticed before, providing perfect privacy.

"Thank you," Dawn said. But A Sist had already moved on, having done her duty.

Before long Dawn was done, and they returned to the handbag. No more was said about the matter.

In the afternoon they reached the area where the Attila siblings lived. Now they could try again to set up their ploy. They decided that limited candor was best.

Fattila the Fun remained at his table. Apparently eating was his main endeavor. Dawn and Woofer approached him and were welcomed, as before.

"We recruited Battila," Dawn said. "He now has a girlfriend he likes. She has a bovine head, but is a nice person with a nice talent. We would like to recruit another brother, for another woman. Do you think any of your brothers would be interested?"

"Gattila the Gun," he said immediately. "He's quite a man for the ladies. Is she pretty?"

"Oh, yes. But her personality can be vicious."

"So much the better. He likes them lovely and tough."

"At present she associates with a vicious monster. That monster wants to abduct and marry me, and she encourages him. So I want to get her interested in somebody else, so that she won't be able to help the monster come after me. That is my personal interest. Do you think Gattila would understand?"

"He doesn't care about social complications. All he wants is a tough, good-looking creature who likes him back."

"Then I think he's our man," Dawn concluded.

"Here they come now," Fattila said.

The other siblings appeared, bearing harvested pies and pods. They settled down around the table.

"You will remember this pretty lady and dog," Fattila said. "She found Battila a girlfriend. Now she's back."

"Gattila," Dawn said. "I know a pretty woman who might like you."

"Bring her on," Gattila said.

"She will arrive soon. But she will be with a monster. The monster may not like losing her."

"Maybe a whiff of grapeshot will make him amenable." Gattila brought out his gun and a cluster of purple grapes. He loaded a grape into the gun.

"I'm not sure that will suffice," Dawn said. "This is one tough monster."

"No?" Gattila aimed the gun at the nearby beerbarrel tree. He pulled the trigger. The gun fired with a loud bang and a puff of smoke. The tree sprung a hundred small leaks, spraying beer onto the ground. It seemed annoyed as it labored to plug the leaks with tendrils.

"That is impressive," Dawn said, "but it might only annoy the monster and make him come after you. You don't want that. You see, the monster attacks with paralyzing music that can reach you at a distance."

Gattila produced a cherry and loaded it into his gun. "A greater distance than this?" He aimed the gun at a distant spire of stone. He fired. The top of the stone exploded, sending fragments and red cherry juice raining down around it.

"Possibly," Dawn said. "It also might not be set back by an explosion of that magnitude."

"This might be a challenge," Gattila said zestfully. He produced a slice of pineapple and pressed it into the gun. He aimed at a distant boulder. He fired. The boulder became a ball of fire that converted to roiling smoke and ascended into the sky in a vaguely mushroom-like configuration.

"I think it would be better simply to impress the woman, and take her away with you," Dawn said.

"Not if the monster chases me to get her back," Gattila said. "Better to dispatch him at the outset and be done with it."

"The monster is really after me," Dawn said. "The woman has a mirror that enables her to locate me. But if she deserts him, he won't be able to follow me—or you. That should nullify him."

Gattila shrugged. "I don't care about personal complications. You say this woman is pretty?"

"She is. You will be able to verify that for yourself when they show up. If you don't like her, you can ignore her."

"Does she pack heat?"

"Yes, but not in the form of a pistol. She's a fiery creature, and loyal to her man. She once dated Attila, until he self-destructed."

"I like her already."

"Then here's what you should do," Dawn said persuasively. "When they show up, stand up straight and call to her so she can see you. Ask her to come to you. If she does, kiss her and take her far away, immediately, before the monster realizes what's happening. Once you have her alone, you can surely do what you want with her."

"That sounds great! But why should she come to me?"

"Because you look a lot like your brother Attila, whom she loved. Be like him, act like him, and she should be more than ready to have you in his place."

"That makes sense," Gattila agreed. Like most fleshy males, he had an exaggerated notion of his appeal.

Joy'nt turned to Picka, in the handbag. "She can really manage a man."

"So I have discovered," he agreed. "She can manage a skeleton too."

Dawn talked Gattila into separating from his brothers so that they would not be in danger. She brought him around to the handbag to meet the others, who obligingly climbed out.

"Walking skeletons!" Gattila exclaimed.

"Tame ones," Dawn said quickly. "Here is Picka Bone, my fiancé. He plays music on his ribs."

"I can play music by bouncing bullets off different rocks," Gattila said.

"This is similar," Dawn agreed. "This is his sister, Joy'nt, and her boyfriend, Skully Knucklehead. We also have an invisible giantess in our party, but you can't see her."

"Where's this woman I'm to get?"

"That's Pundora. She should be along soon. In the interim we will entertain you with some music."

They did. Gattila was plainly bored but put up with it.

Then there was distant pipes music. Piper was arriving.

"Remember," Dawn said hastily. "Wave to Pundora. Make sure she sees you. You want her to come to you."

"I got that," he agreed.

The music grew louder. The local animals fled. The monster was clearing the area of anything that might interfere. All he wanted was Dawn. And to be rid of any competition for her.

They came into sight. The monster was flowing rapidly across the terrain, with Pundora riding on his back. He was heading straight for Dawn. His music shifted.

Dawn started to walk toward him, compelled.

"Go for Picka first," Pundora reminded him. "Get him out of the way so he can't balk you with his music."

Reluctantly Piper obeyed, knowing she was right. It did not require much of a change, since Picka was standing beside Dawn.

Picka took off his clavicles and started to play. That blocked the summoning music, and Dawn stopped walking. "Call to her," Dawn said to Gattila. "Now!"

Gattila had been distracted by the sight of the monster. Now he remembered his own mission. "You're right! She's beautiful." He took a breath. "Hey, Pundora!" he called. "Come give me a smooch!"

Pundora looked at him and almost fell off her perch. "Attila!"

"No, I'm his brother. Gattila the Gun."

"His brother! I didn't know he had one."

"He has several. I'm the manliest."

"You look just like him!"

"Built just like him too," Gattila said proudly. "Come here and I'll show you."

Pundora considered half a moment, no more than two-thirds of a moment. Then she jumped off the monster's back and ran toward Gattila.

Meanwhile Piper, focusing on Picka, didn't notice. That was fine. Picka increased the tempo of his music, not only nullifying the monster's music but causing the fleeing animals to pause. His object was not to beat the monster back so much as to distract him long enough for Pundora to leave him, if she was going to.

Pundora ran right to Gattila. "What's your talent?" she asked. "It can't be abolishing puns."

"It's my gun," Gattila said. "I can shoot anything." He drew his big pistol. "Do you want me to shoot something?"

"Not yet. Let's see how you kiss."

"No problem!" He holstered his gun and grabbed her. He pulled her roughly to him, put his hands on her bottom, and smacked her face with a huge sloppy kiss.

"Uh-oh," Dawn murmured. "No halfway decent girl will go for treatment like that."

After a moment and a half he drew back. "How's that?"

"That's pretty good," Pundora agreed. Then she put her hands on his bottom and planted an even more slobbery kiss.

"She's not halfway decent," Joy'nt said.

"Great!" Gattila said. "Let's go somewhere else and get serious."

This time Pundora pondered only a quarter of a moment. "Yes, let's."

The two started walking away together. "I counted on her fickleness," Dawn murmured.

But now the monster caught on that Pundora was no longer with him. He played an angry note.

"Oh, go away," Pundora said carelessly. "I have found another man, so I don't need revenge for Attila anymore. I never liked you much anyway."

Picka, Dawn, and the others remained still. Could their ploy be working this well this soon?

The monster played a louder, angrier note.

"Well, that was then," Pundora said. "This is now. I'm out of here." She resumed her walk with Gattila.

But Piper wasn't having it. He needed Pundora to track Dawn. He did not want to let her go before he had completed his own mission. He played loud music, of another variety.

Fire bombs exploded before Gattila and Pundora, barring their escape. Picka recognized the strategy: Piper did not want to hurt Pundora, because he needed her. Once he had Dawn, he would not care at all about Pundora, who had now betrayed him twice. He might destroy her with his kill-music. But at the moment he needed her with him, and unharmed. So he was fencing her rather than attacking her.

Battila, however, was not one to quit either. "So it's like that, eh, slug bomb?" he asked, drawing his gun. He put in a grape.

"Don't do it," Dawn murmured. "You can't prevail. Just run around the fire and get away before he can react."

"Good advice," Pundora said, agreeing with Dawn though it probably annoyed her to do so. "Let's run."

"The bleep," Gattila grated. He aimed the gun.

The monster was evidently not familiar with guns, which were rare in Xanth because most preferred Mundane science. He ignored this one, as he maintained a curtain of fire hemming the two in.

Gattila fired directly at Piper. A spray of grapeshot struck the monster's flesh.

Suddenly Piper understood about guns. He slid back, smarting. Goo oozed from multiple little holes.

Then the monster blasted Gattila with music. The man staggered and would have fallen, had Pundora not caught him and propped him up. And now Gattila understood about kill-music.

"They need help," Dawn murmured to Picka.

So they did. This was an odd temporary alliance, but what was needed at the moment. Picka played some notes of his own, and Gattila recovered mobility.

"Now run!" Pundora told him.

"The bleep," Battila repeated. He put a cherry into his gun.

"You're so pigheaded," Pundora told him. "Just like Attila. I love it. But we really must go now." She pulled on his free arm.

The monster fought off Picka's interference. Battila stiffened again. But before he fell he pulled the trigger.

A section of the monster was blasted out of the middle. Goo flew up and around. But the splotches that landed flowed back to the main mass, which healed as if it had not been injured.

"Run!" Pundora cried, pulling Gattila along. This time he yielded. He had not yet picked up on the fact that the monster wasn't dead.

Piper soon disabused him. More fire appeared before the couple, entirely surrounding them.

"I'll handle this," Pundora said. She drew her sword, which she had somehow concealed on her body. She sliced at the wall of flames, and the flames were cut off, leaving a gap. The two of them leaped through that gap and fled.

Piper played other music. The flames vanished, but this time both Gattila and Pundora stumbled, half stunned.

Picka played more nullifying music. The two people righted themselves and resumed running—until more flame appeared before them.

Gattila whirled, drawing his gun. This time he put in a slice of pineapple.

"No, you can't—" Pundora cried.

He fired. This time it wasn't just a section, but most of the monster's body that sprayed up in a roiling fireball. The fried fragments fell again, and reformed again, but by the time Piper was ready to resume action, the guilty couple was gone. They had made their escape. Gattila had gotten smart, and played for time rather than total destruction.

The monster evidently realized that, and gave up on the fruitless (apart from the pineapple) chase. Now he turned his attention to the true cause of this mischief: Dawn and Picka. His music intensified.

Dawn dropped to the ground, unconscious. Piper slid toward her.

Picka quickly put his clavicles back in place, bent, and picked Dawn up. He ran, carrying her.

The monster didn't dare hit them with fire, because that would burn Dawn. But by similar token, Picka could not defend them with his music, because his arms were occupied. All he could do was run.

Piper, it turned out, could slide faster than Picka could run. In three moments the forward extensions of goo were licking around Piper's feet. They curled around his ankle bones, tackling him. He dropped.

But Skully was there. He took Dawn and ran on with her. That freed Picka's arms. He unlimbered his clavicles and beat on the sides of his ribs. His music speared out, striking the tentacles that clung to his ankles with null magic. They shriveled.

Picka yanked his ankles from the mess and got back to his feet. He concentrated on his music. It blasted at the monster at point-blank range. And fire erupted amidst that flesh.

Piper recoiled as he hastily stifled the flames. Picka had caught him by surprise, and scored. But singed flesh was no worse than blasted flesh and almost immediately he was back on the attack, his music countering Picka's attack while his body advanced.

However, the break had enabled them to rescue Dawn, and it was clear that she was now beyond recovery by the monster. Skully would carry her to Granola, who would take them both well away from danger.

Piper raged at Picka, focusing his deadly music. The very ground Picka stood on fragmented into sand. But Picka fought back with his own music, and the ground the monster slid on fragmented similarly, unbalancing him. Every time Picka invoked the kill-music, he was better at it, and he was achieving parity.

Evidently realizing this, the monster veered away from Picka and cruised toward the table where Gattila's siblings remained clustered.

"Run!" Picka called. "Scatter! Don't let him get near you!"

"But we haven't finished our meal," Fattila protested.

"You'll never finish anything if he gets you," Picka warned. "He's mad because Gattila got the girl. He'll take it out on you."

"Now aren't you exaggerating just a little?" Nattila asked calmly as she bit delicately into a slice of angel food cake. None of them moved from the table as the monster bore down on them.

What folly! He would have to try to protect them despite their unrealistic attitude. He ran to the table, racing the monster. He played his ribs, balking Piper's deadly pacifying theme.

The monster arrived first. He plowed into the table, his juices starting to dissolve the wood. A streamer of goo flung out and looped Nattila's waist. She screamed, belatedly getting the point.

Sattila concentrated on the streamer. A sunbeam focused, becoming burning hot. The streamer sizzled and fell away, releasing the woman. She scrambled clear.

But now the music changed. Nattila straightened out, then moved toward the monster, compelled.

Did Piper want her for assistance, or eating? Was he looking for a replacement for Pundora? A nun was unlikely to be effective.

Picka countered the summoning music, and Nattila backed away. But Pattila was also approaching, similarly compelled. Picka extended his theme, and she too halted. "Get away!" Picka cried to them all.

Now at last they understood the personal danger. All of them backed away.

Fireballs appeared behind them. They couldn't retreat. Picka doused one fireball, then another, but new ones appeared faster than he could dissipate them. He had to come up with something more effective.

How did he douse individual fires? He explored the parameters of his own music, and discovered that it was water. He was conjuring splashes of water that struck the fireballs and extinguished their centers. That aspect was adaptable.

He worked on it, adapting his tune to make more water. That didn't help douse new fires, but did splash the old ones more effectively. He worked harder, locating and clarifying the key themes.

Water flowed. It overflowed. It spilled to the ground and coursed along the slope, soaking the ground. It spread in a minor flood, intersecting the other fireballs and extinguishing them. One by one they hissed angrily into steam. Soon all of them were gone, and the burning grass was also clear.

He had come up with a way to stop any amount of fire! The monster would no longer be able to use that against him.

However, Piper still held the several siblings captive by musical summoning and pacification. They looked uncomfortable, but stood in place, facing the monster. They were about to become slaves and/or food.

Piper held the monster off with his music, but he couldn't directly help the others while doing so. It was another impasse.

"Picka!"

It was Joy'nt. He had forgotten her in the throes of combat. "Yes?" he called over the dueling music.

"You can't beat him," she said. "He's a better musician than you are. But if you can slow him down long enough, I can carry these poor folk to safety. Woofer is guiding me, and Tweeter is guiding him from above."

"Do that," Picka agreed. It was easier to impede the monster than to defeat him.

Joy'nt went to Nattila, whose expression was one of divine horror. She spoke a few reassuring words, then picked the woman up and carried her away from the table. Piper fluted angrily, but his mesmerizing music could not control the skeleton, as it affected only living creatures. He could not stop her physically, because Picka was balking him with distracting music. It was tricky to do different types of things at once, as Picka knew.

Joy'nt walked away, following Woofer. Somehow they knew where safety was.

The monster intensified his music. The other siblings started to move toward him. Picka intensified his own music, playing so hard and fast that his clavicles almost seemed to blur. He was improving, but it was largely because of desperation; without it Piper would wipe him out.

The monster's music shifted. The ground under Picka's feet blasted out, leaving a small crater. Picka shifted his own music, and the crater widened until it undermined Piper's forepart. He was amending rather than excavating, turning part of the monster's power against him. It was the best he could do.

It worked. Piper backed off slightly, and ceased blasting sand. He returned his attention to the siblings, and they began to walk forward again. Pattila was closest, and a pseudopod wrapped around her thigh and drew her in closer. She opened her mouth to scream, but was unable to get the sound out.

Picka was fully occupied musically, and could not divert any notes to rescue her. So he stepped forward physically. He lifted a foot and kicked the pseudopod repeatedly until it was knocked loose. It tried to connect again, but he kicked it away again, this time pressing it down into the dirt and stomping on it.

Joy'nt returned. She picked Pattila up and carried her away. The monster seethed, but could not prevent it.

In similar manner Joy'nt was able to carry the rest of the siblings to safety. Only when the last was gone did Picka relax, letting his music fade.

The monster faded too. Stage by stage their music subsided, until at last there was silence. Picka did not trust this, but of course he trusted nothing about the monster except his viciousness. Was Piper tired, magically? Certainly Picka was.

There was a minor flash. Picka braced, but it did not seem to be an attack. Where had he seen something like that before?

"Picka Bone," the monster said.

Picka jumped. Had the thing actually spoken to him? "What?" he asked.

"I invoked the spell I got from Pundora, to make my notes intelligible as human speech, for a limited while. I want to talk with you."

The communication spell! They had seen it in the Caprice Castle History. "Yes." It was better to talk than to fight, though Picka did not trust any part of it.

"I give you a choice. Deliver the princess to me. Or else."

There was no way Picka would turn Dawn over to the monster! "Or else what?"

"Or else I will destroy you and take her anyway."

"Lotsa luck with that."

"Will you turn her over?"

"No."

"Then you must be destroyed."

There was something about the monster's attitude that made Picka believe it was not a bluff. Nevertheless, he bluffed it out. "Then do it."

The music resumed. This was a new and eerie theme. Something about it made Picka's very marrow uncomfortable. It intensified, and his joints felt strained. It intensified further, and his skull bone felt loose on his neck bone. In fact, his bones were disconnecting!

He played his ribs, trying to counter the theme, but it didn't work. His tune was wrong, and his limbs were losing cohesion, spoiling his ability.

Much more of this, and his body would be vibrated apart. He had to stop it. But how? This was a new theme, and while he might copy it, that would not nullify it. The monster did not seem to have bones, so would not be vulnerable to a reflected attack. Yet if it didn't stop soon, Picka would fragment, his bones falling in a loose pile, and the monster would be able to cover them and dissolve them in acid. He would indeed be destroyed.

And if that happened, there would be no one to stop the monster from taking Dawn, because only countering music could do that, and Picka was sure that he was now the only practitioner with the power.

The music became overpowering. His own music collapsed; he could no longer wield the clavicles. He jammed them back on his shoulders, lest he lose them. He seemed to be helpless before the onslaught.

Could he flee while his legs still worked? Maybe, but what would be the point? The monster would follow, and Picka would not be able to outrun it. Not even if his legs worked perfectly.

Then he got an odd notion. He was playing by the monster's rules, and losing. Could he change the rules?

He bent down to the ground. This was easy to do, as it was a collapse. But he had something else in mind. He put his two hands to the sand around him, pressed his finger bones together, and clutched two handfuls. Then he lifted his hands and flung the sand into the vibrating vents of the monster.

The notes soured as the sand fell in and clogged them. It was not a lot, but it didn't take much sand in the works to mess up a musical instrument other than Picka's own bones. The interference made the devastating melody less effective, and Picka was able to move more freely. He scooped up two more handfuls and threw them, fouling more pipes.

The music became grainy. The monster tried to blow out the sand but it was hard to clear, and Picka kept throwing in more. He had found his own attack that could not be used against him, using the same sand the monster had made by fracturing the ground around Picka. It would take Piper many hours alone to get all the sand clear. Even then he would have to beware of future encounters, making sure there was no sand.

Piper, stifled, had to withdraw. He pulled back, then fled. Picka had won this encounter, or at least made it another draw.

Just in time. His weakened joints could no longer sustain him. He sank to the ground.

Joy'nt returned. "Picka!" she cried, alarmed.

"Just get me out of here," he said, hugely relieved to have her back.

"Immediately," she agreed, picking him up.

18
CARNAGE

Soon enough they were back with the siblings, who were duly grateful for being rescued. "I never thought much about walking skeletons before, and never about dating one," Fattila said. "But I'd almost consider this one."

"I'm taken," Joy'nt said.

"Then all I can say is thank you for rescuing me from the monster," Fattila said. "We did not take him seriously enough. It was almost too late before we learned better. But you, Picka Bone, held him off, and you, Joy'nt Bone, carried us away. We wish we could repay you."

"You already have," Picka said. "Battila took Adora Bull, and Gattila took Pundora. That greatly improves our position with the monster, because he can no longer track Dawn." He sent an eyeless glance toward her. She smiled.

"However," Dawn said, "the monster remains dangerous. If you ever see him again, flee immediately."

"We will," Fattila said. He shook his head. "Who would ever have thought that such beautiful music could be so ugly!"

Soon they returned to the handbag, and Granola lifted them up, up, and away. She had stayed clear of the action, knowing that the monster could readily bring her down. She had been more useful keeping Dawn safe.

The giantess strode rapidly across Xanth until she came to the coast. She waded across to one of the temporary islands that appeared and faded on their own schedules. "I don't know what's here," she said, "but my feeling is it is where we want to be now."

They looked out on a nice landscape, girt with flowering trees. There was a lovely little house by a small lake. The handbag came to rest beside it.

A young woman emerged as Dawn climbed out and became visible. "Hello. Do I know you? I'm Sara Nade."

"I don't believe we've met before," Dawn said. "I am Dawn, a member of an unusual party in need of isolation for a while. Are we intruding?"

"That depends. Are there any men in your party?"

"No human men. Why is that important?"

"Because I'm avoiding them. Every man who ever sees me wants to serenade me. At first I thought it was romantic, but since they all do it, it soon became tedious."

"Is it the music you object to?"

"Not at all. Just being the center of attention, when I know it's not really me they care for."

"Then we should get along perfectly."

"Just how unusual is your party?" Sara asked, not entirely satisfied.

"It consists in part of three formerly Mundane pets who are learning magic talents," Dawn said. "A dog, a cat, and a bird. They are all nice."

"I love nice pets!"

"Then you must meet them." Dawn signaled the invisible handbag, and Picka and Skully lifted up the groundbound pets so they could join Dawn. Tweeter needed no assistance; he simply flew up and across to perch on Dawn's shoulder. "This is Tweeter Bird," Dawn said.

"Pleased to meet you, Tweeter," Sara said.

"Tweet!"

"He returns the sentiment," Dawn translated. "He also says you're a pretty girl."

"Are you making that up?"

"No. It is my talent to know about living things, so I understand him. He understands human speech, and is a sharp observer."

"Now I don't want to seem unduly suspicious, but—"

"Tell him to do something unusual," Dawn suggested.

"Fly to her other shoulder and face the other way."

Tweeter did so.

"I apologize for doubting," Sara said.

Woofer arrived. "This is Woofer Dog, who also understands you."

"Hello, Woofer."

"Woof."

Midrange arrived. "And Midrange Cat, ditto."

"Do you like catnip, Midrange?"

"Mew."

"He says—"

"I got that. I have a patch of it growing wild behind my house, and not much use for it. You can have any you want."

Midrange bounded around the house.

"We also have three walking skeletons," Dawn said.

"Walking skeletons! Are they haunting you?"

"Not exactly." Dawn signaled the handbag again.

Picka climbed out and approached them, giving Sara time to get used to him. "Hello, Sara," he said politely.

"Uh, hello." She was clearly taken aback, as most living folk were.

"This is Picka Bone, my fiancé," Dawn said.

"Your what?"

"He's a musician. You might say he serenaded me, and I fell for him."

Sara considered. "I've heard hundreds of serenades. He must be really good."

"Do you care to demonstrate?" Dawn asked Picka.

Pick took off his clavicles and played an intensely moving love song. Dawn melted visibly. So did Sara. Now he realized that there was an element of Summoning in it, compelling emotion beyond simple appreciation. He had had the ability before he understood its nature.

"That the most moving music I've ever heard," Sara said. "If any of my suitors had been that good, I'd be married."

"We face a musical monster," Dawn said. "Picka has to practice hard to get good enough to beat the monster. Otherwise I'll have to marry the monster. We thought this would be a good place for him to practice."

"It's the perfect place," Sara said. "I could listen to that quality of music forever."

"Picka's sister Joy'nt is also with us. And her boyfriend Skully." Dawn signaled, and the two climbed out and came to join them.

"Are you musical too?" Sara asked.

"We just play along with the others," Joy'nt said. "Were not musically talented ourselves."

"And finally we have an invisible giantess, Granola," Dawn said. "We traveled here in her invisible handbag."

"She's welcome too, if she watches where she steps," Sara said doubtfully.

"I am careful," Granola said.

"All we need is a place to practice," Dawn said. "We can go to a far edge of the island if you wish."

"I wouldn't think of it! I love music, as I said. I even sing."

"Then you are welcome to join us," Dawn said. "We'll teach you our signature song." She brought out her ocarina.

Before long they were doing "Ghost of Tom," and Sara sang one of the parts. She was good; her voice was clear and firm and exactly on key. It was a beautiful rendition.

That was the beginning of a very nice interlude. Sara took an interest in Picka and sang with him while he played, encouraging him to tackle the more difficult themes and effects. He could feel himself improving. Dawn showed no trace of jealousy, knowing that Sara's interest was purely musical. In fact, Dawn obviously appreciated the assistance. She still had more confidence in Picka's potential than he did.

Sara had a guest room, and made it available. Dawn and Picka took it. She made him invoke the transformation spell, and it had the same

effect as before, causing him to indulge in all manner of fleshly gratifi-
cation that she eagerly accommodated. If he had had the slightest incli-
nation to doubt his love for her, this would have abolished it. The next
night she invoked the spell, and had at him as eagerly in skeletal form.

How could he ever yield her to the monster? Yet still he doubted his
ability to prevail.

They worked more on "Ghost of Tom," because Sara liked it as well
as the others did. They used it as relaxation between bouts of serious
practice. Picka learned to play parts one and two while Dawn and Sara
did parts three and four. Then he tried parts one, two, and three, and went
to pieces, figuratively; it was just too tricky to manage.

At other times he practiced the kill-music. Sara needed gravel for
permanent paths around the island. She had a little quarry, but it con-
sisted largely of stones and boulders, the free sand having been taken
long before. Picka went there and played rock-cracking music, reducing
stones to sand with increasing proficiency. He now knew that this ability could be especially useful against the monster.

There was also a patch of mean-spirited thistles that liked to stab
any legs that ventured within range. Picka practiced pacification music
that intensified and made the thistles wilt and shed their prickles and
finally vacate the premises entirely. He likewise tried the reverse, to make
tougher and meaner thistles, though he wasn't sure they would impede
the gelatinous monster. It was best to be prepared in any possible way,
just in case.

Sara was also a willing subject for attraction/repulsion music, knowing that Picka had no designs on her living body. She tried to resist,
to give him practice, but could not; she came toward him when he
summoned, and retreated when he repelled. Then Dawn and Sara got
together, and he attracted one while simultaneously repelling the other.
That was precise control, another step forward.

And the fire and water balls. They made a pile of brush, and he practiced igniting it with fireballs, then extinguishing it with waterballs. When
he was able to light one side of it while wetting the other side, they knew
he was there.

"You are better at kill-music than at melody music," Joy'nt remarked.

"It's cruder," he agreed. "Just a matter of invoking the correct themes. But real music takes years to perfect, and I haven't had those years."

"And the monster has," Joy'nt agreed. "So you had better focus on defeating him with kill-music."

"But I'd prefer to be a great musician!" he protested. "Rather than a destroyer."

"You won't be anything if you can't stop his kill-music."

She was right. Reluctantly he returned to practicing the deadly forms. But between times he practiced quality themes, just for the joy of it. Sara always came to listen to those, and so did Tweeter, who turned out to be a fair connoisseur of music. The bird did not sing much himself, but song was evidently in his bloodline, and he liked it.

Picka also practiced the healing music GoDemon had taught him, simply because it felt better to heal than to hurt. He obviously was not cut out to be a warrior, regardless of the weapon.

As it happened, he got a chance to use it. Woofer sniffed too avidly at an obnoxious plant and got scratched by a thorn. The wound wasn't dangerous but it was painful, perhaps because of caustic sap. Picka played healing music, and slowly the pain became discomfort, and the discomfort faded, until the dog was better. "That's wonderful," Sara said. "The cure music is prettier than the kill-music."

They were safe from a raid by the monster, because now he lacked Pundora's magic mirror. But that meant that soon enough things got dull. Joy'nt and Skully weren't bothered, because they had each other and liked boning up on mutual interests. Picka and Dawn also had each other. But the other four members of their party became restless.

"Maybe you should go out and check on the monster," Dawn suggested. "Just in case he's up to something he shouldn't be." As if there was any proper monster pursuit.

Granola consulted with the pets, and they concluded that this might indeed be worthwhile. She could carry them to some likely site, where the others could spread out. Her talent could not take them directly to what they wanted, but she could show them interesting places, give up the search, then back off to the prior stop, where there might indeed be something worth checking. The pets had come to know and trust Granola, and she was getting better at interpreting their woofs, meows, and tweets.

They got together with Dawn and the skeletons to present their decision. "So we aren't deserting you," Granola concluded. "Merely going out to check. We'll return often to report on what we have seen."

A ball of smoke formed over the outdoor hearth they had, but there was no fire in it. Had the monster found them and hurled a fireball?

"No, it's only Demoness Metria," Dawn said with resignation.

A head poked out of the smoke. "Are you contemplating something evaporating?" she inquired.

"Something what?" Sara asked innocently before the others could caution her.

"Heating, blowing, gripping, drying, absorbing—"

"Interesting?"

"Whatever," Metria answered irritably.

"No," Dawn said. "It's absolutely dull."

"So it wouldn't relate to monster searching?"

"You've been listening!"

"I admit to nothing," the demoness said. "But that monster is some character, and he thinks you will marry him. That seems like an interesting development."

"The pets and I mean to go out looking for him," Granola said. "You are welcome to come along."

"Why would I want to go anywhere I was welcome?"

"Because otherwise you might have to stay here where we don't want you and listen to us practice music," Picka said.

The rest of the demoness formed, a dusky figure with overflowing bra and panties stretched to the tearing point. Unfortunately the show was wasted on women and skeletons. "But if they find something awful, then you would have to go there too," Metria said. "That would be interesting."

"Why?" Dawn asked. "I mean, why would we go near the monster? We have no business we want to do with him."

"Oh, I can think of a reason," the demoness said.

"What reason?" Dawn demanded.

Metria shook her head. "That would be telling."

Trying to question her would be a waste of time. "I think we should let them go, while we practice," Picka said. "With luck, both groups should be utterly boring."

"Maybe sew," the demoness said.

"Maybe what?" Picka asked before he caught himself.

"Stitch, fix, fasten, secure, tailor—"

"So?" Dawn asked impatiently.

"Whatever." The demoness smiled, knowing that Dawn had not intended the word as an answer, but as a "what's the point?" demand. "So I had better see about making it interesting."

"How could you possibly do that?" Dawn snapped.

"By serving as liaison, instantly communicating to you whatever important discoveries the explorers make."

"But that would be useful," Picka said.

"A side effect. Mainly it would stir things up, and put me in the center of remarkable action."

"I don't see how." Picka was normally even tempered, but the demoness was getting to him.

"That's because your empty skull lacks brains," Metria explained helpfully.

"Oh, she'll do what she wants to, regardless," Dawn snapped. "We'll just ignore her and get on with our business."

"Or so you think," Metria said slyly, and faded out.

"That creature can be so annoying!" Dawn said.

"We'll be on our way, then," Granola said. She flattened the handbag so Woofer and Midrange could readily enter it, then lifted it up, making them invisible. Tweeter flew down into it, disappearing in midair.

"Farewell!" Joy'nt called, and was answered by a medley of woof, meow, tweet, and "Thank you" run together, followed by a stirring of the water as big invisible feet displaced it at regular intervals. They were on their way.

"Do you think she really will?" Skully asked.

"There's no telling," Dawn said. "She will calculate the path of maximum annoyance, and follow that. But I simply don't see how acting as liaison will accomplish that."

"You will," the air said, followed by a whiff of brimstone odor. The demoness hadn't quite gone, as was often the case.

"That's some character," Sara said.

"Oh, Metria has her points," Dawn said. "She was stepped on by a Sphinx centuries ago, and it fractured her personality. Her alter ego D. Mentia is a bit crazy, but doesn't foul up words, and her other alter ego is a rather sad, sweet child named Woe Betide. Metria's married, though you wouldn't know it by her escapades." She paused, listening, but there was no response from the air. The demoness was really gone this time.

They resumed music practice, and thought no more of Metria. Picka was steadily improving, but still doubted that he was good enough now, or would be in the likely future.

Evening came. "It seems quiet," Joy'nt said.

"Granola and the pets are gone," Picka reminded her.

"Oh. Yes. I miss them. They're nice folk."

"They are," Sara said. "So are you folk. I never got to know giants, animals, or skeletons before. Now I know they can be decent people, pretty much like regular humans."

"They can be," Dawn agreed.

Next morning Metria appeared. "Tweeter Birdbrain found an awful mess for you to disintegrate."

"To what?" Dawn asked.

"Decay, decompose, modify, alter, change—"

"Fix?"

"Whatever. It's urgent."

"Why should we accept that?" Picka asked.

"Because it's true."

"How do we know that?" Dawn asked.

"Because I brought a witness." The demoness made a flourish, and a man appeared. "This is Brant, who can answer any question without confusion."

"Brant, what is the situation?" Dawn asked grimly.

"A horrible monster raided an innocent girl's valuable beehives and ruined them, scattering the bees." He spoke with such clarity and authority that it was impossible to doubt him.

"What kind of bees?"

"Bumble, honey, sweat, spelling, and others. They are desperately needed by many communities for everything from pollination to schoolwork. The ripples will spread outward, doing increasing damage, unless the situation is repaired immediately." Again, there was no doubting him.

"So there," Metria said.

"I remember when my grandfather Prince Dor made a spelling bee help him," Dawn said. "It was a disaster. We do need tame spelling bees. And the rest." She sighed. "We'll have to go there. It's our fault the monster is on a rampage."

"But by the time we get there, more damage will have been done," Skully said.

"No. I have a motion spell I have saved for emergency use. This is an emergency. Gather round; you must be in contact with me."

"I'm so sorry to see you go," Sara said.

"We will return when we have done what we can," Dawn said. "We really like it here with you, and Picka needs to continue his progress on his music."

"That's a relief," Sara said. "I will be expecting you."

"Metria, if you are serious, guide me," Dawn said.

Then the three skeletons closed in around Dawn, and she invoked the spell.

Suddenly they were standing in a field of flowers. Beehives were overturned and broken apart all around. A young woman was amidst them, weeping.

"See?" Metria said, and faded out.

Tweeter was there, hovering helplessly. "Tweet!"

"I know," Dawn said. "You did right to summon us. This is a bad scene."

They separated, and Dawn approached the woman. "I am Dawn, and these are my assistants," she said. "We are here to help you."

"I'm Emily Bee Keeper," the girl said. "It's too late; my bees are scattered, and I fear I'll never recover them."

Dawn reverted to her princessly organization mode. "Picka, summon the bees back. Skully and Joy'nt, rebuild the hives. I will get more information from Emily."

Picka unlimbered his clavicles and started playing summoning music, attuning to bees. Skully and Joy'nt got to work on the hives, collecting their pieces, righting them, and fitting them together. Sometimes pieces needed to be cut apart and reassembled; Skully did that with his saw-edge arms. Combs were scattered across the ground, smeared with honey and clogged with tangles of hair; they fit these inside their hives. It wasn't perfect, but the bees would know what to do with them. The skeletons were far more efficient than living folk would have been, because the disturbed bees were stinging any living folk they encountered. Except Emily, whom they knew, and Dawn, who understood them so well that they had to understand her back.

While he played, Picka listened. Dawn, knowing all about Emily, had no need to interview her; she was actually diverting and reassuring her while the others worked.

"It was horrible," Emily was saying. "This ghastly blobby monster came sliding along on its goo like a giant slug and knocked over the hives. The bees stung it, of course, but it didn't seem to notice. It just seemed to be trying to do as much damage as possible, just for the bleep of it. I never saw anything so utterly malignant."

"That was Piper the Music Monster," Dawn said. "He is mad because I won't marry him, so he seems to have gone berserk."

"Who would ever want to marry him?" Emily asked.

"Well, if he marries a princess, he will revert to a handsome human man and get to live in a marvelous traveling castle. He won't be the monster anymore."

"You know this? You're a princess?"

"I am."

"Then why won't you marry him? It doesn't sound so bad."

"Because I love another."

"Oh."

Soon the hives were reasonably restored, and the bees were flying in in swarms. When they reached the hives Picka released them. Bees were quite useful creatures, but not phenomenally smart; when they saw the hives they went to them, forgetting what had happened. They resumed their normal activity, visiting flowers and tending to the combs. Some even did dances of joy.

"There," Dawn said when she saw that the job was complete. "Your bees have had a traumatic experience and will need comforting and supervision, but they should be all right now."

"They're back!" Emily said. "How—"

"My friends the skeletons are very good workers," Dawn said. "And not bothered by bees." She introduced the three of them to Emily, who after seeing what they had done, was not at all afraid of them.

"Thank you so much!" she exclaimed. "I thought all was lost."

"All has been regained," Dawn said.

"I must tell my best friend Erin," Emily exclaimed. "She was so sad she couldn't help."

"Erin?" Dawn asked.

"Erin Kitty Litter. She's a were-kitten, conceived at a love spring. Actually she's a were-cat now."

Picka saw Dawn's sudden interest. "Could I meet her?"

"Certainly. Here she comes."

A tawny cat was bounding toward them. When she arrived she transformed into a tawny-haired young woman. She was nude, but that didn't matter to Dawn or the skeletons. "The bees are better!" she exclaimed.

"These kind folk did it," Emily said. "Dawn wants to meet you, Erin."

"Sure. Any friend of Emily's is a friend of mine."

Dawn had taken her measure immediately, of course. "Erin, you're single. I'd like you to meet another friend of mine. He's a talented cat."

Erin frowned. "I don't necessarily get along with straight cats. I was banished from the Isle of Cats & Dogs for violating their littering law."

"They *have* no littering law," Dawn protested.

"Except against impure crossbreed litters. I'm not a pure enough cat for them."

Oh. "Midrange won't care about that. He's a special feline with a developing talent."

Erin caught on. "What about my human half?"

"He's tolerant."

Erin shrugged. "It won't hurt to meet him."

Picka realized that the pets were lonely for girlfriends, and Dawn had just acted to secure one for Midrange. It would surely work out.

"Now we must move on," Dawn said. She signaled the skeletons and they came to cluster around her. So did Erin. Tweeter remained aloof; he would be searching out other mischief. "Farewell, Emily."

Then they were back on the island. There were Sara and Brant, the straight talker, standing close together.

"We forgot about Brant!" Dawn said. "He got left behind. He must be furious."

But as they approached, and Emily and Brant faced them, they saw little kiss marks on their faces. "They're getting along!" Joy'nt murmured, always quick to pick up on romance.

"He's tone deaf," Sara explained breathlessly. "He can't serenade."

"I never considered it an advantage before," Brant said.

"And he is most expressive about . . . things," Sara said, blushing.

"I can imagine," Dawn said. Then she introduced Erin, who reverted to cat form.

They went to their place for musical practice. It felt incomplete because of the absence of Granola and the pets, but the point was to drill Picka, rather than simply to relax.

A smokeball appeared. "Ha! There you queue."

"Hello, Metria," Dawn said with resignation.

"You queue?" Skully asked.

"El em en oh pee—"

"Are!" he said. They were letters of the alphabet.

"Whatever. I have another report."

And the prior one had been valid. "Spit it out," Dawn said wearily.

"Your cat picked up on it."

"Midrange is slightly psychic."

Erin's ears perked.

"The demon's retreat has been messed up. It's a dream realm tailored to their needs, generated by a mortal woman the monster freaked out. Now they're getting into all sorts of mischief, lacking their place to go."

"But aren't *you* a demon?" Joy'nt asked.

"I get into mischief anyway. I specialize in it. I don't like the competition."

"One is more than bad enough," Dawn agreed. "We don't want hundreds of mischievous demons." She glanced at Metria. "Who is the mortal woman?"

"Nicola."

"Then we'll go to see Nicola."

The skeletons and Erin closed in on her, and they went to the site. There was the woman, sitting on her doorstep with little planets and squiggles circling her head. Demons were all around doing mischief.

"See?" the demoness said, as before, and faded out.

Midrange was there. "Meow."

"So it seems," Dawn agreed. "We'll do what we can."

"Mew." It was Erin.

Midrange reacted as if mentally electrocuted. "Mee-yow!"

"Exactly," Dawn said. "Midrange, this is Erin Kitty Litter. I'm sure you two will get along."

Erin arched and purred. Midrange seemed smitten. It was surely the beginning of a marvelous association.

They spread out, studying the situation. "It must have been just the sight of the monster that did it," Joy'nt said, "because the landscape is not torn up."

"Nicola," Dawn said.

The woman didn't answer. She was sealed in her freakout.

"I know all about her and her talent," Dawn said, "but I have no experience unfreaking folk. Normally I'm the one doing the freaking, flashing village louts. Eve and I used to do that for amusement."

A village lout happened to be passing by. Dawn hoisted her skirt just enough to flash half her panty, and the lout went into a half freak, staggering away.

The Demoness's cloud formed, in the shape of half a panty. "I can do that."

The lout staggered by the cloud, looked, and freaked out the rest of the way. He crashed into the brush, out of it.

"But can you unfreak a lout?" Joy'nt asked.

"Why would I want to?" The cloud faded.

"Normally a finger snap will do it," Picka said.

Dawn snapped her fingers. The lout recovered and lumbered away. The woman did not. It was evidently a more serious freak.

"We had better explore the situation," Dawn said. "Something may offer."

Now they focused on the surrounding demons. One was making disturbing music. That got Picka's attention. "Who are you?" he asked.

"Ban D," the demon said, and continued.

Another demon was generating small clouds that floated away, obscuring and wetting innocent things. "Who are you?" Skully asked.

"Cloud D, of course."

Another demon was intercepting villagers who were walking along the village path. They looked sober until they reached him; then they looked inebriated. "Who are you?" Joy'nt asked.

"Bran D."

Dawn approached a sugary, sweet-looking demoness. "And you?"

"Can D."

"I think I am beginning to appreciate why the villagers are annoyed," Dawn remarked.

They continued to check out the demons. There was Han D with many hands, Ran D who was sex crazed, Un D with panties, Win D who blew them off, and San D who spread beach sand all about. There was Gau D wearing high-fashion clothes, ID with many eyes, DDT killing mosquitoes, and DUI, who was chronically drunk. All were a nuisance.

"We're not getting anywhere," Dawn said morosely. "We need to somehow snap Nicola out of it. Then she can restore the dream setting, and the demons will flock back to it."

A hollow bone bulb flashed over Joy'nt's head. "Dreams are from the dream realm. We skeletons are from the dream realm. Disasters and panties freak people out. Walking skeletons freak people out. We should be able to connect to her, in a dream mode, somehow."

"But *how*?" Dawn demanded.

"Maybe by acting out a bad dream to get her attention, then leading her out of it. Picka's healing music could help."

"Healing music," Dawn said thoughtfully. "That may be worth a try."

"Maybe a song and dance," Joy'nt continued. "Skeletons in a grave-yard, like the standard opening bad dream."

"I'm not exactly a skeleton," Dawn said.

"Oh, but you could be, for long enough. Borrow Picka's spell, or I'll lend you mine."

"I could," Dawn agreed, seeing it.

They worked out a routine. Then Dawn borrowed Joy'nt's spell, and became a skeleton. That made two males and two females. They formed two couples and danced. Picka was able to dance, guided by Dawn-skeleton, while playing his healing music.

Midrange gazed on the scene. "Meow," he said approvingly.

"Nicola!" Dawn called. "Nicola Dreamer! Your dreams are back!"

The woman looked, vaguely startled.

They danced to Picka's healing music, two synchronized skeletal couples. Picka loved dancing with Dawn in bone mode; she was lovely and flexible, and she was an excellent dancer.

"This can't be real," Nicola said, "so I must be dreaming."

"Or making a new dream become real," Dawn called. "We know what happened: a monster came by and spooked you. But he's gone now, and you can return to your normal dreams."

"Now my dream figures are advising me!" Nicola said in wonder.

"We value your dreams and want them back in order," Dawn said. "The demons need their retreat."

"I wonder." Nicola focused, and a dream setting appeared, replete with all manner of things demons liked.

Immediately the surrounding demons took note. They piled into the dream setting and started entertaining themselves. The crisis was over.

They left Midrange and Erin to search out other mischief, and returned to the island just in time for Dawn to revert to fleshly mode. "That was fun," she said. "Mind if I keep the spell a while?"

"Welcome," Picka said. "I don't want to use it anyway." For one thing, he feared it was dangerous, because he could not play his music when his ribs were covered with meat. Suppose the monster came when he was in that state?

Brant and Sara were happy to see them back, and happy to leave them alone, having an interest of their own to pursue. So they had a quiet night. That was just as well, as it turned out.

19
RULES OF ENGAGEMENT

Because Metria was back in the morning. "Weaver found a mess," she reported.

"Who?" Dawn asked.

"Loomer, clother, spindler, threader, wefter—"

"Woofer!"

"Whatever. You have to get over there pronto."

"Get there how?" Skully asked.

"It's the right word, airhead. It means immediately."

"We'd better go," Dawn said grimly.

They gathered together and Dawn invoked the spell.

They landed in a crowded arca. There was music and food and laughter. No one seemed alarmed by the unexplained appearance of the skeletons. That was odd.

"Oh, my!" Dawn breathed.

None of the skeletons recognized it. "Where are we?" Picka asked.

"The North Village," Dawn said. "Where Great-grandpa Bink lived as a child. It's completely unimportant, except historically."

"These are North Villagers?" Joy'nt asked.

"No. I'm pretty sure most are visitors. You see, in an effort to make this dull village seem more interesting, in recent years they have sponsored a celebration. It's called the My Lady So Fair, and it is a fair sponsored by the local women, who hope among other things to attract the notice of handsome men from more civilized places. I don't know how well that works, but certainly many visitors come to compete in the games, win prizes, stuff themselves on pastries, and flirt with the girls. Many wear costumes, which is why our party isn't attracting attention."

"They think we're in costume!" Skully said.

"That's right. Maybe that's fortunate."

"But there's no disaster here," Joy'nt said.

"Woofer wouldn't spoof us," Picka said.

"But Metria might," Skully said.

"I did not!" a smokeball said.

"So what is going on?" Dawn asked evenly.

"Woofer tracked the monster to the edge of this village," the smokeball said. "He knew there was about to be a disaster, so I fetched you in time to avert it."

"Where is Piper now?"

"Just over the ridge to the north. Better hurry." The ball faded out.

"We have no choice but to trust her," Dawn said, obviously ill at ease about it. "We have to warn the people."

"But we don't want to generate a stampede," Picka said. "That would be mischief of its own."

"True. We'd better tell people individually, and ask them to spread the word, quietly but rapidly."

They tried. They spread out, bracing individual people. Picka approached a group of grease monkeys hanging out with fuel hogs. They were all in costume, of course; real grease monkeys were made of grease, and fuel hogs of fuel. "Danger is coming!" he told them. "You must get away from here!"

"Wonderful costume," a monkey responded. "It almost looks real."

"I'm serious," Picka said. "There's an awful monster coming."

"Great act too," a girl with a large belt said. On it was written CON-VEY HER BELT, and she glided as if being transported.

Picka realized that in this context, a costume fair, nothing would be taken seriously.

But he tried again. He approached a friendly-looking man, though he carried a sword. "Hello. I'm Picka and I have a warning."

"I'm Buddy. My talent is to become your best friend."

"There's a deadly monster approaching. You must spread the word and get well away from here."

"Yeah, sure," Buddy agreed jovially.

"But it's true!"

Buddy clapped him on the backbone. "Great act!" He moved on, making other friends.

Picka tried again. He approached a young woman. "I must warn you that there is great danger about to strike."

"Oh, I'm sure," she agreed, and kissed him on the cheekbone. "Ooo! You even feel real! My compliments on your costume."

"But—"

"I'm Shadow. My talent is to become a shadow." She winked. "It's real, not just a costume. So don't try to get too fresh. I'll disappear into darkness."

What use to continue? No one was listening. He wasn't sure he could blame them.

"Woof!"

"Woofer!" Picka said as the dog ran to him. "What's the news?"

"Woof!" he repeated urgently.

Picka took a not-so-wild guess. "The monster is just about to get here?"

"*Woof!*"

"Right. Bad news. We'll find Dawn. Maybe she'll know what to do."

They wound through the crowd in search of Dawn. But there were too many people; she was lost amidst them. So Picka unlimbered one clavicle and played a simple version of the summoning melody.

In barely two and a half moments Dawn found them. "That's a relief! At first I feared it was Piper, until I realized it was bonged rather than blown. Woofer! What's the news?"

"Woof!"

"Oh, bleep! Piper is bearing down from the north? Then we're too late. No one's listening to our warnings."

"Woof!"

"Oh, we still have a few minutes? Then we'd better try to use them well. I don't want to have to announce my status, but this time I fear I will have to. If I can just get the attention of the whole crowd, somehow."

"Woof!"

"You do? Well, bring them in, Woofer." She turned to Joy'nt. "Go with him, to explain verbally. We can't afford to waste any more time."

The dog ran off, following his nose. Joy'nt followed. Meanwhile Dawn set about making herself princessly. She reversed her jacket so that it became a royal robe, and produced her little crown from her purse. Picka wasn't sure how it had ever fit in there, but that was just one of the mysteries of the feminine state.

"Skully, form into a platform structure I can stand on, to gain elevation."

The skeleton obeyed, making a hollow box several feet high. Dawn climbed onto it and stood overlooking the throng.

Woofer returned, leading Joy'nt and three other people. They were young men whose eyes widened when they saw Dawn. Picka understood why; she was manifesting as a princess, and she was beautiful. If she breathed too hard they might even freak out. But she was being careful not to inhale deeply, and her gown was close about her chest, showing only an approximate outline.

"These are Justin, who can make a bubble of silence," Joy'nt said. "Alex, who has a rain bow. And Tuck, who can pause time for others, not himself."

Dawn looked dubious. "I'm not sure how such things can help."

"Woof!"

She looked surprised. "You're right! That may work."

Then there was the sound of pipe music. Oh, no! "The monster is arriving," Picka said.

Dawn looked at Tuck. "Can paused people still see and hear?"

"Yes," he said. "They can't react, but they can understand."

"Can you make an exception for me and my friends?"

"Only if you are touching me while I make the pause."

Dawn smiled. "We're used to that. Gather 'round, friends." She glanced at Justin and Alex. "You two too."

They closed on her, each touching her legs. Justin and Alex did so also, though they seemed diffident about touching a princess. Picka understood perfectly.

"Tuck, raise your hand." He did.

Then she reached down and took Tuck's raised hand. Now he seemed on the verge of freaking, but managed to hold on. "Uh, say when," he said.

"Now."

He concentrated. The sounds of the crowd quieted. Picka saw why: they were all paused in place.

"Alex, I need your rain bow," Dawn said.

Alex handed it to her. It was simply a colored bow of the kind that might decorate a package or a head of hair.

Dawn put it on her head. And suddenly it was raining on them all, but especially on her. Now Picka understood: a rain bow made it rain on the person wearing it. Of course.

"Is that the best you can do, Bow?" Dawn asked scornfully. Stung, the bow increased its effort, and the rain became a small storm centered directly above them. Lightning cracked, and a peal of thunder sounded. The rain completely soaked her.

What did she have in mind?

"Now release the pause briefly, Tuck," she said.

The hubbub resumed as the people reanimated. They turned to face the thunder, which was now the main noise.

"And restore it," she said. The people paused again, this time facing Dawn.

"Now, Justin, make your bubble of silence around the storm."

There was sudden quiet. Jags of lightning still flashed, but in eerie silence.

Dawn raised her voice. "Your attention, please," she called. "I am Princess Dawn. I am sorry to interrupt the festivities, but I have reason. I am here to warn you of a severe emergency. A destructive monster is bearing down on us all, and will do much damage if we don't flee promptly. So as soon as you are free to move, run, don't walk, south. Do it carefully so you don't trip and fall, and make sure your families and children are with you, but keep moving. Only when you are safely south of me can you afford to pause and look back, because the monster is really after me. I hope you understand, but if you don't, do it anyway. Now go!"

The pause ended. There was a flurry of motion. Then the crowd oriented and forged south.

But so did the monster, who had also been paused. Picka realized that they couldn't pause one without the others; otherwise it would have been a handy way to stop Piper.

"I can pause them again," Tuck said.

"No, that merely postpones the problem. Thank you for your assistance; now you should head south." She glanced at Alex and Justin. "Here is your rain bow back, Alex; it served well." She removed it from her hair and the rain ceased. She remained soaking wet, her clothing plastered to her torso, but seemed not to care, though the three young men were having trouble keeping their eyes clear of glaze. "So did your bubble of silence, Justin. Thank you."

The three headed south, gratified perhaps as much by the wet view of her as by their ability to assist her.

Unfortunately, the main mass of people did not move smoothly. They were panicked and not making the best judgments. Some banged into others; some got separated from their families in the crush. Overall they could not move efficiently, and the monster was gaining on them.

"Play pacification music," Dawn told Picka as she stepped down from the Skully platform so he could reassemble. "Just enough to calm them down."

That made sense. Picka took his clavicles and started playing as loudly as he could. He made the theme moderate so that it would take the edge off panic without eliminating concern.

It worked. The people started moving sensibly, and the misqueues eased. But the monster was still gaining, and would soon catch the rearmost people.

"We have to distract him," Dawn said. "Lead him somewhere else, so the people can get away."

"How?" Joy'nt asked. "The only thing he wants more than fresh living food is you."

"Exactly. I need to get over there."

"No!" Picka cried.

"I don't mean to give myself to him," Dawn said. "I mean just to show myself so he'll follow me. Then when he's well away from the crowd, I'll invoke the travel spell to escape him."

"But he will stun you!"

"True. Or summon me in to him. I'll need help."

"I'll go with you."

"No. You need to keep the crowd in order. Joy'nt or Skully can help me."

Picka was not much reassured. "Maybe you can get a faster ride. I see a centaur."

"Maybe," Dawn agreed.

Skully ran out to intercept the centaur, who was moving perversely north rather than south. The skeleton led him to their small group.

"Hello," the centaur said. "I am Checkoff Centaur. I am cursed to get everything wrong on the first try. So I don't know whether I can help you, unless you have some perverse need for failure."

"What about your second try?" Dawn asked.

"That I can usually get right. But you see, my first try is usually automatic, and by the time I realize it I am committed to a wrong course. I have banged into more trees I tried to avoid, and insulted more fillies I meant to compliment, and loosed more arrows at wrong targets than I can check off." He shrugged. "So I no longer carry a bow; it's dangerous."

"Can you carry me and my friend Joy'nt Bone to the monster? We could direct you, so you would not have to make directional decisions."

"That would work," Checkoff agreed. "But I can't see the monster from here."

"Neither can we. But Woofer will lead us."

Dawn and Joy'nt got on the centaur's back. "Move toward the monster," Dawn told Woofer. "Follow that dog," she told the centaur. Woofer started off at a dogtrot, and Checkoff moved that way without a problem, since it was Dawn's decision rather than his. Dawn, knowing everything about any living thing, knew how to neutralize his curse.

Picka and Skully watched them go. Picka continued playing, and Skully remained near to guard him in case of mischief. "I am not easy about this," Picka said.

"I think Dawn has something in mind," Skully said. "She's smart, for a meat figure."

"See if you can track their progress," Picka said, still nervous about their prospects.

"Kick my tail."

Oh. Yes. Picka gave him a good kick in the rear.

Skully flew into pieces and reassembled in midair. Now he was a tall pole with his skull at the top. "Hold me upright."

Picka couldn't do that and continue to play, so he paused his music, grabbed the pole, and jammed the bottom foot into the ground to that the pole could stand alone. Then he resumed playing just in time to prevent the moving crowd from messing up.

"They're moving along okay," Skully said from on high. "The centaur is running now, moving swiftly. They are closing in on the monster."

"Oh, I fear that!" Picka said.

"That's odd."

"What's odd?" Picka asked nervously.

"I thought Dawn was riding in front, but it's Joy'nt there. Not that it matters."

"Maybe they switched places."

"Maybe. But why would they take the trouble?"

That was curious, but they surely had reason. If they really had switched places. Picka couldn't remember which way they had mounted. It wasn't worth being concerned about.

"They are reaching the monster," Skully reported. "I see him orienting on them. Now they are dismounting. Dawn is bare."

"But he can catch them afoot!" Picka protested.

"He can as readily summon or stun the centaur," Skully pointed out. "Maybe they want to separate so Checkoff is not in danger."

"But what of Dawn?" Picka asked in almost living pain. "Going bare won't freak out the monster; he can control it. What is she thinking of?"

"Now she's standing there. Now she's walking toward the monster. Now—well now!"

"What?"

"Joy'nt is picking Dawn up. She's carrying her away. Woofer is with them. And the centaur is galloping right toward the monster."

"He must have bolted," Picka said, "and gone the wrong direction."

"Yes. Now he's colliding with Piper. He's stomping him with his four hoofs. He's not attacking, just running through the monster. Ooo, that must smart!"

"Indeed," Picka agreed. "That acid will burn his legs."

"I mean the monster, getting stomped like that. He's disorganized as the centaur runs to the north. Joy'nt's running north too, carrying Dawn. Maybe they'll rendezvous."

"So they can all outdistance Piper," Picka agreed. "That's a worthwhile strategy."

"But now the monster is moving again. He is closing on them as they rejoin the centaur. Woofer seems to be barking a warning. Dawn is dropping to the ground and running too. Oh!" He sounded surprised.

"What?"

"Joy'nt leaped onto the centaur's back and they are charging away. Dawn remains afoot. She's running east with Woofer. The monster is veering to follow her, of course."

"Of course," Picka agreed, feeling ill. Why had they done it? Not only was the monster not after the skeleton, he couldn't do her much harm anyway unless he played his joint-fracturing music, and what would be the point of that? So it should have been Joy'nt who ran, and Dawn who rode away to safety. What had ever possessed them to reverse it?

"The monster's gaining on Dawn," Skully said. "All that jiggling meat on her bones makes her slow. She'd better invoke the travel spell soon."

Oh. That was right. Dawn *could* escape alone. So the centaur would not be stunned and maybe eaten for trying to help her. It made sense after all.

"The monster's catching up to her," Skully reported. "He's throwing out a pseudopod. He's got her!"

"Invoke the spell!" Picka exclaimed.

"She isn't doing it. She's just standing there talking to him. Woofer is listening. And—I don't understand!"

"Understand *what*?" Picka cried in anguish.

"He's letting her go. She's walking away with Woofer."

"Impossible!"

"But it's happening. What could she have said to him?"

"Apart from agreeing to marry him?"

"Um, that would do it, yes."

"She wouldn't do that!" But Picka wasn't quite sure. He had never completely understood the complicated thought processes of meat heads or of females, bare or otherwise.

"What else could it be?"

The dialogue lapsed. What, indeed, else?

Meanwhile the crowd of people was still moving, now well away from Piper. Whatever else the diversion had or had not accomplished, it had given the people time to get clear. That had been Dawn's object. A number of them were now looking back, seeing what it was they had escaped.

Picka ceased playing his music; there was no longer need for it.

The centaur galloped up, with the skeleton still aboard. "Joy'nt!" Picka cried. "You were supposed to help Dawn! Why did you leave her to the monster!"

"Are you sure?" the skeleton asked.

"We saw—" He broke off. That was Dawn's voice.

"I'll be disjointed!" Skully said. "You're not Joy'nt!"

Now Picka saw what he had somehow missed before. Those absolutely lovely bones. It was Dawn in skeleton form.

He worked it out. "You invoked the conversion spell. Joy'nt invoked hers. So you became skeletal and she became fleshly. The monster thought you were each other."

"And chased Joy'nt," Dawn agreed, "while I escaped on Checkoff." She swung her leg bones over and dropped to the ground. "Thank you, Checkoff. You really helped."

"Glad to have been of service," he said. "That's one fearsome monster."

"Don't go near him again. He was distracted by what he thought was me, so didn't stun you, but he will next time. He won't forget that stomping you gave him."

"I was trying to run away from him, but got it wrong."

"Nevertheless you helped distract him, and I do appreciate it." She patted his shoulder affectionately. "I'd kiss you, but I don't have lips at the moment."

"That's all right," Checkoff said, his hide faintly blushing. He moved on before she could get any other ideas.

"So when the monster realized he had caught Joy'nt, all he could do was let her go," Skully said. "Because she would simply revert to bones soon anyway."

"And the time taken to try to dissolve her would simply keep him from his other business that much longer," Dawn agreed. "Woofer will be leading her back here soon."

"So we stopped another monster rampage," Picka said. "But there's bound to be another."

"Do you know what the cunning beast is doing?" Skully asked. "Since he can no longer track Dawn, he is making *us* come to *him*. He'll keep doing it until we settle with him, one way or another."

"That's right," Dawn said. "We can't let him go on this way."

"But I'm not strong enough to defeat him," Picka said.

Dawn considered. "It seems we must choose between letting him continue marauding, maybe doing real damage, and tackling him directly. I can stop it in a moment simply by agreeing to marry him."

"No!"

"Then it seems we must tackle him," she said.

Picka was unable to argue with that.

In due course Joy'nt and Woofer returned, and the group of them transported back to the island.

"We need a strategy," Dawn said, displaying her princessly management skill. "We also need to meet with the monster and establish the rules of engagement."

"Engagement!" Joy'nt said. "But if you don't want to marry him—"

Dawn smiled. "I mean the terms by which we deal with Piper. We have to establish where and how the combat will be, and what the consequences are, depending on who wins. Such as the combat will be musical and, win or lose, no more marauding."

"Why would he agree to that?" Skully asked.

"Because he wants to win the prize, which will be contingent on his agreement to those rules. He'll do it."

"Prize?"

"Me."

"But—" Picka started ineffectively.

"I will marry the winner without further protest."

"But if Picka loses—" Joy'nt said.

"Then I will marry the monster. He won't maraud after that; he'll be too busy collecting and storing puns. Xanth will be safe."

"And if Picka wins—" Skully said.

"I will marry Picka, and he will be too busy collecting and storing puns to maraud either."

Skully and Joy'nt chuckled.

"I don't like this," Picka said. "Not just because he's a better musician than I am. It's that music appreciation is subjective. Who is to say who is better, really?"

"Good point," Dawn agreed. "We'll need a judging panel. Maybe one member we nominate, one member Piper nominates, and a third we both agree on. They will decide, if the merits are not obvious. We must both agree to abide by the panel's decision, whatever it may be."

Picka still wasn't easy about it, but saw no alternative.

A smoke cloud appeared. "Ah, you're front," it said.

"We're what, Metria?" Dawn asked.

"Side, obverse, reverse, rear, aft, butt—"

"Back?"

"Whatever," the smoke agreed irritably. "The huge has a crisis."

"The giant has found another crisis," Dawn agreed. "Of what nature?"

"Fires starting everywhere. They'll soon spread if not stopped—but the monster won't let firefighters near it."

Dawn sighed. "Guide us there."

They gathered, and in a moment they were there.

Dawn looked around. "I know this region," she said. "It's near the Faun & Nymph Retreat. Princess Ida took my sister Eve and me here once. She grew up nearby."

Ahead of them was the fire. Fauns and nymphs were pausing in their endeavors to gaze at it, not understanding it. It would soon spread into their retreat, because the wind was that way.

And there of course was the monster barring their access. They couldn't even start to fight the fire without first dealing with him.

"I'm glad you're here," Granola's voice came from above. "Every time I try to fetch water to douse the fires, the monster stuns me."

"What is causing the blaze?" Skully asked.

"Jesse makes greased lightning bolts. He forges them with his anvil and greases them so they can slip through thick clouds, and stores them until a client like Fracto comes for them. But the monster charged though, broke open his storage bin, and all the stored bolts flew out. Now they are starting fires wherever they land."

Dawn nodded. "I will deal with Piper." She strode toward the monster.

"Wait, you'll need someone to speak for you, when he stuns you," Picka said, running after her.

"He won't stun me when I'm coming to parley." Then she froze. She had been stunned.

"The monster doesn't yet know you have come to parley," Picka said belatedly. Then he stepped in front of her. "Piper!"

The monster waited.

"We have come to negotiate," Picka continued. "To establish rules of engagement. Free her so she can talk with you. Otherwise I will defend her with my music, and you will lose your chance."

Dawn reanimated. "Thank you, Picka," she said as if this were routine. "Piper, here is the situation: you want to marry me. So does Picka. Only one of you can do so. The two of you must battle it out musically. I will marry the legitimate winner, and live in Caprice Castle with him and be a perfect wife. But only if the contest is fair. You can't cheat and win me; I will suicide if I have to."

The monster played a note.

"I am coming to that. Suppose we form a three-judge panel. We will select one judge. You will select another. We both must agree on the third. The majority decision of the judges will be final."

Another note. Dawn responded to what she knew the monster was thinking, rather than the music. "Yes, you may compete with kill-music if you prefer. In that case no judging will be necessary; the loser will likely be destroyed. But if it comes to melodic music, judging will be necessary, because of the subjectivity."

Another note.

"We will agree on a contest site," Dawn said. "Here, if you wish. But first we must put out these fires. I suggest a truce for that purpose."

One more note.

"Yes, I hereby commit to the contest, and to honoring its result. I will marry one of you, on my honor as a princess."

The monster retreated toward the fire. "He agrees," Dawn said. "It is a truce for this purpose. We will not attack each other. We will fight the fire together."

Could it be that simple? Dawn surely knew.

They advanced on the fire. "Fetch the scattered lightning bolts," Dawn said. "Toss them to the monster, who will extinguish them."

"I will fetch water," Granola said.

Once they were working together, it went rapidly. The skeletons fetched and threw the slippery bolts and stamped out their spot fires. The monster put them out and stacked them safely. Granola brought water and doused whatever smolders remained. The fire crisis was over.

The three pets, now four with Erin in cat form, had reassembled, realizing that the need to track the monster's depredations had ended.

Picka was privately amazed that they had worked alongside the monster without any problem. Piper was not a mindless thing; he knew what he wanted, and could do what was required to achieve it.

But now it was time for the contest. And Picka still wasn't ready.

Dawn faced Piper. "There remain some details. I suggest we schedule the competition for tomorrow morning, here. I see you agree."

A reprieve of a few more hours! But Picka did not feel very much relieved.

"Now the judges. Picka?"

He had thought about it, and made his decision. "I choose Tweeter Bird, who has a considerable musical sense and is fair-minded."

Tweeter tweeted, surprised, but accepted.

Dawn addressed Piper. "Whom do you choose?"

The monster considered, then blew a note.

Dawn's jaw descended a degree. "Do I misunderstand? She's on our side!"

Another note.

Dawn shook off some of her amazement, which scattered in little dissipating beads. "Piper chooses as his judge Joy'nt Bone."

Now Joy'nt's jawbone dropped. "But—"

The monster blew another note.

"He says he is satisfied you are objective."

Joy'nt spread her arm bones. "If that's the way it is, then I will do it, and try to be fair-minded. But I am likely to prefer my brother's music."

"Now we must agree on the third," Dawn said.

There was a silence of one and three-quarter moments. Then Midrange spoke. "Meow."

"Midrange nominates the Demon Pundit," Dawn said, "if he will serve. How do the two of you feel about that?"

Picka considered. This was the Mini-Demon who had built Caprice Castle and started the collection of puns. His interest was in getting that project resumed. He should be reasonably competent and objective. "I agree."

Piper pondered, then decided. He blew a note.

"Piper agrees," Dawn said. "Now the question is whether Demon Pundit will agree to serve."

Caprice Castle formed on the burned-out section of ground. The door opened. The Demon appeared in human form. "Yes. Meanwhile, for the night, the castle is yours. All of you. It will be a neutral site; you will enter it under enforced truce. The winner tomorrow will take possession of Caprice and commence the mission. I shall return on the morrow." He vanished.

An amazed look circulated among the eight of them and the monster. Granola surely shared that look. Then they walked toward Caprice Castle.

20
DECISION

The monster happened to be closest. He slid up to the front gate and crossed the threshold—and became the handsome human man they had seen in the History.

Piper turned. "Welcome to Caprice Castle," he said, then stood and waited for the rest of them to enter.

The skeletons and pets hesitated, but Dawn did not. "Thank you, Piper," she said, and walked on in. She knew he could be trusted in this context. Demons did not fool around.

The others hurried to follow. In another moment they were all in the entry foyer.

"It is good to be here again," Piper said. "I remember it so well. This is the perfect residence."

"Yes, it is," Dawn agreed.

"I am sorry I can't enter it," Granola said from outside.

"Ah, but you can, madame giantess," Piper said. "The magic extends to any the castle welcomes, and the Demon included you in that number. Merely approach and enter."

"But I'm way too big!"

"Try it and see."

The ground shook as she stepped close. An invisible foot touched the threshold.

A nude human-sized woman with a handbag appeared. "Oh!" she said with Granola's voice.

"We will wait while you dress," Piper said graciously.

Granola scrambled and found her bra and panties and a simple dress and slippers in her handbag, all correctly sized. The transformation evidently included everything in proportion. Soon she was clothed: a handsome matron with graying hair.

She joined them. "I am astonished to be on this scale," she said, "but it's a delight to be able to interact with the rest of you on a more personal basis."

"When I recover the castle," Piper said, "and marry the princess, she will of course be able to entertain any guests she chooses. I'm sure she will welcome you, and so will I, our issue having been settled."

"And what of Picka?" Granola asked dryly.

"He will be destroyed. That is the nature of this contest."

"And if Picka wins?"

"Then I will be dead. Either way, the issue will be resolved."

Picka did not comment. Piper was correct. It was a duel to destruction. There would be no rejected suitor hoping to reclaim Princess Dawn.

Piper clapped his hands. "Dinner in half an hour," he announced. "Please show the assorted guests to their chambers so they can clean up and change."

Lines appeared on the floor, leading from each person to the stairs. Picka's line was blue. So was Dawn's. He had to admit that Piper's familiarity with the castle was facilitating things. He knew tricks they had not imagined.

Their line led to the same bedroom they had shared before. Picka saw that Piper's line led to a different wing of the castle, so he would not be close by. That was a relief.

Dawn stripped and stepped into the castle shower. "Select something nice for me to wear," she called.

Picka looked in the closet. There were a number of dresses. He selected a nice one.

She emerged, took one look, and frowned. "This is a formal occasion, Picka. I need a formal gown."

"I'm sorry," he said, embarrassed.

She kissed his skull. "You're a typical male. I'll have to dress you too."

"But skeletons don't wear clothing."

"When you transform to man form for the dance."

Oh. He wasn't sure that was wise, but knew she would not be denied.

They went down to the ballroom. The others arrived at the same time. Granola was garbed as an elegant matron. Piper took her arm, guiding her, as she had never been inside a castle, or indeed any human domicile, before.

The table was laid out with a suitable banquet: food for the three living people and the four pets, none for the three skeletons. But all had places set.

"There are name tags for all," Piper said.

So there were: Dawn and Picka at the head table along with Piper and Granola, while Skully, Joy'nt, and the four pets were at the second table. It seemed that Erin was quite satisfied to remain in feline form, so as to be with Midrange. She was a cat who could assume human form, rather than vice versa.

Covered dishes were already there. Dawn's turned out to be a fine repast of exactly the kind of things living folk liked, like beefsteak tomatoes, mild boot rear, and sugary pastry. Picka's contained a little bone-rolling puzzle he could use to divert himself in the interim.

Granola looked uncertain. "No, this food will not interfere with your invisibility when you depart the castle and revert to your normal form," Piper reassured her. "It is wholesome throughout. Indeed, this whole castle is wholesome, the perfect royal residence."

Reassured, she began eating with gusto.

"Delicately," he murmured. "So as to give the impression of royalty."

She nodded and ate more carefully.

"You seem to be quite the host," Dawn remarked.

"It is the way I will be when I am with you," Piper said. "I am not royal, but you are, so I will be your consort, and wish never to embarrass you."

This dialogue made Picka uneasy.

In due course Dawn and Granola repaired to the ladies' room, with Dawn taking over the quiet instruction for the giantess. Picka was not sure what ladies did there, but understood it was not polite to inquire.

"It has been interesting to interact with you, Picka Bone," Piper said. "You are a fine musician."

"Not as fine as you are," Picka said. He did not like complimenting this person, but it was the truth.

"Ah, but you overlook the subjective element. That is of course why we have a judging panel. They may well prefer your style."

Picka found this awkward, so wanted to change the subject. But what he said surprised him. "I think you were treated unfairly."

"Oh?" Piper inquired, surprised.

"You were doing your job. You trusted a woman. She betrayed you. You were horribly punished for that, while she wasn't."

"Not so," Piper said. "I understood my mission. I allowed personal preference to expose my mission to risk. The woman had a mission of her own, which she accomplished. That forfeited what I had accomplished, and so Demon Pundit rebuked me. I had it coming."

"Rebuke! He transformed you into a monster!"

"Demons have ways to make their annoyance known."

"Wouldn't a simple verbal rebuke or penalty have been enough?"

Piper shook his head. "Not when dealing with a Demon. I was criminally foolish. I will not be so again. That was the real lesson here."

"And Pundora. She betrayed you again."

"Ah, but I knew her nature. I never trusted her. I merely traded favors with her for our mutual convenience. She had a very fine body, in contrast to her sneaky mind. There is a lot to be said for access to such a body, when one's own form drives away most women. I knew she would be gone again when she found a suitable nonmonster to be with. You were shrewd to arrange that; I congratulate you on an effective ploy."

"I don't like that ploy. We simply had to try to stop you from following us. But you outsmarted us; you made us follow you."

"And I did not like *that* ploy. Many innocent people suffered. But we all do what we have to do."

"I don't want to fight you."

"Ah, but you have to, Picka. If you simply walked away, the princess would follow you, much as Pundora followed Attila. I respect you, but I need to be rid of you, so that she has no choice but to marry me. I know you will not be corrupted, and I know it is not cowardice that repels you, so you have no choice."

"Bleep," Picka muttered.

"A worthy sentiment. However, our personal feelings have little relevance when we interact with Demons."

Worse, Picka discovered that he was beginning to like Piper. The man did have a case.

Dawn and Granola returned, cutting off any further dialogue. Picka was satisfied with that.

They finished the meal and adjourned to the dance floor. "I believe we have two couples," Piper said. "Granola, would you care to make a third?"

"I don't think I know how to dance," she demurred.

"Not so. In Caprice, any person who sets foot on the dance floor develops the capacity. You will not embarrass yourself. It is one of the many nice things about the castle."

She considered only half a moment. "In that case, yes. I have never had the chance to interact on an even physical basis with ordinary human beings, so I might as well indulge while I can."

Piper took her hand and led her to the floor. Music sounded. Then he moved into the couple position, his arm around her waist, and they danced. Sure enough, she was perfectly in step. "Marvelous!" she breathed.

Skully and Joy'nt embraced and moved out onto the floor, similarly competent. Even the pets participated, with Midrange and Erin matching motions and Woofer and Tweeter doing individual dances.

"That wipes out any excuse you had," Dawn murmured to Picka. "Now come with me."

She took him to the bedroom, made him invoke the transformation spell, and efficiently dressed him in living flesh clothes. She combed his hair and neatened his cravat. "You will do, handsome."

They returned to the dance floor. The others were still dancing; the two of them had not been gone long. Now Picka danced with Dawn in fleshly form, and he was indeed competent, while she was surely the source for all human dreams.

Suddenly there was a tap on his shoulder. It was Piper. "May I cut in for one dance?" he inquired.

Reluctantly Picka stepped back, and Piper danced with Dawn. They made a lovely couple. It was clear that if Piper won the match and Dawn, he would indeed not embarrass her. Since Picka expected to lose, that was perversely reassuring.

"Dance?" It was Granola. So he danced with her, and she was graceful despite her age. In fact, she did not seem old at all; she seemed to have youthened since entering the castle. "I think he is trying to weaken your resolve," she said, "so you won't fight as well. Don't let him do it."

"The man's a better musician than I am!" he protested.

"Yes, but that doesn't guarantee he will win. You do your best, so as to maximize your chances."

"I will try," he said humbly.

In due course the dance concluded. That was just as well, because Picka's hour was almost up. It was time to retire. Skully and Joy'nt linked hand bones and walked to their bedroom. Dawn took hold of Picka's hand.

"It seems that there are two of us left over," Piper said to Granola. "Would you care to share my bedroom this night?"

"Thank you, but I have one of my own."

He merely waited.

Then she caught on to the nature of his invitation. "But I'm old!" she protested.

"Have you looked in a mirror? You don't look your age. That is part of the enchantment."

She walked to a hall mirror. "Oh!"

"You would not embarrass yourself in that manner either," Piper said. "It is an opportunity for another kind of normal human experience you may not often have a chance for in the future. There is, of course, no other commitment implied. It is purely for fun."

"And you?" she asked. "What is your interest in this?"

He laughed. "You forget, I am a man. I am always interested, and my temporary woman decamped with Gattila the Gun. I am eager to be with any willing woman, for an hour or a night."

This time she considered a full half moment. "Why not?" She went with him to his bedroom.

"It's really quite a castle," Dawn said.

So it seemed.

As they entered their room, Picka's hour was up and he reverted to skeletal form. "Bleep!" Dawn swore.

"Bleep?"

"I wanted to make love with you before you reverted."

"Maybe tomorrow, when the spell renews."

"That's right! It should renew after midnight. That's only a couple hours away. Picka, I'm not going to sleep now; I'll wait for it."

"But why?"

A look passed across her face that made him nervous. It hinted of devious living-female wiles he was not equipped to understand. "Isn't it enough that I want to do it?"

"I'm not sure it is."

"I may explain in due course. Now let's just enjoy each other's company. Have you anything to say to me?"

"Yes, actually. I talked with Piper. He's really not a monster. He's a man with a mission."

She frowned. "That was not what I meant."

Evidently he was not being clear. "Piper seems halfway worthy, and he is alive. He will treat you well."

"Bleep."

"I don't understand."

"If I have to, I will marry Piper, and be all that he desires. Those are the terms of the deal we made. But I don't want to marry him, I want to marry you. Because you are worthy also, and you can be alive for key aspects."

"Key aspects?"

"Such as summoning the stork. And I can be a skeleton for making a skeleton baby. Maybe we can have one of each, and raise them together, brother and sister. It might be Xanth's most unusual family. But one other thing overrides all others."

"It does?"

"I love you, you numskull."

Oh. "And I love you, Dawn."

"*That* was what I meant."

Oh, again. "But I am not at all sure I will win tomorrow's combat. So I want you to be secure regardless."

"That's nice, Picka. I am making sure I will have at least some happiness, regardless."

"Making sure? This must be a fair contest, or it won't count."

"By getting what part of you I can, regardless of the outcome of the contest."

"I don't understand."

"I will signal the stork for your baby. The contest outcome will not be able to undo that."

"But—"

A clock bonged in the castle. "Midnight. Invoke the spell, Picka."

"But—"

"Do it."

Overwhelmed by her intensity, he invoked the spell. She was right: it was restored, and he became fleshly again.

Then it was a blur of activity and pleasure. He lost count of the number of times she got him to summon the stork. There might be a whole flight of storks arriving with their bundles. He was almost relieved when the spell finally expired, because he was exhausted.

"But I would rather marry you," she murmured as she went to sleep.

He was left holding her, realizing that she had indeed made her move. She might marry Piper, but her first child would be Picka's. Only she would know, perhaps, but that was enough.

Living women could indeed be devious.

In the morning they all shared a nice breakfast. Piper remained urbane, and Granola looked refreshed and amazed.

"We have certain things to arrange," Dawn said briskly. "I expect to govern Caprice Castle regardless who wins today's contest, and I want my friends close. Skully, Joy'nt, I presume you will marry in due course." She paused, but there was no dissent. "I would like the pair of you to take up residence here, and assist me in managing the incoming puns. Is that satisfactory?"

Both nodded. "We'd rather be doing something useful," Joy'nt said.

"We had no plans," Skully said. "I'm still new to Xanth proper, and this would make settling in easier."

"Piper, Picka," Dawn continued. "You are amenable?"

Again, no objection. Dawn was being princessly.

"You four pets," Dawn said. "You were wandering, looking for adventure. If you stay here you'll be seeing all corners and edges of Xanth, spying, sniffing, and identifying puns to be collected by the musician, whoever he may be. It should be interesting. We can use you. We will keep an eye out for suitable lady birds and dogs. Are you interested?"

"Woof!"

"Meow."

"Mew."

"Tweet."

"They have agreed," Dawn said, glancing again at Piper and Picka. "Amenable?"

"I can see already that pun collecting and processing will be a good deal more efficient than it was before," Piper said. "I will no longer have to do it alone."

"I like the pets," Picka said simply.

"And Granola. You are, in your natural state, an invisible giantess. You have been somewhat lonely. If you joined us you could have our company, and still be free to exit the castle, revert, and roam alone or with us as you choose. You would not, I think, have male company, but it is possible that if you found an invisible giant who was interested in becoming young, handsome, and human while within the castle, that could be arranged. Speaking for myself, I would like to have you here, as a woman not in awe of my status, a friend. You could also be quite useful working

with the pets to bring in far-flung puns without attracting outside attention. Are you interested?"

"Yes."

Dawn glanced at Piper and Picka.

"I like her too," Picka said.

"She could be extraordinarily helpful," Piper agreed. "And yes, I
would encourage her to find a male companion. The castle will accommodate anyone the princess approves."

"Then I think those loose ends have been tied," Dawn said. "It is
understood that the contest will determine the future master of Caprice
Castle, and past enmities will be laid to rest if not forgotten. I have made
clear that I would much prefer to marry Picka, but if that is not to be, I
will accommodate Piper in a manner that warrants no complaint. We
will all work together to accomplish the castle mission." She glanced
around again. "Agreed, all?"

They all agreed.

"This is exactly the kind of gracious competence I value in a princess," Piper said. "It will be a far better situation than I had before. I
know that none of you are my friends now, but I hope in the course of
the future to win at least your respect." He glanced at Dawn. "This will
be a marriage of convenience, as royal liaisons tend to be. Love is not
necessary, or even always desired. But it can be earned, and I will sin-
cerely try."

"I am sure you will," Dawn said. "It is fortunate that your expectation is low."

"The lowest expectation is still infinitely better than what I have
faced in recent years."

A nod of understanding went around. He was correct.

They went on with their meal. Picka found his respect for Piper increasing. The man was his enemy, who would probably destroy him
before the day was out, but he had qualities to be respected. Indeed, he
might in time win the respect of the others, and Dawn's love.

"Now, unfortunately, it is time," Piper said as they finished the meal.
"I will exit first and take my position. When you exit, Picka, it will be a
duel to destruction. You do understand."

"I understand," Picka agreed. He hated it, but he accepted it.

They walked to the front door. Piper walked out, crossed the threshold, and became the monster. He slid on through the blackened terrain, turned, and took up a position facing the castle.

Dawn walked out, and went to a chair set on the edge of the castle abutment, where she could watch the proceedings.

Granola emerged, having removed her clothing, passed the threshold, and disappeared. She had reverted to her normal state.

The four pets went out and joined Dawn.

Skully and Joy'nt walked out, and took two more chairs on the verge. The audience was ready.

Picka walked out, unlimbering his clavicles. He walked resolutely toward the monster.

Piper blasted him with kill-music. The battle was on.

Picka felt his joints fraying; they had not completely recovered from the prior damage. But he had faced this theme before, and played the countertheme that stifled it. Then he shifted to a fire theme, and sent scorching fireballs at the monster.

Piper shifted his own tune, dousing the fire. Then he played the rock-fragmenting music that undermined Picka's footing. Not enough to make sand, just enough to interfere.

Picka countered that, and played a theme that melted the earth on which the monster rested.

Piper lurched forward, advancing on Picka, corrosive acids glistening on his surface.

Picka played pacification music, causing the monster to slide to a halt. He was unable to approach Picka physically.

Thus they fenced with variations of kill-music, neither gaining an advantage. They were evenly matched in this respect. Picka's practice was paying off.

Demon Pundit appeared. "This is a stalemate. Proceed from kill-music to skill music. Each victory of melody is one point. A lead of two points will be decisive." He vanished.

They had been indulging in mere preliminaries, knowing there would be no decision there. Now they moved on to true music. This was the phase Picka feared, because Piper could play more notes and chords, and play them better. He really was the superior practitioner.

There was a brief silence. Then Picka led off with a simple melody. What else could he do?

The monster waited silently until Picka was done. Then he played the same melody the same way, except that he blew sustained notes instead of percussion notes. He had matched the melody. After that he played it again, this time elaborating. His version was beautiful; this confirmed his expertise.

After that Picka played the variant the same way, then played it again with his own flourishes, making it about as complicated and pretty as it could be.

The monster matched that, but did not take it further; that theme had been embellished as far as was feasible. So the first melody was a draw.

Piper played a new theme. Picka matched it, then embellished it. Piper matched that and enhanced it further. Picka matched that and let it be. Another draw.

The first melodic round was done. It was really more like a practice session, establishing the format. Picka had held even, but that meant little. The contest would be decided on the more challenging tunes.

The monster played a piece with four voices: soprano, alto, tenor, and bass. This was considerably more sophisticated than the prior single-note melodies.

Picka matched it, using both ends of both clavicles. This was a technique he had mastered in practice. Because his clavicles were a fixed length, he could not readily play adjacent ribs with a single clavicle. He did it by angling the clavicles between the ribs, playing the front end of one and the back end of the next. The notes were the same for each rib, regardless where they were struck. So if the monster had thought to mess him up this way, the effort had failed.

But if Piper played more than four voices, Picka would be lost.

Piper did not. Apparently he had been so sure that four parts would suffice that he had not practiced more complicated ones. Picka was in luck. So far.

Then he noticed something. The animals that had fled the scene of combat were returning. They were sitting around the scene of the contest, quietly listening. There had been no summoning music; they had come to appreciate the beauty of the melodies.

Picka played a different type of theme, one that gradually quickened its tempo. Piper matched it, accelerating similarly. That was Picka's disappointment; he had hoped the monster would not have had experience with that type of music.

Then Piper played another kind: two merging themes, each with its own tempo. Five beats of one matched six beats of the other. That was more sophisticated. Picka barely matched it, but only because Dawn had drilled him on the type, and because he could play anything he heard. But then the monster played a 3-5-7 beat combination, and that was beyond Picka's means. He might master it if he had time to work at it, but couldn't manage it now. He lost the melody, and was behind one point.

"Monster's point," Joy'nt said. There was a tweet of agreement. They were merely confirming what Picka already knew.

The ground beneath his foot bones softened, and he sank into it up to his knee bones. This was not Piper's doing; it was a signal of his disadvantage. If he lost again, he would sink out of sight and be gone. But his skill remained; he was not yet finished. He knew that Dawn, the other skeletons, and the pets were watching, knowing he was in trouble. He couldn't disappoint Dawn! She had trusted him to win Caprice Castle for her and save her from the monster, and he had to do it if it was conceivably possible.

They went back and forth, each matching the other, neither gaining any clear advantage. Picka was playing better than he ever had before, as if Dawn's faith in him was charging him up. Piper was still better, but it was by a narrow margin that few others would be aware of. Picka had almost closed the gap between them.

The surrounding animals remained rapt. They didn't mind who played, or who won or lost. They simply appreciated the music.

Suppose this contest ended in a draw? Who would get Dawn and the castle? Or would the Demon Pundit, disgusted, wipe them both out? Picka suspected that the monster was no more comfortable with that thought than he was. There had to be a winner. Yet there seemed to be no advantage to be had.

Picka tried a tweedle. That was a fast alternation of the two ends of a clavicle, one end striking one rib, the other the adjacent rib, making a kind of double note. He had heard the effect once, and made it his own. The monster matched it with alternating pipes. Picka added the second clavicle, so that four notes alternated rapidly, a double tweedle. Piper tried to match it, but his pipes were slower and stalled out with a tangled tweedle.

"Skeleton's point," Joy'nt said, with a tweet of agreement.

He had won a point! The ground pushed Picka back up and firmed beneath him. He was even again.

The monster went into an interactive piece. He played it once, complete, then played it with every second note missing. Picka had to supply the missing notes. Well, this was something else he could do; Dawn had practiced such pieces with him, possibly anticipating this.

Picka filled in the notes when Piper played it again. Then he played his own elaboration, with every third note missing. Piper matched it when Picka played it again, and sent it back with two notes played, two missing throughout. Thus it was two organ pipe notes followed by two clavicle notes, a rather nice effect.

Picka duplicated that, then played a variation with one note, the second note missing, then two notes, and two missing, then three notes, and three missing. This was fun!

But it wasn't fun for the monster. This was evidently a new pattern, and he hadn't practiced it. He was superlative when playing familiar music, but uncertain when it was new. When he tried to fill it in, he hit one sour note.

"Skeleton's point," Joy'nt said, with the tweet of agreement.

Picka had gained the lead! He was ahead, against his expectation. If he could just win one more point he would have the victory. But he knew he needed to do it now, because he was unlikely to get another chance.

The ground beneath the monster shifted and sank. He was in a hole. He could still play well, but he was in trouble.

They continued matching themes and variants. Neither found any further advantage. The prospect of a draw loomed larger.

Then Picka thought of something. He had, as a frivolous exercise, practiced variants of "Ghost of Tom." Could he now make use of that peripheral skill?

He played the melody through. The monster readily matched it. Then Picka spoke. "This is a round, normally sung by four voices offset. Like this."

He played the first line as before. "Have you seen the ghost of Tom?" Then, continuing the next line, "Round white bones with the flesh all gone," he added the first line for the second voice, so that they overlapped. It was like a two-voice melody, except that the first line was overlapping the second line. Then the second line overlapped the third, "Oo-oo-oo-oo-oo-oo-oo-oo!" And the third overlapped the fourth, "Wouldn't it be chilly with no skin on!" Finally the second voice finished, the first voice silent.

The monster tried, though it seemed he had not done this before. He managed to overlap the voices, but his notes were ragged and it was not very melodic. However, after finishing he tried it again, and this time did it better. He had lost style points, perhaps, because he had required two tries, but he had done it. That was what counted.

Then Picka played it again, this time with three voices. He carried it through to the end, suddenly glad that he had tackled this supposedly irrelevant exercise.

The monster did well on the first voice and the first overlap, but the third one threw him. He had obviously never practiced a round done this way, and had trouble balancing the offset melodies. He got through again, but in an inferior manner.

Then Picka played all four voices. He covered them perfectly, making a lovely song with the "Oo's" sounding above the other parts, providing a special flavor. He tapered off at the end, as each voice finished in turn.

When he finished, he looked at Piper—but there was not much to see. The monster had melted into the earth, and was now no more than a messy pool of goo-soaked dirt. He had not even attempted the four-voice variant, and had been defeated. He had paid for it with his substance.

Picka was, in his fashion, sorry. Piper had been a worthy opponent, and probably should have won. Picka had just happened to find the variants that gave him the edge. Maybe in time he would truly become a superior musician, but he owed his victory mostly to luck.

The animals, aware that the music was done, faded back into the forest.

Demon Pundit reappeared. "The verdict?"

"Picka," Joy'nt said.

"Tweet!"

"And I agree," the Demon said. It had been a formality, considering the fate of the monster. "Picka Bone, take possession of princess and castle and commence your duties collecting and storing puns. I will expect to see steady progress." He frowned. "And no messing up."

"No messing up," Picka agreed. Then he surprised himself by trying something dangerously daring. "Demon Pundit, I beg a boon."

The Demon was surprised. "You dare?"

Picka plowed ahead. "Piper is worthy. He did what he had to do. He made a mistake trusting a treacherous woman. He has been punished. He does not deserve extinction. I beg you: spare him."

"I'll be bleeped," the Demon said in wonder. "You are a more generous being than I took you for. But if I spare him, he may interfere with the pun-collecting mission."

"Not if you put a geis on him not to interfere. He might even help, making the job go faster."

The Demon pondered a micro-moment. He cared not half a whit for any person, but did want efficient collection. Then the gooey dirt where the monster had melted heaved, and formed into the man, Piper.

"You are spared by Picka's request," the Demon told him. "You will retain existence as long as you labor diligently to assist in pun collection. If you enter Caprice Castle you will transform to monster form until you depart it. If you touch Princess Dawn you will dissipate in smoke." He turned to Picka. "Is that satisfactory?" The sarcasm fairly dripped. "Will you now get to work?"

"First we will need to report to the Good Magician," Picka said, still dazed by his sudden victory, "so he knows Dawn has completed her mission to tame Caprice Castle and fetch Pundora's Box."

"Caprice will take you there, and anywhere else," Pundit said shortly. He vanished.

Piper spoke. "Thank you for a favor beyond anything I would have done for you. You are not only Xanth's greatest musician, you bid fair to be Xanth's best person. You and I have been enemies. That is over. I will support you in every respect to the best of my ability. I will go collect puns." He turned and strode away.

Dawn jumped up and ran to him. "I knew you could do it, Picka!" she exclaimed, kissing his skull so hard that little heart-shaped skulls flew out.

The Demon reappeared. "One other minor thing: either of you will be able to assume either form at will for as long as you desire, while on the castle premises. The same is true for the two other skeletons, and the giantess if she chooses. You no longer need the transformation spells. Return them to the Good Magician." He faded.

"Thank you, Demon," Picka said belatedly.

"Enter the castle, all of you," Dawn said, also beckoning the sky where Granola stood. "We have a trip to make, and a job to do." She glanced around. "Plus a phenomenal victory celebration, a royal wedding inside Caprice Castle, and anything else I happen to think of." She glanced at Picka. "You will assume fleshly form for the wedding, and for the wedding night, until I am quite satisfied." She winked in a manner that would have unsettled a stork. "I may even tease you by becoming a skeleton while you are in amorous flesh form. Any objections?"

"No, dear," he agreed dutifully. In fact, her notions threatened to be quite intriguing.

"I knew that," she said, and kissed him again.

Author's Note

I planned to start writing this novel SapTimber 1 (Ogre Calendar; their months are more descriptive than the mundane ones) 2009. I cleared all my projects and tag-end chores by the end of AwGhost, so as to have no distractions. It is said that nature abhors a vacuum. Well, nature must have considered that clearance to have been a vacuum, because things came in from left field to take my time. Such as the copyedited manuscript for my historical novel *Climate of Change*, which I had to page through and check. Such as a necessary blood test for a doctor's appointment. Such as material to review for the high school writer I was mentoreeing. I also answered four or five fan letters those two days. But on the second day of the month I did manage to squeeze in five-hundred-word notes organizing the novel.

The third day was busy. I use an adult scooter, the kind you push with one foot, to fetch in the morning newspapers, a round-trip of just over a mile and a half. On the way back the rear tire popped, and I walked the rest of the way. My wife's front bicycle tire also went flat. So I dismounted both, and discovered neither could be patched; we would have to buy new tubes and a new tire. That took an hour to ascertain. We also had shopping to do, another generous hour. A novel manuscript arrived, for reading and comment. I planned to read the first ten pages, getting it started, then start writing my novel.

Then came The Call: our elder daughter, Penelope Carolyn Jacob, in treatment for cancer, who had recently had brain surgery to remove tumors that were paralyzing her right side, had suddenly died. Her forty-second birthday would have been the next month. That wiped out the rest of my day, and in fact it was four days before I could return to this novel. It wasn't just the emotional turmoil. We were busy notifying family of the tragedy and setting up monetary and practical help for her widowed husband and eight-year-old daughter; their loss was greater than ours. Fortunately our younger daughter, Cheryl, had taken time off from work and flown there to assist for the month. Three days into that, Cheryl suddenly had a lot more responsibility.

So this novel was written under a cloud. Penny was constantly on my mind. I really wasn't in the mood for funny fantasy. But neither was I in the mood to curl up and suffer. Writing is what I do, and it was time for this novel. My wife and I maintained our activity, consoling each other, and supporting the others. There is no need to belabor this further. It will be two years later by the time this novel is published. Anyone who wishes to get more of the story can check my blog-type column for OctOgre 2009, at www.hipiers.com, where I give a sort of memorial life history of my daughter.

But I will mention here that Penny had impact on Xanth. She was ten when the first Xanth novel was published. She contributed the pun about the dirty mind of Jordon Barbarian, after his skull got split open and his horse used his hooves to scrape his brains back in, along with some dirt. Every time thereafter when Jordon saw a pretty girl, that dirt got stirred up and colored his thoughts. That also happens, oddly, to many mundane men. Penny said after her own brain surgery that, yes, there was some air and dirt from that, so now she was an air head with a dirty mind. When I made up the Xanth calendar, with the Ogre Months, I was stumped on February. She suggested FeBlueberry. I laughed, dismissing it, but soon realized that it was perfect: the month when the red berries got blue with cold. Penny's horse, Sky Blue, became the model for the Night Mare Imbrium, with the hoof print on the moon named after her, and for Neysa unicorn in the Adept series.

In fact, I had Penny in mind when I crafted Princess Ivy and followed her as she grew up over the course of several Xanth novels. When Penny made a friend her exact same age, she demanded that Ivy find a twin sister; thus Princess Ida came to be. When Penny got engaged, so did Ivy. But then Penny didn't marry for eight years, so neither could Ivy. I finally lost patience and divorced them, freeing Ivy. She immediately married Grey Murphy. *Then* Penny married. It seemed the character had started leading the way. Ivy went on to have triplet princesses, but Penny was satisfied with just one mundane daughter. Ah, well.

However, this novel is not about Penny. It just happened to be the one I was writing when Penny died. Because her death colored my world while I was writing it, Penny gets this recognition here. And no, Ivy will not die, any more than will my memory of my daughter.

The writing started slowly, but gained speed as I recovered my equilibrium. Life does go on, though the hole in my soul will never completely heal. Before the novel ended, I had dental surgery to remove five teeth, setting up for partial dentures. At this writing I'm seventy-five, and my teeth have never been great; I'm tired of pouring money into the aching cavity. I thought my recovery from the extractions would have me zonked out on pain pills, but it wasn't that bad, and I continued to write, and completed the novel on schedule. But I remain in doubt whether it is as sharp as prior novels; that will be for the readers to judge. Meanwhile I had to wrestle with the dread Soft Diet while my mouth healed, and lost weight before bouncing back.

There are the usual half slew of puns. There may be fewer in future, as the puns are methodically collected and locked in the Caprice Castle dungeon. But I suspect that more will continue to leak in from Mundania, so there won't be much difference for a while. We'll see. The title itself is a pun on *The Well-Tempered Clavier* by J. S. Bach. The clavier is the keyboard of any musical instrument; think of it as a piano. Bach's piece is about four hours of gentle piano music. My second daughter,

Cheryl, gave me a four-disc CD set with the complete preludes and fugues, and I listened to it while working on this novel. To my untrained ear it's just music, but I understand that knowledgeable musicians consider it to be a pinnacle of this form, the "Old Testament." So we have even-tempered Picka Bone playing his ribs as a keyboard, and yes, his music sounds just like Bach.

Before I started writing the novel I had a problem: I did not remember how walking skeletons reproduced. That information was buried somewhere in a prior novel, and I was not about to reread several novels to locate it. So I went to the readers of my monthly column and asked, promising a credit in the Author's Note. They came through. The most comprehensive early answer was by Erin Schram, who identified the novels and even quoted relevant passages. Others were by Russell Leverett, Heather Hatch, Sean Draven, Jan Perlmutter, Bridget "Bee" Allen, and Kerry Melissa Anne Garrigan. Thank you, one and all. Oh—how *do* they do it? He strikes her so hard she flies apart. This is known as knocking her up. He selects small bones from the collection and assembles them into a baby skeleton. I was not sure how Princess Dawn would go for that, nice as her bones may be—women can be fussy about the darnedest things—but in the course of the novel I learned that Dawn could handle it. How are the genders distinguished? Girl skeletons have one more rib.

That settled, I proceeded to the writing. I have a list of reader suggestions that keeps growing; I try to use them up, but some readers send in pages at a time, and so I never quite catch up. But I try to use one suggestion by each contributor before using more than one by some. That means that a number of available notions were not used here; I ran out of room. They should find homes in future novels. I don't want to annoy readers unduly, but the truth is that I would find it easier to write the novels without reader suggestions. I know, because I do write non-Xanth novels, even if many readers seem not to know that. It can be a challenge to fit in so many reader notions without disrupting the flow of the story. At any rate, here are the credits:

Appundix: the list of contributors to the novel—suggested by Ken Sundvik. Bring back the Baldwin pets, Woofer, Tweeter, Midrange—Michael Putch. F & G gravestones, Flight of Stairs chained down—

Taz Spivak. Cody deciphers codes or languages—Cody White. Think tank, Chopping Chop Sticks, Gorgon's marble cake, Isle of Cats littering law—Robert. Astonish- and fig-Mints—Olivia Davis. Coco-nuts with cocoa inside—Nicole. Iron Maiden, Talent of changing the color of trees, boy with hot hands, Snowshoe Tree—Aaron Jackson. Psycho Path—Cassandra York. Rob, who robs—Robert Tobara. Talent of making balls of light—Aaron Amberg. Lending strength of body, substance, or character—Champion. Meaty Oar—Logan Addotta. Curse Sieve—Sophia Hanson. Glitch in the spell making Bink's descendents magicians, makes most female too, Chameleon gets split into Fanchon and Wynne—Matt Yarnot. Riding a day mare—D.B. Bone-headed ideas—Kerry Melissa Anne Garrigan. Sound Barrier, Diplo-mats, woman makes dreams real—Nicolas Birchett. Key Limes that unlock doors—Adrian. Jack in the Box, Occu-pie, crack-hers, crack his—Jennifer Macleod. Frayed Knot—Dave Gomberg. Evil Devil Tree, Blood, Fog, River Banks, Salad Bar, Infini Tea, petroleum jellyfish, jellyfish bean, many pun demons—Tim Bruening.

Thought Projection, Worry Wart, absorbing talents, answering a question without confusion, pausing time for others—Brant Tucker. Box containing all puns (Pundora's Box)—Belgarion Kheidar. Caprice Castle—Ron Leming. Attila the Pun, Hairdo/Hairdon't, finding something in the second-to-last place looked, Greased Lightning—Jesse Mc-Beth. Punisher—Jamie Conner. Tom Boy, SOGA (Sea of Gruesome Arms), Walking skeletons have desiccated souls, the woman Steel who becomes a weapon, Buddy who is best friend—Bithor. Aliena—name borrowed from Aliena Scarlet. Bass Fish—Chris Hamilton. Drift wood makes thoughts drift—Kyle Martin Paddock. Ci-Gar, Ci-Garette—Donald Dickerson. Water Shed—Anna Pool.

Khari Saia—Khari Saia. Cow peas, reci peas—Darrel W. Jones. Pop fly (soda)—Wes Didier. Finger Prince (finger prints)—Rusty Burkett. Matter Horn, Turn Coat—Thomas Pfarrer. Pastree for pastries and paste, razor tree—Webster Neely. Window Pain—Richard Dickerson. Pie in the Sky—Wes Didier. See an Enemy (anemone)—Ian deJoode. Aphid David, the legal bug—Misty J Zaebst. Poultrygeist, Doris who sees the truth—Deneen Jardstam. Rockchuck—Kelley Gililland. Car

Pet—Cathy Priller. Have a female giant—Jareth. Granola = Granny Ola—Chris Dalton. Wear-Wolf, Where Wolf—Laura C. Punishment—cursed with a pun to live with—James Kollinger. Demon Litho fragmenting into asteroid belt—Kim Delaney IV. Furn, Airic, Peat, Wyck, Quantum—Wade Moriarty. Skully Knucklehead—Joe Birchett. Ports of Xanth: C, D, M, X, Car, Pass, Purr, Trans, Rap—Avi Ornstein. Smart Bombs—Richey Birchett. Crymea River—Adria Nyxx. Common Tater—Amber Hamm. Skyler making gray days bright, Sky Violet blending into scenery—Audrey Willoughby. The two Claire Voyants meeting—John D. Heinmiller.

Mim Barbarian, changing her wings—Maddragon. Eunice, who adds the silent E. Text Tiles, Text Us—Dragonlord. GoDemon making music from anything—Benjammmin St. Rebel. Talent of making any rolling object come up as wanted—Mike Kloss. Tracy Berry McLain—Tabby McLain. Anthony Liaw "Pirate"—Kara Ogushi. Talent of summoning cheese from the moon, summoning stink horns—Dan Clarke. Adora Bull, minotaur maiden, with door talent—Jamie O'Neill. D Sist, A Sist—Chris Bullard. Sara Nade—Kari Lambert. Emily Bee Keeper, Erin Kitty Litter—Lora Beuoy. Grease monkeys, fuel hogs—Russell Styles. Convey-Her-Belt, Transparents—Emma Schwarztans. Talent of becoming a shadow—Noah Goodman. Bubble of Silence—Justin Hernandez. Rain Bow—Alexander Jones. Centaur gets things wrong—Sparrow.

Thus concludes Xanth #35. I have not yet decided on the next, but suspect it will be *Luck of the Draw,* wherein there is a Demon contest to determine the ideal man for Princess Harmony as she comes of age. Xanth has many princesses, as noted, and finding suitable men for them is a continuing project. They do not like to be denied. Meanwhile, readers are welcome to catch up on my current events at my website, www.hipiers.com, where I have a monthly blog-type column and maintain on ongoing survey of electronic publishers and related services. That's because it seems that about half my readers are aspiring authors, and they need to find suitable publishers. That's almost as difficult as finding situations for princesses.